Educated at Oxford University, Dr Ian Wilson joined the J. Walter Thompson advertising empire before establishing his own fiefdom: WEXAS International, the UK's leading business travel company, of which he is owner and chairman. His passions are psychology and travel, and he spends much of the year skiing or surfing, sailing, diving and windsurfing in exotic locations. He is a qualified masseur and photographer, and the author of books on travel and political philosophy.

IAN WILSON

Black Jenny

Paladin
An Imprint of HarperCollins*Publishers*

Paladin
An Imprint of HarperCollins*Publishers*
77–85 Fulham Palace Road,
Hammersmith, London W6 8JB

Published simultaneously in hardcover
and paperback by Paladin 1992
9 8 7 6 5 4 3 2 1

Copyright © Ian Wilson 1992

The Author asserts the moral right to
be identified as the author of this work

A catalogue record for this book
is available from the British Library

ISBN 0 586 09204 8
ISBN 0 586 09161 0 (paper cover)

Set in Baskerville

Printed in Great Britain by
HarperCollinsManufacturing Glasgow

All characters in Black Jenny *are fictitious and bear no resemblance to
anyone living.*

For
Mary Mowat Muir

Thou princely judge here mayst thou see
What force in error doth remain,
In envious pride what fruits there be
To write the paths that lie so plain;
A double darkness drowns the mind,
Whom self will make so willful blind.

*The Victory of English Chastity
under the Feigned Name of Avisa*
Thomas Willoughby [Anonymous]
[1596]

1

How can you term her then obscure,
That shines so bright in every eye?
How is she base that can endure
So long, so much, and mounts so high?

The Victory of English Chastity
under the Feigned Name of Avisa
Thomas Willoughby [Anonymous]

Show me a woman in love and I'll show you a whore. That was Lord Byron, I think, and he recognized a spot of rumpy-pumpy when it was handed to him on a silver plate. Not for him waking up with an armful of cellulite playing neighbors with a belly as taut as a post-coital condom. Nor racking his brain for a way to wriggle out of trading names and phone numbers the morning after. He pushed them out before dawn with a King George shilling for the cab fare home.

There was a lurch. I snapped to attention and squinted up as the senior stewardess in first class reached for my seatbelt. 'There, Dr Bosworth,' she crooned. A touch of Irish brogue, maybe? Her hand brushed mine and lingered a moment. I took it but she slid her fingers away. A spot of turbulence and strong headwinds, the captain announced in the hyperaccent of the British Airways flightdeck. The daytime flight from London to Boston would be twenty minutes late. I didn't regret leaving the high-octane cocoon of Heathrow Airport, but the cloying scent from the ventilators couldn't mask the fug of aviation fuel. Jeezers Christ I hated flying – the dry air, the microwave body fodder and who knows, being blown to smithereens by a terrorist who didn't know my name.

The seatbelt sign winked off minutes later and I unclipped myself and strode toward the lavatory carrying a pouch that contained my cut-throat razor. When I returned, morning shadow gone, a Perrier bottle was rolling in the aisle. Out the window a gouache sun lay daubed across the cloudline. I pulled down the blind and tugged the advance but already rumpled copy of *Nature* from my briefcase. Within hours the journal's contents would be front-page news.

I stretched restlessly and gave the pretty stewardess the once over, to which she quivered receptively before straightening her body language with a pat of her strawberry curls. *No, someone else will light my candle tonight.*

The past eight months had been too hard on my nerves. Memories rang in my head: Oxford . . . the International Conference on AIDS . . . The House that May afternoon . . . The venerable hall off Peck Quad . . . My paper on sexually transmitted diseases and immunodefense systems . . . Strawberries and cream afterwards in the Dean's Garden . . . And then . . . Amelia.

As I maundered about the lawn pretending to listen to the jeremiads of other underfunded scientists an eye-catching woman materialized. She looked to be in her mid-twenties. *Save me* she mouthed over the top of her glass, indicating an assiduous man with a flick of her lashes. Even then there seemed to be something familiar about her. *Amelia, with your bumpy nose and your contact lenses and your laughing light-green eyes.* She was tall and coltish. It was lock-on to target.

'Hi,' she called out loud. A group of undergraduates bimbled around playing at croquet on the far side.

Slightly blotto in the summer heat I waved my glass and with my rapist's eye for opportunity I zoomed in and steered her across the sward. She too was plastered and a Yankee to boot, a tawny blonde with a Boston drawl.

She purred something in slow motion. I nodded and supported myself against the drinks table where a white-jacketed scout was filling glasses. I quaffed from mine and in a muzzy voice I asked what her field was. It was there again: the beatific smile. It reminded me of someone, but I couldn't put my finger on it.

She ignored my bantering tone as I hovered in front of her. Her reply was laconic. 'I'm into Shakespeare. I really don't know beans about the things you were talking about. I shouldn't be here at all.' And she pursed her lips to meet the rim of her glass, but stopped short, slopping a little down the side.

I was puzzled: drawn to the dimples at the corners of her mouth. She brought to mind my first and only wife. The same sublime cheekbones, eyebrows. Even below the neck she and the preternaturally buxom Lucy shared common contours. I sneaked a long look up and down. This woman had a *racé* frame that was playing all hell with my libido. She was kitted out in leaf-green cotton: not a lot of it. I tore my eyes from a tiny diamond-shaped birthmark peeping from a declivity that advertised no mortal breasts.

There was a remote cast to her, more pre-Raphaelite handsome than beautiful. As she spoke she twirled her free hand in the air. 'Would you be shocked if I told you I came to England to see you?' That sultry timbre would haunt me for months to come.

Her breezy question left me foraging for a reply. I hoisted one eyebrow and narrowed my eyes.

She stood there jiggling, waiting for more reaction, but I held back, so she went on: 'I'm staying at the Randolph. I'm here to do some research in the Bod. I heard about your theories on syphilis.'

I opened my mouth to say: 'What's the connection with Shakespeare?' but nothing came out. I screwed my features up tight and finally I got there. Not that I've got a speech impediment.

'I thought you'd never ask.' The rest of the party was background and fading fast. She brimmed with smiles. 'I'm into syphilis too,' she said, 'figuratively speaking. Y'see, I've got a lot of theories about Shakespeare. One is that he had syphilis: even died of it.' Her voice was rising in her excitement as she added: 'When I tried to find out more about syphilis, everyone pointed to the great Dr Daniel Bosworth.' She told me she'd found out I was the molecular geneticist who'd used syphilis to identify a new gene. She even knew I'd got a First at Cambridge and done my doctoral thesis in venereology – on the molecular history of syphilis. Then she added: 'I like your name. We had a Daniel in our family. That was in the eighteenth century.'

I looked up and gut reaction made me move closer. There was something asymmetrical about her face. Later as we got acquainted I'd learn that this was enhanced by her left eyelid. When she was tired or excited it would droop a fraction. It was drooping now. There were laughter lines to her eyes, but her bumpy nose was a stroke of genius. Without it she'd definitely have run the risk of being beautiful.

9

I set down my Pimm's, none too steadily, and folded my arms. 'We don't encounter syphilis much anymore. And I've switched to viral diseases . . . immunovirology.' Christ, did I surely sound pompous. *Daniel, you bloody scug.*

She looked to be rapt in my words as she hashed over this piece of information.

'Basically I'm hunting for an AIDS vaccine.' My hand trailed in the air at the sea of scientists. 'The competition's getting tighter all the time.'

'I've got a theory,' the girl was saying. 'It's something you could help me with.'

I didn't have a lot of time, I told her. Which was true.

She moved close to me and laid one hand on my chest. 'Daniel – d'you mind if I call you that?'

Out of the blue I was feeling way up there. 'What's yours first?'

'Amelia.'

'Amelia who?'

'Amelia Hungerford.'

I stared down at her signet ring on one taper finger.

Here's the picture the way I got it later. God, she could be patronizing too, the way she played you her life history like some old gramophone record: she grew up in Cambridge, Massachusetts. After spells at Shady Hill and Miss Porter's she descended on Harvard to do English Lit. In Generals she graduated *summa* and won a Sheldon Fellowship which took her to Paris for two years. Her application to the Harvard Graduate School of Arts and Sçiences followed a meeting with the German emeritus, Saul Lindenbaum, the world's undisputed authority on Shakespearian biography. When she was appointed a lecturer in her third year in GSAS the old academic honored her in *The Shakespeare Quarterly* by describing as 'seminal' her work on sixteenth-century cosmology. Now Lindenbaum was her mentor.

Her family background and striking looks, the contrast of blond hair, green eyes and freckled *teint mat* skin ensured her welcome in New England society, but she was a reluctant socialite at the best of times. One evening in a confessional mood she told me some plonker columnist from *Details* magazine had described her as 'an estrous gadabout'. When I found out more about her I had to admit maybe there was something in that description. After all recreational sex wasn't all it was cracked up to be and wasn't everybody somebody's second-hand slapper when all was said and done?

The only reputation she valued was her academic one. Around Cambridge, Massachusetts she was inseparable from the Hungerford name, itself apparently a Harvard legend, however little she resembled the archetypal bluestocking.

I sipped from the orange juice the flight attendant had placed beside me. Amelia was waiting. She'd sent me a map of Harvard and details of where and when to find her. The only other contact I had in the vicinity of Harvard was Ben Talbot, the gifted Nobel laureate who was Director of the Whitehead Institute on the fringes of MIT.

I rose to get my jacket from the bulkhead closet and took out the wallet Lucy my ex had given me in happier days. As I flipped it open a dog-eared photograph fell to the floor. Before I could pick it up the stewardess was stooping at my feet, handing it to me with a smile. I snatched it from her. The gesture tore the edge of the black-and-white print and I cursed under my breath and sank back into my seat, holding the picture with reverence between thumb and forefinger. With a snort the stewardess pivoted on her heel and departed. I fingered the small tear. It had barely gone beyond the margin.

The picture was faded and grainy but I made out the familiar features. The black coat was calf-length with the padded shoulders of the Fifties. The eyes held a glint of fire. She was slim and memorable with an elusive smile. I touched my lips. The resemblance was visible if you looked hard. She had the same cleft chin and upper lip. Her hair was swept up at the front. It took no gigantic leap of faith to see she'd been a stunner. Only I was ignorant of almost every fact about her except the words written on the back of the picture: 'Oxford October 1956'. That and the certain knowledge she'd been murdered three years later. I struggled to button up my feelings and slipped the photograph back into my wallet.

I didn't even know her name and this was my mother. My real mother. Did anything else matter apart from finding who she was? It was too late now to rewrite my life the way it should have been.

*   *   *

11

For half a second I saw myself at school togged out for a photograph in what I used to call my 'fancyman's waistcoat': irredeemably an outsider. From school I'd got one of the last closed scholarships to Trinity. You could say I was a gregarious loner and maybe there was a lot of the ringleader about me. Others didn't warm to me easily, but when I made the effort and opened up, people usually respected me. It had crossed my mind before now that the rest of my department thought of me as an eccentric visionary. At least I wasn't a weedy back-room boffin. My mother would have wanted my life to add up to something. Well the world would fall at my feet one day.

Not that I'd always been unhappy up to the age of fourteen, though there were times when the feeling of not belonging had been pretty unbearable. It was only when I was summoned by the Colonel a month before my fourteenth birthday that things really got out of kilter. The blimp of a man I'd assumed was my father took me into the smoking room and in a welter of embarrassment informed me I was adopted around the age of two. Just like that. It might as well have been a death sentence. The Colonel plucked the photo from the pocket of his jacket. Mrs Bosworth had gone to tea at the vicarage.

I was informed that Matthew and Sue were only my adoptive brother and sister: the Colonel's flesh and blood. They were also out of the way. It still rankled after all that time.

The photo was probably my real mother, so I was told. I was dumbstruck. Very likely she was dead, the Colonel said flatly. I looked at the attractive woman. There were a thousand questions. Who was she? How had she died? Where had she lived?

'Your mother' – the Colonel meant Hattie, his wife – 'and I adopted you in nineteen-fifty-nine.' My legs were buckling, but you didn't sit when the Colonel was standing, any more than you called him 'Dad'. He was always 'sir' – a little man in more ways than one – a dotty diehard of the old school: emotionally bankrupt. The Colonel rambled on: *two months at an orphanage in Oxford: they closed the place in the Sixties: woman found you in a supermarket trolley: carpark at Cowley: clean clothes: mind you it was summer: photo tucked into your dungarees: a kind afterthought? Nothing else to go on.*

Hattie Bosworth was the good-works type and she and the

vicar of the day had been behind my adoption. She saw more of the current vicar than she did of the Colonel, who farmed eight hundred acres of Berkshire countryside with a professional manager and four laborers. Two of them, Jake and Roy, had virtually grown up with me at Forest Spring.

My rebellious streak seemed to date from age fourteen. At school it led me from one scrape to another. When Bambi Tresham my housemaster surprised me against the potting bench with the Dame's precocious niece – boobs as big as the Ritz – *in flagrante*, only my track record in class saved me from getting sacked. That wasn't the only incident. It was how I'd always been, things like that. Mostly women. Call it impulsive. But I had a good creative brain and that was my saving grace. That and being an incorrigible romantic. Only it was poor compensation for being forced to grow up as an internal exile in the nimby Bosworth family, aside from Matthew. My adoptive brother, an architect, was the family's only redeeming feature.

There was one man who was sort of a father-figure. Sir Maurice Humpherson was an ancient Trinity don. Being a Celtic archeologist he'd press-ganged me some years earlier into joining a dig near Canisbay in Caithness. The expedition was a turning point. We discovered the body of a man preserved for four thousand years in a peat bog. By then I'd published one paper on heredity and the sex-linked chromosomes and, as another archeologist had already found two such bodies, Maurice had got round to wondering if human genes could really be cloned, something he'd read somewhere.

I was on the spot in his own college, we both played chess, and when the old widower was in his rooms, which wasn't often, we'd play into the night as we sipped questionable quantities of an amazingly mellow port, of which Maurice had a limitless supply, despite the fact that it was antediluvian. Perhaps I liked him more because he usually won. He was a gentle, affable man with skin like *chamois* leather after years of toiling in hostile conditions to unearth the artefacts that meant so much to him.

When his daughter Lucy had come home from secretarial college, oozing nubility, it was inevitable that she and I would be in bed together in under a week. The rest was Trinity College history. Lucy and I were married in the college chapel under the eyes of Isaac Newton and divorced three years later in the local council office under the eyes of a bureaucrat with a war-surplus mustache not unlike the Colonel's. It was divorce that prompted my brief departure for Paris then Sydney. But Maurice and I stayed friends, and I still looked him up on the rare occasions when I was in Cambridge. His eyesight was almost gone and we didn't play chess anymore, but we still drank the port, only now it was even mellower.

In the British Museum lay Canisbay Man in a glass case, just in case I needed to remind myself of one chapter on the road to meet Amelia.

But it was the woman in the Oxford photo who was the real obsession in my life, apart from my work. I spent a lot of my school and university holidays vainly combing Oxfordshire and Berkshire graveyards armed with the words on the back of the picture: 'Oxford October 1956'. It was not a part of Oxford I recognized, even today.

At the time the Colonel had asked the powers that be his own questions, but he knew no more than he'd told me. They'd coaxed only my name out of me at the orphanage, so Daniel I continued to be. I looked about two years old so they made the day of my christening into my second birthday.

That was that: fourteen, orphaned and there was sweet Fanny Adams I could do about it. I'd had more than my share of bad luck . . . except when it came to women and that was something I put down to being born lucky in that department. My life hadn't been the same since the photograph.

Lucy wasn't what you'd call a 'good wife.' For one thing she wasn't able to accept the little I'd guessed about my real mother, though God knows she pretended to. Lucy only cared about her position as the wife of an eminent scientist. That and my jumbo wowzer and the fact that I knew how to use it. There was only one way human beings had penetrated her carapace and it wasn't intellectually or emotionally. When it came to the usual variations under the covers, Lucy, at twenty, had already been an old trouper. Where the muse between her legs was lacking in imagination, she made up for it in sheer experience. I, a relative novice at the time, received the hand-me-down grace of her promiscuous past. But what an education that was, as if she'd spent all her teen years practicing just for me.

There was a lot to be said for the English dislike of awareness.

14

For a long time I'd refused to face our interpersonal problems. Lucy hid her feelings in a bell jar built to withstand a helicopter gunship. Look, don't touch. It would have taken nuclear arms to get through to her. She gave you nothing of her core. She could only suck like a deep black hole. Therapy saved Lucy's life, brought swift divorce and, thus salvaged, she took off with a friend called Sophie. We all called her Sappho. Lucy in disguise. Now in her carefully reconstructed happiness she was running a gallery on Sydney's North Shore, one that specialized in tribal stuff: still childless. Maurice missed her a lot but there was no part of her I missed except her breasts. The sort Lucy had were the sort that some men died for: the real McCoy. You could suffocate there if the fancy took you. I could still visualize their quick wobble as she brushed her teeth up and down in a finishing frenzy. Sweet Jeezers, how that relationship hurt for a time. And there I was, with Amelia, infecting myself with love's sickness again. I must have needed my head examining.

Something in my wallet caught my eye. I pulled out the sprig of blond hair tied with a ribbon and glanced at the neighboring seats. A ferret-eyed man with a bulging belly looked away as our eyes met. Amelia's parting gift, this golden tuft came with a card: 'For my Crusader from your own sweet angel'. She'd left it on the pillow without waking me the day she left Oxford. On the phone later when she rang from America I found out the meaning of her pledge: knights going into battle carried an erotic favor: a lock of their lady's most intimate hair.

I was thinking that angels were meant to be male, but I'd poked around in cemeteries quite a bit since I was a kid and I'd looked into the vacant eyes of a hundred angels, not one of which, gazing soulfully down under lofted wings, had looked remotely as if they had a penis hidden in their stony folds. There was no suggestion of breasts, mind you. I could see that the sex of angels used to worry me a lot.

But when it came to my own guardian angel – I called her Janey – there was no doubt about her sex. Janey was a *she* all right. I could sometimes feel her watching over me. But when she wasn't there other eyes followed me and bored through my back.

Janey had been known to save me from a fate worse than hell. Take one incident. There might have been a spot of bed-swerving, but the only woman I'd ever got pregnant was Lucy, my lawful wife. Lucy miscarried in her fourth month and for a few weeks I fell apart. It was my angel Janey I had to thank for the way the psychiatrists stepped in again and saved me.

After that I could handle the voices talking about me unctuously . . . and the invisible eyes drilling into my back. I found out that the voices and the eyes really belonged together, but it was always one or the other. They never came at the same time. And they never came at all when Janey was watching over me.

Janey didn't often leave me, thank God. And Janey had breasts aplenty. When Amelia and I fell for each other across a crowded lawn I knew Janey had laid it all on for me specially. No woman ever got that close to me before. Maybe that's why I liked to call Amelia 'angel' when I was feeling close to her.

I squinted up to catch a particular expression in the eye of the stewardess. Here was I meant to be involved with Amelia – the first serious woman in my life since the brain-dead Lucy and I went our separate ways. I tilted my seat and went back over those four summer weeks.

The day after Amelia ran into me like that we took my ram-shackle DB6 and hammered out to the Perch with the top down and my pecker up. After a pint of scrumpy we pootled up the back of the Isis, me feeling like Mungo Park hunting the headwaters of the Niger. *Some lunch.* She said it was yumbo, but I was hacked off sitting at the Trout in semi-drizzle trying to sound serious against the screech of free-range peacocks. I didn't see the funny side till a couple of pints later, by which time I had a first-class stonker on and third-degree lover's balls. Though I didn't know it then, I was already terminal in the heart department.

Why she'd come to Oxford to find me she wouldn't say, though I asked her over and over. Just that first mention of Shakespeare and syphilis. Tight as a clam.

The Saturday of Eights Week we hustled a punt at Magdalen Bridge and ploughed up the Cherwell through a miasma of drunken undergraduates. We edged into the landing stage at the Cherwell Boathouse where some dickhead was caulking the bottom of a boatshell on the slipway. Some wet bob she knew. After she'd exchanged the weather with him we grabbed the last table in the boathouse restaurant and lunched on microscopic snails before punting on. At the Vicki Arms we clambered onto the grass

16

in sodden garb and got wrecked on a Tesco muscadet that Amelia produced like a white rabbit from a voluminous waterproof she'd brought along just in case. So like an American and unlike her.

Apart from the punt expedition and the Trinity Commem – Amelia dazzling in a flouncy affair she'd tarted from some guy called Jasper Conran; the mind boggled – there was one night never to be forgotten. As dusk fell in Magdalen's Deer Park we squirmed together on hard cushions to watch an open-air performance of *Salad Days*. It was easy in the comfort of the plane to forget how cold we were by half-time, clinging sweaterless to each other in the dark of the scaffold amphitheater and finding a closeness that was more than physical.

That was the night Amelia turned vulnerable and her face filled with caring. 'I want to spend the night with you,' she whispered as I steered her the short distance to All Souls. We were passing under a streetlamp across the road from the Schools. For me it was strangely intense but without lust. I wrinkled my nose at her and danced a little jig while she stood and snickered. To show off my Shakespeare I compared her to a summer's day and it was almost midnight.

Romantic just wasn't the word for it in the beginning. I was the wind and Amelia was Preciosa. Our feet hardly touched the ground. After that she moved out of the Randolph and into All Souls unofficially.

Even now I could capture the shades of twilight spilling through my leaded window two nights after we first made love. So different from Lucy. That had been physical, nothing more. So much for my late lamented marriage. With Amelia there was this subtle energy that fed you deep inside, making sex almost transcendental. From the very beginning we were comfortable just being together, leaving so much unsaid.

'You need someone to look after you,' she whispered in my ear. 'D'you think if Shakespeare had syphilis he'd have gone fooling around?' The switch brought me down to earth. She'd stopped in the middle of a torrid moment. No modern condom: just her old-fashioned pill. So much for safe sex. Twin cupolas hung over me jostling generously for air. Better than a pig in the eye.

'Half the women he went to bed with probably had it anyway. It could take years to kill you.'

'So he could have had lots of illegitimate children after he got syphilis?' Her mouth flickered the way I found irresistible.

I agreed with her. 'It probably would have made him sterile eventually.' I didn't want to talk. I could taste musky bodies that clung to the air.

'There's still no absolute proof he had syphilis.'

'Why does it matter so much?'

'You wouldn't believe how many so-called authorities take the view he was a paragon of virtue. Don't ask me how a puritan could write some of the bawdiest bits in the English language.' She put a finger to my lips. 'Shhh. Don't move.' She extricated her body, grabbed my towel dressing gown from the chair and disappeared into my cubbyhole that passed for a pantry.

There was a thud like a stiffy coming through the letter box. 'Irish coffee,' she announced, jettisoning my dressing gown as she swanned back and plonked down a cup. In the five minutes she'd been away I'd almost dropped off. Twilight had turned to darkness. Her voice brought me round. She perched cross-legged on the end of the bed while I struggled to a sitting position and took the cup. She stretched her arms, flaunting her breasts. 'I have a confession to make. Like I said, before I came over to England I knew about this gene you've found. Just as well. My dodo brain didn't understand a word of your paper the other day.'

For three weeks I'd waited for her to give me the full story behind why she'd come all this way to get my support. That it had to do with Shakespeare and syphilis she'd made clear in the beginning. I widened my eyes in an effort to stay on the ball. 'Stop me if I'm wrong,' she said, pushing back an errant ringlet. 'You've got this technique where you can trace descent through several generations, thanks to this syphilitic gene.'

'More or less.' A sleepy tone from me. Bleary-eyed I stretched out a leg and massaged the sole of her foot with my big toe. I was almost alert again.

Making love had flown out the window. *There's more to life than sex, Daniel.* I shrugged off the voice and launched into what she wanted to hear, giving it to her in layman's language: the full picture. No interruptions.

Basically my new gene was carried by all males near the end of one particular chromosome in pair twenty-three. Quite a few men carried it in a mutant form, a sure sign they had an ancestor who'd caught the Great Pox. In this mutant form the gene could only pass from father to son. It couldn't pass from father to daughter. If a man with the mutant gene died without a son, the mutant version of the gene died with him, so the gene could only be used to trace ancestry in an unbroken male line where an ancestor – the first generation – caught syphilis.

I knew that sounded simple but in fact it was a lot more complicated.

I explained how I'd followed the disease back to the middle of the eighteenth century, but regression modeling had allowed me to reconstruct some strains back to the early sixteenth century. Nowadays venereal syphilis had been partly defeated by penicillin, but the spiral-shaped syphilitic bacterium or spirochete known as *Treponema pallidum* was still doing the rounds, so genetically mutable that the Great Masquerader, as the Victorians called it, now had more varieties than Heinz.

I wanted to know how Amelia had found out about the mutant gene since hardly anyone had known it existed before the conference, but she sidestepped my question before I asked it as if she seemed to see it coming. 'Give me a pillow.' She feigned a wicked look and sizing up my loins, added: 'Is this a dagger I see before me?'

I made a priapic gesture from below and threw a pillow playfully. At least that was the intention. It hit her in the face. 'Sonofabitch,' she said huskily, plumping it in the nest of her legs. She steepled her hands and rested her chin firmly on the summit. 'Tell me if I've got it right. This gene changed – mutated – when it was exposed to syphilis. The mutation got passed on identically in each generation to all male descendants.'

I grunted agreement.

'Is it true you've traced descendants by ... cloning –' she struggled with the unfamiliar vocabulary – 'genes from bodies buried hundreds of years ago?'

'Up to two hundred years.' I explained patiently how I'd followed the work of Dr Svante Paahe at Uppsala University, who'd worked on genes isolated from an Egyptian mummy two thousand four hundred years old, growing its cells in tissue culture and cloning them by inserting them into micro-organisms. Now, thanks to the polymerase chain-reaction method, a piece of DNA could be cloned millions of times over in a matter of

19

minutes. Other scientists at Berkeley had had success with a forty-thousand-year-old woolly mammoth preserved in ice. At the MRC molecular genetics unit in Cambridge – stop me, I told her, if I sound pompous again – I'd replicated suchlike experiments, starting with tissue from the mummified remains of two English sailors who'd died in 1844 on Franklin's expedition to find a North-West Passage and been buried in the arctic permafrost which had preserved their bodies – even their organs – as if they'd died almost yesterday. Swampy ground was the next most promising territory for well-preserved human remains.

After two years of working with exhumed animal and human tissue I'd been fortunate to spend some time with Dr Fred Sanger. Later that had led to co-research in DNA typing techniques with my friend Professor Geoffrey Alton, the man who pioneered genetic fingerprinting at Leicester University in 1984. I explained how success at Cambridge had led to a year at the Pasteur Institute in Paris, then a brief spell in Australia before my All Souls Fellowship. At Oxford while working with the MRC immunochemistry unit on the so-called HOT method of analyzing genetic defects I'd made my breakthrough with the new gene. For the first time male lineage beyond the previous generation had been proved biologically – by digging up the bodies of men whose present-day descendants were known and had been tested. This work was now being verified through a research unit at the John Radcliffe Hospital in Oxford.

There wasn't much light from the lamp in the bathroom but I could see that her eyes never moved from mine. She came out with it. Dead serious. 'If we had physical proof that Shakespeare caught syphilis would it be possible to trace a descendant now?'

'Yes, in theory, if there were males in every generation right back to Shakespeare. But even if you had a copy of his version of the gene, where would you start to look for a living relative? And that's assuming Shakespeare did have syphilis and didn't become sterile from it. It also assumes he fathered a bastard son who went on breeding. There's a lot of "ifs".'

Her left eyelid was drooping. In combination with her bumpy nose – the Bump, I called it – it gave her a hooded look. She threw me a crumpled glance and, pushing the pillow aside, leaned forward to reach her coffee on the bedside table. The argument she came up with was simple. Too simple if I really wanted to be

20

rational about this. What was the greatest drawback, she asked, to progress in my search for an HIV vaccine? I had to admit more money would help, but even more vital was a greater supply of HIV samples covering the full range of subtypes for the plotting of antigenic drift, since this fragile virus had a notoriously variable molecular structure. I splashed my cup down in a coffee-filled saucer. It was still too hot. As she fondled the hair on my chest I asked – demanded even – that she explain what she was on about. Oh that Bump. I've always been a sucker for noses shaped like that. I wanted to eat it.

She described – pausing over her choice of words – how she wanted a major discovery in her research, apart from the identity of Shakespeare's Dark Lady which, for her, was the Holy Grail. She wanted evidence of Shakespeare the adulterer in the shape of a direct living kinsman: for faculty kudos and to cock a snook at holier-than-thou's among Shakespeare hunters. She snuggled under my armpit and rubbed her nose against my side. 'Have you heard of the World Health Rostrum?'

'Mmm.' I nodded wiggily.

'They've made a commitment in the war against communicable disease . . . they've taken a stand on AIDS . . . to get more Americans screened. Maybe you heard they've got these mobile diagnostic units, over four hundred, going round America giving free screenings to thousands of people.' She wriggled against me.

I'd read all about the World Health Rostrum . . . how it was a spin-off organization from the Rostrum Training Centers. Their AIDS Campaign had been news everywhere. What had made it possible was the Cambridge BioScience diagnostic test for the immunodeficiency virus. This test, which directly detected HIV's enzyme reverse transcriptase, had only been around for three years, but already it had replaced the HIV antibody tests known as the ELISA and the Western blot. I'd been using the procedure on groups of Oxford prostitutes. It was sensitive, fast, cheap and accurate.

She scrutinized my face, demanding a comment that didn't come. I propped myself on one elbow and tried my coffee again. I'd been stirring it for two minutes. Mmm, the bitter taste was good. What struck me was how she could appear to be so open and still leave me feeling I hardly knew her; the schizy way she could swing from little girl lost one moment to full-bodied woman the next. It was chaotic and tantalizing. The channel-changer in her personality would catch me wrong-footed time and again.

'The guy behind it's a friend of mine,' she said.

'What's-his-face . . . Marcus Freeman?' I knew the founder of the World Health Rostrum by reputation: everybody did. An American cult figure with an aura of showbiz and a flair for marketing. The AIDS Campaign had made him famous. He'd capitalized on the Cambridge BioScience test and used the publicity to raise charitable donations from the public at large. This funded the free screenings while the surplus went into blatantly hyped medical projects.

'In a year's time,' she went on, 'Marcus's AIDS Campaign will be running out of steam. That'll mean less money to cover the cost of screenings.' I was fully awake. Suppose, she suggested, I were to do something that would help my work and hers at the same time. Maybe she'd get to prove Shakespeare did have syphilis and eventually a descendant would be traced. More people would be screened for AIDS – free of charge. The boost for the AIDS Campaign could raise millions of dollars.

She hesitated before coming out with what I'd get for my pains. If I went to America the Rostrum would supply me with all the HIV samples I could ever hope to get my hands on to build a complete set of restriction maps – boy, did she have the jargon for a dodo brain. Marcus would also provide me with a well-equipped research lab. She promised. I trusted her and I didn't want to pour cold water on her idea yet. Not until I knew what she wanted in return. I didn't dare to ask.

Nor did I ask where all this would leave my relationship with her, or about her friendship with Marcus Freeman, if friendship was all there was to it. Something in her tone made me suspicious. The way she could be so secretive about bits of her life. I just scrunched up my face and asked again how she'd found out about my gene. My skepticism was leaking out.

She crooked her little finger beside her ear. 'My little finger's telepathic,' she said. As I reached out to take her hand a wry grimace crept over her face. Funny, but I believed her, about telepathy. It's something I felt I had too. Almost like I could will things to happen.

'I love your Bump,' I said. I meant it. Her nose was fine and straight but for that slight Roman bulge.

She replied by stretching the tip of one finger to touch my nose. 'Your Bump,' she whispered urgently. 'Give me *your* Bump.' Then, more urgently: 'Now.'

She set down her cup and moved closer to nuzzle my ear. I ran one finger up the inner side of her leg, flirted for a moment at the moist wedge and seconds later she sprawled supine, quivering, the hollow between her thighs cradling my head. She rested one hand on my hair, pressing gently as I buried my face, refusing to surface. Her breath was panting, interlaced with small sounds that quickly turned to a strangled skirl.

Ten minutes later I came up for air and wiped my nose with the back of my hand.

As she smothered me with her breasts, she whispered how she liked dark men with the kind of looks a woman could feel comfortable with, then her fingers were fossicking in the mat of my chest and her head was working down on me. She smoothed her cheek against my navel and took me between her lips on an out-of-body trip like no other I'd experienced before. I felt as if she was a part of me that I'd only met before in those rare dreams – the ones where you run into your ideal lover and you recognize each other instantly without saying a word.

I'd thought I could see her coming a mile off, but it turned out my hunch was light years off the mark.

I spluttered and choked and called it preposterous when she finally came up for air and presented me with her plan and Marcus's to tunnel into Shakespeare's grave. My breath caught in my throat as I protested there was no way you could justify illegal disinterment, but with her lips glistering like that in the moonlight she was pleading personified and I but putty in her hands.

When I'd done all that research on DNA from bodies buried in the eighteenth and nineteenth centuries . . . come to think of it she seemed to know anyway . . . that had been above board, permits, the lot. This was the twentieth century. I wasn't a resurrection man delivering cadavers on contract to some crooked anatomist.

But if I *were* to do it I'd need help: maybe Jake and Roy, the gardener and the handyman from my father's estate. At a price, knowing them. I dismissed her harebrained plan again and rolled over to face the wall.

I agonized over her half-baked proposal for the next few days, raising every conceivable objection. Aside from legality there was

23

the cost, the valuable time it would take . . . just when my vaccine work was looking good . . . and the all too obvious chance of failure that such a hit-or-miss operation entailed. She was the one who drew my attention to the electronic surveillance equipment that had been installed in the Stratford church in the Seventies after the failed attempt to steal Janssen's bust of Shakespeare. The question was: would the sensors reach so deep below the floor?

I dug up another objection: Shakespeare's corpse, if I could locate it, would be no more than a skeleton. That was before she produced the archeology thesis on Jacobean burial caskets. Anthony Treloar's research, which I was unaware of, at least made it conceivable the cadaver would be well preserved. Still there were always enormous problems in reconstituting badly degraded DNA. Treloar had excavated a tomb in Gloucestershire dated 1622 and the remains had turned out to be intact inside an airtight coffin: not a pauper's casket, but lead, solid and sealed.

I mulled over this tomb-robbing idea till I felt possessed by it. By this time Amelia belonged to all my thoughts of present and future. I could hear her voice cajoling in my sleep. She'd done her homework all right and I found I was gulling myself to believe the plan might, as she suggested, be the shortest cut to a vaccine for HIV. It was the only rational excuse left to me after she swallowed me whole and became part of me. I couldn't admit I was obsessed with her. Hooked was as far as I dared to go. I never called it love. Not yet. Not aloud.

In the end I could say no to nothing . . . the head of John the Baptist, even the remains of William Shakespeare. You name it.

Our idyll lasted a month as Oxford flowed through the sybaritic rites of Summer Term. On our final night together we strolled across Port Meadow a little tipsy. A harvest moon guided us to the village of Wolvercote across the grass, leaving the town silhouetted in the sky. Back in bed afterwards she glowed deliciously. I said I'd do it and she turned herself inside out for me. No words can describe the way it felt.

2

OTHELLO: . . . Then must you speak
Of one that lov'd not wisely, but too well;
Of one not easily jealous, but being wrought,
Perplexed in the extreme; of one whose hand,
Like the base Indian, threw a pearl away
Richer than all his tribe.

> *Othello*, Act V, Scene 2
> William Shakespeare

'Jeezers, geddown!'

Three shapes ducked their heads. The rotten beam groaned, followed by a crack as it split across the grain. *Death-watch beetle.*

Sweet Jesus, would the Church of the Holy Trinity, dead overhead, render the bones of William Shakespeare? 'They have laid him full seventeen foot deep, deep enough to secure him,' I recited to myself.

Eyes pricked white out of black locked into the hole. I caught the crease of a smile, then it was gone. The stench tore into me. Wrestling back the urge to throw up I signaled the next beam with a jerk of one thumb. Jake went to work. By degrees it twisted back, rotten also.

I found I could just breathe the chilly air in shallow breaths. The fetid gases made me dry-heave. A muffled gasp.

'Bleedin' hell!' Roy spat into the ground.

Straining to support the weight of my kit I peered into the void. Above in the so-called Weeping Chancel a few feet from the north wall lay the dramatist's chanceled stone with its malediction:

GOOD FRIEND FOR JESUS SAKE FORBEARE
TO DIGG THE DUST ENCLOASED HEARE:
BLEST BE YE MAN YT SPARES THES STONES,
AND CURST BE HE YT MOVES MY BONES.

25

I removed my helmet and pushed a hand through my hair. I knew the doggerel lines by heart and mumbled them under my breath as the light from three helmets washed over the darkness. A buttress loomed into view supporting oaken joists.

The crowbar levered away two further beams that blocked the way as Jake and Roy crouched under the dank tunnel roof, swallowing the stench as if they would rather choke. I coughed and straddled my tall frame over, paused and listened.

I looked back just as the others heaved their shoulders through the hole and craned their necks to follow my progress. A fallow smile. I lurched ahead.

My skin crawled and I shrank back. Some ghastliness . . . the beam from my helmet picked out orbits staring from row upon row of skulls that had lain in this charnel house for centuries. I squared my shoulders and shuffled toward a stone sarcophagus. One arm swept over the top of a slab caked in grime. It was unmarked.

A fine dust veiled the air like muslin drawn across my shaft of light, and filtered into my nostrils.

My God, this cramped necropolis felt vast; this mortuary beneath another vault. And above that the Shakespeare family stones laid out in the chancel: those stones were no guide to their bodies and where they lay.

Avoiding stabbing eyes I weaved from one filthy tomb to the next, more desperate with each failure to uncover a giveaway sign as I wiped away the dirt.

How many were there? Fifteen, twenty cadavers in lengthlong repose?

Unmarked stones. Others bore lapidary cuts: coats of arms. I made out chiseled letters. Initials and more initials. Inscriptions. Blackened hands: yellow light.

God give me a sign . . . for Amelia.

I avoided the eyes of my companions. Another failure.

A rough outline. Another trick of arms cut in stone. I supported myself on one nervous hand and traced the faint weapon's edge with my index finger.

I froze. Delayed reaction.

'Gold on a bend sable,' I whispered. 'A spear of the first steeled argent, and for his crest of cognizance a falcon. Let it be, dear God.'

With my fingernails I scratched the dust out of the rough outline.

'. . . his wings displayed argent, standing on a wreath of his colours, supporting a spear gold.'

'Shakespeare's gold,' I yelled under my breath. My words seemed to boom round the place. How small this catacomb was suddenly.

Jake and Roy were at my shoulder. After so many months . . . They caught my look of thanksgiving.

Grunting with the effort the three of us hefted the slab that formed the top of the sarcophagus. It moved slowly, grinding its way round.

'Shine your light here.'

The vault ached with cold. My hand shook as I probed inside.

'It's lead all right; cast lead.' I could hear the gloating in my voice.

A cruciform casket lay in my light. I peered at the gabled lid. Jake shot me a look which might have been deference behind the dirt.

Unzipping the front of my overalls I tugged out a bundle and laid it on top of the slab. From it came an implement like a miniature rapier with a serrated edge. When I plugged it into a handle and pressed a button the blade whined. I prayed the lead had been sealed airtight in 1616. The place was damp as a witch's arse. Was this the way Howard Carter felt when he came to his rendezvous with Tutankhamun?

At the first insertion there was a hiss of escaping gas. I held my breath to avoid the putrid aroma.

'More light.'

My hands were steady now. Fancying myself as a surgeon, total control, I cut round the edges of the coffin and halfway down made an incision across the center. Jake produced a spatulate instrument and wedged it under the top end. Roy and I brought out similar tools. On the count of three we levered up a piece of Jacobean lead weighing over a hundred pounds and manhandled it to the top of the slab.

'Holy Jesus!' My heart almost stopped.

The ghoul before us made no answer. It grimaced horrifically from ear to ear. Foul air climbed up from this grisly corpse and clung to the roof of my mouth. Roy turned his back and vomited.

In color the Bard's face was not unlike our own dirt-stained features, but with a hint of yellow. Only this face was bearded and mustached, hoary old, the cheeks sunken and pitted with deep ulcers. Scrawny lips were shriveled back to display a set of peg-shaped teeth, chipped and blackened. The head and body were wrapped round in a winding shroud that had begun to fall away as flesh shrank over time. William Shakespeare face to face, culminating in the shroud's top-knot lying tattered above a parchment pate.

I broke the silence. 'Hold the bag open.' I had the fancy that if I didn't move fast the cadaver would crumble into dust.

I prodded the Bard's chest. It was firm. The rise of the water table in the Avon basin hadn't filled the sepulcher with mud. That much I'd gambled on, though the Avon's surface lay only four feet below floor level in the church. Down here only damp had entered.

The success of the funereal craftsmen in fashioning an airtight casket had guaranteed the absence of outside air and saved the body from the worst ravages of bacteria, ensuring an almost perfectly preserved mummy. This was a man who believed in his undying reputation and invested in it with the best lead money could buy: a man with pretensions to gentility and all its trappings.

The corpse fleered back at me out of sunken eyes like dried olives. I registered the smoothness of the facial skin in those areas that were not ulcerated, the tracery of wrinkles in the leathery surface: a face barely touched by putrefaction.

But it was the nose – or what little remained of one – that held my concentration. It was a remnant of a nose: two holes like a little florid trumpet, with the bridge flattened in a way that to my regret I'd seen so often before. This disfigurement had nothing to do with decay. The collapsed bridge and splayed nose were the blazon of advanced tertiary syphilis.

I tried carefully to push back the remaining bits of cere-cloth in which the corpse was wound but the calico and wax of the withered raiment disintegrated as I touched them. Above the ears lay the fluff of a tonsure. Two teeth were missing: one upper incisor and one lower canine. This wizened face was totally unlike the plump bourgeois of the monument in the church. This ghoulish Shakespeare with his smile of the blissfully demented looked for all the world like a satyr transfixed at the climax of a maenadic revel.

I parted the shroud where it clung below the chin. The burial chemise underneath was crisp as a cracker and seemed to dissolve as I touched it. Over the midriff hands seamed with their own grain and aged to an ebony hue clasped at something.

'What in the name of God . . .?'

With difficulty I coaxed the object from the poet's clutch to place it in the bag.

The body's soft tissue was dry but not brittle. It had the texture of pemmican, almost supple. I divided the shroud at thigh level and palped one bony leg still wrapped in scraps of pitted skin. A shriveled knot in a rope was all that remained of the sartorius muscle. Taking a scalpel from the kit I excised a blackened strip. The blade touched bone. I turned and dropped the sample into a jar of formaldehyde held by Roy.

As I withdrew my other hand more calico crumbled and something broke away from the corpse just below its hands. I picked up a small desiccated lump and examined it under Jake's lamp: a shrunken penis, so atrophied it looked like a cross between a lugworm and a tumor.

Despite the condition it was in, the tell-tale scarring of syphilitic lesions was plainly visible. When I probed the groin I could find no trace of testicles. I dropped the Bard's manhood back into place more or less where it had come from.

'Let's move.'

The lead top was replaced and the slab shunted back into position.

Bent double, we retreated the way we had come, past pinewood struts shoring up our secret tunnel.

At 0422 hours we emerged into the fog that enveloped Stratford-upon-Avon that January morning. The trapdoor entrance in the riverbank was reconcealed. Gear was loaded into the boat tied a few yards away.

The plane's cabin seemed suddenly very still. I opened *Nature* and ran over the easy-to-read introduction that preceded my scientific paper on the syphilitic gene that from then on would be called

29

the 'weeping gene', after the Weeping Chancel of the Stratford church. After announcing the gene at the Oxford conference and meeting Amelia, I'd postponed the naming of it to coincide with my 'confession' of the Stratford incident if I pulled it off and succeeded in cloning the Bard's DNA. The piece closed with an apology for what I'd done. *If I have disturbed the bones of the Swan of Avon, I am sure, understanding my motive, he will forgive my intrusion.* James McFadden, *Nature*'s editor, had kept the secret for three weeks. My advance copy had reached me at Heathrow.

I recognized the bits that Amelia, by phone from America, had helped me compose: *After the death of his son Hamnet, Shakespeare had no direct legitimate male descent. The direct female line ended with his granddaughter, Lady Elizabeth Bernard. However by-blows – children born 'on the wrong side of the blanket' – were common in Elizabethan times.*

Then the textual evidence on Shakespeare the whore-lover. Some scholars had a theory he'd died of Bright's Disease, that this accounted for the shaking signature in the poet's last will and testament. But I'd seen that it was syphilis. The trumpet nose caused by a mucosal gumma, the peg teeth, the cutaneous ulcerations and the cicatrized penis had said almost everything. An autopsy would have told the rest of the story: the thickened bones, the infected eyes, liver and lungs. Neurosyphilis would have ravaged the central nervous system and a cerebral gumma would have formed causing 'walnut brain' and general paresis. Locomotor ataxia caused by tertiary syphilis would account for the wobbly writing, just as Amelia argued in one of her papers.

By the time I'd written my own paper I'd devoured every available book touching the little that was known about Shakespeare's life.

The Bard had amended his will on 25 March 1616, declaring himself to be 'in perfect health and memory', which was obviously a whitewash, given what tertiary syphilis could do to your brain and the signs of advanced infection that I'd seen for myself. Shakespeare must have been bedridden and going downhill fast. It's no wonder his will left his second-best bed to his wife. He would have been horribly incontinent by that stage, so the best bed he was lying in would probably have been in such a state that everyone agreed it had to be burnt.

Four weeks later Shakespeare was dead, and though it looked to me as if syphilis killed him I tended to think something else might have got to him first: mercury, the chemical that was one of the period's favorite cures for syphilis. One that frequently finished off the patient before the disease did. In fact the struggle in Shakespeare's testamentary signatures could also have been the effect of acute mercury poisoning. If I'd had a chance to autopsy his body, I reckoned I'd have found traces of mercury.

The lead coffin was a work of such craftsmanship that it could well have taken a month to make. It might have been ordered the same day as Shakespeare summoned his notary to his bedside to amend his will. The sealed lead kept air out after the poet's body had been hastily buried, but syphilitic bacteria would have gone on ravaging it for a time until they too died like their host. The only thing that had survived was the crucial DNA – enough of it for me to carry out, over two weeks in January working day and night, the painstaking job of cloning those cells in a culture. And coming up with gold: Shakespeare's gene mutated by syphilitic spirochetes.

The crux of the introduction to my paper was the argument to convince readers of *Nature* and the world at large that a flesh-and-blood descendant might be walking the streets of England or the United States at that moment.

Thinking back to our last night in Oxford together, Amelia told me she loved me, in the early hours, as we lay sprawled like Siamese twins in a sticky afterglow and all I said back was: 'Love me or need me?' She didn't reply, but in the middle of her silence she went down on me under the sweating sheet and raised me to a higher plane with the tip of her tongue. I thought hard about why I didn't want to run from her. I wanted to taste her saltlick skin and eat her bumpy nose and suck her soul out of her mouth, then burrow into her brain.

I expected too much of my relationships, so was it any wonder I wound up disappointed? So much was new with Amelia. I wanted to spend time with her doing things. It was as if I'd found a place where I could belong, skin to skin. No more hit and run.

Amelia was no wide-eyed virgin. She too had a past. A good many as I later found out. What was odd was how short all her relationships had been, considering she was attractive, ultra-intelligent and almost as rich as Croesus. Despite that, she said she was the one who got left behind. Men couldn't seem to handle her; they got scared off. Men who came on all macho and wound up wiping their eyes in your armpits was how she put it.

That morning I'd got talking to Matthew about it as he drove me to Heathrow. For all our differences, like Matthew was born legitimate, he and I were close friends. He was four years younger than me and had also come out the other end of a messy divorce. Some people reckoned he was a bit of a plonker, but he was okay, really, even if he did squitter through life in the slow lane. With money, tight just wasn't the word. Matthew was the kind of closet straight who'd be into DIY bondage if it'd save a few quid on eating out. I dare say some of us spend our lives looking for our mothers. Only with the namby side of Matthew it wasn't his mother, it was his nanny. Someone to hurt him – exquisitely.

There was the usual traffic snarl-up on the M4 and the congestion got so bad once we turned off that I almost missed the plane. Still, it gave me time to update him on Amelia and me and what we'd planned. I knew he could be counted on to keep his mouth shut.

'She had sex written all over her face,' I said as we crawled into bottom gear.

He flicked his eyes off the road to answer me. 'Don't you ever see *people* out there,' he demanded to know, 'instead of tits and bums? Someone should lock you up before you cause serious harm.'

I tend to work on the jealousy theory when I get suchlike comments, only with Matthew and me it's just a game we play. Off to starboard a 747 was about to touch down, so we were getting close. 'Look, I can't help it,' I said, 'if there's this hungry hole inside me that needs to be fed, otherwise I'm only half there.'

'You can say that again,' he sallied back, casting his chuckle about the car for an audience. 'When I look at what you've done – all your women and glory . . . well, Lucy was right.'

I made a go-on noise in his direction, but he took his time, stalling at a confusion of signposts as he tried, without his glasses, to figure which was the turn-off for Terminal Four. Without his glasses, Matthew had the hang-dog look of a menopausal hippopotamus.

When he'd deciphered the right road he explained what Lucy had told him. 'She said your definition of a woman was something soft and warm that you wore on the end of your wonker.'

If I hadn't known Matthew better I'd have thought he was trying to twit me. I answered his pet question before he could launch it. 'I *was* faithful to Lucy . . . for a bit.'

'Ten minutes.'

'If she chose to turn a blind eye that was up to her. I didn't ask *her* who she'd been with all day.'

'With Lucy you knew she wouldn't have told you.'

'Look, Lucy got what she was asking for. Can't you see it's different with Amelia?'

Matthew knew a rhetorical question when he saw one. There was a lot to be said, I told him, for the one-night love affair, safe sex and all things considered. So long as you escaped before you were gobbled up.

'Maybe this time,' he said, 'you've found someone you're prepared to respect and settle down with.'

The idea of settling down and becoming an item, even with Amelia, left me feeling out of control. Matthew was asking when I'd grow up and I was saying: 'Women have an organ between their legs that looks and operates like a plant called a Venus flytrap. The female organ's also pink and sticky and it's called a brain.'

'Sexist shit.'

Still, we both laughed. I wasn't really sexist. He liked to play the game too, where we put all women in the same box and pretended to poke holes in it. Isolation was the price he and I paid for our independence and it didn't come cheap. But what else was I to do when Lucy grew frigid and started turning off the tap?

With Amelia it was different. The feeling of being trapped with Lucy just wasn't there. After we'd made love I didn't come crashing down like a lead balloon.

You understand that, Matthew, you of all people.

He pulled the car to a halt outside the terminal and two porters leapt improbably to attention at the sight of his beat-up Morris Minor.

I glanced across at the cardiac candidates snoozing off lunch around the cabin. The callipygous stewardess was still chilly, but she wasn't the one my thoughts were on, nor Amelia.

I saw myself again: a small boy knelt in the lush grass at the edge of the lake and scooped a jamjar full of frog spawn. One muddied hand came up to take the string tied tightly round the jamjar's throat. The air was warm. This was his secret place where he came to cry the day Hattie turned away the gypsy woman cradling the baby that had scarlet fever. The lake held sticklebacks – he dreamed of catching one, but not the iridescent green dragonflies of high summer that would soon be coming.

The tree stood at the far side of the lake in Dorrell's Wood, holding a plank between two branches so that Jake and Roy and the other boys could dive into the water and make the girls watch – and come up yelling, shivering, like heroes. He sat on the bank and looked at them until they all went off without him to steal the speckled green-brown eggs in the hedgerows. Then the lakeside, as often, was deserted, but the trees were alive with rooks, and one different call: the double note of a cuckoo, the bird that always stayed invisible, no matter how hard he tried to see it.

The sun stroked his hair and beat through his T-shirt when he set off home. There was trouble with the frog spawn though. There was too much in the jar and gobs of it kept spilling. His eyes moistened when he scooped it back, aware that this was life and to abandon one of those brown dots was to let life die.

He felt special in that place and sat down again in the knee-high grass and cried for something that was missing. It was a hole as big as the world and it could not be filled, no matter how tight he tied himself inside his sheet each night and peeped at the blue light out in the hallway.

I took the All Souls Fellowship and left the University of New South Wales so that I'd have more chance in Oxford to look into my mother's death.

I saw her again and again, being suffocated by anonymous hands, a man's hands: her bulging eyes, her tongue bitten till it bled, her blood vessels bursting in her cheeks, her silent gasp as air escaped when her head was finally released . . . dead.

'Hot towel, sir?'

I refused snappily and went over things one more time. Through the weeks of planning and tunneling – Jake and Roy's help had cost me the predicted arm and a leg – Amelia and I had stayed in touch by phone.

She brought Marcus Freeman up to date the moment she returned to America and it was arranged that I should meet him in London if the Stratford operation turned out a success. That way the World Health Rostrum's peripatetic founder would have time to gear up secretly for the search for Shakespeare's weeping gene that would spearhead a relaunched AIDS Campaign: assuming the gene – dutifully mutated – was found and nothing happened meantime to scupper the plan. To date everything had gone as forecast. Even Shakespeare, much to my surprise, had cooperated.

A meeting was scheduled with Amelia's father, then a second meeting with Marcus – in New York this time. But first there would be three weeks in hiding at Amelia's house. The thought of Lawrence Hungerford made me go tight in my throat. Amelia said she could twist her father round her little finger. But she admitted that under the patina of old money he was totally barbaric. She said it almost jocularly. He was an art historian and lobbyist who handled congressional relations for the World Health Rostrum; they were his only client from outside the international art world. I had an impression, from what Amelia said, of a man who was seriously rich and had clout in important places. As art advisor to the White House he had access to the Oval Office. She said Lawrence and Marcus were friends as well as business associates and it was through Lawrence she'd got to know Marcus in the first place. Lawrence was giving the AIDS Campaign a lot of moral support and would back the Shakespeare Search. Marcus had already picked that name for the hunt.

I couldn't fathom whether Amelia's father was getting in on the act for professional reasons or because Amelia wanted him to do it for her research or for Marcus Freeman. I found myself forcing the thought of Amelia with Marcus out of my mind. I'd carried out a careful check on this character and his cultish movement and been forced to give them a clean bill of health. And if Lawrence Hungerford was going to be involved, his supposed influence might protect me from any nasty repercussions of breaking into a famous grave.

When Shakespeare's version of the weeping gene had been extracted, purified and cloned in my Oxford lab, I hadn't been totally on my own. Two colleagues I trusted were in on the secret: Roderick Tillman, a retrovirologist; and Alistair Cunliffe-Jones, a molecular biophysicist – a bit of a fruitcake really but otherwise okay – from Caltech whose expertise in high-speed gene sequencing and DNA profiling would be crucial if large numbers of DNA samples were to be tested for the weeping gene in its Shakespeare format. Both men had been sworn to secrecy. Both were smitten with the possibility of a stake in the fame . . . or infamy . . . that would follow if the Shakespeare gene was found in a living man. Tillman had agreed to rejoin me in America and form the nucleus of a Rostrum-sponsored team to work on a vaccine for HIV. Cunliffe-Jones had flown over to England last October and helped conduct the covert operation in Stratford, using an optical fiber camera on the end of a long probe to pinpoint the mysterious second crypt below the newer, higher one in Holy Trinity. He would spearhead the laboratory search for a Shakespeare descendant in the US.

At the first hint of success in my lab I'd called Amelia and she'd put Lawrence and Marcus in the picture. That was when Marcus had flown straight to England to introduce himself and hold three days of clandestine meetings with me. Now the Rostrum's plans were dead on target.

To move to America at this point had all the signs of a bad career move and I realized I'd laid myself on the line like some woebegone lover, along with my reputation as one of the front runners in the vaccine stakes. I could hear the tattletale stories going round with the port after dinner in hall: words like 'fugitive' and 'on the run'. I'd be forced to lie low for a time. My plans for a six-month sabbatical had come as a surprise to everyone. Not that I hadn't been due time off. They'd just thought it odd for me to be taking leave when the race – with over eighty competitors worldwide – was hotting up to be first over the line with a vaccine that actually worked.

I peered out through the twilight at a snowswept Newfoundland and stretched back for the final hour of the flight.

Sweet Amelia, so giddy in love.

3

All of her that is out of door most rich!
If she be furnished with a mind so rare,
She is alone th'Arabian bird . . .

Cymbeline, Act I, Scene 6
William Shakespeare

I picked a path over frozen slush. From the campus map I reckoned I'd got the place wired. In the middle of the Yard I scooped up a handful of not-yet-dirty snow. Removing my dark glasses I crumped the crystals into my face and the tingling sensation woke me up. A girl coming the other way gave me a knowing twitch of her mouth. Ahead lay the edifice of Sever Hall. I headed for it and took the steps three at a time. Bodies swarmed everywhere as I pounded up the stairs.

One thing I hadn't reckoned with at the beginning of February, which Amelia would soon explain: Shopping Week after the four-day intercession, when the chance to sample Harvard's best before signing on brought the horde to many lectures. I squeezed in the door of Room 202. *Standing room only.* My eyes darted across serried heads. Amelia stood on the podium in a plaid skirt and bulky knit. On her feet were serious shoes but her clothes could do nothing to cover voluptuousness bursting under the genteel exterior. A handful of students sat in obeisance at her feet. I dismissed the idea that a man of thirty-five must look conspicuous and wedged myself half inside the door, the closest I could get. An opal light filtered through dirty Venetian blinds. Amelia had a home-made lectern: her attaché case upended to form a wedge on top of the table. The voyeur in me caught sight of her breasts and I sank my head deep in the fissure.

Amelia had quite a track record from everything I'd been able to piece together. She'd been a popular Teaching Fellow during the first two years of her PhD program. The invitation to apply for lecturer came from Professor Alexandra Hufstader, Dean of GSAS, with the full endorsement of Professor Bob Carr. The appointment was exceptional. Her thesis was still more than a year from completion. But as early as her first year in graduate school the 'iconclast of Shakespeare studies', as Bob Carr had dubbed her, began to turn upside down the shibboleths of Shakespearian dogma. Now scholars were beginning to validate her totem-shattering revelations and take a new look at the canon to find the writer. There was something about Shakespeare, I had to admit. He even had a hold on me now.

I sucked in my breath and scratched the side of my nose at the sight of her back view. She had turned to the board and peeled off her sweater. When she spun round to face her audience she glanced my way and I caught a look in those green eyes that might have held a glimmer of recognition.

As I inclined my head she smiled conspiratorially for half a second and checked her notes. Taking a piece of chalk she drew two symbols on the board, the first of which made me sit up straight as I registered the resemblance to the artefact I'd taken from Shakespeare's hands: 'In hermetic tradition,' she pronounced, 'the most powerful of all fertility symbols – the male pudendum – is commonly represented by the Tau cross, a capital T. The Tau is the symbol of Mercury the great confounder . . . Hermes in the Greek pantheon . . . Hermes "who divideth not 'tween good and ill", Hermes the Ithyphallic or Hermes with erect phallus who sows the seeds of cosmic confusion. The Tau

takes many forms. The one drawn here is the astrological symbol of Aries the Ram, the herald of spring renewal.'

There were sniggers from the front row.

'Let's look at another arcane symbol: the Arabian bird. In Elizabethan poetry the phoenix is often the symbol of married love. In alchemical mythology on the other hand the phoenix stands for resurrection through the golden elixir of the Holy Grail. This rare bird that nests on top of a palm tree can also represent Venus, goddess of the vagina, which is why we can substitute the female cross I've drawn here for a phoenix. The

Tau or palm is Mercury, ruler of Aries in the esoteric Zodiac. This she-Mercury or Rebis is an androgynous figure, male in sex but male and female in gender. In the alchemical process Mercury holds the key to the freeing of white masculine *spiritus* from black feminine *chaos*. As we'll see in a later lecture many of Shakespeare's sonnets to the Friend have a lot to do with the theme of truth and perfection. These are key aspects of the androgynous ideal in the late Renaissance.

'Let's go back briefly to Shakespeare's poem: *Venus and Adonis*, published in 1593. It celebrates love, the fourth fury, and love's power to resurrect. Mortal Adonis, preferring the hunt to dalliance with immortal Venus, is killed by jealous Mars in the guise of a wild boar. The red-and-white anemone that springs from Adonis's blood is a symbol of the androgyne and human perfectibility.

'Three is the number of the Hermetic Trinity, commonly represented by the trefoil or triangle. With the point one way the triangle represents Man. With the point the other way it represents Woman. Combined in a hexagram or six-point star – the Kabbalists' Seal of Solomon – we get another symbol of androgynous Mercury, the Hermes Trismegistus so dear to Renaissance alchemists. Now let's look at another hermetic figure.'

She turned and drew a hieroglyph on the board:

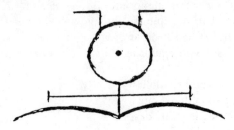

'The *monas* of Dr John Dee: a symbol of the archetype we call the cosmos. It holds the Tau cross split in two and the female or Egyptian cross, the *ankh*, the most powerful symbol of the vagina. Notice the twin crescent moons and the sun . . . the dot in the center is an alchemical symbol to indicate transcendence of the world of duality: the sublunary world. We'll be discussing sun imagery and the sexually ambiguous role of Diana and her various moons in a later lecture.

'It's almost time to finish.' Her glance crept once more in my direction. 'I'd like to remind you that in my last lecture I intend to take you over what still remains the most baffling mystery in English literature: who was Shakespeare's Dark Lady? See if you can identify her for yourselves. The Elizabethans loved to bury clues in wordplay, especially clues to names. Look in the *Sonnets* and Willoughby's *Avisa* and *The Victory of English Chastity*, which we touched on last week. If there are textual clues to the Dark Lady's name, that's where you'll find them. We'll be examining the half-dozen or so recognized candidates, so make sure you've read up on them. Any Student Cards still for signature, see me in my office Monday between four and five.'

The lecture had ended with unseemly haste. The clock on the wall still showed six minutes to the hour. I retreated outside the door while the class dispersed. As I reentered, Amelia was passing her attaché case to a girl in a woolly jacket. The girl hurried past me and I took off my dark glasses and stepped onto the podium. Amelia gazed into my face and took my hand, but kept me at a distance. After a glance at the open door she threw her arms round me, stopping my next words with a short kiss.

I managed to say: 'Where did you get the suntan?' Her teeth positively gleamed out of a tan complexion.

She said it was skiing in Vermont at the weekend. It sounded so trite. Where had the epic language of love disappeared at this of all moments? It had been at least half a year.

'Vermont,' she said again, as if there was nothing else in the world to say.

I made a sign and she followed.

Collar up, I shouldered our way through the doors to the Yard. It was frisky weather but despite a biting wind that raked the Common, Harvard Square was noisy with the throng of late afternoon. When we passed Out-of-town News and Tickets on Nini's Corner it was Amelia who caught sight of the front page of the *Boston Globe*'s night edition. A caption announced: SHAKESPEARE'S GRAVE VIOLATED. I looked round the Square before stepping forward to buy a copy which I tucked under one elbow.

As we swung onto Brattle Street she clasped my arm. A trail had been blazed in the slush along the sidewalk. When she slipped on an icy patch she steadied herself against me, laughing. I checked my watch. The temperature was falling fast under a pallid sun. 'Bodysnatcher!' she said and gave me a wicked poke in the ribs. I leaned on her and snuffled her ear till she giggled archly and tugged at my elbow. 'C'mon,' she told me.

On the corner of Ash and Brattle she halted and came round in front of me. She removed her mittens and reached into my pockets to draw out my gloveless hands, which she raised to her lips. I saw her fingernails. In Oxford they'd been erotically long. Now they were chewed to the quick, almost bleeding. For one frozen moment she was a shadow linked to me by fingers, then she was pressing my hands between flattened palms and palping each mound of Venus with her thumbs. She intercepted my gaze and tensed.

A dog barked. Freeing myself I pulled her to one side. A woman went by in sweat suit and headband, dragged after an Irish wolfhound. My hands were feeling like parts of someone else. I chafed them together. I was close enough to catch the smell of Amelia's hair. She squizzled her nose at me and gave me that smile I'd come to know as her call sign. Baneful clouds raced overhead.

41

'Take off those crazy sunglasses,' she ordered, exploding into mirth, 'unless you think you're getting snowblind.' Before I could reply she reached out and removed them. She was serious again. I pulled her to me. Words stuck in my throat. She stiffened, her eyes held mine, then with a murmur of 'I love you, baby' she buried her face in my shoulder.

'Welcome,' she said in jest at the gate, 'to the ancestral demesne of my family of merchant scholars.' She snuggled against my side. 'Robber barons really.'

My first sight of Hungerford House sent my heart into my mouth. I was looking at a herringbone path leading up to the place and wishing in vain for a yellow brick road. The path led to a short flight of steps and a tall black door crowned with a triangular fanlight.

From this prospect Hungerford House was a feat of eclectic craftsmanship. It dominated the neighbouring Harvard and Radcliffe mansions along the former cart track that was Brattle Street, better known to early Cantabrigians, she told me, as Tory Road. Apparently of all the houses erected in old Cambridge by the town's merchant Brahmins, only Elmwood, the home of Harvard's President, was more grandiose.

It was a gaunt mansion on three floors, surmounted by a cluster of unmatched chimneys. One wing had a gambrel roof. A gust of wind knifed round the corner, sending a badly latched shutter crashing into the wall. The place was a feast of windows: bay on the ground floor and casement on the next, panes in diamond-shaped lead lattice, the kind that defied penetration by the world outside. An attic dormer jutted above the eaves. I stared up at it and it stared back at me. It didn't blink. Instead I thought I saw someone's shadowed face pass across it.

She fumbled with her keys. On the third attempt the right one went in and she pushed the doorknob shaped after its designer's vision of a pineapple. Inside I took stock of a parquet floor and a dark oak-paneled hallway furnished in the style of the late nineteenth century. It was lit at one extreme by a stained-glass window. A grand staircase disappeared up to the first floor.

She took my coat and guided me through to the sitting room. Its French windows overlooked the terrace out back and a desolate garden. A low table stood center of a group of seats in crushed velvet. Beyond these a Sheraton chair confronted a rosewood desk. One half of the room gave pride of place to an ebony Bösendorfer grand, matched with a fretted harp beside it.

Amelia crossed to the desk and picked up the phone, trying to reach her service, pen poised over a scratchpad.

I took stock of an oil painting on the wall beyond the piano: a tropical dreamscape peopled by naked women. She was off the phone. Who was the painter? I asked.

'Me, in the Virgin Islands at Christmas.' There was a touch of authority that hadn't been there in Oxford.

Other paintings covered the walls. I turned and looked at the sheet of music on the piano: a Chopin ballad. She caught my questioning air. 'How about a stiff drink?'

I noticed she ignored the tantalus with its crystal decanters sitting on the music desk in the other corner. As she disappeared I picked up a photo album lying beside an ormolu clock on a console table. I stopped at one picture, taken in Gstaad: Amelia standing in snow in front of a hotel I recognized as the Palace. Beside her slender form was a tall man in his late forties or early fifties. His eyes were dark, unlike Amelia's, but I saw the resemblance in other features, especially the commanding nose. I knew I was looking at Lawrence Hungerford. Every inch of him, even in a snapshot, betokened dynastic power. There was intelligence too, but no trace of humor.

As she returned with a bottle of Krug, the phone went. She gave me a roguish look. 'Let it ring.'

I poured her a glass and another for myself. 'You know, angel, you're guilty of sheltering a felon?'

'With a saintly objective,' she retorted. 'But vigilante ethics.'

'Do I look like a felon to you?' I brandished my glass.

'Mmm, maybe. Your eyes are kind of manically intense.' It was a poker-faced reply.

She slid her eyes up the front of my trousers before walking to the window with its bleak view, in the gathering twilight, of an icing-sugar lawn. I refilled my glass, drained it and sauntered across to her. She spun round. I pinioned her in my arms and she shut her eyes, rocking heel to toe until my mouth brushed the Bump on her nose. She murmured something and cupped my jaw in her hands. Her face turned up to meet me. For several seconds

I was startled to glimpse a faraway look in her eyes. I took in the glazed expression, the pursed lips.

'Would you change me if you could?' she asked finally.

'No, I like you fine the way you are.' I told myself there was nothing I would change: the haunting contradictions, the mixture of fey and feisty. There was something about her that was out of place with time. Children saw things that other people never noticed. Amelia saw things that no one else saw at all. I was still under her spell. I took in her impish air.

She kicked off her shoes and taking my hand led me to the sofa and sat me down. She put a record on the stereo turntable and Lucia Popp erupted to the strains of Mozart at his pastoral best, accompanied more softly by Amelia in the aria *L'amerò, sarò costante*. Just when I'd decided I liked her voice it tailed off leaving Lucia Popp to continue alone. When I twisted round to check why she'd stopped she was standing motionless, except that she blinked and her head nodded a couple of times. Then I saw it again: an unfocused look gazing into the distance. Her pupils were dilated. The faint smile at the corners of her mouth was frozen there. A moment later she was shaking her left arm as if trying to restore circulation. Her smile dissolved into laughter that sounded somewhat forced. I quickly discounted the idea that she was hiding something. From one minute to the next I wasn't sure where I stood with her. We'd had only four weeks together in Oxford and almost eight months had passed since then. In many ways I hardly knew her.

She sat down beside me and, resting her head against my shoulder, walked the tips of her fingers across my thigh, arousing me despite the alcoholic imperative to lie low. She giggled and took a snickering bite at my shoulder. My cheeks were burning. She made small purring sounds and kissed my ear: hot sharp kisses that left a burr of excitement.

She'd been gone for several minutes. When she sailed back in wearing a maroon spinnaker of a nightshirt she found me hunched over the *Boston Globe*. A clock chimed out in the hallway. I took the pastrami sandwich and cup of strong black coffee she was holding out and continued reading without looking up as she spread one arm across my shoulders and rested her chin in the hollow of my collarbone. I felt distanced from the Stratford story, as if it was about someone else.

Early the previous evening, as planned, Reverend Adrian Mannering of Holy Trinity had received my letter – my apology – by courier from my lawyer. By dawn that morning Mannering had investigated the tunnel under his church with a detective from Scotland Yard. Mannering had immediately got on to the national media and called a press conference. Several dozen reporters had turned up at the Swan Theatre in Stratford around the time my flight took off from Heathrow.

I took a sip of coffee and studied the photo of Mannering and the detective sitting behind twin microphones. The detective's name wasn't given and the picture was pretty fuzzy, but I thought I recognized his face and when I looked at it harder my heart started pounding so hard it was almost fibrillating. I wondered if it could just be coincidence . . . I'd said nothing to Amelia yet about my mother's murder. I read the article again, letting my heart rate return to normal.

Mannering hadn't wasted any time. I was staggered to learn they'd brought the police into it – this detective or any other. A lot of people would thank me in the end, maybe, but in the meantime I was a common criminal. They'd called me 'the self-confessed grave robber' and set up an Incident Room at New Scotland Yard. No mention of my article in *Nature* or the weeping gene and its significance.

Amelia straightened up. 'I suppose you know Mannering's the chairman of the Shakespeare Birthplace Trust. I don't mind him personally. It's what he writes that I just can't stomach. He's a tunnel-vision type, an amateur biographer of sorts; writes smartass articles about how Shakespeare was an orthodox believer, stuff like that. He'll go to any lengths to prove Shakespeare was whiter than white.' I looked up and saw her expression. The sympathy in it was too hackneyed to be real, surely. There was silence between us, then she turned away and I glanced up to hear her say, 'Back in a minute. I've got to go take two Tylenols.' Almost inaudibly: 'I can feel a headache coming on.'

I scanned the report a final time. The journalists had left angry and almost empty-handed. Mannering had told them only that the Bard's body was still there after this foolhardy escapade, that

45

an archeologist called Gillespie had resealed the coffin and the tunnel to the new-found crypt was being filled in. There was no description of the grave, the corpse. The end of the article didn't augur well. It had always been too much to hope that the church authorities and the police would regard my mission philosophically. It was looking more and more like a case for the Crown Prosecution Service.

Amelia slipped back into the room, rousing me from my thoughts, and we talked of the Shakespeare Search, its chances of success. One point was scored already – for establishing that Shakespeare had syphilis. Now Amelia needed a descendant. More than that, she confided again, she needed to know the identity of the Bard's Dark Lady. She had a pretty good idea who she was – lots of circumstantial evidence – it was just that she didn't have something yet that added up to proof. She appeared to be so preoccupied with this unknown floozy that I was amazed she'd only mentioned her once before. When I asked her who her hunch was, she said: 'Mind your own beeswax,' and looking teasingly enigmatic added that I'd just have to wait till she'd gotten proof, like everybody else.

Three more hours passed before Dan Rather made the connection with the *Nature* report and broke the story of Shakespeare's possible descendants breathlessly on *CBS Evening News*. The other networks covered only Mannering's press conference. When the CBS anchorman ended there was uneasy silence as we sprawled on the sofa.

Amelia tried to talk about something else. 'I'm directing Fry's *Phoenix Too Frequent* for the Harvard–Radcliffe Dramatic Club. Pity you won't see it. It ties in nicely with today's lecture.'

'So do I get to see less of you?'

'Most nights I've got reading meetings at the Loeb, but they can manage with my assistant for a while. I've cleared a lot of my calendar. I had back-to-back appointments.' She wriggled round and propped one arm on each of my shoulders.

'You didn't have to change anything for me,' I said with a dry catch in my voice. I could just see her bare feet tucked under her where she was kneeling.

We ended the day on a crescendo, coupling in Amelia's bed. As a clock outside the door struck a quarter after one in the morning I pleaded jetlag and admitted privately I couldn't make it a hat trick tonight. When I told her the second coming had been sheer Heaven she didn't smile on cue. I could see her face pale in the moonlight pouring in the window. In our haste we'd forgotten to pull the curtains. I liked to make love with the lights on to watch their faces, but Amelia preferred it off. She did give me a look though, a strange one that I couldn't work out. The thought of time, for some reason, would not leave me: time surging by like a fast poison.

The next morning I watched *Good Morning America* on Amelia's bedroom TV while I shaved, and nicked my chin. My features loomed large at me. Someone had found a photograph, probably the one from *The Sunday Times* feature on AIDS. Dr Daniel Bosworth, I heard as I sat on the end of the bed and massaged after-shave into my skin, was a much-sought-after man in England. I pulled on chinos and suede brogues and after channel-hopping for a minute headed downstairs.

In the old-fashioned kitchen Amelia held out a steamy mug of chocolate – real hot chocolate made the Spanish way from a solid block – and a plate of fresh *brioches* from a bakery called Au Bon Pain. Morning had barely arrived. The snow flurries to which I'd awoken beside her had turned to a blizzard. A few inches had already built up on the sills.

'C'mon,' she coaxed, 'it's virtually the middle of the afternoon where you come from. Drink this for me. I've put off the Saturday Morning Club and called Logan. Your bags'll be on their way over this morning.'

There was a cry of '*Dios Mío*' from the porch beyond the screen door and a small woman flew in, sixtyish, covered in snow. She was laden with shopping which she banged down on the counter. Amelia had already warned me about Maria-Guadalupe, her trusted housekeeper from Guatemala, a real godsend round the place. The woman removed a waterproof hood to reveal a tight gray bun. Her teeth gleamed in a deferential smile. She stamped her feet to get rid of snow and said: '*Encantada*,' bobbing and holding out her hand. It was the closest I was to come to having a conversation with the chirpy woman who'd been the Hungerfords' Cambridge housekeeper for twenty-odd years. Amelia spoke Spanish like a native. Me, I was okay on French, but my Spanish was nix.

When she'd hung her coat up to dry next to the stove and

47

removed her overshoes, Maria returned to the porch where scratching noises could be heard. A second later a snow-coated Saint Bernard with an outsize jowl and a brindled coat bounded into the kitchen and jumped up at me in a slobbering welcome. I quickly put down my mug.

'I almost forgot,' Amelia said merrily, 'this is Falstaff.' Falstaff could recognize a dog-lover. I'd grown up surrounded by retrievers and labradors. Maria started to unpack the bags she complained she'd had to carry all the way from Sage's Market. I noticed how she kept clicking her tongue as Amelia translated for me.

'C'mon.' Amelia motioned me to follow her. 'I'll show you round this ancient pile.' She smiled savvily. 'Sorry there wasn't time last night.' Maria was preparing to venture back outside to sweep snow from the front path with a birch besom.

I put a hand on the newel post at the foot of the banister and followed her up the burnished staircase. On the half-landing we passed a clock fixed to the wall beside a portrait of Amelia's mother. Below the clock's face swung a bob pendulum. I asked if Maria could be trusted to keep our secret.

'Don't worry about her. She's utterly dependable. She's also discreet. She won't come barging in on us in the middle of . . . well, you know.' She blushed. 'She spends all her free time watching soaps. There's also Cissy, my assistant on the play. She's a friend in GSAS. She comes over for workouts in the gym upstairs. Cissy won't breathe a word.' We'd reached the first-floor landing.

'There's a monumental Victorian toilet in there,' she indicated with a nod to her left as we passed one door. The floorboards creaked underfoot in the central corridor, lit only from a casement window at one end and a stained-glass window, an oriel, at the other. For the first time I noticed the moldings and deep cornices along the light-green walls.

Back in her room I threw myself down on the bed – what would have been called a marriage bed when it was made – and stared up at the ceiling. The mattress was about as modern as a charabanc seat and almost as hard. It was made from horsehair. The sensation triggered memories fresh from last night. I sat up. Amelia was at her vanity bench.

The portrait of Sarah Hungerford I'd stopped to look at earlier prompted me to ask about her mother.

Amelia came and sat beside me. 'Mummy died of cancer when I was twelve. I've got what's called "traumatic amnesia", so I don't remember anything about her except what Lawrence and a few other people have told me. I had a brother once,' she added. 'He died almost as soon as he was born. What Lawrence calls a chrisom-child.'

I stroked her cheek, then, since it seemed opportune at last, I went to dip into my jacket draped over a chair and produced the old photograph. So much had remained unsaid in Oxford. There hadn't been time or it hadn't seemed right. Or else we'd just taken each other's thoughts and backgrounds so much for granted. Falstaff was rolling on his back on the floor making woofing noises.

She noticed how carefully I handled the photo and as I told her the little I knew she studied the warm face and the black coat prettified with a claw brooch. One moment I was too embarrassed to say more but she coaxed it gently out of me. She touched my sleeve and asked if I knew what her name was. I was resting my forehead in the palms of my hands.

My voice was hesitant. I'd hunted for her for years; eventually found her in 1984; an unmarked grave near Swindon; then the police – that detective – had said they'd never found out her name; she'd been discovered dead; murdered; choked to death in 1959. *God, sometimes if only* . . . I stopped myself and jumped to my feet.

'Did you find out anything else?' She could see how much it tormented me to talk about it. She said she was sorry she'd asked.

I faced her with a miserable look that turned to appeal when our eyes locked for a second. 'That's all there is. Anonymous woman dies anonymous death in anonymous fucking hotel room.' Maybe, I thought, they'll kill me too . . .

'One last thing. How did you figure for sure that she was your mother?'

My answer shocked her all too clearly. 'It isn't that difficult, with the right credentials, to get a permit to dig up the bodies of people whose identity's unknown. It's called scientific research.' A hollow laugh. 'I disinterred five women who'd been buried around the right time. Who they were, nobody knew. All in Oxfordshire, Berkshire or Wiltshire.' Amelia had no answer to that. I told her:

'Shakespeare's body was perfection compared with the viscous skin and bones in that rotting coffin in that marshy graveyard. She'd been there a quarter of a century.'

Amelia came to put her arm round me, but I turned away and spoke with my back to her. 'It was early days. Genetic fingerprinting was just starting to happen. I'd done some work on the myoglobin gene with Geoff Alton, the guy who really got it off the ground.' When I turned to face her she seemed to want to stop me, but I went on. 'The police weren't very coöperative. They told me about their original report, but they wouldn't let me see it. Said it was too shocking, so of course I filled in the lurid details with my imagination and that made everything worse. It wasn't pretty. I identified which woman was my mother by matching her genes to mine.' A pause. 'That doubled the agony. I still couldn't find her real name. Nothing. The police had closed the file years ago on the unsolved murder of an unknown woman. Now they opened and closed it again.' I couldn't go on; couldn't explain what I'd guessed about her. It choked me up never being able to talk about it to anyone. I wanted to tell Amelia, about that too, everything, but the words wouldn't come. I'd been staring at my feet. I glanced up. How could I tell her my mother was probably a prostitute?

'C'mon on,' she said, extending a hand, 'I'll take you round the rest of the house.' At that moment I felt again that she could read my mind.

I followed her up to the third floor where she showed me her studio, cluttered with paints and an easel and part-completed canvases – all *art naïf*. At the end of the corridor she opened a door. 'This is how Cissy and I stay in shape,' she announced. 'Lots of bodywork.' I looked at the array of Nautilus machinery. 'It's mostly for Cissy. She's got this personal trainer who comes over from Le Pli. After her workout she gets a massage and a loofah scrub.'

I noticed the rugs as we went downstairs. The house had no fitted carpets except in the sitting room and the bedrooms. Rugs were everywhere else: Persian, Moroccan, Afghan, Turkoman and priceless Aubusson. Where there were rugs there were family portraits. Amelia halted on the stairs to point out two: Edgar and Lawrence Hungerford, her grandfather and father.

Lawrence Hungerford's portrait gave me a prickly feeling of *déjà vu*. Maybe it was the resemblance to the photo.

I looked at her grandfather, a mustachioed young man with mutton-chop whiskers posturing in a wing-collar and gold chain that disappeared into the fob of a brocade waistcoat. The inscription read simply: 'Edgar Hungerford'.

'Tell me about your family,' I said. Amelia looked at me doubtfully, but when she saw I meant it she sat down on the stairs and patted the place beside her.

Edgar Hungerford had inherited old Yankee money, a fortune built on investment banking. Marguerite, his wife, was a French Rothschild and despite her early death the marriage did a lot to expand an already substantial capital. One Chairman of the New York Stock Exchange was on record as saying that Edgar Hungerford was the only man in America feared by J. Edgar Hoover. Amelia's grandfather moved easily in the highest social circles and devoted most of his long life to art. His friends included Bernard Berenson, Kenneth Clark and, briefly, Joseph Duveen. For generations the Hungerfords had combined erudition with a flair for business. Edgar wrote the definitive book on Titian and when it was published in 1953 his preface acknowledged his debt to Lawrence.

Lawrence belonged to Harvard's Class of '53. Each June from 1950 to 1952 he spent the summer vacation with Edgar in Europe, visiting art collections of the slowly recovering continent. While still a Freshman he acquired a reputation for being headstrong, even unstable, what Amelia described as the Hungerford wild streak that had haunted the family for generations. He was also a dyed-in-the-wool Lothario.

Sarah Barnard Carlton was a 'Cliffie' Lawrence Hungerford met at a Harvard–Radcliffe Democratic Club dance. From the moment she fell for the dashing Eliot crewman she was a woman under a spell. She had a pedigree that stretched back to the seventeenth century and it was not long before Lawrence proposed to her and was accepted.

Lawrence turned out to be a gifted art historian. From Harvard he went straight to Oxford while his fiancée stayed in Boston to look after her elderly mother. In his Oxford vacations Lawrence was the houseguest of some of the most prominent art-owning families in Europe. By that time he already played a role in a practice that went back to Pierpont Morgan. Through his dealings scores of paintings, mainly Old Masters, crossed the Atlantic to find permanent homes in America.

Lawrence took his B Litt degree in 1955 with a dissertation on Rembrandt and the attribution dilemma and his Oxford College, Brasenose, offered him a Research Fellowship which he accepted. In the same year Edgar died at the age of eighty-one and Lawrence inherited the Hungerford fortune. It was not until 1957 that Lawrence and Sarah finally wed.

Unlike his father, Lawrence was a collector. The Hungerford Collection was housed in his Dumbarton Street mansion which passed more easily for a museum than a family home in Washington's Georgetown district. In contrast, at his Long Island estate, now a hobby farm where he bred polo ponies, there were no Old Masters, only a valuable collection of early American furniture.

Though he never sought political office the scion of the Hungerford clan – as Amelia called him with a smirk on her face – grew into a conservative Democrat lionized by the wives of politicians in both parties. Lawrence was on the A-list of every Washington hostess. His name appeared in the Washington Green Book among its handful of patrician families. The one-man lobbying firm which he founded in the capital specialized in the upper echelon of the art world. His firm's reputation for integrity in a profession notorious for back channel relationships gave him such an aura of respectability that new clients were never hard to find. Over the years the firm flourished, earning him a further fortune. By the early Eighties his client list included not only the White House but the National Gallery, the Getty Museum and the Walters Art Gallery in Baltimore.

As a member of the Visiting Committee of the Fogg Art Museum Lawrence was tacitly assured a place for life on Harvard's Board of Overseers, a sinecure endorsed by gifts totaling eight million dollars to the university Fund Raising Campaign.

Amelia recited the facts with practiced ease, but became more animated, her left eyelid droopy, when she talked about the house itself. When we reached the dining room it turned out to be enormous. Once the ballroom, it had a minstrel's gallery at one end and a maplewood floor in marquetry. Down the center was a claw-foot American Chippendale table. I counted sixteen chairs and noticed bare patches high along the walls.

'Those were Albert Hungerford's trophies. My great-grandfather. He went hunting in Africa with Teddy Roosevelt.' She stood arms akimbo. 'So that's it, apart from the cellar. It's the only part of the old house that was saved when my great-great-grandfather James Hungerford built this one in eighteen-fifty-seven.'

'Show me.'

She rolled back a red woolen drugget beside a teakwood chest at the end of the hallway. Underneath, a trapdoor was set in the floor with a brass ring for a handle. When I bent to help I found the door came up easily, soundlessly assisted by a concealed counterweight. Amelia went down the first stone steps and flicked a switch. A ruddy glimmer came from below.

As I followed her shadow down the worn treads she was saying, 'One legend has it the house was used to hide runaway slaves not long after it was built. The Hungerfords were out and out abolitionists.'

For no obvious reason I felt dizzy. Maybe it was jetlag still. It was so strong I hesitated, unsure of my footing, but Amelia had already disappeared into the darkness below, still reciting the history of the house: 'According to legend, there's a passage that leads under the street to the church on the other side. If the story about the slaves is true, it must have been meant as an escape route. I've never seen it, though. There's even meant to be a hidey-hole. Houses like this have so many stories attached to them. One goes that in April seventeen-seventy-five Paul Revere rode into Cambridge from Concord and spent the night in the old Hungerford House. Some of the Minute Men were billeted here – at least that's a fact; we've got letters to prove it. Adam Hungerford was a fanatical patriot. He mustn't have been too popular with his neighbors. This was a very Loyalist part of town.'

I put a hand to my head. There was a musty smell in the air.

'Are you all right?'

'Just felt kind of weird.'

She looked at me by the glow from the bulkhead light. I was peering from side to side. It must have looked odd. 'You insisted on coming down here,' she was saying. Then, more complaisantly: 'Are you sure you're okay?'

Something was nagging at the back of my mind. Amelia's voice seemed to come from a distance. I thought I heard a footfall on

53

stone, but when I turned there was only the long staircase. I alone was real. Other people were marionettes, in another sphere of existence. Even Amelia.

Feeling rattled I walked over to where she stood by a walk-in fireplace that contained an iron stove. 'It's kind of like being a tourist guide,' she exclaimed. 'In there you can see the baker's oven built into the side of the inglenook. Under it that's the oak chimneyseat where the servants would have kept warm in winter.' I steadied myself against the stove and squinted at where she was pointing. There was a dark hole in the brickwork above the snug. Now the musty smell was so strong it was overpowering. A flush of nausea swept through me and after a long moment was gone.

My hand had gone up to my mouth and I was turning hastily to look at the rest of the cellar, more visible now that my eyes had settled to the semi-darkness. The joisted ceiling that made me think of another older vault stretched the length of the house. Along one wall were rows of wine racks, most of them loaded with dusty bottles. Opposite was a four-poster bed. I went over and peered up at the underside of the tapestry. It was like one of those eyesight tests. If you relaxed you could see the numbers. If you tried too hard all you saw were dots. I relaxed and saw in the faded purple what I recognized as the constellation of the Great Bear, woven in gold stars. A black cloth covered the bed like a pall over a funeral bier.

I could sense Amelia behind me, pressing herself lightly against my back. 'My grandfather had it shipped over from Venice. Mummy and Daddy slept in it when it was in the master bedroom.' She added: 'It's been down here since Mummy died,' but I was hardly listening. I had this weird feeling of being outside myself, pushing away those moony arms, but when I spun round to face her, Amelia wasn't up against me at all. Now I was shivering and my skin went clammy. Amelia was no longer talking. She was facing me from several feet away, blinking strangely and shaking her left arm.

I fought for control and tentatively crossed the floor to look under dusters draped over early-colonial chests and a stack of horned and antlered trophies on ebony plinths – Albert Hungerford's spoils. Among this old lumber I unearthed two Purdey shotguns in mahogany cases. Maria's cleaning hadn't extended to the underbelly of the house. Though cool the cellar

54

was surprisingly dry, with only the faintest hint of mildew. As I moved, my feet stirred up the dust. Near one wall was something black and shapeless. I peeped behind the duster and found a standing mirror.

The place had an out-of-time atmosphere. When Amelia hugged me again – it really was her this time – I steadied myself against one upright of the mirror. I was numb with cold for half a minute then the sensation ebbed. I unclasped her hands from round my waist.

'Did you feel it getting chillier just now?'

Ignoring my question she gave me a peck on the lips.

The cellar was not my idea of a nice place to spend the night alone. Halfway up the stairs I glanced over my shoulder, still feeling queasy. When we reached the hallway the delicious aroma of Maria's cooking – a gamey casserole – was wafting along the corridor. Amelia gestured me toward the dining room.

Since I arrived there I'd really become interested in Shakespeare and all the things that Amelia was researching. Even the Dark Lady. In fact I was beginning to like the house in a bizarre kind of way. The pictures didn't answer back. I was already best friends with the mahogany seat in the Victorian loo. Best of all, there was an endless supply of liquor, courtesy of Maria, in the library.

On the Monday I spent the day alone in the library boning up on Renaissance alchemy and the Kabbalah, jotting down points of interest, though from time to time I found myself fretting after a laboratory. In genetics three weeks of downtime is a lot of downtime, but Marcus needed those three weeks to ready the Shakespeare Search for launch. I'd thought it was going to be three weeks in purgatory. The library, like the cellar, was creepy, but now I was relishing that feel, almost erotically. I was aware I was chewing on the end of a pencil as I reclined in a green wing chair, my ankles up on the arm of a leather Chesterfield. The bronze of Sarah Bernhardt that stood nearby on a walnut table reminded me of Amelia: cloaked and mysterious. The Mars Vallet figurine revealed the actress's left breast. For a second I saw Amelia as an incarnation from *art nouveau*.

The library was a bibliophile's heaven. Books were one of the few things Amelia indulged in with her fortune. She bought regularly from Wordsworth the Cambridge dealer, corresponded with antiquarian bookdealers worldwide and in sixteenth-century cosmology had amassed a collection that was reputed to be more valuable than, if not as extensive as, Widener Library's. Many of her acquisitions were rebound in split calf and carried her *ex libris* bookplate inside the front cover.

Rising and crossing to the fire that burned in the grate behind a screen I pumped it with leather bellows and replaced them in the hearth beside a poker, slightly bent, and a pair of eagle's claw tongs supported by a blackened firedog. The sides of the fireplace were lined with ceramic tiles depicting New England whaling scenes from the early nineteenth century.

Thursday her father would be there. I shrugged.

There was a family crest carved in the stone lintel over the hearth: two crossed keys like Amelia's signet ring and underneath, the Hungerford motto: *De caelo per umbras*. I raised my eyes to scrutinize the portrait of James Hungerford hanging over a chimney-piece hand-carved in maple with creeping dogwood and dainty scrolls. Amelia's great-great-grandfather was crippled with polio in his youth and found fame as a philosopher, endowing a Harvard chair of metaphysics shortly before his death at ninety-four. Allegedly he was the mentor of William James, Harvard's great nineteenth-century psychologist. No sign of polio there. The eyes of the man were hard with the same intensity I'd observed in the paintings of Edgar and Lawrence. James Hungerford, Amelia had suggested, passed away in the wing chair in 1911. They embalmed him and left him propped in the chair for a year while his widow and Harvard debated the fate of the oddly deformed corpse its owner had bequeathed to medical science. Finally it found a new home in the family mausoleum in Mt Auburn Cemetery. 'The Hungerfords were like that.'

I moved away from the fire and unlatched the bay window over the box seat, but five minutes later the place was still stuffy. It made my throat dry. I marched to the armoire in the corner. Inside, cleverly disguised, were a fridge and a liquor cabinet. I mixed myself a vodka martini and sank it in two gulps while I watched myself in the mirror let into the paneling at the back of the cabinet.

On a nearby desk lit with a tiffany lamp stood a huddle of daguerreotypes and a Thirties photo of Edgar by Man Ray. In front of them was a silver-framed photograph of Lawrence, twenty-fivish. Next to him was the instantly recognizable face of Robert F. Kennedy. At the bottom someone had scrawled in black ink: 'Lawrence and Bobby – Ida Lewis Yacht Club.' Two go-getting men in striped sweatshirts with windswept hair. It made me think of my own modest yacht in Poole Harbour. No sailing that summer. That was two in a row.

I squared my shoulders and poured myself a short of Southern Comfort before tacking back across the floor, careful to skirt the polar-bear rug. Another of Albert's kills she'd pointed out, emphasizing 'kills'.

I tossed a log on the fire, where it crackled and spat, and hovered for some while nursing my glass. I could see why she relished the sanctum of the library. It had a comfy feel with its floor-to-ceiling shelves surmounted with scalloped cornices. Turning back to the fire I gazed into it.

———— • ————

Amelia's advisor on her PhD program was Professor Nancy Bretton, a brittle individual of a certain age. As the most senior woman in Harvard's once notoriously chauvinist English Department she had her own elegant office in Warren House, a good step up from faculty of Amelia's rank, who shared the annexe on Kirkland. Amelia had been foisted on her by Bob Carr and there was nothing Nancy Bretton had been able to do about it despite all the power women now had around the department. The rising star had landed on Nancy's doorstep with her proposal to take apart half the received laws of Elizabethan literature and turn Shakespeare back into a man of his own times.

Nancy Bretton's aspiring Doctor of Philosophy came with no mean equipment for the job, never mind her influence in places that counted. Amelia was so steeped in the hermetic traditions of the Renaissance that she would have been equally at home in the History Department. There were times, she thought, when Nancy Bretton wished her there . . . or anywhere else.

It was a cold but clear morning when Amelia, having newly abandoned Daniel to his reading in the library, poked her nose round the door of Nancy Bretton's office without an appointment, just as the old termagant was dabbing a final puff of powder on her vulpine face before launching off to a committee meeting in Widener that would decide next year's budget for sixteenth-century acquisitions. Nancy Bretton had the build if not the demeanor of a square-rigger whose sailing days are over. Her special field was Shakespeare's *Sonnets* and fortunately for Amelia they both held that this the most famous poetic sequence in the English language was largely autobiographical. However Nancy Bretton firmly believed that the *Sonnets* were dedicated to Henry Wriothesley, third Earl of Southampton and that the Dark Lady could be identified with Emilia Bassano, also known as Emilia Lanier.

On this occasion Amelia marched in with triumph written across her face and banged down a copy of *Nature*. Nancy Bretton had already read the article, as had many others in the civilized world. Amelia was insisting that Dr Bosworth had demonstrated beyond a shadow of doubt that Shakespeare had syphilis. Probably – she stressed 'probably' – he'd died from it. He could, she went on, have fathered several children outside his marriage and have direct living descendants today. No one, she said pointedly, would dispute that he'd had the opportunity to do so in London while that homemaker Anne Hathaway whiled away her days in her Stratford kitchen. Shakespeare might even have made the Dark Lady pregnant . . . and she wasn't Emilia Bassano; that much Amelia was convinced of.

Unable to conceal her rage at this interruption Nancy Bretton stuffed her powder compact into her bag and rose from her desk. Despite her width she was not a tall woman. She looked tall, however, standing on the stool she kept hidden at her feet. Amelia was one of the few women that Nancy Bretton could not intimidate, try as she might.

'Dr Rowse,' Nancy blustered, 'has shown convincingly who the Dark Lady was and there's no evidence that *she* had syphilis . . .' adding: 'or any illegitimate children for that matter.'

'I say bunkum to Dr Rowse.' Amelia looked at her tutor with no visible sign of malice. 'Shakespeare probably had lots of women. Only this one was special. Sure, I don't know . . . yet . . . who she was, but I'm telling you she wasn't Emilia Bassano . . . or Lucy Negro for that matter . . . or Mall Fitton . . . or Mistress Davenant . . .'

'At least we agree on three women that it wasn't.' Nancy Bretton sat down again and Amelia took her chair opposite.

At once the committee meeting was forgotten. When the knives were out the bellicose Professor Bretton was the last person to beat a retreat. This particular feud had been going on for some months . . . since the day Amelia declared she would not rest until the Dark Lady was identified to her satisfaction.

'This woman,' Amelia continued, 'was special. Sure it was sexual with Shakespeare. But something else was going on that brought Shakespeare into contact with the secret world of one of the courtly circles in the fifteen-nineties. And the Dark Lady is the key to what that circle was doing. I'm convinced of it.' She did not add 'intuitively' though that was what she was thinking. Instead she banged the edge of the desk with her fist.

Nancy Bretton, who could have been any age from fifty to seventy, and had long since given up competing with anyone outside the academic arena, brought her own fist down in reply. 'Back to a secret society, are we?' There was the hint of a sneer. 'I suppose Shakespeare and his Dark Lady went for country weekends at Wilton and Longleat and Titchfield . . .'

'And Brook House in Wiltshire,' Amelia said, interrupting in a tone that silenced Nancy Bretton for several seconds. Her tutor had never heard of Brook House. Amelia seized on this silence to press her point. 'Through his grandmother Anne Willoughby, Brook House was inherited by Charles Blunt who became the eighth Lord Mountjoy. He had occupancy from fifteen-ninety-three to fifteen-ninety-nine.'

Nancy Bretton listened intently. Prejudice was not among her long list of inadequacies.

'The old Willoughby manor of Brook House was the scene of some pretty strange goings-on if I'm not mistaken, even in fifteen-ninety-three when Blunt was overseas . . . perhaps especially in fifteen-ninety-three. Blunt's interest in alchemy and hermeticism probably came from his father. He was a close friend of the nearby Herberts at Wilton.'

Nancy Bretton replied without hesitation: 'You're going to need some pretty hard evidence if you go round telling people Shakespeare spent weekends attending séances at a place called Brook House . . . or Wilton . . . or wherever. I don't think for one minute Shakespeare came close to dabbling in these things. There's not the slightest evidence, apart from a few dozen allusions in the plays and a handful in the *Sonnets*.' Nancy without thinking had delved into her bag and was dabbing at her face with a bright lipstick.

Amelia couldn't help but smile as her advisor deftly rouged a mouth round the line where in her youth lips had once appeared. 'What about *The Tempest*?' There was a streak of violence in Amelia's voice. Her smile vanished. 'What lay full fathom five? A flesh and blood father? What is a sea-change?' she asked, alluding to the famous lines from Ariel's Song. 'Are you telling me Shakespeare didn't play around with alchemy?'

'Shakespeare enriched our language in a thousand ways . . . a sea-change is one of them. It's just a dramatic change, that's all . . . the way the sea can switch in mood from one moment to the next.'

Amelia composed herself, but her voice was thin and high with anger. 'A sea-change, dear Nancy, is an alchemical change at the level of sea. "Sea" is a standard metaphor for the alchemist's *materia prima*, the matter with which the alchemical process begins. Why five fathoms? Because at the fifth level, beyond the four elements, lies the quintessence, the etheric element, the subtle astral plane. Shall I go on? Do you want to hear about the hermetic trinity all over again, the divine ambrosia, the philosopher's stone, the *aurum potabile*, the Holy Grail? Do you want the whole goddamn list again?'

Nancy had dabbed once too often with her lipstick. The jagged red line was an insult to what was left of her dignity. Amelia burst out laughing.

At the first hint of mirth Nancy sprang surprisingly nimbly from stool to floor. 'Get out of here,' she screamed. 'Get out this minute.' It was not the first time and would not be the last. 'Stop trying to turn a pretty little lyric poem into something it isn't.' She calmed herself a little as Amelia made for the door and banged it shut behind her.

———— • ————

I was dozing by the fire when there was a crackle and spit and the dying embers burst into flame then just as suddenly subsided. A draft had sprung up from nowhere, a chill that darted this way and that between the legs of the furniture and round my ankles. I could feel its nip going up and down some subtle channel in the back of my legs. When it moved to the nerve fibers in my spine and radiated out to my shoulders it dissolved in a flash of blue. The draft had departed.

'Hi!'

I spun round. Amelia was back from teaching her Monday afternoon seminar. 'Have a good day?'

'Horrendous. Another goddamned argument with Nancy then everybody wanted my opinion on Shakespeare's grave.' She told me all about a fight with her advisor.

After all, I'd got my own rivalries to contend with, like the recent three-way prize fight between our Immunochemistry Unit, the Molecular Biophysics lab and the Institute of Molecular Medicine.

A girl ghosted without warning into the library.

Amelia was quick to play the hostess. 'Daniel, this is Cecilia Wotherspoon. Watch out. She's a Taurus!'

Through owlish glasses the newcomer's eyes took in my crumpled clothes and five o'clock jaw. She presented a petulant child-woman's face and a clipped voice that said 'Hi!' as if it were an accusation. She reached out one hand. 'You can call me Cissy.'

I clambered to my feet and took her hand. 'Why's Taurus so dangerous?'

'We're totally physical,' Cissy replied with an upmarketly modulated Georgian twang as she held my eye for a second.

I noticed how she was fractionally shorter than Amelia, dressed in a bulky mauve cardigan. The eyes behind the lenses held intelligence; I sensed the force of her personality under the variable front. She was standing almost on tip-toe. Amelia put her arm round her friend's shoulder and gave it a squeeze. I didn't like the way Cissy prissed her lips. She was pumping her hands together in awkward silence, so I asked her what she planned to do after Harvard.

'Twyla Tharp Dance – if they'll have me. I've got to get out before there's another pogrom in the English Department.'

Amelia pointed out that Cissy was her assistant on the play. Reading meetings had been moved from Hungerford House to a practice room at the Loeb to protect my privacy.

Cissy was addressing Amelia exclusively: 'I've got a dance rehearsal at the Agassiz. Can't be late.' She flounced toward the door.

Amelia followed and I could hear the thrum of their voices in the hallway. A moment later they both returned. 'Cissy's got half an hour before rehearsals.'

'I'll go over the press stories with you.' This time Cissy looked at me directly, but her voice was disdainful, her hands still nervous. All the sweetness, I was realizing, of a Siamese fighting fish. She was giving me a Semtex smile: smooth and light on the outside.

Amelia who was watching me carefully said: 'Boy, have I got something for you.' She headed outside and came back with an armful of newspapers and magazines. 'Let's spread them on the dining-room table.'

Next door Maria was busy laying places for dinner. She tssk-tssked and clicked her tongue at the sight of the papers.

It was a changed Cissy that trailed in and sat down opposite. She'd disappeared long enough to let her hair down and remove her glasses and cardigan. Her breasts swelled against a skinny blouse. I frowned in Amelia's direction and glared at her friend. Cissy wore a fixed expression and I realized that her confident side brought out the aggressor in me.

Most of the stories we clipped over the next half-hour covered the feasibility of finding someone carrying the atavistic gene. A few mentioned the hunt now on for me in England and these went into a separate pile. Overnight I'd become an invisible celebrity. *Am I really a sucker for fame?* Maria brought in a jug of hot chocolate and a pecan pie.

Amelia waved a copy of *Time* magazine under my nose. They'd labeled me 'the polymathic pundit of the new genetics'. Yet another photograph. This one was two years old – a press handout from the Singapore colloquium on sexually transmitted diseases. It struck me how much I'd aged meantime. The hours in the lab and the stress of masterminding the Stratford operation had taken their toll.

I stretched my legs under the table. One foot accidentally touched Cissy's and I withdrew it hurriedly. She said nothing but gave me a determined look as she sipped from her cup. I sent her back an inaudible snarl and tucking my feet under my chair pressed clenched fists into my cheeks.

'I've been wondering,' Amelia was saying, 'how long we can go on pretending I'm unconnected with all this. It just needs one nosy reporter or someone who's seen you and me together.'

Cissy was looking my way out of the corner of her eye. Her mouth curled into a half-smile, but on contact her eye squirmed away from me.

I gobbled the piece of pie on my plate. It was a large one and I almost choked. Amelia came round and gave me a slap on the back. She didn't sit down again. 'I've got a *vernissage* at the gallery at seven.'

Cissy jumped up. 'I'll walk with you some of the way.'

'See you for dinner round nine,' Amelia said. She was pursing her lips, looking at Cissy as she spoke to me.

Cissy shot me this drop-dead look. Amelia was obviously embarrassed.

When they'd gone I stalked back to the library and stood with my back to the fire.

4

Or why is Collatine the publisher
Of that rich jewel he should keep unknown
From thievish ears, because it is his own?

Perchance his boast of Lucrece' sov'reignty
Suggested this proud issue of a king;
For by our ears our hearts oft tainted be.
Perchance that envy of so rich a thing,
Braving compare, disdainfully did sting
His high-pitch'd thoughts that meaner men should vaunt
That golden hap which their superiors want.

The Rape of Lucrece, 33–42
William Shakespeare

Amelia came into the third-floor bedroom where I'd been banished for the duration of Lawrence's stay. She promised Maria would move my things back down as soon as her father left. Lawrence, she said, would be staying two nights in the room that he alone used, the master bedroom next to hers. He had other plans while he was in Cambridge besides meeting with me. The following evening he'd be taking her out to dinner.

I finger-combed my rebarbative hair and, grumbling about jealous fathers, pulled on a battered tweed jacket before following her downstairs.

A curtain bellied out in the draft as I opened the library door. Maria was scuttling about laying things out for tea. Lawrence and I took the measure of each other as we shook hands. For one thing we were the same height and build. It was his turn to stand heels to the fire looking every inch the patriarch with his daughter fawning at his side. She was knitting her fingers in front of her, the way she did with me too sometimes if she got into one of those passive moods that would sweep all her larger-than-life assertiveness straight out the window from one moment to the next.

Lawrence huffed himself up to his debonair six-two and rammed his paws deep into his pockets. There was a hard edge to his jaw, set in an irregular face. His skin was shiny smooth: the complexion of a man who shaved with a blade and got the best kind of facial twice a week: his eyebrows as manicured as his nails. He clearly belonged to that caste whose trademark was half an inch of hair no more no less curling over the collar when it was swept back each morning after ministration of a little something to turn white to gray. His mouth presented mankind with scarcely more than a slash that hooked at either extremity as if it wore a permanent sneer that would need hard work to get it into neutral, let alone a smile. When I hunted in that face for a suspicion of warmth, I spied it in the nose. The rest all led there as roads led to Rome: the fine bridge with parabolic profile, the flared nostrils and a good clear skin over it all. His features had weathered well in sixty-odd years. Amelia was watching him in unswerving fealty.

The impenetrable eyes missed nothing of me, whose blood pressure till now wasn't so easily elevated. How in hell had I gone and got myself saddled with this smug poseur for a – who knows? – father-in-law?

Amelia had filled me in only last night on the old boy's background. He had few if any close friends, but fewer enemies than might be expected of a man in his position with a reputation for vindictiveness. The sharpest barb deemed fit to print had come from the typewriter of an embittered member of the Washington press corps who'd described him as omnipotent, immortal and irresistible. One competitor, less forgiving, had called him a pathological hedonist to his face and found himself bankrupt the following year. I disliked the man from the word go, but felt strangely drawn to him, maybe as the tortured was drawn to his tormentor.

A teapot stood on a silver tray on the sideboard. Amelia, who'd said nothing after the pleasantries of introduction, went dutifully to pour. Lawrence made a feudal gesture and I sat down, careful not to take the green wing chair which I guessed was where he liked to sit.

'I've got a busy program while I'm here.' As Lawrence spoke

he looked over in his daughter's direction. 'When you and I have done talking, I'd like to spend a little time with Amelia.' His voice carried menace.

It really struck me the way his daughter knelt on the polar bear in discreet silence, missing nothing as our joust got underway. If I hadn't seen her suddenly act so passive and dependent with me on the odd occasion, I'd have been amazed. She rose again only to pass round the cake that Maria had baked. As she bent over, her father paused to glance at her viola shape.

'I'll be happy to sit down and talk with you whenever's convenient,' I said. My eyes lingered on the portrait of James Hungerford above Lawrence's head. There was no mistaking the resemblance.

When a formal tea had been taken Amelia made signs of appeasement to both of us and toadied off to the kitchen to help Maria organize the weekend's menus. I noticed Lawrence seemed to relax when she'd gone. And God, he certainly knew how to bring the almighty Amelia down from her throne. There was an inner quality to him which I found ambiguous.

The bumpy nose he'd inherited from Marguerite Hungerford and passed on to his daughter gave Lawrence his hawkish air of breeding, but there was something of the Latin in his mien that must have owed more than a little, I reflected, to time spent in the great *palazzi* of Italy. I noticed his signet ring, like Amelia's but bigger, with its crossed keys that matched the escutcheon in the fireplace; the silk stock and tailored hacking jacket. A burgundy handkerchief spilled from the breast pocket. Sartorial panache: almost a dandy.

Falstaff was napping in front of the fire. Lawrence broke the lull with an attack, a characteristic I'd been warned about. The gentlemanly tone had vanished. 'One thing first, Daniel. I care a lot about Amelia. I've got no illusions what the pair of you are up to. Goddamnit, get this straight: if you're fooling around together just don't mess with her affections.' Irritation flared in his face. 'Is that clear?'

I swallowed and cleared my throat. 'She and I understand each other.' I immediately regretted my reply.

'For halek's sake don't tell me you understand women.' For a gentleman, Lawrence had a rare way with expletives. 'In my book that's a hanging offense,' he spluttered, and added: 'by the balls.'

As I crawled back into my chrysalis he continued without waiting for comment. 'Why did I let myself get roped into this damn fool idea?' He pursed what remained of his lips and raised a fat Havana to moisten the head before turning briefly to the fire and flicking the cap off with one well-aimed fingernail. As he clamped his mouth round the cigar and lit up he said out of the corner of his mouth: 'Amelia and Marcus have given me a complete run-down. I'm prepared to endorse your little hunting expedition – strictly from the wings. The rest is up to you and Marcus. He'll have put the finishing touches to your Shakespeare Search in two weeks time.' A match was tossed into the fire.

A whisper of smoke rose from the end of Lawrence's cigar. He took a meditative puff. I knew when I was being sized up. There was something patronizing in Lawrence's approach, wasn't there? He didn't talk, he speechified. The old whacker would have to find someone else who would kowtow to him.

'My God, don't make the mistake of thinking Marcus is some kind of a flaky guy just because his approach is unorthodox,' Lawrence continued, throwing me a seering glance. 'He's got a nothing's-impossible approach to life and he's a genius when it comes to public relations. I wouldn't back the whole thing if I didn't know he was rock-solid.'

He took another puff. 'Nor do I want you to think I've got any doubts about you personally.' He made an expansive gesture with both arms. His hands cut the air when he brought them down. 'I had your credentials checked out. I was at Oxford too, y'know.' There was a pause. 'I had my doubts to begin with – about you, or anyone, including Marcus, with such a pie-in-the-sky idea in their head. Ultimately it was your professional credibility that sold me – and will convince millions of others to buy this gimcrack plan.'

'I'm glad to hear it,' I blurted. *Screw you*, I thought, but then I also thought: *first blood to Lawrence*. A tiny facial muscle twitched below his left eye. I noticed it for the first time as I got to my feet. I sensed a trap. It was time to gird my loins. 'I've had a few months to think the whole thing over and here's my rationale.' I spoke carefully this time, pacing up and down for the next few minutes, expounding the strategy as I saw it.

I'd liaised with Marcus by phone before and after our meeting in London the previous month. When I got to the part where I admitted I wasn't happy about the location Marcus had selected for my hideaway lab Lawrence looked amazed. 'Why the hell not? For godsakes, you and Marcus come up with an insane plan to bust into a grave and start looking for some guy who probably doesn't exist.' His face was an apoplectic puce. I watched the tic under his cantankerous left eye and smiled inwardly. The flicker was so small it was barely visible. He took a pill from what looked like a snuffbox and turned to face the fire, but I saw him swallow it surreptitiously half a minute later. When he swung back he found me eyeballing him. His livid hue had abated. 'What the hell difference does it make,' he said, 'whether you work in an ashram or a scientific institution?'

I couldn't find anything to say to that. Lawrence was right. In any case they'd already built most of the lab. I'd agreed to the Northern California location. The place might turn out fine. I realized I'd objected just to get the old boy worked up a bit. 'I suppose you're right. It just seems an odd place to build a sophisticated laboratory.'

Lawrence was mollified but he still had a frosty look. 'You're going to need all the seclusion you can get your hands on.' He moved away from the fire to pour himself a Scotch. 'Look, Daniel, I understand how frustrated you feel, an active man, twiddling your thumbs while other scientists are out there working their butts off on their own vaccines. Believe me, with Marcus behind you no one's going to beat you to the punch.'

'I know next to nothing about this guru who runs the ashram.' I straightened up. The wind had evidently shifted but there was no clue to where Lawrence was headed.

'I'm assuming you don't object to being the guest of an East Indian. I've met Baba Dayananda a few times. You'll have plenty of freedom so long as you stay away from prying eyes. Mendocino has a perfect climate . . . a little Xanadu with a view of the sea.'

I knew the lab set-up was costing the World Health Rostrum two million dollars – the kind of research money I only dreamed of, but I would have preferred Lawrence out of the whole thing. It made me uncomfortable about my relationship with Amelia, but I'd learnt that her father's influence in Washington was vital if interests hostile to the Rostrum were not to filibuster the Shakespeare Search. It was Lawrence who'd negotiated an intermediary role for the American Red Cross, and that had given Marcus's screening units the 'Good Housekeeping Seal of

Approval.' The Red Cross was supporting the AIDS Campaign right down to the release forms that screenees signed – consent and confidentiality guaranteed – when they took the Cambridge BioScience test for HIV in one of the mobile units. Marcus's plan was to put an extra box to check on the form: a request for the sample of blood to be analyzed for Shakespeare's gene. Any male getting screened could ask for the test for the weeping gene. Publicity would stress that only men with an old Anglo background – worded more diplomatically – should check the box. That would keep time-wasters to a minimum. Among AIDS Campaign screenees a small proportion would be Shakespeare hopefuls, maybe one in twenty. Their blood samples – whether or not they were HIV positive – would be sent to my new lab in Mendocino, batched by four hand-picked hematologists who'd be working through Marcus's office in Santa Monica. The samples served two completely separate functions. Enough would be seropositives to give me a more than sufficient spectrum of HIV strains to work on after the weeping gene test had been carried out by the lab technicians next door. I knew Marcus was building the ashram lab to my specifications. Tillman and Cunliffe-Jones had reconfirmed their willingness to join me, as would another molecular geneticist of serious repute and half a dozen lab technicians. All sworn to secrecy. According to a gung-ho Marcus that side of the operation was going smoothly.

'The thing that worries me about the Shakespeare side of the AIDS Campaign,' I was saying, 'is that I'm supposed to be part of all the publicity.'

Lawrence drew on his cigar and frowned and hummed and hahed. 'That's why you've got to have somewhere really isolated to work. You're Marcus's trump card: a scientist of your caliber. It wouldn't be the same if the hunt was on for this Shakespeare guy without you. The way Marcus sees it people are interested in Dr Daniel Bosworth.' People, he went on, were like that in America. They put someone on television because he was a scientist – and suddenly he was famous for being famous. Ordinary people wanted to know what brand of toothpaste he used, did he sleep nude, had he had a vasectomy? The more personal the better. 'Believe me, when you're rich or famous – or both – you've got one helluva cross to bear.'

I guessed he was speaking from experience. I made my tone

acid and said: 'Join the celebrity circus? Is that it?' Every time that word 'celebrity' came up I thought of money and women. Especially women. That surely couldn't be what I was doing all this for. For AIDS sufferers, yes. For Amelia, maybe. But not for Money and Women and Fame. When you were famous you still got forgotten in the end. It just took a little longer, that was all.

'A successful man like you is going to get a lot of adulation. My God just take the news media this week. You're already halfway there. Marcus thinks the Shakespeare Search needs you to be famous for being elusive. If you're interviewed every which way the whole thing will dry up in a few weeks. The Rostrum's going to need you longer that that . . . maybe six months.'

'That's the bit that worries me. I don't see myself staying holed up like some hermit in a cave.'

Lawrence's sharp eyes were on me and I caught the trace of a tight smile. 'I'd hardly call it a cave. Dayanandpuram's famous for its free-living attitude. You'll be out of sight of your eager public. If you find a new Shakespeare that's fine. If you don't find him that's even better, at least for some months. It will keep the excitement going longer.'

Lawrence stood with his back to the fire looking frighteningly familiar – the resemblance to Amelia was larger than life. Before it had only featured in that sensual nose. And that feeling of *déjà vu* was back. His cigar was wedged defiantly between two fingers as he peered into his highball. I crossed the room to fix myself a drink. When I came back, glass in hand, I sat down in the wing chair without thinking, but it was already too late. The damage was done. From the hearth Lawrence uttered some profanity which he garrotted before it fully escaped. He shot me a look of utter disbelief before marching over to press a button on the wall.

I remained seated in *his* wing chair, toying with my glass, and allowed myself an astringent smile. Lawrence and I had summed each other up. It was standoff.

The pernickety Maria came trotting in to clear the tea things. The fire was getting low. With a small cry she rushed at it, crossing herself, and began to pile fresh logs in the grate.

I remained seated where I was, but I flushed as the *paterfamilias*, without a word, proceeded toward the library door.

*　　*　　*

The curtains were open. The half-moon through a rent in the clouds scattered a pool of bluish light on the rosewood vanity.

Falstaff growled edgily where he lay on the rug. I opened my eyes and found myself standing naked at the side of Amelia's bed. *Christ, how did I get here?* The coverlet was peeled partly back and I was looking down at her sleeping shape. My head was seething. Maybe it was the two bottles of '53 Margaux. I'd got no recall of leaving my second-floor bedroom where I knew I'd gone to sleep soon after midnight. Sleepwalking wasn't my style. Not since I was a child. I glanced toward the door and climbed into the bed that was forbidden to me while Lawrence was staying.

Under the covers I felt something small but lumpy pressing into my hip. I pulled it out and held it up. In the half-light I made out the features of a rag doll with gimlet eyes and Hecate hair. This juju transfixed me with a look between a frown and a glare. It was repulsive and I let it fall to the floor.

As I lay there I caught a glimpse of a dream . . . so it seemed . . . from earlier in the night: I was down in the cellar, then following a tunnel in solitary darkness. The place was wet with something unspeakable, then I was wrestling with a faun-like creature perched on its hind legs. It was laughing in my face as I grappled with its horns, two on either side of its head. I shuddered, opening my eyes, and this specter vanished.

There was a vague impression of a voice. I teetered at the edge of sleep. Open one eye. Falstaff rose and stretched before padding out to the corridor through the half-open door. The next moment there was a long canine wail and he rushed back, hair bristling, and squeezed his bulky shape under the bed. I listened. There was no sound apart from Falstaff's whimpering. Amelia was sprawled on her side with her knees drawn up. Lying on my back I peered sideways at her huddled outline.

I pulled up the coverlet. As I turned my back on her I heard her voice murmuring, like a whispering in her breath, but it didn't sound like her. 'Amelia, what is it?' The voice – or voices – paused for a second then continued in a different tone: still not Amelia's voice. It had a dreamy quality. I watched her sleepily. Her body hadn't moved. Nothing of what she said was clearly audible. I cocked my head and strained to pick up her words. I couldn't even tell if it was English. It came out as a disjointed rambling. I snuggled toward her as close as I could get with her knees

71

sticking up between us. Her hair brushed my chin. As I fumbled my way back to sleep the last thing I remembered was the rustling of the sheets.

I woke with a jolt. I felt for Amelia and found the bed empty where she'd been sleeping. I got up and groped my way into the dressing gown that hung over a wicker chair in the corner.

When I tried the light switch nothing happened. The electricity had either failed or been cut off. Falstaff now lay peacefully at the foot of the bed. In the bathroom I found what I was looking for: a pocket torch. The batteries were going but it gave some light.

On tip-toe I passed the closed door to the master bedroom which Lawrence occupied that night. Was it locked? I'd tried it before and found I couldn't open it. I tried it again, slowly, gently. Still locked. Why should Lawrence lock it when he was inside? Amelia had mentioned something about his bodyguard never coming to Hungerford House. The only sound in the long corridor was the soughing of the wind and an unpruned oak, moved by the breeze, scrabbling at the panes of the stained-glass window.

At the top of the staircase I groped for the dado rail and felt my way down. The woody texture under my fingers sent small shivers up and down my skin and I transferred my hand to the banister on the other side. *Slowly, Daniel.* 'Amelia,' I said in a carrying whisper, then louder, '*Amelia.*' I seemed to become detached from myself and I panicked, recalling my experience in the cellar. Somewhere I heard a distant echo, calling back. Not Amelia. It was my own name . . . I thought. A voice was calling *Daniel.* I tried to get a grip on myself and wondered whether Janey was watching over me.

At the half-landing I shone my light up at the only portrait in the house of Amelia's mother: those relentless eyes, so like Amelia's. I paused to listen. Only the white sound of nothing. The house was prowling all round me now. I put one hand against the wainscoting and read the dates. Sarah Hungerford lived from 1932 until 1979. The wind outside had risen. I lingered to listen and heard – was it imagination? – a plaining and keening like a woman's voice . . . or a castrato male's, like the cry of a part of you long forgotten, a lych-owl's call in response to the tear-stained face, a widow's weeds, a woman's corpse washed and dressed and laid out on a catafalque, the bombazine mort-cloth folded back

72

to reveal the waxy pallor of death. This memory that did not belong to me . . . again . . . was harrowing . . . an unsubstantial presence . . . a wraith. I quickly moved on down the stairs, stumbled, picked myself up and felt my way through the hallway. The batteries were almost dead. In the kitchen I found another torch on a shelf beside the sink.

I tried the library, checking stealthily behind all the furniture. I shone the beam up at James Hungerford and flashed round at James's chair. I was helped by shafts of a fitful light coming through the window from the moon which hung one moment in a crisp starless sky, the next came riding in, or so it seemed, and flooded the library, dazzling me. When I dared to open my eyes, outside in the hallway a clock was striking a quarter of the hour. A heap of embers still glowed in the grate.

'Amelia?'

Steady, Daniel. I whistled to myself under my breath and looked at my watch. It was 3.52 a.m. Close to the midnight of the soul. Shakespeare's curse, are you there? Then a hush in the cry of the wind and I was so keyed up I started upon hearing a faint noise, a soft thud outside in the hall. Five minutes I waited, ten? fifteen? With a glance at the wing chair I headed for the door and stepped through. A clock chimed in the library behind me, losing time in its old age.

In the hallway I shone my light down the corridor. The chest still sat beside the rug, now askew, covering the trapdoor. I gave a shiver that sent every hair atingle and raised a sleeve to wipe my forehead.

Easy, Daniel. Your head spun slowly and you felt yourself floating on air as you watched a dissevered hand hover into view, remove the rug and descend on the ring. *Janey, are you there?* The light in the other hand, also adrift from your body, was fading fast.

5

So is it not with me as with that Muse,
Stirr'd by a painted beauty to his verse;
Who heaven itself for ornament doth use,
And every fair with his fair doth rehearse,
Making a couplement of proud compare
With sun and moon, with earth and sea's rich gems,
With April's first-born flowers and all things rare
That heaven's air in this huge rondure hems.

Sonnets, 21
William Shakespeare

Light riffled over the cellar floor from the candle burning on top of the stove, its translucent sides shading through ocher to menarcheal red. The wick burned inches from the bottom, but the outer lips stood a foot high, engorged and crusted with their own drippings. Veins webbed the tissue, barbled with rivulets of wax.

She floated close to the four-poster canopied by a damask half-tester and whipped off a black duster to reveal a scarlet coverlet. At the head of the bed lay a bolster with a satin sheen.

She skimmed across the floor to where a form loomed out of the dark and another duster was conjured away, disclosing a full-length looking glass in a boxwood frame. She glided up to it and stood there preening, turning from left to right with one hand behind her hair.

From the gloom behind her a naked man emerged. She spun round and staring at him without a word she plucked a vermilion rose from her corsage. It fell to her feet. The figure watched as she undid her busked bodice, all cringles and hooks, and tugging it off, flung it away. Underneath she had on a camisole of filigree embroidery. Everything she wore was black, even the *fleurette* garter round one thigh.

Her face was expressionless. She reached a hand behind her

head. The emanation stared at her. Nothing was said. She pulled the bow which held her hair and it tumbled in ringlets round her face. Her eyes gazed at the man and for a moment her mouth curved into an icy smile.

Her fingers spent an age creeping upward. She loosened the laces, one row at a time, and wriggled the garment down to her feet before stepping neatly out and throwing it to one side. The candle's glow ruddled her skin. Her nipples stood out in the cellar's coolness.

The man leered at her legs rising to the croup of moulded buttocks and dressed her down from the contours of her neck to her plush thighs. With a careless gesture she discarded her undergarments.

The fleece over her love mount went higher than most: dense wiry hair. A fine line ascended to a flat navel. A hint of axial hair showed under either arm.

The figure followed every detail as she turned her back. All she wore were single hose and shoes and her garter with its tiny flower. Discarnate eyes explored her dimpled rump. She stood tossing her head, her hair flaming blond around it, and spun to face him across the floor.

In a remote voice she asked: 'Will you come to bed, my lord?'

'Think on thy sins,' he rasped back.

She replied without hesitation, 'Why I should fear I know not, since guiltiness I know not, but yet I feel I fear.'

The apparition advanced on her and stopped two feet away.

She looked down at his loins. At first his virility was not upstanding. He seized her hair and struck her across the face with an open palm. 'Perjur'd woman!' He spat the words. 'Thou dost stone my heart, and mak'st me call what I intend to do a murder, which I thought a sacrifice.'

'O, banish me, my lord, but kill me not!' she entreated him.

'Down, strumpet.' Jerking her hair, the figure dragged her to the bed and threw her on the coverlet where she lay sobbing, face down, legs spread apart. Her buttocks trembled.

His eyes gloated over his own now flailing instrument, and he bent to pull off her shoes, which he tossed on the bed beside her. Her sobs turned to panting. A small gasp. Her gorge heaved.

Her left hand slid between her belly and the coverlet in search of her most intimate part and soon her breathing was rhythmic, matched by the rise and fall of her rump. Her legs were twitching.

The figure worked his hand over his organ and stared all the while at the tips of her fingers where they came and went at the moist apex. The movements of her buttocks grew quicker. She started to moan.

In his left hand the figure wielded a long black pizzle. He raised his arm and lammed the strop down on her pert haunches.

She screamed. Her body writhed.

'Filth,' he roared back at her and threw away the scourge.

'Now,' she pleaded, on hands and knees, legs parted urgently. 'I prithee, my lord.'

She reached between her thighs to guide him, crying out, her body bucking to receive him as he took her glistening by the hind. Her breathing came in gargled puffs. She thrust out her posterior, arching her back and lowering her head into the bolster pillow, scattering her hair, and pushed hard back to meet his cadence. Sweat gleamed on her shoulders.

A scraping sound came from the darkness behind him. He paused to throw a glance over his shoulder, then recommenced his onslaught. His fingers clawed her dainty flanks.

She hovered before giving herself with a scream to climax as he shunted deeper to bury the utmost length of himself inside her. At the same moment he seized the nape of her neck and rammed her head deep into the pillow, muffling her cries. She struggled but he was too powerful. Her movements grew less. He continued to smother her.

He watched the weal on her skin and his organ red with the blood that trickled down the cleft in her rump, and he forced her head deeper into the pillow.

When the backs of his legs began to quiver he drove himself faster till he reached full spate and exploded with an animal cry.

There was no sound in the cellar. The candle had guttered and drowned. There was only darkness.

6

O, blame me not, if I no more can write!
Look in your glass and there appears a face
That overgoes my blunt invention quite,
Dulling my lines and doing me disgrace.

Sonnets, 103
William Shakespeare

Lawrence had left early for Washington and Amelia had rushed off
to a Sunday-afternoon tea and sherry at Warren House. She had
denied all knowledge when I'd asked her where she disappeared
to in the night. I was reluctant to admit I couldn't remember
how I'd come to be in her bedroom anyway or anything after I'd
gone to look for her and caught sight of the rug over the trapdoor.
What had happened after that I didn't want to imagine. Had I
had a blank spell? Could it have been the wine after all? My skin
crawled just thinking of that ghastly cellar. I'd woken late the next
day in my own spacious room on the second floor.

Now I knew that she'd had her rag doll since childhood. She
hugged herself to sleep with it when she slept alone. I'd refrained
from asking how often that happened. The doll's name was
Rosaline. The fire that Maria had lit in the library before going
to Mass was almost dead. I fanned it a few times with the journal
I was reading. There was a snap from the embers and a flame
sprang up. I worked on it and soon a new fire had taken hold.

With a tall Scotch and Perrier I settled myself deep in the wing
chair to study Amelia's paper on Doctor Dee and Edward Kelley
entitled: *The Skryer's Stone*.

Some of it was pretty interesting, especially the bit about this
hermetic circle that Dee the Elizabethan magus seemed to have
been involved with, and maybe Shakespeare and the Dark Lady
too, whoever she turned out to be. I reread the part about the
priestly whore-virgin – apparently you could be both at once

– and the idea that maybe the Rosy Cross of the Rosicrucians was actually a hermetic version of the Roman *rota*, a spinning wheel used to test slaves for epilepsy. Amelia seemed to think this secret sect in England and maybe elsewhere had used one of these devices to experience a kind of transcendental high – to vivify the pineal gland – all in the name of resurrection, experiencing God directly through reunification, things like that. Maybe they'd also used drugs to reach this state of exaltation. There was something about occult initiation and the mystery of the conjunction and the part about Christ resurrected as an androgyne rang a bell . . . something she'd been saying in her lecture.

I was sitting there scratching away on my thigh. This was pretty far-fetched, but she admitted a lot of it was speculative and the evidence was only circumstantial, like the central female figure being introduced to the rites of the sect at first menses. She went on at great length about what she called the metaphysical use of sex in ceremonies like that. There was nothing prurient. Still it was horny-making just reading about it and thinking who wrote it.

At seven the author herself came tilting into the room full of smiles. I slewed round as she glided across the floor brandishing her scarf. Around her shoulders she had on a navy cape which she peeled off upon reaching the fire. She cast it across the nearest chair and twirled round skittishly before halting in front of me. She stretched her arms out.

I got to my feet and gave her a peck on the cheek which she returned with a lip-smacking kiss. 'How was the tea party?'

'Deathly dull,' she said. 'Some of us went on to the Skating Club.'

'Care for a drink?'

'I'll get it.' She went to the liquor cabinet and started to fix herself a Campari soda, but I followed behind to stop her.

'How about my special cocktail?' I suggested. I'd planned it as a surprise. My barman act always had Lucy tickled pink in the old days. I disappeared to the kitchen where I knew I'd find egg yolk, cream of coconut and frozen strawberry juice. When I returned I added shaved ice to the shaker with a dash of fresh lime juice and three shots of Mount Gay rum. 'Add a little pizzazz.' I shook gently and popped the top with a flourish. 'Your very own Bondi Bangaroo apart from no Bundry rum. Puts hair on a lifeguard's chest.'

She gave me a pout as I added freshly grated cinnamon. 'Let's sit on the rug,' she suggested.

I charged our glasses and joined her cross-legged on the polar bear. She snuggled up to me, cradling her head on her free arm which she leaned against my shoulder. She gazed into the tongues of flame.

For several minutes I looked too, enjoying the feeling of being close to her. It took me by surprise when her body stiffened and her glass fell to the floor and broke. I bent forward to look at her. She was right out of it, her eyes gazing into blue yonder.

'Are you all right?'

There was no reply at first. Her head was her head: a place where no one else could go.

Suddenly there was a voice. Not quite Amelia's, only it was coming from her. It came in sing-song tones. I tensed with shock. In Latin, too:

Ave magister angelorum. Ave mater meretricula. Ave rosa caeli. Ave domine rorispergio.

I stared in stupefaction.

Ave anima mundi. Ave regina virginum.

Another voice interrupted the last, so deep it verged on a man's: *Diana hunts in the palace of Aquarius. Jupiter's realm reaches even into the noble House of the Scorpion, there to be conjoined with mighty Uranus. Beware the Scorpion's sting, thou born within Diana's shining sickle. Bare not thy bosom to the stars, but take heed, for Saturn even now doth return into the Seventh House in the Firmament. There dwelleth Death. Guard thyself. Guard thy beloved.*

I could only look and listen in abject amazement.

A woman's voice called out of her: *Ancilla sum humilis, nata fontis.*

The deeper voice came crashing back: *Beauteous Venus will join with the Scorpion, conjunct Saturn conjunct Uranus. Fill thy longing with the joys of Eros. Beware misprision. Saturn doth lie in the Maiden's House. There will chaos come in the guise of a swain. The Maiden thou wilt find in the House of the Lord of Darkness. Meet not thy sire therein, but serve thy Archon. Thou wilt behold Mercury trine Jupiter in the Ninth House.*

Vale doctor, a lighter voice said in answer.

Then abruptly, Amelia's own voice: *Now she's coming, the black one.*

The light voice again: *Ave regina fornicis.*

By now I was kneeling down beside her, my left knee brushing the broken glass, knowing it must be some kind of a seizure; that I should wait and it would pass. I was watching her body sitting stiffly on the rug. The only sound was her almost stertorous breathing.

Her arms and head moved. She turned and looked into my eyes. The coquettish expression wasn't Amelia's. Neither were the words that came blurting out in a voice and accent I didn't recognize. She stood and curtsied as she spoke: 'Sir, will you visit my velvet garden? Will you pluck a red rose tied with a virgin knot and part the petals of my own sweet flower?' Her eyes focused and there was a raunchy glint in them.

I didn't try to answer. I looked back at her in amazement.

'Will you dance,' she was saying, 'with a daughter of the sugared game?'

On the surface I was only confused and fascinated. Underneath I was struggling to overcome shock. Was she completely out of her tree? All the same I allowed myself to be drawn into her act, thinking that if I humored her, maybe she'd snap out of it. 'What do you call yourself?' I felt guilty as hell. Christ, was I sweating! All right, I didn't know much about Amelia, but *this* . . .

'I am Jenny, sir.' She threw away the words. 'Will you help me fly these reeking stews?'

I was still kneeling in front of her, feeling frantic. When I shifted position her eyes followed me.

'O sir, come, make your heaven in a lady's lap and taste the sweetest almond of them all. I ask no fee for such sweet traffic.'

She rose to her feet and lowered her eyes for half a second. I visualized her assaying my weapon between both hands. That was the kind of look. The beguiling voice went on: 'In faith, sir, my sweet treasure is yours to use at your pleasure.' She did a pirouette and reaching between her legs slipped off her panties. It jolted me. She had on a flossy skirt which she held up as if she was going to dance the can-can and I could only stand rooted there, sizing up her sex.

She gave a small gasp. Her eyes were distant again. Though I still stood anchored to the spot I could almost feel my ploughshare as I tilled and furrowed in my own fantasy. 'O sir, how you disport yourself in Venus' temple.' It was an excited voice interlaced with snuffling breaths, then she shut her eyes and dropped her skirt. She swayed for a moment and sank on to the rug where she lay curled up on her side with her face inches from the damp strawberry stain and the fragments of glass that formed an ugly patch on the parquet floor.

I removed the broken glass quickly and avoiding the glare of the bear's glass eyes and two vicious teeth I leaned over and touched her shoulder. 'Amelia?'

She rolled on to her back and looked up. It wasn't Amelia. 'Would you leave me with child,' the voice admonished. 'Would you lie with me still were I covered with the blains?'

I should be so lucky. There was a faint noise over by the door and I turned my head. Cissy stood there dressed in a blue sweat suit and matching pumps. How long had she been skulking in the background? 'What the hell are you doing?' My question was almost a shout.

'I'm just hanging.' She shrugged and stomped out, slamming the door.

'Jenny' had risen to her feet meanwhile and stood scowling opposite me. All at once her scowls departed and there was a minute's blankness. Then from the metamorphosis in her look I knew she was Amelia again, looking distressed, biting her lower lip, then her blunted nails. I held out my hand but she refused it.

'Get me a drink will you – no alcohol.' It was Amelia speaking, Amelia's voice.

I got up and poured her a Canada dry. She took a big gulp and said, 'I had one of my attacks. I can't remember anything.' She picked her panties off the floor and struggled back into them.

'Is your arm okay?' She was shaking it.

'Yes, just a bit stiff. It's not too bad this time. Be a honey and get me a Tylenol from the medicine cabinet.'

When I returned she was sitting in a chair crying. I realized I'd never seen her in tears before. Her face looked childlike. I popped the caplet into her mouth. With a shaking hand she took the glass of water.

'Do I look terrible?' She said it in a way that didn't sound right.

Her cheeks were blotchy. 'You look fine to me. What in God's name was that all about?' I tried to make light of the whole episode. 'One minute you're Amelia: the next you're talking like some old-fashioned tart. Then suddenly you're you again.' I thought of Lucy. Her eye shadow would have been slipping. But Amelia never wore any. No make-up except the faintest touch of lipstick.

'Tell me what I said.'

'You seemed to be having fantasies, sexual ones, about me, like you were making love to me. At least in your imagination you were.' I explained in detail, leaving out how I'd almost been fantasizing too that we were making love. For the next minute she said nothing. She sucked her lower lip between her teeth and twisted trembling fingers round her glass.

I tried to fill the embarrassing silence. 'You said a lot of stuff in Latin, then a name: "Jenny".' I gently took the glass from her.

This time the silence was longer. She seemed to be thinking, at the same time avoiding my eyes. 'Y'see, I've got this kind of problem. It's never happened in front of anyone before.' She sniffed. 'At least not out loud. Usually it just happens inside me. I didn't want to tell you about it. I'm sorry.' She managed a smile. 'Only you'd have thought I was some kind of a screwball. It's happened more often since we were in Oxford together.'

I grabbed the journal that was lying on the wing chair and sank into thought with my back against one arm and my legs over the other. When she continued I had to strain to hear her voice. 'Before last summer my life wasn't going anywhere except in my work. I thought it wouldn't matter if I didn't tell you, but I guess you have to know – I've been seeing this analyst for the last four months.' She was weaving her hands together in a ball like a potter working up a lump of clay for the wheel.

I tensed. 'Have you been sleeping together?'

She smiled thinly. 'You've got it wrong. I mean I'm a client of this analyst. She's a woman. Uncle David, that's Dr Bendix, referred me to her when I told him I was getting dizzy spells. She's meant to be the best analyst within a hundred miles of Boston. Apparently she gets results.'

I gave her a look of deep suspicion. I was already half prepared for what came next, but it still jolted me. Probably it took one to know one.

'Daniel, baby, I get these voices in my dreams. I call them my gods. There's four of them. They're like a part of me. Sometimes too they pop up in my head from time to time – in what I call my "missing seconds", like just now. Afterwards I can remember things sometimes, the way you remember things from dreams. Other times I can't recall anything. It doesn't happen often when I'm not in bed and when it does no one notices. They just see a blank look and it's gone in next to no time.

'Don't think I'm schizophrenic,' she went on, her voice begging. 'I see this analyst – Katie Barber's her name – three hours a week. She says it's a rare kind of hysteria. That's not psychotic. Borderline really.'

I was looking at her hands. At least that explained the distant looks and the arm shaking.

'I thought it might go away and I wouldn't need to say anything to you, only now it's getting worse all the time.' Her voice was trembling. 'I can't stand that, baby – knowing there's part of me that I can't really meet. I don't feel complete. I feel empty . . . like a desert. That's what's so maddening. You don't think I'm mad, do you?' She looked at me with teary eyes. 'Shouldn't I feel more whole with you, not less?'

I raised an arm and rode a finger along the studded back of the chair. 'How long's this been happening, angel?'

'Since I was a kid, but not so often then. I couldn't bring myself to tell you, baby. Promise not to laugh or be upset?' She brightened.

'Promise.'

I noticed she was growing more hyper by the minute, unnaturally vivacious considering the circumstances. Her face was spry as she spoke. 'There's Hermie and Maggie. They're really Hermes alias Mercury, and Maria Magdalena. Hermie's a real honey. He makes me melt and I want to give myself to him body and soul.' She giggled. 'Maggie's a kind of cheerleader. And there's DeeDee. He's Dr Dee the wise old man. He tells my horoscope for me.'

'And Jenny?'

'Black Jenny's a whore. All she talks about is sex. She's really harmless. At least I thought so until now. I mean she never came out of my head before. That's really awful. I'm sorry, baby. I wouldn't have wanted you to find out this way, believe me. It's really embarrassing.' She was laughing wildly.

'Tell me more.'

'Well Katie says it's hysterical, but it's kind of confusing because she also says it may be epileptic, just temporal lobe epilepsy, nothing serious – very mild really. Sometimes I get this great light-headed feeling for a few seconds. I told Uncle David about it just since last summer and he said it's too soon to say if I'll need epilepsy tests and anticonvulsant drugs. He said it isn't life-threatening. It's still okay to drive, stuff like that.' Her left lid was drooping but I could see that both her eyes were swimming. 'I shouldn't drink too much alcohol,' she added. I knew alcohol and Amelia were close. Too close really. I knew the feeling.

She took in my perplexed expression and began to sob again, then wiped her face and though she was still in a state her story continued, more bizarre: How could she tell me, she said, about her fifth god, who held Black Jenny in his dominion and subjected her to the ignominy of his subtle congress, descending like an incubus in the night to rob her of her soul? But she told me anyway. Her memory of those dreams was so out-of-focus. Black Jenny had no option but to play the whore. Her master treated her like one in every way, leaving her sick-feeling when she woke up shivering and perspiring to find that time had disappeared. She hadn't dared tell anyone, not even Katie, about the fifth, the one with no name, no face. She shuddered, she said, to think of the liberties he took in return for her pleasure. Why did this monster remind her of Othello for no reason she could put a finger on? Katie would only have said her dreams were a safety valve for the dark fantasies of the unconscious seeking a harmless alternative to acting out. Just how real could fantasy get?

I was utterly confused. I quested for an opening but changed my mind. Hadn't I heard a warning voice in the back of my head: one I hadn't stopped to listen to before? The other thing that was beginning to get to me was the way she sometimes took me for granted. At times she was totally wrapped in her own urgencies and I was left feeling as if she was talking to herself. Shifts in her personality happened all the time, for no apparent reason, and I was unable to shake off the feeling that I wasn't there except to provide the audience and applaud at the end. At times like that trust flew out the window. She'd only asked about Lucy once and switched off straight away. I softened when I glanced at her sitting on the rug looking so pathetic. Now wasn't the time to interrogate her.

'Katie Barber thinks she can cure me. She says it's serious but treatable. She says it's to do with depression and poor parenting and maybe it's triggered by my absence seizures. She agrees with Uncle David there's no need for drugs unless it starts happening outside my dreams.'

I noticed the dimple that formed on her chin when it puckered and the fugitive smile that came and went round her eyes and would turn into crow's feet in twenty years. It made me want to hold her tight. 'Isn't this outside your dreams? You weren't in bed and you weren't sleeping when it happened.' She didn't reply, but she did accept my outstretched hand. I coaxed her to her feet. 'You need to lie down and get some sleep. You haven't told your analyst about us, have you?'

'I'm sorry.' She mopped her puffy face with the back of her hand. 'I haven't told Katie about you and me. Please take me up to bed, baby. I'm sorry if I screwed up.'

She was completely wiped out. I got her unsteadily to her feet and she leant on me as I led the way upstairs. One of the clocks that threw up chimes at all hours erupted as we reached the first floor. Something screamed at me that I refused to acknowledge. Hadn't Lucy been halfway bonkers by the end? Perhaps the three of us had more in common than Amelia realized. Did it really matter? She recognized the problem, she could talk about it and she was getting help. So I wasn't the only one who could lose his grip now and again.

I helped her undress and she flopped onto her bed. I laid her out and moments later she was asleep. I took the hand that trailed over the edge and tucked it under the coverlet before going downstairs again to clear up the mess from the broken glass. Later I mounted a long vigil over her sleeping form.

———— ● ————

'I say she's fucking her father,' Katie Barber emphasized again, scattering ash from her Gauloise across the table as she picked up her notes. She had doubts in the back of her mind, but she wasn't going to admit them to Rosalind Kahn, her junior partner in the psychoanalytic clinic which they ran on Farrar Street. On the other hand Katie appreciated second opinions and Rosie had been introduced to Amelia for just that purpose.

85

A week had gone by since Lawrence's brief stay in Cambridge. Amelia had made her own decision to visit her analyst for five hours a week instead of three.

Rosie, born Jewish and recently born again in Christ, was a dilemma professionally for Katie. With her direct line to God the younger analyst was having increasing difficulty these days reconciling Sigmund Freud and the deity who had empowered her to move in the gifts of the Holy Spirit. Without Katie's incessant commentary on the problem Rosie would have seen no contradiction in interpreting the same neuroses analytically or charismatically. Katie however made no inner concessions at all to Christ, though on the surface she sometimes admitted with some irritation that it ought to be possible. Katie had times when she muttered darkly to herself that Rosie's days with her were numbered and might God help her when the last day came.

Rosie listened in stubborn silence as Katie presented her theory. What annoyed the younger analyst was that Katie could go on like that, sounding so sure of herself when it was clear to anyone who'd met Amelia that her problem was a lot more complicated and Satan probably had a hold on her. But Katie was twelve years her senior. Rosie listened respectfully then put her own case. When she had finished she crossed her arms.

Katie lit another Gauloise, shook out the match and sat back in her chair, two furrows of concentration showing between her eyebrows. The eyes behind her spectacles were permanently screwed up, the way it happened to people who had spent half a lifetime hooked to the end of a cigarette as if it were a life-support system. She was a big woman, some would say obese, and her spectacles did nothing to enhance her homely looks. In fact Katie Barber looked an unlikely candidate for the tag of 'best analyst within a hundred miles of Boston' accorded her by Dr David Bendix. But beneath the unprepossessing exterior was a kind woman unembittered by her singlehood.

Katie had trained as a doctor at the Harvard Medical School and after a further year studying neurophysiology had moved to New York to be analyzed by the renowned Otto Morgenthal. She had paid her way working in clinical psychiatry at Queensborough State Hospital.

Rosie Kahn was a graduate of the University of Illinois Medical School. Though she was by no means pretty, in comparison with

Katie she was not a mile short of ravishing. People said they made an odd pair. Rosie was thin, of medium height. Katie was taller though her plumpness disguised her height. It was when the two of them appeared together, which was often until Rosie became an evangelist, that they looked 'odd', the older woman beaming and roly-poly, the younger sharp, almost bird-like. In her flowing gowns with her frizzy hair and a cigarette invariably hanging from the corner of her lower lip, Katie looked like the last of the great earth mothers – Mama Cass twenty years too late.

They often discussed their cases. Rosie had just spent two hours with Amelia, one alone with her and one with Katie as observer. If only, Rosie thought, she could hypnotize too as Katie did regularly, but hypnosis wasn't part of her own repertoire and now anyway she felt there was something diabolic about Mesmer's art. Amelia it seemed was a perfect subject. In the month since Amelia had consented to hypnosis Katie felt she'd made considerable progress in uncovering the darker layers of her unconscious.

'Her ego defenses,' Rosie said when no comment came, 'are staying in place whether she's hypnotized or not.'

'This is true,' Katie admitted, always thankful when Rosie's remarks were entirely rational. She knew only too well that when an ego with poor boundary definition – what she called 'a depleted personality' – set up its survival mechanisms, these were often continued, sometimes in another form, under hypnosis, which was a useful but limited tool. It was certainly no highway to the truth. But in combination with the free associations of the couch it had its uses. With Amelia it had taught her something about her client's traumatic childhood. It might have taught her more if she had regressed Amelia back to that early period in her life, but regression under hypnosis still seemed too risky.

'Do you think it helps,' Rosie asked, 'not telling her afterward what she said while she's hypnotized? If you did then maybe she could accept Christ and His love so that He can heal the underlying trauma.'

As usual Katie addressed herself only to one part of Rosie's remarks. 'Oh I confront her with some of it. The rest will come up as insight in its own good time.' She stood up from her easy chair and went to the window. 'It looks like spring isn't far off.' She opened the sash window a fraction at the bottom.

Except where food, cigarettes and her soul were concerned Katie was a sage in Rosie's eyes. 'Are you still hoping to present the case at the symposium?'

'That depends on where Amelia and I have gotten to by then.' Katie knew she already had enough material for an interesting paper and it would be a good excuse for a vacation in Fort Lauderdale. Her paper to the American Academy of Psychoanalysis the previous year had been published in the *Journal of Abnormal Psychology*, making her an overnight authority on the difficult subject of internalization of the father-figure in the female psyche. By contrast the pinnacle so far of Rosie's writing career was a piece on her own hobby-horse: damage limitation in personal relationships. It had appeared pseudonymously in *Cosmopolitan*. That was before Rosie teamed up with Jesus.

Katie returned to her seat, tamped out her half-smoked Gauloise and lit up another which she waved in the air as she spoke. 'What do you make of this other personality that came out of her?'

'It's got all the signs of hysteria and demonization.'

'This is true as far as hysteria is concerned.' Katie strained to remain tolerant. 'Let's look at what happened again. She's lying there on the couch talking. Something I said must have triggered it because then there's a pause. I look down and her pupils are wide, her head's pulled over to one side and after a few seconds there's a kind of gulp from her throat – just once. Her arms are stiff by her sides and her body's rigid.'

Rosie made as if to speak, but getting a cold look she hemmed and paused, changing her mind. However, Katie seemed to expect a comment so she said: 'All the signs of a convulsion?'

'Right, only the rest is different. Out comes this weird voice – don't say speaking in tongues – that I can't understand. After two or three minutes it stops as suddenly as it started. She's pale and anxious; her head's aching. Except for a slight recall of aura there's amnesia, including what I said to her before it happened. She's lying there shaking her left arm. All the after-effects of an epileptic seizure.'

'What about her conversion symptoms? That would suggest hysteria not epilepsy.'

'Sure, like her tension headaches. And there's sleepwalking too. She seemed doubtful about that, but under hypnosis there's a lot of evidence she does. You'd expect some signs of fugue and hypnogogic trance, especially in someone so vulnerable to post-hypnotic suggestion.'

'Nothing that can't be healed in Christ's name.'

'On the one hand we've got symptoms of epileptic absence and on the other we've got fugal amnesia, symptoms of hysteria and this weirdo voice that comes out which isn't her regular voice at all.'

Katie was conducting the conversation like a tutorial, Rosie thought resentfully, and made a mental note to ask God for a gift of the Spirit that would help her to pray for Amelia.

'Dear Rosie, does it not add up to multiple personality disorder, the rarest and possibly the most serious subgroup of borderline personality disorder. Let's look at the less obvious parts of the syndrome. It's worth remembering that when Amelia had her seizure I'd just drawn her attention, very gently, to the fact that she unconsciously associated Shakespeare with her father.'

'That's got to be possession,' Rosie said.

'It's got to be pathological, but that doesn't explain about Shakespeare.'

The magisterial tone left Rosie feeling miffed. Inwardly she asked God to forgive Katie for the sin of pride.

'Something's happened to her that I can't put my finger on. It's whatever precipitated the crisis that brought her into analysis.'

'I'd say she's very mediumistic. She's got that quality of the mediatrix. Excuse the Jungianism,' Rosie added.

'That's very insightful.' Rosie knew this time it wasn't a putdown. 'Amelia *is* very mediumistic. Magical thinking may be a symptom of the dysfunctional personality, but it's also a quality that's not uncommon in epileptics. They sometimes have a kind of sixth sense, telepathy almost. Rosie, you really ought to have gotten into bed with Carl Jung, not Freud and Jesus Christ.'

'I also got that she fakes her orgasms.'

'Did she tell you that?' Katie was startled.

'We talked a bit about sex and I kind of guessed. When I asked her she said "yes". She said at school they called her "Hotty".'

'This is true. She's been extremely promiscuous for years. What I call pseudo-sex. Mechanically good, but lacking the real feeling that makes loving sex so much more rewarding.' Katie stopped to sigh. 'Yet sometimes she does have real orgasms. They're linked to her vivid fantasy life. In it two figures loom large: her father and William Shakespeare. Y'see her father's the only love in her life . . . except that love is exactly what it isn't. It's infantile dependence on a powerful controlling and messianically narcissistic father figure. He's god in her universe and she's in thrall to him . . . or to William Shakespeare. It comes to the same thing. In her dream-like fantasies which she can't recall clearly afterwards she explodes in all-too-real orgasms that depend on her psychological fetish.'

'What fetish is that?'

'Shakespeare of course. Anything to do with him. As an addictive personality type she's been obsessed with Shakespeare since adolescence, perhaps longer. With her mother it was alcohol. With Amelia it's Shakespeare . . . and work of course, but that's Shakespeare too. Her whole life is driven by the need for symbiotic attachment to a single mother/father figure.'

'Where does her mother's death fit into the picture?'

'I think when Amelia was twelve and her mother died she felt responsible . . . a case of inappropriate guilt. The roots of her disorder would go back much earlier though . . . to somewhere between the age of one and two. There's a failure of separation from the mother there.'

Rosie seemed to make up her mind about something. 'I think there's a strong masochistic tendency, one that God may be able to heal.'

'I never thought I'd hear that coming from a feminist,' Katie said with a chortle, ignoring the remark about God, 'but you're right on target. The orientation needn't be sexual of course, but in Amelia it probably is.'

'With her father?'

'Now you're putting me on the spot again. There's no doubt she idolizes him. She can't say "no" to him: quite literally. Not surprisingly she's learnt to manipulate him from her position of subservience and this way she has power over him. Of course she hates him underneath, but without his recognition of her she ceases to exist. Isn't that what masochism is all about? When all's said and done Lawrence Hungerford's the one in the driving seat. He's her overlord and her prison keeper. Psychopaths like him,' she added, 'are a danger to everyone.'

'That's a bit over the top.'

'You'd be surprised. The malignant narcissist in extreme cases becomes the psycho who makes the headlines. He can be charming, witty, intelligent. But invariably he uses people and he's indifferent to the feelings of others. He's without the capacity for love . . . or for guilt or remorse. The psychopath can be a brilliant actor using a false persona to fake all the emotions which he never really feels. Some are Walter Mitty types who go through life chameleon-like, adapting to circumstance. They're impulsive loners with few real friends, always seeking instant gratification for their infantile needs.' Katie shifted uncomfortably in her seat.

'And her demons that you mentioned before: she didn't say anything about them to me.'

'Gods, not demons. She didn't tell me about them either the first couple of months.' Katie looked pensive for a second. 'When she did say something I thought they'd come out under hypnosis . . . but they didn't. I thought they were fantasy for a while then she told me some of the things they say to her. When she had her seizure the voice I couldn't understand was probably one of them.'

'Who are these gods? They sound like demons to me.'

'Amelia sees them as aspects of her research into hermeticism and alchemy. I see them as dissociative parts of her ego which is what multiple personality is after all. It's fairly rare, which I suppose is why I haven't encountered it before. Isn't it incredible to think the unconscious can invent new personalities, however incomplete they tend to be? Think of all the publicity surrounding *Sybil* and *The Three Faces of Eve*. Usually these personalities have a parallel past and an ongoing existence. That's what makes it even more amazing.'

She gazed into thin air. Rosie could tell when Katie was deep in thought. It wasn't a good idea to interrupt at such moments. 'The literature tends to be pretty inconclusive,' Katie continued. 'One thing it highlights is how different the symptoms are from one case to the next. There are dozens in the textbooks and Amelia doesn't resemble any of them much.' She was extinguishing another half-finished cigarette and wriggling round to get comfortable in her chair. Her dewlap chin rested on one balled fist.

'How much does she remember after the event?'

'What recall she has is pretty limited. If she gets one of her seizures while she's with someone all they'll see is a faraway look. She won't answer to questions. But it only lasts a few seconds so it often goes unnoticed or the other person shrugs it off as a "blank spell". A lot of us have moments of day-dreaming when we drift off and don't seem to hear when we're spoken to.'

'Don't I know it.' Rosie thought of Rick, her librarian boyfriend from the Law School, a fellow Christian.

'The split-off parts of her personality must go back to some traumatic event in the past, something she can't face. It gives her an outlet when the build-up of guilt gets too great to bear.'

'But surely multiple personality disorder is symptomatic of psychosis or possession by demons?' Rosie liked straight answers. This time she got one.

'There's no true delusions. Amelia recognizes her gods as part of herself. She doesn't see them as "other". I'd like to think that at worst it's borderline. It's not as if she's schizophrenic . . . or in need of exorcism,' she added with a dry laugh. 'Her reality testing is basically normal, even if there is an element of the false self masking her core personality . . . an element of power that she takes on from her father.'

'Do you still think *you* can cure her without the power of the Holy Spirit?'

'As usual, "cure" isn't the word. Our job is to help people along the difficult path to self-actualization. Not so they'll be happy. Just so they'll take responsibility for their own lives and won't drive themselves into an early grave through depression and illness. When you look at the kind of world we've got, all our survivors are a success story. Y'know something, I love that girl to death, almost like she's my own child. There's such love there under the surface, burning to grow with the right man; someone who would act as the catalyst that the deepest part of her needs to begin the long painful journey out of emotional infancy. But if she could grow to the point when she found *real* intimacy with a significant other, it would amount to a giant act of infidelity to her father.'

'Don't you think she needs more help than analysis is able to give her?' Rosie put her question in the closest she ever got to an aggressive tone of voice.

'Of course she does. But the extra help needn't necessarily come from God.' There was a pause. 'Whatever skeletons she's got lurking in her childhood cupboard won't be a pretty sight, but in the end she's going to have to face them with her own inner resources. Otherwise, what a waste! Hell's bells, d'you realize what a gifted scholar she is and a good musician and painter into the bargain?' Katie slumped in her chair. 'She's highly motivated. I just hope she stays the course. Borderlines so rarely do. There'll be a lot of pain, a lot of resistance.'

'What about the incest issue?' Rosie was burning to get back to incest. It was a subject on which Katie was a recognized authority.

'I still say she's fucking her father. An incest trauma is often involved in cases of multiple personality disorder.'

'Couldn't it just be psychological incest?'

'It could, but I say it's for real,' Katie said emphatically. 'Until a few days ago I wasn't sure. I still have nothing concrete, but on Monday the impression that came through under hypnosis was overwhelming.'

'Maybe it's just hysterical fantasy.' Rosie refrained from bringing up possession again.

'An Elektra complex is one thing, but diddling your dad when he's sixty-two and you're twenty-six is something else. If she is it's going to have to stop.'

With an air of finality Katie Barber opened another packet of Gauloises.

———— • ————

With astrakhan collar turned up and a following wind Lawrence hiked bare-headed the few blocks from the Olympic Tower, yielding en route to the temptation of a foray into Bijan, then it was on to the Pierre for a seaweed cleansing mask at Gio's. When he reached the Knickerbocker Club a block away there was no time in hand to read the *Wall Street Journal*. He loathed Manhattan, especially Fifth Avenue, but the 'Knick' was handy when he was consulted by the Metropolitan Museum. He dismissed Jasper his chauffeur-bodyguard who had tailed him all morning and at the hatcheck he deposited his white silk scarf and black vicuña topcoat before proceeding up the stairs to the dining room. Here the *maître d'* showed him to his habitual table in the corner by the south window whence, with his back to the wall, he had a good view of everyone who came and went. The Frenchman inclined his head and withdrew.

Two elderly men at the next table gave the aristocratic-looking lobbyist a familiar nod which he returned. The wine waiter arrived on cue carrying an ice bucket that held a bottle from Lawrence's private reserve. A little champagne was poured. He gave his preferred tipple a summary sniff and set down his *flûte*.

A familiar figure appeared across the table ten minutes later. 'Good to see you,' said Lawrence and put down his napkin as he rose to welcome his lunch guest. 'I've already ordered for both of us. Hope you don't mind.' Marcus Freeman had flown in late the previous evening and dined at Elaine's before retiring in the small hours to his suite at the Algonquin.

Lawrence raised a finger that brought the wine waiter scurrying back as he took in the intelligent, slightly effeminate features. The all-American guru was forty-seven years old, lean and hale with close-set eyes. He wore a pinstriped suit in navy mohair and a blue buttondown shirt. His tie bore an emblem that meant nothing to Lawrence.

'What the hell's that tie you're wearing?'

'The Rostrum Training graduate tie,' Marcus shot back stiffly. It still got to him when people said things like that. Marcus was better known than Lawrence to television audiences. In the Western world thousands – described by one critic as 'the psychologically crippled' – had fallen for the lure of the Rostrum Training Centers which had wide support among businessmen and educators attracted by Marcus's claim that anyone could become a TV star or a Formula One racing driver if they placed total trust in their own potential and the power of risk.

Launching the Rostrum Training at the peak of the hippie diaspora of the early Seventies Marcus had borrowed from most of the assertiveness and growth therapies from Scientology and est to encounter and Gestalt. To a generation in a hurry the Training had offered easy enlightenment larded with smatterings of Zen Buddhism. Since the heady month in 1968 when he had sat at the feet of a maverick Alan Watts on his Sausalito houseboat Marcus had spoken of the way of Zen. His real fillip had come in the late Seventies with the launch of the World Health Rostrum.

Marcus still had more charisma – in one journalist's words – 'than John Lennon and Mahatma Gandhi'. Thousands hung on his every dictum as if it were holy writ. He exuded confidence but he was wiser now, his hair graying. He operated a bicoastal lifestyle shuttling the New York–LA axis between his principal centers. The previous week he had lunched with Lawrence in the Bar Room of Le Cirque and Lawrence had passed him the calling card of two ritzy black hookers.

He had pocketed the card and later thrown it away. As a man twice divorced and still wearing a wedding band he suffered from a largely deserved reputation as a lover, described by his first wife at dinner parties as a 'black belt in cunnilingus'. He found it easy to remain single but difficult to stay celibate for long. The hookers' card had not changed his view of Lawrence. They had had too much to drink that day and Lawrence had admitted he found it hard to 'get it on', except with high-class whores. Nothing surprised the onetime chemicals salesman from Columbus, Ohio.

'You know, Marcus, I might not be doing this except I still owe you one big bunch of favors.' Where Lawrence was concerned there were no gratuitous gifts. Marcus knew from experience everything came with a rubber band attached.

'There's one thing I still haven't figured . . . why Bosworth agreed to Amelia's proposal in the first place?' Marcus knew the answer anyway. He just wanted to hear Lawrence confirm it.

Lawrence obliged with a none-too-friendly look. 'Grade school chemistry. He fell in love with her.' He gave a short laugh.

'What's he got that others haven't?' Marcus's voice was huffy.

'Women are like doorlocks, Marcus. You can waste hours messing with the wrong key. If you've got the right one you slip it in easily first time round.' Lawrence pulled out his cigar case and offered his guest the last Havana – Zino Davidoff's best, a personal gift. When Marcus declined he moistened the head, sliced off the cap with a silver cutter and placed the cigar beside his untouched *bisque de crabe*. 'You want to know something? Everybody's asking how they find out if they've got Shakespeare's gene – every white man in America besides a few of a darker shade of pale.'

Marcus sat back as a waitress removed his soup plate. 'What else have I been doing for the last month if not living and breathing the whole shebang?'

'The hell with whether we find this Shakespeare guy,' Lawrence went on. Marcus sat up. 'Listen, you'll be pleased to hear I've gotten you the backing of the director of NIH and you're home and dry with NORA as well as the chairman of the FDA advisory committee on AIDS and no one's ass was even kissed. As you and I know Bosworth's got credentials like you'd never believe. With that kind of reputation and the prestige of the American Red Cross, the Shakespeare Search won't turn into some halfass farrago.' Lawrence took a sip of champagne and with a pair of crackers broke open a lobster claw on the plate that had newly arrived in front of him, subtly dissecting the hapless crustacean before devouring it with gusto.

Watching him Marcus found he had lost his appetite. The Rostrum had run an education program with the AIDS Action Council before launching its own AIDS Campaign with its fleet of mobile screening clinics. The prognosis from Marcus's business-school lieutenants wasn't looking too good. With two million dollars committed to Bosworth's new lab they'd be out of money in six months if the Shakespeare Search wasn't a success. He already felt as if he'd hit rock bottom, but it didn't show.

As if he could read Marcus's mind Lawrence reached for his inside pocket and brought out his billfold, from which he produced a piece of paper. Marcus cast an eye over the Chase Manhattan check for five million dollars made out to the World Health Rostrum Shakespeare Search. 'It's no big deal,' Lawrence said. 'Think of it as a start-up gift from the IRS.'

'Are you serious?' Marcus looked dubious.

'Damn right I am.' Lawrence didn't bat an eyelash. He twisted his neck and jabbed his index finger at the check.

Marcus thanked him and laid the check on the table. He could see the difference it would make.

'You're gambling on a helluva lot of guys wanting to find out if Shakespeare was their grandfather,' Lawrence said with a chuckle.

'Up to two thousand a week. The market research team's been busy working out what we can expect. Some big gifts should be in the pipeline soon . . . on top of this one.' He touched the check.

'I've got to hand it to you, Marcus. You're the best goddamn publicist in the whole damn country.'

If Marcus sensed a slur he was too diplomatic to say so.

'D'you think you can keep Bosworth's involvement a secret much longer? Amelia feels the media will sniff out where he's hiding in the next few days.'

'I'm doing my damnedest. The Search is already leaking out but no one knows Bosworth's in it too. People think we've capitalized on *his* idea.'

'How's his competition?'

For a second Marcus looked unwontedly flummoxed. He pulled himself together. 'That's not going to be our problem, not with enough insider muscle in DC?' He eyed Lawrence pointedly, putting half a query into his inflection.

'How d'you mean?' Lawrence harrumphed back.

Marcus backed off from pushing his point. 'I mean there's serious influence behind outfits like Biocal and Technogen. Let's just say the likes of vaccine-makers such as Bristol-Meyers and Hoffman la Roche.'

'Are you referring to Greenberg and Sardou?'

Marcus heaved his shoulders. Lawrence was better informed than he thought. The big vaccine-makers were all backing AIDS research via biotech proxies and their pet scientists: men like Robert Greenberg at George Washington University and Bernard Sardou at the Pasteur Institute.

Lawrence saw the same characters as Marcus but he placed them in a different setting. Daniel was the thoroughbred they were entering in a select race. He knew he could head off congressional hustlers aiming to stymie the Shakespeare Search, whatever Marcus suspected to the contrary.

Marcus thought he could read people too, though admittedly Lawrence was harder than most. 'Everything's legally watertight,' he said. 'Especially the new releases that screenees will sign.'

'Whether they want the Shakespeare test or not?' Lawrence was looking out the window as he spoke. Across Fifth Avenue in the Park two gangly black teenagers were aiming passes with a football across the head of an irate parkman. One whose white scarf sailed in the wind laughed as the parkman saw the joke and leapt up to intercept the ball. He too was laughing. Lawrence envied all three of them.

'Either way.' Marcus gave a succinct nod.

Lawrence returned his attention to his guest and mulled over this piece of information. 'I think I'll mosey over to the Met.' He was impatient. He could tell when Marcus was about to launch into one of his diatribes on risk and that was a pleasure he could forgo.

Marcus was looking at the check for five million. 'Hey, you forgot to sign it.'

Lawrence pulled out his pen and signed. He was left-handed.

'Do you really think we'll discover someone out there related to Shakespeare?' Marcus was eyeing Lawrence's signet ring.

'Amelia seems to think so and she ought to know. There could be dozens of descendants out there.'

'What if Bosworth gets cold feet and pulls out early?'

'He won't. I promise you.'

7

So am I as the rich whose blessed key
Can bring him to his sweet uplocked treasure,
The which he will not every hour survey
For blunting the fine point of seldom pleasure.

Sonnets, 52
William Shakespeare

Hungerford House was all mine while Maria went shopping. I'd been unable to get Black Jenny out of my mind. She'd not reappeared – or the voices, except in a dream I'd had – and I was disappointed. The dream had been wildly erotic – me and Black Jenny – or was it the Dark Lady? I wished Amelia wouldn't make me think so much about my mother. It was that bloody photograph . . . the way Amelia looked at it.

I snatched a light breakfast and charged up the stairs in shorts and T-shirt for my daily workout. It was Sunday and Amelia had gone off to a meeting at Warren House. I threw my towel across a radiator as I surged into the gym.

I wasn't the first to arrive. I didn't have the place to myself after all. Cissy the vestigial virgin worst luck raised her head and leveled her eyes sideways from the training mat. Did she have a stripped-pine approach to sex and intimacy? The corners of her mouth pulled back in a look so intense I couldn't tell at first whether it was hostile or not. She lay naked on her back with her Amazon of a fitness trainer kneeling beside her in nothing but pink panties: a trim breastless woman with a muscular back and platinum hair. She was looking askance.

'Sorry,' I stammered.

'Feel free.' Something in Cissy's voice stopped me from leaving. I fixed her with a puzzled eye. The trainer was continuing with her massage and muscle toning routine. She reached over Cissy for a bottle of baby oil and poured a little into one palm.

A sweatshirt hung over the lateral bar as if it were a coathook.

Cissy carried on speaking as the trainer massaged her larger-than-life breasts. 'Glad to see the back of Lawrence? I've learnt to stay out of the way when he's here.' There was more than a grain of arsenic in her innuendo.

I said nothing. So I wasn't the only one who couldn't stand the old sod. Cissy seemed an unlikely ally in view of our unconsummated hatred.

'You either put up with that kind of situation,' she was saying with her eyes shut, 'or you're hell and gone out of it. That guy's a shaman looking for an erection the size of a totem pole. I know what I'd do, but I'm not a man. If you're prone to jealousy better stop phutzing around and quit while you're ahead.'

Was I hearing what I was hearing? She was saying that in Toraja in Sulawesi big noses equaled big penises; that Torajan men were totally concerned about their noses. I leaned back against the doorjamb feeling out on my own. I was smiling awkwardly. I could feel a hard-on coming . . . merely at the thought of a little touch of Cissy in the night . . . something too lewd for words. Me and two women: Amelia and Cissy in some romantic no-man's-land.

She sat up and turned over on her stomach. I watched her back arch as she supported herself on both elbows. Her breasts that I'd imagined so Sloppy Joe hung gracefully, her nipples almost touching the rubber mat. The trainer was hacking and chopping at the smooth cheeks of her rump.

'You wouldn't be the first,' Cissy said. 'Daddy's girl brings something out in all her boyfriends.'

At that remark I strode over and glared down at her. The trainer ignored me.

'The trouble is,' she said, 'Amelia's so rich and attractive. Few enough people can live with that kind of tension. Only on top of everything else she has a load of academic credibility going for her. All that kudos doesn't go down too well with some faculty come-and-goners and other marginalia. They'd dance in the street if she got cashiered tomorrow . . . particularly Nancy Bretton.'

'What's that got to do with Lawrence?'

'I said it already: jealousy. It follows her round like a shadow. Did you never read those stories where two knights battled for a lady's favor?'

'What the hell are you getting at?' I was over by the window

100

talking with my back to her. There was no reply. Feeling none too gruntled I raised my voice and asked again.

'Why settle for two,' she called over, needling me in her prima-donna voice. 'Why not make that three, four, maybe half a dozen. All her yinnies end up in the garbage . . . apart from Lawrence. The mofinch round here got daddy's girl figured out long ago.'

Screw this for a game of soldiers. With Cissy's charms no longer dazzling my imagination I marched across the floor and whipped up my towel. Tumescence gone, I stole a final look at the George cross badge of her buttocks as I closed the door.

My encounter with a nude Cissy left me shaken. On top of that the feeling of being imprisoned was getting to me despite the fact that I now shared Amelia's passion for the Dark Lady and had all day on my hands to wade through books rummaging for a clue to who she was. It occurred to me to phone Ben Talbot at the Whitehead Institute just for a change of human contact, but on reflection it wasn't such a hot idea. Instead I phoned my lawyer in London as promised. He reported that the police – he had inside contacts at New Scotland Yard – were surprisingly keen to find me, considering busting into a tomb, albeit a famous one, wasn't that big a deal in the statute books.

I replied that I'd seen who was in charge of it: Detective Chief Inspector Tom Drake. I let him know how that scared the hell out of me and puzzled me too. I could still see Drake's blunt features and hear his blunter voice in 1985 as he gave me a rundown of the 1959 police report on my mother's death. He only did that on condition I gave him a copy of my own findings on her – the complete genetic profile, all the blueprints.

We'd argued, but Drake was insistent I shouldn't see the report. A year earlier the police had tried to stop my permit to go round exhuming bodies, but I'd had too much influence in that department. So I never saw the 1959 report, just got Drake's surprisingly detailed account. But the astonishing thing was that Drake admitted in 1985 that he'd been in on the 1959 investigation as a young Detective Constable newly promoted from copper on the beat. His details weren't second-hand from the old report. He'd actually been there and examined her body.

They'd found her clothed, full of some unspecified drug, underwater, including her head, in the Victorian bathtub down the hotel corridor. It was Drake, working with someone from forensics, who'd come up with the evidence to show she'd been slowly suffocated with a pillow, then strangled, and her body had been dragged from bedroom to bathroom and dumped in the bathwater. In the lavatory next door they'd found a used and knotted condom. Someone had flushed the loo and left without checking to see it had gone.

There was Drake in 1985, a very senior detective in the Metropolitan Police, reopening and reclosing the file. And now this. Tom Drake was in charge of tracking me down.

Peter Dunkley – that was my lawyer's name – had something disturbing to add as I was about to hang up. Drake had again reopened the investigation into my mother's murder through the same Incident Room at Scotland Yard that was looking for me. Dunkley wouldn't tell me where he got his information, but I knew he was 'on the square' – a Freemason – like most of the big guns in the Met's CID, so I had little doubt where his facts came from and even less about their reliability. He swore to God though that he knew nothing more than he'd already told me. I felt leery of Dunkley, even, but dismissed the feeling as unreasonable.

I hung up wondering what the hell was going on, as if reopening that file would help them find me or for that matter identify who my mother was after all those years. If that was the reaction of the police it was out of all proportion. I didn't even take anything from Shakespeare's grave apart from some body tissue and that silver sodding T-cross and frankly that had been a lot more exciting for Amelia than for me. I sat back and sifted the facts but there was no obvious explanation.

At eleven I made up my mind to take a walk outside, at the risk of being recognized. Donning my dark glasses I hunched my shoulders and strolled into the real world, cutting across Radcliffe Yard in the sharp air to explore the Old Burying Ground. Nosing among the graves uncovered by a momentary thaw I searched for early Hungerford headstones but found none. Most of the inscriptions had been effaced by wind over the centuries.

I rewound my scarf tight under my chin and trudged on to Harvard Square to forage in the Coop bookstore for half an hour. Passing a shop window I glanced at my reflection in the glass and ran a hand through my windblown hair. When I returned to the house I was armed with a couple more books on Shakespeare. I only had to switch on the TV to see what a pitch interest in the Bard had suddenly reached. Now everyone was a Shakespeare buff. Amelia's love of Shakespeare was infectious and it made a change from AIDS, however guilty I felt not to be at work.

I was back indoors long enough to look at a map of Cambridge then on to Brattle Street again, heading west in the direction of Mt Auburn Cemetery. I whistled into the wind and followed the winding street, replaying mentally the half-dozen conversations I'd had with Marcus on the phone since Lawrence departed. Despite meeting the man at some length in London I still had only a vague impression of what he was really like. I resigned myself to getting a better idea in New York in a few days' time.

The cemetery was vast and desolate, an agoraphobiac's nightmare. I hadn't a clue where to start. Under a solitary beech I made out two figures digging a grave. The elder, a man with hands wizened to crêpe and a chined face, turned out to be eager to ply me with information. When I'd pumped him dry and was thanking him I noticed a curious twist lingering in the void that represented his mouth. His unfettled companion was half his age, a dwarfish man with hyperthyroid eyes who looked to be mute and probably had the same world-view as a Lambeth bag lady. He sized me up from waist deep in the grave he was digging. It was all too familiar a scene, reminding me of graves I'd legally opened with research students in my early quest for the weeping gene, long before Shakespeare came into my life. Graves, too, excavated in search of my mother's remains.

After this coruscating exchange it took only a couple of minutes to find the Hungerford mausoleum, a baroque affair half-covered in lichen at the far perimeter. Bronze plaques clustered on the east wall, weathered green. Albert and Edgar were there and the belated James and a handful before them – names I recognized from their portraits. Marguerite Hungerford shared her husband's plaque. The newest was Sarah Hungerford's, inscribed with the name of the son she'd lost a few months before she died. There was also one I hadn't expected: 'In Memoriam Joanna Naresby Hungerford'. There was no one by that name I could remember seeing among the Hungerford portraits.

A gust of wind blew across from the river, bringing a dull rain. I stamped my feet and puffed into my bare hands. I should have found some gloves by then. Despite my overcoat and scarf it was bitterly cold. Raindrops were trickling inside my collar and seemed to seep right through me. A dreary dusk was falling. I took the steps down the south side of the mausoleum and the turning at the bottom brought shelter from the wind. Here there was an iron grille. I seized hold of two bars and peered into the gloom and imagined decaying corpses: Amelia's ancestors. Immediately to the left I could make out a patch of tiny dark – maybe purple – deathstools growing in a mossy patch on the stone floor. A catafalque was visible supporting a bronze casket. No I didn't scare easily, but now I felt I was being watched. The cracks that had begun to show in my life after *that time* had turned to chinks since the divorce. I didn't want them to open any further. Someone might notice. When I tried to take my hands from the bars my fingers were locked there. I couldn't let go. I'd been edgy to start with. Now I was panicky. *Get a grip, Daniel.* The voice seemed to work wonders. Only it was much darker suddenly. How long had I been down there? My hands came free and I stuffed them into my pockets and hurried up the steps with only one thought in mind – to get out of that place and return as quickly as possible to the haven of Hungerford House.

There was no sign of surprise from Amelia when I told her about my visit to the cemetery. I was about to query who Joanna Hungerford was when, to my astonishment, she answered my unasked question. It wasn't the first time she'd double-guessed what was going through my mind. Now I was convinced she could read inside my head like she said she could. I sometimes thought I had the gift, but she really had it. Joanna Hungerford had been Lawrence's younger sister – she was meant to have drowned somewhere in Europe in her twenties – before Amelia was born. They'd never found her body. She was just one of the women in the family that they never talked about. She'd been banished to boarding schools in Europe and Lawrence had expunged her from the family history. I asked about photographs. No not a single one. And had the other women been expunged? To which she said there'd been quite a few over the years. It had always been that way. The Hungerfords, she added with a hint of bitterness, had always been devoted to the idea of producing sons, preferably only one per generation. In Hungerford history daughters had frequently been banished like Joanna, written off from the day they were born. There had been family feuds. She wouldn't elaborate when I pressed her. In fact she clammed up completely and started getting angry until I changed the subject. I'd bottled out of pushing her – again – but she'd only have sidestepped, the way she always did when questions got too personal, especially questions about her family.

'By the way, what's a mofinch?' I asked casually.

'Did Cissy say that?'

I came back at her with: 'How d'you know she said it?'

'Because it's Georgian slang. It means the motherfucker-in-charge.' There was a hint of mirth and we were friends again. 'Who was she talking about?'

'Who else but your old man?'

Silence.

'Don't you think maybe you and he are . . .' I hesitated . . . 'a little too close?'

'Oh we're close all right. Would you expect it to be any other way when he's been unmarried so long and I'm his daughter?'

'You know how I mean . . . unhealthily close.' *So much bloody shilly-shally.*

She flushed. 'If that's a dirty innuendo, the answer is it's none of your goddamn business.' Pause. 'But the answer's "no" anyway. It's not like that. We're just very close, that's all, and I'll thank you not to talk about it.'

I gave her my best shrug and suggested a game of backgammon, to which she agreed, brightening, mercifully. Now wasn't the time either to ask about her relationship with Cissy. I knew what she'd say without even asking: that Cissy and she, like Lawrence and she, were completely above board. Whether it was true or not was another matter. With Amelia there were times when I felt as if I could just about trust her, and others when it was like I was with a stranger. As if her life divided into neat compartments and I could only look into one of them. At times like that I knew my angel Janey was around and I kept my thoughts to myself. Serendipity would take care of me. Amelia might be good at having her cake and gorging on it, but if either of us was really lucky in love, it was me. I was the born survivor.

Amelia was a one-off all right: independent and hyperactive, a real origami type . . . all over the place, as if she was several people at once.

The sound of her voice trilling *arpeggios* in the shower roused

105

me before dawn the following day and my diva dragged me
downstairs and played the piano while I slumbered on the carpet
with a cushion under my head. I fell asleep halfway through the
first movement of a Beethoven sonata she was attacking with
bravura.

When I woke up she was still playing. Between the shadows
of the room she was an ethereal portrait hung in the air. Then I
blinked and she seemed more substantial. She left the piano and
came to sit beside me where I lay marooned on the carpet.

From my half-world I listened to her telling me about the
correspondences between all things. There was, she was saying,
a symmetry, a synchronicity. When I opened my eyes she was
looking down at me, holding a pack of Tarot cards in her
left hand.

'Would you like a reading?' she was saying. 'This is a Frieda
Harris deck. It's rather special . . . an original. Lawrence gave
it to me for my eighteenth birthday. It used to be Edgar's.'

'My horoscope?'

'Kind of. This reading's for you.' She shut her eyes. Her right
hand was suspended over the cards while her lips moved silently.
Then while her mouth still flickered she shuffled the cards. 'These
are the twenty-two major arcana,' she explained. 'We'll do a
quickie three-card spread. I shouldn't really be doing this for
you. I know you too well. I can feel your anxiety trying to get
in the way.'

'Am I meant to do anything?'

She was still shuffling as she said: 'You've got to say what
questions you want the Tarot to answer. Think carefully.'

'I want to know if I'll find the vaccine.'

'I can tell you before I put the cards down that you'll find truth,
a truth. Whether it will be the vaccine I won't be able to say.'

'Will you and I stay together?' The question came without
thinking. She'd never said it, but I sometimes sensed she felt
trapped by our relationship – ours or any other – as if she could
be committed, even clinging, and yet running away from me at
the same time, like the two sides of her personality were complete
opposites, at war with each other. At times like that I felt like an
object, as if there was no real feeling in her. She was just going
through the motions.

From left to right she laid out the top three cards from the shuffled pack: face up. 'Art,' she said quietly, 'then the Empress and Death.'

I was on my stomach now, supporting myself on my elbows.

'It will be difficult for us to stay together,' she said, 'but not impossible. The answer will depend on you, not me. Art paired with Death could be very positive; the outcome is positive; there's transformation. But the Empress stands in the way.'

'Who's the Empress? Cissy? Your analyst?'

'No. We're dealing with archetypes, not people. I told you I shouldn't be doing this for you. Art is a clear warning that you mustn't rush into things. The Empress could be your own driving ambition.'

I stared hard at the profiled Empress holding a flower. There were twin crescent moons and a bird that could be a swan or a pelican. The female figure of Art beside her was more sinister: a woman in green with two faces and four breasts pouring liquid into a gold cauldron at the edges of which hovered a white lion and a red eagle. A Latin inscription formed a halo around the woman. The right-hand card, number XIII, was Death, a skeleton with a helmet on, wielding a scythe over a phantasmagoric background of humanoid forms and snake, fish and scorpion.

I asked if I was doing the right thing, going to California.

'Yes. Going or not going isn't going to change any risk that's already been laid down. Nor will that change you and me – our relationship. This isn't about our relationship.'

'What's it about then?'

'The Empress is ill-dignified in the middle position. You must overcome your greatest weakness – your inability to express your feelings. Without that you won't find the answer to the questions that matter in your life.'

'The questions I asked?'

'No. We're talking about the questions that are unconscious and unarticulated. This is your reading, but it's also someone else's and I can't see whose. It's as if there's a still higher force intervening.'

'Will I find out who my mother was?'

I saw the pain fly over her face. I asked again.

She was gathering up the cards and saying, 'I felt something terribly wrong. You should only read the Tarot for a stranger. There was something wrong but I couldn't see it.'

I sat up straight. 'Murdered,' I whispered.

'I felt danger everywhere.'

'For me?'

'I don't know.'

That was that. End of reading.

She talked about Shakespeare after that – familiarly, as if the Bard was a personal friend. Sprawled beside me on her stomach she asked me if I had any idea who Mary Herbert was.

I knew, I told her, she was the Countess of Pembroke and the sister of Philip Sidney the soldier poet. I'd read how she was the center of a talented circle of scientists and writers who visited her at Wilton – some even lived there – in the heyday of the Elizabethans. Her famous guests included her uncle, the Earl of Leicester. There was Dr John Dee the astrologer – did his wife call him DeeDee? I wondered rhetorically. Amelia called him 'the crystal gazer'. And Thomas Digges the Oxford mathematician and Sidney himself, before his death at Zutphen in 1586.

I'd been shut up in the library for the best part of three weeks. There wasn't a lot I couldn't tell her about Mary Herbert's acquaintances, or so I thought.

'Does it not strike you,' she said, 'that a lot of this woman's friends seemed to come from Wiltshire?' She rolled on to her back and folded her arms. I knew when she was sleuthing again for the Dark Lady. She got that burning look in her eyes . . . and her hooded left eyelid.

I said it wasn't surprising if that was where she lived. I leaned over to kiss the Bump gently.

'Wilton wasn't far from Brook House, one of the homes of the eighth Lord Mountjoy, Charles Blunt, in the mid-fifteen-nineties. It wasn't far from Wardour Castle, the home of the Arundels. Henry Wriothesley, the third Earl of Southampton who received the dedication of Shakespeare's *Venus and Adonis* and *Lucrece*, came from a family with Wiltshire origins.'

'Wriothesley's sister married an Arundel,' I said, hoping to impress her.

She turned back on to her stomach and propped herself on her elbows. 'Who else in the fifteen-nineties lived close to Wilton, Brook House and Wardour?'

'Henry Willoughby, who's supposed to have written about the Dark Lady in a poem he called his *Avisa*.' I smiled when I saw from her look that I'd got it right and I leaned forward to push back a strand of hair that had drifted from behind her ear. She thanked me with her eyes. This wasn't the first time I'd encountered Henry Willoughby. I knew he was supposed to have been a friend of Shakespeare's and maybe the missing link in the whole Dark Lady puzzle. The bizarre poem *Willobie his Avisa* appeared in 1594 – about a woman called Avisa, obviously a parody on a real-life married woman and her affairs with six real-life men. One of these, 'W.S.', was believed to be Shakespeare, raising the possibility that if the true Avisa could be identified, so would the Dark Lady. I knew this was Amelia's main line of inquiry in her search for Shakespeare's mysterious lover. I'd read loads about the Dark Lady. The problem was no one had convincingly identified her yet.

'Only Henry Willoughby,' Amelia said, 'wasn't quite the insignificant second son in a bastard line that he's been taken for. A bit of a black sheep maybe. He was Lord Mountjoy's third cousin and a distant relative of Southampton's in-laws the Arundels through the Nottinghamshire Willoughbys. His uncle John Willoughby was involved in a land transaction with Southampton's sister.' Her fingers moved along the edge of a cushion, stroking it firmly. 'Henry Willoughby's family were tenants of land belonging to the Herberts. He probably visited Wilton now and again and was on familiar terms with some of the Herberts' guests, one of whom was William Shakespeare. We know Shakespeare stayed there later in James's reign. Essex too,' she added, 'probably visited there. He was on good terms with most members of the group and married Mary Herbert's former sister-in-law Frances Walsingham.'

Her next piece of information pricked my interest.

'I've got one very interesting Elizabethan document, a letter or the draft of one, signed by a William Willoughby, who I think was Henry Willoughby's son.'

'Can I see it?'

'It's locked away in a vault for safety . . . and it doesn't identify the Dark Lady or give any clues to who she was.'

'What connected all the people you were talking about?' I looked over at the window. A thaw had set in. Drizzle was falling so fine it was little more than morning dew. A cold gray was faintly visible. Soon the first light of morning would be licking over the floor. I hated dawn.

'It was a person and his occult philosophy that connected them
. . . the visionary Dr Dee. He was fascinated by a priest he met in
Paris in fifteen-fifty: Guillaume Postel the Sorbonne's authority
on Oriental languages and philosophy. Postel was a scholar of
the Hermetic and Kabbalistic traditions. He was also learned
in the Tantric scriptures. In fact he was the first man to bring
together the theories of androgyny that are fundamental to the
Tantras and Hermetic cosmology.'

'I thought nobody in the West discovered the thinking of
the East until the last century.' Daylight was crowding into
the room.

'That's a common misconception. Just consider what it was that
Postel was saying to Dee. He believed in a dualist soul after the
Fall, a soul that was part male and part female – in the broadest
metaphysical sense of "male" and "female". The Messiah released
only the male principle. A female Messiah was needed to release
the female principle before mankind could be saved and reunited
in an androgynous godhead.'

'Kind of like Gnosticism?'

'Yes and no. In fifteen-forty-seven Postel became fascinated
by a woman he met in Venice. In his eyes she was a female
Messiah, a kind of Great Mother incarnate. This woman died
in fifteen-forty-nine but Postel didn't hear she was dead until
fifteen-fifty-one. Then he claimed her female soul had entered
him, making him androgynous. Later on he went a stage further
and proclaimed himself the new Messiah.'

'Sounds completely out of his box.'

'Who's to say?' Amelia sat up and crossed her legs in a half
lotus. She swayed as she spoke. 'To get what Postel was on about
you have to understand the trinity of the *Zohar*, made up of the
three *sephiroth* that alchemists know as the *animus mundi*, the *anima
mundi* and the *filius*.'

I pushed myself up and sat opposite her, though I didn't even
try a half lotus.

'Thus reborn Postel called himself Rorispergio the dew spreader.
That made him Rebis or she-Mercury the androgyne. But as the
Venetian woman reincarnate he embodied the spirit of the Black
Madonna whom we now equate with Mary Magdalene, Christ's
so-called wife. Now do you see where my Maggie comes from –
and maybe Black Jenny and Hermie too?'

110

I chewed over this last question. It was something I'd been wondering about for the past few days. 'I don't get the connection with Dee.' I had my hands joined palm to palm under my chin. Only her fifth god was still a complete mystery.

'That side's fairly obscure. It's taken me a lot of research just to get this much evidence. I don't know how many of Postel's ideas Dee introduced to the Herbert household when he came to iive there in fifteen-fifty-two. A lot of it must have come much later, after he visited the Continent with his trance medium Edward Kelley. The labels that get pinned on Dee today are words like astrologer and mathematician. In fact he was the closest thing in Elizabethan England to the Renaissance ideal of the universal man.'

'Like Philip Sidney?'

'Sidney didn't come close by comparison. It isn't surprising Dee attracted Sidney's interest as well as Mary Herbert's and the Earl of Leicester's. When I started hunting for the antecedents of the movement known as Rosicrucianism that burst into prominence in continental Europe in the early sixteen-hundreds I looked at what Dee had been doing in England and what the followers of Postel had been doing in France. The problem's the total secrecy that surrounded the movement before sixteen-hundred. There's little doubt a cult of the hermetic trinity existed in the Elizabethan period, practiced by a small educated and very aristocratic elite. Its adherents were *illuminati* or *perfecti*, those who measured up to the neoplatonist ideal of androgyny and perfectibility that's the outstanding feature of Henry Willoughby as Shakespeare depicted him in one section of the *Sonnets*.

'In number there must have been no more than a few dozen of these men in the whole of Europe. They may even have considered themselves Cosmic Masters, the group rumored to be the so-called Masters of the World. They earned themselves another name: like the Rosicrucians they were the "invisible" ones. Avisa is the bird-woman, the phoenix. But she's also the woman who is unseen, unidentified, invisible. I can't glean much more than that from the documentary record. The cult's rituals are unknown apart from maybe a resurrectionist and a dualist element. But they probably bore almost no resemblance to early masonic rites and had little to do with the mythical Christian Rosenkreutz who's meant to have founded the Rosicrucian fraternity. Who knows,

111

they might still be around now. Think of all the more esoteric orders in Freemasonry like the Rose Croix and the Knights Templars and the Red Cross of St Constantine. Or the Societas Rosicruciana and the so-called Prieuré de Sion and the Hell Fire Club. Even the Ordo Templi Orientis who are supposed to have had these symbolic sexual rites.'

'I never knew any Freemasons – not that I was aware of – apart from my ex-father-in-law and my lawyer,' I told her. 'Never even felt a secret masonic handshake. Your Elizabethans sound like a pretty exclusive bunch.' I lay down on my back again. 'I suppose Mary Herbert's club were all aristocrats apart from the odd meritocrat like Shakespeare . . . He was one of them wasn't he?'

'Maybe that's how he met his Dark Lady. Whoever she was I think she was part of the group . . . and from the popularity of the *Avisa* poem I would say she must have been an aristocrat.' She looked absent for a moment. 'Nancy goes out of her mind when I tell her things like that.'

'Are you still not going to tell me who's your surefire choice? Mary Fitton? Luce Morgan?'

'Not those whores.' She leaned over and with a wicked laugh shook her hair all over my face till I choked and blew it away in a mock attempt to breathe. She lay beside me.

'Okay don't say it.' *Don't trust me*, I was thinking. 'I'll probably work out who she was anyway before you dig up your proof.'

I glanced sidelong and she feigned a hurt look. 'Believe me, I'd tell you if I was sure. But I do think Mary Herbert was a linchpin in this cult apart from Dee in the early days. They got heavily involved in the Kabbalah and the occult arts. They were heterodox Christians really, something heretical that was beyond the understanding of the regular Protestant and Catholic churches.'

'How come you know even that much if it was so secret?'

'No one's looked that hard in England before. When people look for what came before Rosicrucianism and Freemasonry they always look at the German principalities, or the Templars and Cathars in France. Here was a small group in England that probably included the Dark Lady . . . Shakespeare only belonged for a short time.' Then she added mysteriously: 'Sometimes clues just pop up in my head and I write them down . . . a bit like automatic writing. You could say it's psychic. It seems to be linked to . . .' She stopped and hemmed with obvious agitation . . . 'with my gods. Katie says I'm using them to tap the great force of the collective unconscious and that every mental illness can have a positive side and lead to growth.'

'How did people get to join?' I fought off the urge to talk about her 'problem'.

'I think membership may have passed from father to son based on what we know about similar sects. Arthur Dee probably succeeded his father . . . Sir Dudley Digges too. So membership would lapse if someone didn't have a male heir or couldn't prove direct uninterrupted descent in the male line.'

'If members were male how did Mary Herbert fit in?'

'I think she was a solitary female figure at the center of it all . . . a kind of focus for the female sexuality that had to be entered metaphysically and transcended if the two parts of the soul were to be reunited. It's possible the cult involved a Black Madonna . . . a virgin-whore or Venus figure. Maybe Mary Herbert played her symbolically and her place was taken by the Dark Lady later on if the central woman was replaced every few years by a younger woman . . . something like that.'

'Are you serious that such a sect could still exist?'

'I'd be surprised if it didn't. We're not talking about a bunch of eager beavers like most of the Freemasons. Nor even about the early seventeenth-century Rosicrucians or the Templars of the thirteenth century, maybe. My sense of it is that we're talking about a small sect that goes right back in a direct line to one branch of the Gnostics of the early centuries after Christ. This is a group so secret that almost nothing is known about them. The closest they've ever come to surfacing is through my research. Every other group – Rosicrucians, Freemasons or whatever – was just a poor and none-too-secret reflection of the real thing.'

'Could they be in America?'

'They could be anywhere. The oldest Christian cross is the Tau. The rituals of the known esoteric orders involve the modern Christian cross: the four-armed cross. The clue to the Elizabethan sect being much more ancient is the Tau, the pagan and early Christian cross that was in Shakespeare's grave. Jesus Christ was crucified on a Tau cross.'

'What kind of secrets would a sect like that have?'

'Difficult to guess. Definitely Christian Kabbalistic. You've got to remember what keeps all esoteric orders going is the idea that they alone are the repositories of some ancient secret knowledge and this is often identified with a great treasure, like the Holy Grail or the philosopher's stone. One thing the treasure certainly isn't is a tangible one like gold or the earthly remains of Jesus Christ. But the idea that others might have the *real* treasure was why adepts often joined more than one sect. That way you got the interconnecting skein between so many groups.'

'What does the *mors osculi* mean?' I asked.

She raised herself from the floor. There was a puzzled look, a kind of frown. 'Where did you get that from?'

'Just something I read in your library.' I could see she was mystified.

'Not something written by me.'

'You're holding back. I can tell.'

She signaled a kind of agreement with a hunch of her shoulders. 'I guess so. It's not something I've dared to write about yet. Y'see, not much is known about Death from the Kiss ... the kiss of Shekinah. Or the Death of the Just as it's also called. It's one of the best-kept secrets of Kabbalistic ritual.'

'So I've read.'

'My theory,' she was saying, 'is that it's some kind of rite of beatification. Death in the body that's a rebirth of the soul. Death in the body may even be real, not just symbolic as in masonic and Eleusinian ritual ... almost a kind of martyrdom. There may be a strong sexual element ... on the quintessential level. The Kabbalists' Shekinah was God in his – her if you like – female persona.'

I suggested it might be a kind of human sacrifice.

'If it was, it's one that the victim consented to. The sexual element suggests a role for Venus, probably in her avatar of Libitina the Roman deity in whom love and death are brought together. Libitina in this incarnation would correspond with Shekinah.'

'Beats me how you find out such things. It can't just be tuning into the collective unconscious.' I could see she'd caught the mixture of mockery and disbelief in my tone. She chose to ignore it.

'It is and it isn't. It's also solid research and the collective

114

unconscious is really nothing more than a big dose of intuition. Not that anyone's going to believe me at first. There's nothing the Shakespeare world likes more than to savage someone with a new theory. But if *you* find someone living today who's descended from Shakespeare, at least people will sit up and pay more attention to what *I've* got to say, especially if I uncover the Dark Lady once and for all.'

I asked her why the Dark Lady meant so much to her, but as I knew I was locked into the puzzle too I realized at once there was no point in asking. Still I said: 'What difference does it make who she was? She's dead.'

'Everybody's crazy about Shakespeare, partly because so few hard facts are known about his personal life. Aside from you and me even the Japanese are crazy about him.'

'Y'know how you were saying you have this paranormal thing like a kind of sixth sense?' I didn't want to say that madness and the psychic were supposed to go hand in hand.

She looked from the ceiling to my face beside her.

'Is that kind of like angel magic . . . ESP, stuff like that?' I visualized Amelia the sibyl telling fortunes and reading Tarot cards at a fairground.

'It's more like what Dr Dee would have called a "wild talent". It's a gift I've had since I was a kid. It runs in the family. They used to call my great-great-grandfather "the ghost-seer".'

'Could he see ghosts?'

'Mmm, sometimes, right here in this house, or so they said.'

I sat upright with a jolt. 'What does it *feel* like having psychic powers? Sometimes I feel as if I might be psychic too. Especially since I met you.'

'It's hard to explain . . . it's like being everywhere at once, other places, even the future; like I just know something is going to happen and then it does.'

I was gazing down at her feeling odd. 'Not like angel magic?'

'Mmm, well maybe a little bit, only nowadays we call it parapsychology. Wouldn't you like to be able to make time go slower instead of faster as you grow older? Have you ever seen a primary color that isn't supposed to exist?'

I shook my head. She was losing me now.

'That's kind of how it *feels* like. It's not something rational. It's an ability that's latent in everyone. Like you said – you too maybe.'

Then she added darkly: 'When that magic ability's at its most advanced it gives power over the future and people's lives.'

'What kind of power?'

'Total control. It can be used for good or evil.'

'Now you're putting me on.'

She didn't laugh or smile. She didn't say anything for a while. When she spoke, her voice so flat, it was to suggest maybe I'd like to catch up on sleep while she went off to an early faculty meeting.

I went back to bed for a couple of hours. In the library that afternoon with Falstaff for company in front of the fire I tried without success to find a link between Mary Herbert Countess of Pembroke and an occult circle that would lead me to the Dark Lady's identity. When I left Hungerford House, that would be my chance gone to work out the identity of the Elizabethan woman who'd thrown a spell over me. Before Amelia came home I read through the Dark Lady sonnets again, but if a clue to her name was there I wasn't able to find it.

I'd never have believed a year earlier that it was possible to get addicted to Shakespeare. Now I could understand why Amelia was completely tied up with him.

One thing I couldn't forget: the poet's ghoulish stare, every lineament in that face. I poked the fire and went back to James's chair to start on one of the books I'd bought. It was called *Shakespeare's Women*. It was about the women in his plays, but it held no further clues to the Dark Lady's identity. When Amelia came home in the evening direct from Katie I asked her what had come up in her hour, but as usual when I asked about her 'problem' she retreated into silence. This time she was worse than usual, especially after she'd had a couple of drinks. It got my dander up, as usual, and as usual I bloused out of insisting on answers. Pressing Amelia when she was in one of her moods was as successful as pissing into the wind and left you feeling about as good.

In two days time we'd be heading for Manhattan.

I yawned, mesmerized by the windshield wipers. The moon disappeared from one moment to the next behind clouds that brought flurries of a wettish snow. Amelia punched the radio switch on the dash and squeezed my knee. 'You look bushed,' she said. 'Why don't you sleep?' Through my half slumber I noticed we'd come to a stoplight: Storrow Drive.

Her hand was on my knee again. I woke up, startled. Snow still fell. The wipers beat faster. I took in the slick pavement.

'Where are we?'

'The Mass Turnpike. We should make Highway 86 by . . .' She checked the clock . . . 'a quarter after three.'

As I floated between waking and sleep Amelia glanced in the mirror for the second time in a minute. A car parped its horn and went scudding past. A gust of wind buffeted the Porsche. I roused myself from where I slouched. The snow had stopped. The Mass Turnpike, almost empty, passed in a blur of slush.

The radio was down low. When the bulletin came, Amelia turned it up and I roused myself with half an ear to the news.

I'm John Fedorowicz, WEEI 590 News. Burt Auerbach is standing by with a news information update.

England's Shakespeare saga continues with a new twist. US Immigration have confirmed Dr Daniel Bosworth, the genetic scientist with the clue to Shakespeare's genes, entered the United States through Logan Airport three weeks ago. We'll bring you more information on that story as soon as we have details. I'm Burt Auerbach, WEEI 590 News.

Amelia turned the radio off. 'Marcus's controlled information leak. This is where things start to hot up.'

Jesus was my only reply. I speculated how she'd known to have the right channel on at the right time. More of her precognitive powers?

'He promised not to bring me into it,' she said. 'Someone's bound to connect us, though.'

She slid a CD into the stereo and I dozed off to the strains of Salieri's *Requiem* as we headed toward the exit for Hartford.

'Good morning, Miss Hungerford.' The brown-liveried figure held open the door.

In the lobby the Olympic Tower's Head Concierge inclined his head in my direction and handed an unmarked key to Amelia. As we emerged from the elevator forty-eight floors later the operator helped us with our bags and wished us a pleasant stay in New York.

The unnumbered door had a tiny spyhole. Twice the key turned full circle. I found myself in a sitting room with floor-to-ceiling glass on two sides looking up Fifth Avenue toward the oasis of Central Park. Most of the wall on the right was filled with a light *impasto* Ascension by Mantegna hung in a gilt frame in deliberate contrast to the contemporary style of the room. With a cry I flopped into an armchair and stretched my legs. 'Does Lawrence stay here much?' My voice surely had a ragged edge and my nerves jangled from lack of sleep. It was barely dawn.

'Hardly ever. He'd rather be out at Oyster Bay. If he's stuck late he crashes out here. How about a drink?'

'No thanks.' While she poured herself a vodka tonic I stood with my nose pressed against the glass that formed the north wall staring at the specks that were early people and cars on Fifth Avenue. It was going to be an unclouded day. I stifled a yawn.

She was at my side with a glass in her hand. 'Suppose we go to bed?' She slipped her free hand into mine.

'You always make everything sound so simple.'

'At the top where the world's inhabited by power-hungry maniacs everything's simplified – people, places, events.'

I moved behind her and put my arms round her waist, resting my chin on her shoulder. We looked through the glass at the morning skyline till she swung round, careful not to spill her drink and looped her arms round my neck. 'You're my very own mad scientist and I'm in love with you, baby.'

Taking her glass, I set it down on a shelf and within a minute had taken off her clothes. Without removing my own I made love to her slowly, splaying her buttocks against the warm glass with New York spread out below.

Amelia wore a black suit and I was dressed down in crumpled jacket and trousers under an old gaberdine Burberry that had outlived fashion more than twice around. I felt scruffy beside her as we walked through the front entrance to where Lawrence's Bentley was waiting.

'Good morning, Jasper.' The chauffeur stood holding the door open, umbrella in one hand. The car pulled away and turned up Madison Avenue. At 61st Street we swung left and on Fifth Avenue halted outside the Pierre. The chauffeur followed us, keeping a discreet distance.

Inside the Café Pierre a sycophantic *maître d'* in wing collar and black tie greeted us as if we were reigning monarchs. He took my coat, passed it to a flunkey and minced ahead of us across the black marble floor with its inlaid *bronze doré*. I glanced round at the *trompe-l'oeil* murals and caught sight of myself looking raffish in an etched mirror. We were ushered to the table in the far corner. I was feeling far from comfortable when Lawrence rose to kiss Amelia. Shaking hands with Marcus was like the first round in an arm-wrestling contest. I sat down on the gray *banquette* with my back to the wall beneath a bouquet of electric candles.

'Hervé.' Lawrence rapped the table with his knuckles. The wine waiter was beside him in five seconds. 'Hervé, another bottle, please.'

It was Marcus who broke the tension. 'Glad you could make the orientation meeting.' Dapper in two-button blazer and turtleneck sweater, Marcus looked younger this time. 'I see you're not wearing sunglasses.'

'Not much sun.'

'I guess by tonight everyone'll know you're with the Rostrum.'

The neighboring tables were still largely empty. It wasn't yet noon. I looked at Marcus. 'Did you bring the dossier?'

Marcus produced a zipper folder and took out a thick volume. 'The whole gameplan's here right down to your lab and the list of equipment. I'll run it by you on the plane tonight and we can hash over any problems. By then the AIDS Campaign will have been relaunched with the Shakespeare Search.'

Lawrence chimed in: 'After what Marcus has planned every man and his dog's going to want to talk with you.' The wine waiter returned with a bottle, which he opened and placed in the bucket beside Lawrence's chair. I turned my attention to the menu. Lawrence ordered Beluga caviar with sour cream and *blinis* followed by veal and sat back with an air of benevolence. Jasper stood by the door keeping an eye on everyone who entered. I glanced across the table, knowing when it was Marcus's turn to bat.

Marcus outlined tactics. 'From here on media coverage is all-important.'

'You don't expect me to appear on TV, do you?'

'No way . . .' – there was an awkward lull – 'though the media have already gotten wind of the Search. We can't keep the lid on much longer. So far no one knows you're involved. The less scuttlebutt the better . . . all the more reason why we have to

119

move fast. Naturally a lot of people want to know where you are right now. By tonight you'll be connected officially.'

'What time's it due to be launched?'

'Four o'clock. It should be over soon after five. Then you and I will be off to the Coast before it breaks on the tube.'

I considered this last statement as I looked from Marcus to my *feuilleté* of scallops and mussels and found my appetite. Below table level Amelia stretched out a hand and squeezed my knee.

Lawrence asked me what I thought should happen if they found a Shakespeare descendant, a green lamplighter as I'd called it the other day.

'Hey, green lamplighter's a great name,' Marcus broke in. 'I'd like to use that for publicity. It's got just the right touch.' He was referring to the tell-tale green lamp that Cunliffe-Jones had mounted for me on a DNA computyper. These were computer-linked machines that molecular geneticists were using now to speed up the testing of genetic material for the presence of a selected gene. Ours would only light up if the right combination of DNA molecules was identified: Shakespeare's version of the weeping gene.

I refused to be deflected. 'To answer your question,' I said, turning to Lawrence, 'I think if we find someone it's up to him what happens. He may not want to be in the limelight.'

Marcus smiled at 'limelight', swallowed a mouthful of sautéed shrimp and cut in quickly. 'If some guy's the one we're all hunting for he's sure as hell going to want people to know about it.'

'It's still up to him.' I could play hardball too. Marcus moved uncomfortably. I guessed there was another side to him: the kind of man who shot from the hip and aimed for the balls. Lawrence pulled a cigar from his silver case. I'd noticed that while we were talking the other tables had filled except the one nearest our own. 'What's the security like in Mendocino?'

'No problem.' Marcus took a sip of Aqua Libra.

I envisioned myself going from one gulag to another for the rest of my life. Marcus picked up my look of concern and tried to change the subject. 'The strategy's rock-ribbed all the way. On top of the endorsements you know about we can count on the moral support of Dr Arthur Maynard of the AIDS Diagnostic Laboratory at the Centers for Disease Control in Atlanta.' He looked to Lawrence for confirmation.

120

I caught an exchange of smiles between Amelia and Marcus a minute later. It reminded me of the smiles she sometimes gave her father, leaving me feeling as if I was on the outside looking in: the down-and-out with his nose pressed to the window of an upmarket restaurant.

Amelia glanced in my direction as Marcus went on: 'I've fixed to appear on a number of prime-time shows, starting with *Today* . . .'

By the time the meal was finished and coffee had come, Lawrence's eyes had clouded over with some bibulous vision. I noticed he was well into the third bottle of champagne. I turned my attention to Amelia and gave her a look that elicited a furtive wink. 'I'm going to miss you,' she said, picking up the orchid that lay in the middle of the table. 'In fifteen weeks I'll be free to fly out and join you.'

I emptied my cup in one gulp and signaled the waiter for more.

Marcus cleared his throat and took an exaggerated look at his watch. 'Daniel, I'm going to reverse field on what I said about keeping you off TV. I met yesterday with Barbara Walters. I didn't think it would hurt to bring you out of the closet just this once. Donahue got pipped to the post.'

'Who's Barbara Walters?'

'Okay, let's take it from the top. Barbara's the fairy godmother of TV chat. She wants you to do the main segment on her show tonight.' He went over the plan. Barbara Walters had been sworn to secrecy of course. Marcus reckoned that I couldn't make myself too hard to get, but this was the big one – 20/20 on ABC. The ratings were always top of the line. If I agreed, it would be recorded that afternoon and broadcast on Channel 7 at ten o'clock. I'd be interviewed while Marcus was taking care of the press conference at Lincoln Center. A little razzmatazz would whet viewers' curiosity.

'You'll have a dozen reporters in Mendocino by tomorrow,' I said sharply.

Marcus ignored the comment. 'If you're agreeable Barbara will interview you at a secret rendezvous. She won't let us have editorial control or see the questions in advance. Some of them will be tough ones but she won't go for the jugular if you play fair with her. You'll appear backlit so all that viewers will see is your head in shadow, which is a pity because you're very mediagenic. Barbara would agree with me on that but she sure as hell appreciates the reasons why you don't want to become a household face.'

'If that means becoming public property, no thanks.'

'Now you've gotten this far you've got little choice.'

———— • ————

Lawrence put down the snifter of Courvoisier and Grand Marnier he had warmed in one palm and poured Amelia a generous Martini with a squeeze of lemon. Earlier she had stood on the tarmac at Teterboro as Daniel kissed her goodbye and climbed with Marcus into the Rostrum's Learjet bound for Napa Airport.

As she turned to face him, lowering her eyes demurely, Lawrence could not help thinking how much she resembled her mother. He recalled the party his father gave to celebrate his engagement to Sarah Carlton. It had been the social event of the season, like the wedding itself five years later from her family house on the Cape. Amelia was the same height as her mother, had the same hair and eyes.

He recollected the first night of his honeymoon in Rome. On the third night he'd discovered Sarah was alcoholic. The painful years for both had begun, exacerbated later by the discovery of his low sperm count and the possibility he might never father another child.

The dry-out farm had become Sarah's home-away-from-home. *If they dried her out once they dried her out a hundred times* . . . The Manhattans last thing at night to wash down the Nembutal and the tall Scotch when she rose at eleven the next day: eleven or she didn't get out of bed at all . . . The bottles so artfully cached away.

Eight barren years were to elapse before Amelia's birth: years of Sarah's drunken binges and Lawrence's growing desperation. Ultimately Amelia's birth had seemed a miracle. Lawrence himself saw Amelia as the twisted answer to his quest for a legitimate son and heir. It had taken a further twelve years to get Sarah pregnant again.

He settled back into his armchair. Amelia came and seated herself opposite on the edge of the sofa. She nibbled at her fingernails.

Lawrence cared not one whit for the Olympic Tower, but its flawless security, combined with the way it swayed up to eighteen inches at the top and groaned in high winds, were features that gave it a certain charm. In the last couple of years whenever he had been at the Long Island mansion and a storm had been forecast he had headed into Manhattan just to experience the pleasure of a night tormented by the cries of steel and glass and sometimes a prostitute.

Amelia came over and settled herself into the armchair beside her father's. He patted her hand seignorally and kept hold of it. 'Honey, it's getting harder for me to look on you as my little girl while you spread your wings and make your own reputation in academic circles.' He thought of her as she was at twelve – a little Lolita full-bodied like a vintage claret. 'Sometimes I feel I've not been the best of fathers. When I think of you with . . .' His words tailed off. He lurched to his feet, spilling cigar ash on the carpet. 'Honey,' he whispered hoarsely, 'when I look at you I think of your mother the way she was when I first knew her.'

'I know, it's okay, really. I understand.' She stood and slid one arm round his shoulder. 'I was thinking,' she said hesitantly, 'Daniel's the first Englishman I've ever really liked.'

'Probably not the first you've climbed into bed with.'

There was silence. Lawrence was well-known for his outspokenness. It had not prevented John F. Kennedy from offering to make him ambassador to Italy at the age of thirty-one. But Lawrence had always known he could be a more effective political animal outside the straitjacket of an official position. He had distanced himself noticeably from Kennedy in the months before the assassination.

In Lawrence's bedroom which Amelia and Daniel had slept in the pages of the Sunday papers still littered the floor, tangled with a sable coverlet, black satin cammie knickers and an empty carton of rum raisin ice cream. Amelia picked up her brush and swept back her hair in front of the mirror. There was an electrostatic crackle. Then she hastily tidied up and aimed the clicker at the TV as Lawrence settled down on the bed to watch 20/20. A minute later a *soignée* Barbara Walters appeared in blue business suit and red blouse.

Lawrence rarely watched television except when he was on it himself. Amelia checked to see he was comfortable with enough pillows plumped up behind him before cuddling up to watch.

Hi! I'm Barbara Walters . . .

8

Then soul, live thou upon thy servant's loss,
And let that pine to aggravate thy store;
Buy terms divine in selling hours of dross;
Within be fed, without be rich no more.

Sonnets, 146
William Shakespeare

The beribboned tuft of pubic hair was taped to one corner. I gave the photograph a furtive kiss and tucked the edge under the frame of the mirror. It showed Amelia sitting on a dry stone wall, laughing into the camera.

My A-frame, though somewhat spartan, was bigger than most. I tried out the double bed that they'd put in place of the futon and found to my surprise that it was long enough. The comforter was ethnic – Peruvian or something – with rough fabric in multiple colors.

One of the Sparkies, the ashram's PR girls, had given me a lightning tour and left me a map. The unit next door – all shingle and tarpaper – had been converted into a lab. It was marked down as Lao-Tzu House and stood well apart from the main complex, linked to it by a four-wheeler trail called Jesus Way. The Sparkie, who'd said her name was Suresha, had pointed out that all the buildings were temples named by Babaji after saints and philosophers. The whole ashram was what she called a Buddhafield, a sacred place alive with the guru's energy.

I looked at the map as I changed into jeans. At the top it said 'Dayanandpuram Mendocino Ashram of the Dayananda Center for World Peace'. My watch showed five of midnight. There had been little to see as the helicopter from Napa landed in front of what turned out to be Govinda House, the central auditorium.

There had been a special meeting to welcome me to Dayanand-puram, as I discovered when I stepped out of the helicopter to be garlanded with flowers by a girl in a magenta jumpsuit, followed by a hearty embrace from Baba himself flashing a toothy smile. Marcus received the same welcome and held his arm up to the hooting crowd of *sannyasins* before hugging Baba. I saw sweat stains under Marcus's arms.

A woman stepped forward robed in orange and introduced herself as Ma Anand Savita. I'd learn later that she was head of the coordinators – nicknamed the Witches – the small circle of women who ran the ashram for Baba and as mediums channeled his energy to the rest of its inhabitants. Savita was a handsome woman in her thirties with the *tikka* on her forehead, one of the few East Indians in Dayanandpuram. It would take me less than forty-eight hours to find out she carried a Smith & Wesson .38 revolver in her flowing garments. By and large she was the brains behind Baba's throne and according to some the person most likely to head a palace revolt.

I unpacked my things. The lights dimmed and brightened again and I guessed the place generated its own electricity. Taking in my dour reflection in the bathroom mirror I asked myself what the hell I was doing in California. Bruce Hazard's crowd from St Stephen's Hospital in London, I'd overheard on the plane's radio, were now at the second stage of testing a prototype AIDS vaccine based on an artificial protein.

I was still dazed from the flight, the reception in the hospitality suite in Govinda House, the speeches of welcome as I sat cross-legged on a podium facing Baba's golden throne, my back to the assembled *sannyasins*.

I could still picture Baba, his eyes hypnotic, body scarcely moving, apart from the hands, their delicate fingers fluttering in the air to illustrate a point. A trace of something fragrant floated in the atmosphere. Was it the hands or the voice or the mesmeric eyes that made Baba a demagogue of an orator? A resonant voice introduced me to the followers: 'My beloved friends . . . someone to cherish in your midst . . . a learned man from England.'

I turned to study the welter of upturned faces. Beside me on the bare floor of the podium sat Marcus in Ungaro jeans, crocodile loafers and a monogramed shirt of salami red he'd changed into during the flight.

I recalled Baba's rhetoric word for word: 'Here, my friends, you are not shut off from reality. The outer and inner worlds are both real. One cannot function without the other.'

I thought of the plastic wristband the Sparkie had given me to wear as an ID. I'd stuffed it under my socks in the second drawer.

'The world outside our gates is not other. It is part of us. For certain people our Peace Force makes entry difficult. But to those who seek the Truth our gates stand open all the time.'

An appreciative murmur rose from the *sannyasins*.

'You are free to follow the god that lives within each one of you. Deep within we are all gods, all Buddhas.'

I noticed for the first time that Baba had lifts built into the Jesus sandals peeping from under his robe.

'Our guest is an authority on sexually transmitted diseases,' the haunting voice went on. 'Here we take no chances. Make love freely, my beloved friends, with someone you truly care for' – he paused with mischief written in his face – 'carefully.'

There was a tide of laughter.

'Our other guest is no stranger to many of you who have done the Rostrum Training.' He grinned at the all-American guru. 'Marcus Freeman and the World Health Rostrum are responsible for the Shakespeare Search and the laboratory we have set up for Dr Bosworth.'

I wondered if the lab was as well equipped as Marcus had promised. *Anything you need that money can buy.* I'd felt too tired to go over the dossier on the plane. I slid my suitcase off the side of the bed and stretched out on my back. Marcus had been a different kind of speaker from Baba, but the effect had been just as electric.

He sprang to his feet and plucked a microphone from its holder, adjusting the impedance like an old pro. The scene that followed brought to mind prehistoric footage of Dean Martin crooning to a dinner audience at Caesar's Palace.

'My friends, Baba and I go back a long way. We want each of you to be responsible for Dr Bosworth's freedom and privacy while he's here. I empower you to share that responsibility. Do you accept?'

'Yes,' the *sannyasins* roared back in chorus. Baba let out a guffaw and clapped his hands.

I squirmed.

'Right,' Marcus continued, 'you've all spent your lives being who you are not. Wake up.'

A murmur of assent filled the auditorium.

'I have some messages to share with you. They're tough ones and you'll hear me if your inner self chooses to hear. Wake up. There's someone going unconscious over in the corner.' He pointed toward the back.

I looked round but everyone else had their eyes glued on Marcus. He had a smoldering look. So this was the famous charismatic cultspeak.

'Stop being in control. Get rid of the chatter-chatter of your mind. Mind is ego. Witness your emotions. You are not your emotions. And you are not your mind.'

I noticed how Baba's eyes followed every movement Marcus made as he paced up and down.

'There's a special place, a context waiting for all of you. Zen monks call it *mushin*, the place that is no-mind. *Mushin* is a context for transformation. If you choose to make a difference in the world, isn't it time you stopped holding onto your ego and went out of your mind?'

Marcus paused to listen to the hum of approval.

I figured the audience understood more of what Marcus was on about than I did. But the voice was spellbinding. Phoney or not, Marcus had stage presence.

'Create your own future ... get clear ... participate in the work ... are you satisfied with your life as it's currently running you?'

'I'm satisfied,' a voice called out from the floor, followed by roars of laughter as tension snapped.

'Politics is a lie. Religion is a lie. The daily news on TV and in the papers is a lie. All truth is a lie ... except *your* truth, the truth that changes all the time, every moment, every second. Your experience is always *becoming*. It never *is*. There *is* no universal truth. The only truth is *satori* that lies beyond *samsara* in a place where you are the universe. Where you *are* your experience. That is truth, the great *Dharma* of god within you.' He echoed the words of Baba who nodded sagaciously.

I was beginning to get a pain in my backside and cramps in my thighs from sitting cross-legged. I shuffled to get comfortable.

Marcus stood in silent thought, the mike held in both hands a few inches from his mouth. 'Somnambulism is a terminal disease. Each year it gets to more Americans than cancer and heart disease and AIDS –' he paused to nod in my general direction – 'put together. Isn't it time you woke up for the first time in your life? If you do, go easy. Look in the good mirror first. You know, the one that highlights your suntan and hides the wrinkles. Otherwise the shock could kill you.'

The audience sat in awe.

'Did you ever run a mile . . . or a risk. In the end it's the same thing. Running a risk is an authentic act. It's declaring a commitment to your own life. And mine. In the summer are you scared to swim in the sea around Mendocino because of the great white sharks? So swim in the lake. Play it safe. No risk. No life. You want to die? You go swim in the lake.'

Silence reigned.

'Take a risk tomorrow. Open up and give all of you away.'

With the mike between both hands at knee level he bowed and made a *namaste* to the audience and then to Baba, amidst a deluge of applause.

Baba beamed from Marcus to me and I pushed myself shakily to my feet. Marcus passed me the mike. I stood looking blank, wondering how an Englishman could produce any kind of act to follow the showmanship of a home-grown American salesman.

'*Sannyasins*, good evening . . .'

Afterwards Baba motioned to me to sit directly at his feet. Then he pressed his thumb into the middle of my forehead just above eyebrow level while he chanted a litany of Hindi phrases. At the end he intoned, '*Bodhisattva Swami Ramamurti*. Dr Bosworth is now a *swami* like the rest of you.' I looked uncomfortably at the guru's knees. Baba was putting a sandalwood *mala* round my neck.

I turned helplessly and faced Marcus.

'Welcome to the club,' Marcus mouthed back. 'You just took *sannyas*.'

I was almost asleep. I rolled from the bed and pulled my clothes off in a daze. I unclasped the *mala* and it joined the plastic bracelet in the second drawer. My watch showed it was long past midnight.

———— • ————

'*Jai Baba*'.

Shree Baba Dayananda inclined his head in response to the girl's greeting. His facial skin had the texture of stippled wallpaper, cratered with direct hits from a smallpox attack in his teens. Gopi held her hands in *namaste*. On his head the guru wore a cap, one of thousands knitted for him in orange wool by *sannyasins* around the world. Orange flowers lay scattered at his feet.

The devotee intoned the recital she had prepared for her special energy-sharing *darshan* with the guru in the small hours of the night: 'I praise the *Kundalini* who creates innumerable worlds continuously, for she is like a filament of the lotus.'

'May the *Shakti* be with you.' The holy man grinned between his beard and mustache and let out a belly laugh that echoed round the marble walls and floors of Gautama House.

The devotee said nothing but from her kneeling position in front of him she looked timidly up, her eyes moving while her head and body remained motionless. She was blissed out at the sound of his voice.

'Did you feel the energy of the Serpent inside you in the *Tantra* group?' he asked.

She nodded. Her eyes moved to catch sight of the peacock fan resting against the steps. 'Just being around you, the Serpent in me comes to life. Now I feel like I'm connected to you.'

The guru moved his head fractionally. His eyes were grave.

'My whole body feels like it's vibrating. It's like I'm a violin string and you are the bow.'

The guru laughed and said in his rich voice, 'I have many strings to my bow.'

He spoke with slurping vowels and sibilant final s's, but his accent was mild. Shree Baba Dayananda was an educated man who had once taught philosophy at Bombay University. In those days when he lived in a modest house in Bombay's Bandra district his name had been Madan Ramji Shastri. Marcus had been in India selling soil nutrients for United Oxide and met Baba at a faculty party. At that time the Rostrum Training Centers had been no more than a glint in Marcus's eye, and the Dayananda Center for World Peace barely a vision of a secure bank account for the University's authority on Nietzsche and Schopenhauer.

'Strings to my bow,' Baba repeated. 'Now we are talking of the way of the *Tao te Ching*. The *Tao* and *Kundalini* are one and the same. The opening of the lotus is at the end of either path. Truth is being and becoming as the journey and the arrival are all the same. In the lotus of our divine meditation everything is one. There is no separateness. Give up attachment.'

Baba laughed again. This time the young *sannyasin* relaxed and raised her head to look up at the man: fifty maybe, it was hard to tell, but a youthful fifty with his dyed hair and beard, sitting on an orange cushion in the middle of the dais. The canopy over his head was festooned with hand-sewn images of Hindu gods. In the center looking down was Ganesha the elephant god. The devotee met the twinkle in Baba's eyes. It was her turn to smile as she caught a particular look.

'It is written in the *Goraksha Samhita*,' Baba said, his smile turning to a frown, 'that the guru is your mirror, but when you look in it, you will not see the self that you see in the bathroom mirror every day.'

At the mention of bathroom mirror Gopi's mind flashed to the six-pack of Trojans that lay on the shelf behind every bathroom mirror in the place. She blanked out the thought and caught herself double-thinking: *mindfucking*.

'The guru,' Baba continued, 'is the catalyst who allows you to witness your thoughts.' He was groping under his tunic. 'As the serpent awakens the mirror grows brighter. The *Kundalini* rises, coil upon coil awakening to ascend like a fire. On her journey, like a she-cobra, she will dart her fangs through each *chakra*, opening the doors of your etheric body till the seventh will burst into a thousand petals and you will witness the bliss of the lotus pouring forth as a clear liquid light. As *Shakti* springs from the lotus and collides with *Shiva* rushing to meet her your mirror will shatter. The opposites within you will join in the harmony of *ardhanarishvara*. The divine *rasa* will be yours.

'Come, it is time for *maithuna*, the left-hand path of the *Tantras*. You will experience the fullness of *Paramashiva* as Parvati is united with the godhead in me.'

Gopi rose demurely and moved toward the guru. She wore the saffron robe of the renunciate. As she reached the last step she untied the garment at each shoulder and let it fall to the ground. Underneath between her breasts hung her *mala* of one hundred and eight wooden beads. A plastic bubble in the locket on the end contained the guru's photograph. Laminated inside the back of the bubble was a lock of his hair – a *prasad* or special gift from the master to convey his energy to her at all times. A green bead was attached to the locket. Otherwise she was naked. Her blond hair reached to her waist.

130

She lowered her eyes and cast a reverent look toward the guru's spigot of a phallus. He had pulled off his own tunic that a minute earlier had covered his lotus-crossed legs. Underneath he wore only a white bulletproof undershirt done up with eight buttons: seven black and one red, the third one down. This garment he now removed, releasing a ventricose abdomen swollen from years of yogic breathing exercises. He made a come-to-me gesture, indicating she should lower herself into the hirsute cradle of his legs with its becondomed centerpiece.

His eyes were commanding. For a second Gopi saw all the devils in hell dance in those eyes, then he laughed and the twinkle was back. She stepped forward to straddle his legs. She lowered herself, and taking the twitching *linga*, for all the world like some figure from a Khajuraho mural, worked the nub into her Eden, now running with the honey of her adoration. A groan came from the lips of the master as she sank down on him, driving his shaft inside her soft wet *yoni*. Her legs wrapped themselves round his waist and her ankles crossed in the small of his back.

Her arms circled his neck the way he had taught her. She remembered how he had put it, word for word, the previous night: even the part about *vajrolimudra*, the withholding of semen by the man as he absorbed the female secretions.

She rocked back and forth, her rump nested in the center of the lotus, her cheek couched in the gray hairs of his chest. The guru's eyes were closed, his body motionless, his hands resting beside him on his knees, index and thumb circled in 'O'. The tips of her breasts rubbed up and down against the rotunda of his belly.

After several minutes tears streamed down Gopi's cheeks and her body shuddered as the bliss of the valley swept over her. The guru opened his eyes for a second and took a deep breath.

'*Kala*,' he said, referring to the subtle energy Gopi generated at the moment of her orgasm, and he intoned a *mantra*: '*Hum Hamsa*.'

———— ● ————

The Lotus Lab had everything I'd ordered: the best on the market. Dr Walter Nieberg of the Institute of Molecular Biology in New Jersey, a Yalie I'd met once before, had been retained for a substantial fee to equip the lab. IBM had been persuaded by Marcus to contribute the top of their new range of biological computers. The machine was waiting to be activated in Lao-Tzu

House alongside a pair of DNA computypers built by DuPont under licence from Caltech. I was impressed with the way Lawrence and Marcus were able to influence people.

Roderick Tillman, the dynamo of a man from my Oxford lab who'd joined in the secretive process of cloning Shakespeare's genes, had agreed to take sabbatical leave and was due at the ashram in a few days time on a healthy stipend from the Rostrum. Tillman was a retrovirologist with an international reputation at the sharp end of the game: genetically engineered viruses. He and I would concentrate our energies on a vaccine for AIDS, working alongside John Fryer, a researcher in monoclonal antibody technology from the University of California School of Medicine, San Diego. Fryer was only twenty-eight, but this young immunogeneticist would turn out to be heaven-sent. Unlike Tillman, Fryer had been forced to break his contract with his department in order to join the team. In the process he risked being sued. It was a lot for Fryer to gamble in the hope of finding a vaccine and I felt flattered.

Another heavyweight was coming with Tillman: the man I'd called a fruitcake: Alistair Cunliffe-Jones of Caltech, formerly of Manchester University Institute of Science and Technology. His work in biotechnology had been crucial to Hitachi's second generation of high-speed gene sequenators. From genetic linkage mapping he'd gone into more advanced development work in automated DNA scanning and typing. He'd be in charge of the daily search for the green lamplighter, manning the lab's two computypers with the help of half a dozen lab technicians, all molecular biology graduates from the University of California, San Francisco. They'd be working round the clock in shifts in the hunt for a descendant in Shakespeare's bloodline. Cunliffe-Jones would also be responsible for liaison with Rostrum HQ in Santa Monica and their number-one hematologist, Arnie Schiff.

Gene-typing devices had made startling progress in the previous couple of years. Now they were a far cry from the laborious manual procedures Geoff Alton and I toiled with for days on end in the mid-Eighties: fumbling RFLP techniques to get DNA sliced and into the old agarose gel that was the only way in the early years. These days, linked to a biocomputer, the state-of-the-art machines could scan thousands of pieces of DNA in microseconds and detect a single gene in under three minutes. Personally I was still more comfortable with the manual method, but thanks to Cunliffe-Jones's expert instruction in Oxford in January I was beginning to learn how to handle computyping equipment. For one thing it was more than a thousand times faster. Though DNA computypers weren't essential to my vaccine work, I was painfully aware that without them there wouldn't have been any Shakespeare Search or samples for me to work on in the confines of the ashram.

My first day in Dayanandpuram was a busy one. It began with a call from Amelia. My feelings ran high as I answered the phone.

'Daniel, baby, I can't wait till after Commencement.' When she'd calmed down I told her about my welcome to the ashram and she laughed when I got to the part about taking *sannyas*. Then she was reminding me that Barbara Walters had called me the next Messiah and a zealot of the new genetics, out to preserve the world from Armageddon. Flattering stuff, only she'd asked viewers to consider which I was: crank or crusader? Then more flattery. She'd said I was almost as big a celebrity as Shakespeare. But Amelia went on to say Marcus's campaign launch looked like a total success. When I asked if reporters had been prowling round Hungerford House, or if anyone had connected her with me, she said she'd questioned Maria and so far no one seemed to have made the link, but she didn't hold out much hope. She asked what I thought of Baba and I dropped my voice and told her I called him 'the fucking old fox'. Amelia snuffled softly down the line, then with a 'Luvya, baby' the phone went dead.

Twenty minutes later I pushed open the lab door. Everywhere, half unpacked, lay test tubes, high-tech equipment, bottles, a lightbox, packs of latex gloves, petri dishes – a morass of color. In one corner between an electronic microscope and a pathogenic microbe cabinet the two computypers squatted with their shiny green globes on top. The stately shape of the IBM computer stood inside the door with a couple of monitors perched on the bench beside it, next to a laser microscope, a gift from Biorad.

Someone who didn't know a lot about genetics had done the unpacking: not the early crew put in by Nieberg, who'd come and gone a week earlier. *Christ what a bordello.* But it looked as if everything was there. Nieberg's crowd had even constructed a room with hermetically sealed doors.

Before leaving the lab I picked a handful of plastic straw off the vinyl floor and stuffed it in the wastebasket. Marcus was nowhere around. The Rostrum's mercurial head, I learned later, had flown out at dawn, bound for his Santa Monica headquarters.

The sea was less than two hundred yards away. I could smell the tang of ozone carried on a light wind. The grass was ankle-deep, wet with dewfall. It was just after eight. I sat on the step outside the lab door soaking up the sun in the balmy air and examined my crumpled map. All round there were signs of industry: dirt roads and irrigation ditches being built, crops being planted and A-frame units going up. Wild flowers swaying in the breeze carpeted the grass as far as a wall of fir trees. On the edge of the ocean a lighthouse perched beside a white structure with a russet roof. Not far off solar panels lined up in neat ranks in front of three windmills, whirling furiously. I got to my feet and set off for the central complex in the distance.

Sannyasins smiled as I passed and one with a pock-marked face called out, 'Ramamurti'. From my right came a cry of 'Hey dude', followed by easy laughter. An erogenous blonde hovered there with a radiant look.

'Hi! I'm Gopi. Baba said you need someone to help, y'know, generally. I had spare time on my agenda so I got the job.' I could see she was bursting with vitality.

'Hi. Where do I find food round here?'

'I'll take you. Breakfast's in Siddhartha House.'

She was almost skipping beside me. Her *mala* bounced over a diaphanous T-shirt in bright lavender. Her baggy meditation pants failed to hide a man-friendly figure and I guessed at nutcracker thighs. In the wind her hair flew back revealing a clear complexion and bright-blue eyes. I put her at nineteen or twenty.

'My real name's Polly Ann. What's yours, besides Ramamurti and Dr Bosworth?'

I told her.

'Hi, Daniel,' she said with a grin, brazenly appraising me, adding: 'Your accent really cracks me up.'

Her leather sandals made my sneakers look out of place on the dusty trail. She said, 'It's great being around Babaji. You pick up on his energy. Did you know he's a self-realized being?'

'What's that?'

'It's a perfect master, someone who's totally enlightened. That means you're kind of high the whole time. Baba generates all this positive energy in the space around him and it gets focused in the *mala*. It kind of collects there.'

'Sounds too scientific for me. What d'you do all day?'

'I've just done *japa*.'

'Does it do a lot for you?' I refrained from asking what *japa* was.

'It helps me get centered, y'know.'

'Is that what people come here for?'

'Oh, some come to do the therapies and stuff. It brings money in for construction and farming. That part's called the Dayananda Institute of Kinetic Therapy. Then there's workshops and intensives and dynamic meditations and group therapies and stuff. Of course work's really meditation too, and service to Baba is meditation.'

'What's group therapy?' There were a lot of *sannyasins* around, many in couples – man and woman. In the light of day they looked older now; more in their thirties than twenties. My own age. There was a lot of hugging and kissing going on and a lot of lingering eye contact. We passed one group sitting in a circle on the grass and stopped to watch them. They were taking it in turns to hold a green crystal the size of a cricket ball and as it came to each they talked about themselves in loud voices and sentences that always began with 'I'.

Polly Ann explained that group therapy was a kind of collective letting-go. 'It's really bizarre,' she said as we strolled on, 'but it's kind of fun, y'know.'

'What kind of fun?'

She laughed and halted. 'Y'see these bruises?' She lifted her T-shirt and gave me a flash of nipples on the tips of her resplendent breasts. She was pointing unself-consciously at a blue-black bruise over her sternum. 'That's what I got in the last one, I kid you not. It got kind of violent: y'know what I mean?'

'I would've thought therapy was something peaceful,' I said, trying vainly to focus on her midriff.

She laughed again and pulled her T-shirt down. 'Not round here it isn't. I got attacked by this dweeb Niren – he even tried to bite me. Everyone was hyperventilating and kind of shaking.

135

Then – he's a real basket case – he hit on this friend of mine called Suddha and he kind of raped her.'

'In front of everyone?'

'Sure. It got real wild. The girls were cheering him on and I'm like: somebody stop this guy.'

'Did Suddha not mind?'

'Sure, at first she did. She fought like crazy, like I mean it was a really shitty thing to do; like Niren almost got one eye scratched out, y'know, but in the end she was laughing and crying at the same time and that shitface Niren looked pretty weirded out.'

I wasn't sure whether to believe what I was hearing.

Our path led into a gaggle of unpainted buildings, one of which was a refectory with rows of tables and benches. At the counter I followed Polly Ann's example and took a tray. I helped myself to yoghurt from the ashram's dairy and a plateful of home-made granola with lashings of apple purée. From the array of drinks I picked a glass of whole milk. We took seats at the empty end of an otherwise crowded table. A few faces looked in our direction and turned to smiles.

I liked Polly Ann. Maybe she was disarmingly unsophisticated after Amelia but her physical charms were undeniable. She had the lascivious air of a groupie who knew when she was into a sure thing. 'Why are you here in the first place?' I asked her.

'I dropped out of Berkeley when I got trashed on drugs. I just couldn't quit, like suddenly I was on this total kick.' She made an expansive gesture with both arms. 'I was such a fuckup. If I'd have done more freebase or one more line I don't think I'd be here to talk to. This guy from the Oakland ashram found me. They made me do a month of detox in rehab – stuff like that – then they took me in.'

I told her about Shakespeare's nose, how there hadn't been much left of it, and she said maybe he'd been doing too much coke ha ha.

I was looking appreciatively at the robust figure of this former addict. She floated round the place, I'd soon discover, unruffled by the political undercurrents that threatened to tear the harmony apart. I could just picture her snorting her way round Berkeley in her search for an existential peace, until a bunch of *sannyasins* came along and saved her from chasing her dragon down a cul-de-sac. I got my first glimpse of the darker side of Dayanandpuram when I asked why everyone seemed to be talking in whispers. She lowered her voice as she explained about the wiretaps and the bugged telephones. Every call was monitored for negativity by a group of women loyal to the Witches. Ma Anand Savita she described as a *dakini*.

'What's negativity?' I asked as I polished off my yoghurt and remembered how I'd called Baba a 'fucking old fox' on the phone to Amelia.

'Negative thinking, any shit that blocks positive energy. Like getting pregnant.' She looked anxious for a second. 'People don't get pregnant round here. If they do they get classified negative and they have to up and go, the same as people who get ill. It kind of keeps down the numbers in the health center.'

'Is that a proper hospital?'

'Not really. There's a doctor runs it – Arup's his name, a real geeky type – with Veena, his main squeeze. She's the nurse. Mostly they do sterilizations now.'

I got up. 'Are you coming back with me? There's a lot of work you can do if you're serious about helping me.'

She followed, still talking about negativity. 'Gays are negative. A couple died of AIDS last year so now there aren't any.'

'I suppose dying's negative too?'

'That's not funny. We cremated them over by the lake and had a party. A few guys and a couple of girls got freaked and left after that.'

'What's all the kerfuffle?' I asked her, pointing to a crowd that had gathered.

Outside Siddhartha House a large group of *sannyasins* were clapping and waving. Polly Ann grabbed me by the hand. 'Quick. Baba walks down Zoroaster Way from Gautama House every day round this time.'

I craned my neck to see over the heads in front. From all directions *sannyasins* came running, across the fields and out of buildings. The top of the guru's flowing hair appeared as Polly Ann towed me, with a wriggle, to the front. *Sannyasins* on either side of the road were scattering rose petals in the guru's path and making a reverent *namaste* as he passed. There were laughs and cries of 'Jai Baba'.

I noticed the four men walking behind the robed figure, their eyes scrutinizing the crowd. One of them stood almost seven feet tall, a bearded Titan. It wasn't his orange uniform – these were four of the thirty 'Saints' who constituted the Peace Force – that held my eye; it was the walktie-talkie radio and the Colt Commando submachine gun that he carried at waist level.

'Isn't he awesome?' Polly Ann gasped in adulation.

I thought she was referring to the giant bodyguard. 'Why all the hardware on him? Is there a war on?'

'Not Rishi . . . Baba. Isn't he beautiful?' She disregarded my question.

Baba had reached the center of the complex. As he proceeded the crowd opened to let him pass. Hands shot out to him but no one touched him until a girl in an orange gown ran forward and kneeling at his feet kissed the toes of his left foot where they protruded from his sandal. Two guards rushed forward looking to catch the guru's eyes for directions but he waved them back. The girl looked up, tears of happiness running down her face. Baba cast a simian grimace at the crowd and placed a hand on her head for a few seconds. Then he stepped round her and went on his way in the direction of the Gurdjieff Center which housed the boutique and bookshop.

Polly Ann squeezed my hand. 'Everyone works eighty hours a week round here. Are you coming?' I was still gazing after the receding figure in the middle of the throng.

'Boy oh boy, that's charisma,' she was saying. 'Baba and Marcus Freeman are totally amazing, aren't they?'

I grunted something inaudible.

The crowd thinned as we walked back across a meadow that sloped toward the sea. We passed a vegetable garden. 'That's Hill's Ranch over that way.' She was pointing. To the east were clumps of eucalyptus interspersed with Douglas firs and pine trees. From the mist below the cusp of the hills rose redwoods sutured to a jagged sky. 'There's Russian Gulch State Park,' she said, turning, 'and Point Cabrillo's in the opposite direction.' She whirled round and laughed. The wind had veered. Now the smell of resin was in the air.

Embarrassed by her directness I bent to pluck a few leaves from a plant and pressed them to her nose. 'Thyme,' she said. 'Some of the Witches wanted to have a herbarium.' She took me by the hand. 'We've got TV in all the rooms, but all we get to watch is video movies of Baba talking. Like it's totally energizing if you want to max out your time with him, but sometimes, y'know, I could scream for a good movie.' Then she added, 'What makes it worse is everyone knows Baba lies on his bed all day watching old movies on his VCR. Sometimes,' she said in a confidential whisper, 'he gets Gadhi – the dentist – to give him a blast of laughing gas, then he spends hours blissed out in the Samadhi tank. Only like no one's meant to know. Don't tell a living soul I told you this.' She put a finger to her lips.

I added that one to my growing reservoir of Baba-lore. I'd had Dunkley look into him before I left England and found out his organization had made a fortune out of shares in rubber companies, years ago, when he'd seen the AIDS epidemic coming before the market analysts did. He'd cornered a goodly slice of the condoms market, which was just as well, I thought, considering how many gross his ashrams probably went through in a day.

'I don't follow this blissed-out business,' I said.

'It's kind of like being wired without drugs. It's the way you get just being round Baba, he has such incredible power.'

'Power for good or evil?'

'Just power. A master like Baba has *prapti*. He's empowered to do anything he wants. It's kind of magic. Like nothing's impossible.'

Was it Lawrence or Amelia who'd said that about Marcus? *Nothing's impossible.*

A few minutes later there came the roar of an engine violating tranquility. From behind a clump of fir trees a Mitsubishi turboprop shot into the air at an angle so steep I thought it would stall. 'It's okay. It's one of ours. Baba's flying lesson,' Polly Ann pointed out. 'They took away his driving license so he decided to fly instead.'

While we were at the Olympic Tower I'd called Peter Dunkley again, this time to order the despatch, under tight security, of my database and the vital cultures I'd grown *in vitro* and cloned in Oxford. The news on the Scotland Yard front had still been bad and the file on my mother's death had remained open.

On the Wednesday a courier from London brought me an aluminium container. Polly Ann watched as I unlocked it and removed a layer of polystyrene and another of latex foam rubber. Underneath, entombed in dry ice, lay a mass of cotton which my

139

gloved hands lifted out in fist-sized bundles, each of which on being opened revealed a glass dish.

Casually I passed one to Polly Ann. It bore simply the initials 'WS' handwritten on a label. 'Shakespeare's DNA,' I replied nonchalantly as she raised an eyebrow. She held the dish gingerly in both hands and stared through the glass at the viscous fluid. 'Goop,' she said, and made a face.

'It's okay, there's more where that came from. That's just genes cloned from the original.'

She pretended to let the glass drop for a second and snickered at me good-naturedly. Near the bottom of the container were more protective layers. Underneath lay a plastic box that held four hard disks. And finally a dossier in a brown folder: the full findings of my genetic investigation into my mother's remains. I ignored Polly Ann's air of curiosity and hurried to bury it away in the security cabinet with the Bard's DNA. My mother's file went everywhere that I went. Her remains, after the exhumation, were cremated and properly buried in the village churchyard near the Bosworth home.

After lunch the next day we walked the grassy clifftop. Below, a glaucous sea was capped in specks of white by the westerly breeze. The township of Mendocino lay two miles off to the south.

After a few hundred yards Polly Ann gave me a winning look but ignored my hand and was off in the direction of the far perimeter wall, half jogging, half skipping. I ran and caught up with her peering over the lip of the gray cliff which braced itself against the rise and fall of the ocean. When we reached the limit of the property we were confronted by a high stone wall with three strands of wire running above it. My line of vision followed the wall to my left up into the trees. On my right it ended at the cliff edge where a barbed-wire barricade had been rigged down the face to the sea.

'It's to keep outsiders out,' she said simply. 'I heard on the grapevine the Feds were trying to get in yesterday. Probably working with the INS to get Baba busted. Either that or we're still being investigated by the Cult Awareness Network. I get real pissed just thinking about it.'

The wind was cooler now and stronger. 'They're supposed to have doubled the perimeter guards since I arrived. I can't see any of them.'

140

'They patrol outside. They've got these huge Rottweilers.'

'Maybe that'll keep the press off my back.' The police – English or American – didn't bear thinking about. I ran at the wall and jumped to reach the top edge, but my fingers lost their hold and I slithered down.

'For shit's sake don't touch those wires,' she shouted at me. 'They'll electrocute you.'

I could feel myself turn pale. 'Is everybody really so paranoid?'

'A lot of them out there hate us,' she admitted. 'We try to love everybody but sometimes we hate them back. Now we have to get passes from the Witches to go outside.'

I mumbled something about friendly natives and forged a pained look. 'D'you think I could just walk out of here?'

'I wouldn't try. Are you coming to *satsang*?' She set off in the direction of Chuang-Tzu House.

I hurried to keep up. The more I learnt about the ashram, the more bizarre it became, particularly Baba. 'If Baba's perfect why does he need lifts in his sandals?'

'Maybe he's just more comfortable, y'know.'

'Maybe it helps levitation,' I said facetiously.

'Don't be a smartass.' She turned to face me. 'I like you a lot. Just don't spoil it. It really gets me when people come out with shit like that.'

In the days that followed the nine other team members arrived and set about the final stage of organizing the lab. However dippy she might appear, Polly Ann was quick to learn and worked hard, ensuring the smooth running of the office, freeing me from most of the day-to-day administration. She was a good 'zoo keeper' as Alistair Cunliffe-Jones liked to call her. Her tasks included looking after two dozen special mice – squeamishly at first – that were kept in cages at the end of the corridor. Later they would become so-called 'San Diego mice', acquiring a partially functioning human immune system so they could be used for short inoculation trials.

Polly Ann also cared for three rhesus monkeys and Deveraj, the adolescent male chimpanzee flown from Zaire. She and Deveraj had taken to each other from the day the cuddly ape arrived. She'd made a pair of orange Bermudas for him and told everyone with a straight face that he'd taken *sannyas*. The two were inseparable

141

and she looked ahead with horror to the day when Deveraj would be given his first vaccine shot.

Thanks to Marcus's PR team in Santa Monica the Mendocino lab was in the public eye. The Rostrum handled press calls demanding interviews and photo opportunities, and handed out media releases while it shielded my team from the disturbance of visitors from the outside world. When an ABC Television producer called the Rostrum to get me to appear on *Good Morning America*, live this time, Marcus accepted in my place.

Polly Ann was my eyes and ears round the ashram. Calls from Marcus himself were few and far between but Rostrum HQ in Santa Monica was professionally staffed, and Polly Ann and Cunliffe-Jones maintained daily contact with Arnie Schiff.

Within ten days of my arrival the first batch of specimens had been flown in by helicopter, coded by numbers and neatly packed in chilled containers that carried the Search's logo, the head of Shakespeare with a question mark on the Bard's lofty forehead. These samples all came from males who'd signed for the weeping gene test as well as an HIV screening. The Rostrum's mobile units had already carried out the Cambridge BioScience test for HIV.

Around one-third of all the specimens we got came marked HIV-positive. Cunliffe-Jones and five of the lab technicians carried out the testing that might lead to a green lamplighter. All specimens, whether HIV-positive or -negative, were batch-processed through the DNA computypers. Meanwhile with the help of one lab technician Tillman, Fryer and I concentrated our energies on just the seropositives after Cunliffe-Jones's team had finished with them.

The two activities going on in the lab were kept apart and I had little to do with the day-to-day operations of the weeping gene crew. Though I could only nurture faith at the outset, within a month the number of HIV strains under examination would number forty-two, giving a wider spectrum than I or any scientist had had before. For a geneticist trying to obtain a complete picture of a virus's antigenic drift they were manna from heaven.

However, early hopes of a green lamplighter had not been fulfilled.

Giving only a few hours warning, Lawrence arrived by helicopter the second weekend after my own arrival, ostensibly to inspect the lab. After closeting himself with Baba in Gautama House he joined me in the lab for a look around. It was already late afternoon and the two of us had the place to ourselves.

I was feeling more ambivalent than ever about the old bastard. Nor was I any closer to gauging what Lawrence really thought of me. Maybe his dislike of me and his possessiveness about Amelia were all in my imagination.

I wondered aloud whether he would like to try out the test for the weeping gene and his nostrils flared with suspicion as he declined. He suggested instead that I might like to try him on the test for AIDS. As he spoke he caught my eye. The feeling was uncomfortable. I looked away and buried my embarrassment. Hadn't Amelia said something about Lawrence and prostitutes: *an antisocial habit.* Having sat him down I gazed steadfastly at his venous blood as I drew one cubic centimeter from his left forearm. I wiped the sweat from my face, washed my hands for the second time and put on a pair of gloves. It took three minutes to prepare a solution.

'One thing, Daniel. Whatever result you get from this test, you tell no one about it. Is that clear? I obviously don't want publicity . . . either way.'

I nodded and left Lawrence waiting in the office as I disappeared into the room next door. The Cambridge BioScience test wasn't something I usually did in the lab. That was up to the mobile clinics of the AIDS Campaign. But everything needed was there. The diagnosis was almost one hundred percent reliable . . . almost. You never could be absolutely sure.

'Negative,' I said, taking the seat at my desk five minutes later. 'You don't carry HIV.'

'What did you expect?' Lawrence was already rising. There was no clue to his feelings. He looked at me long and hard and muttered something that didn't sound like 'thank you'. Before I could ask after Amelia he turned and marched outside to rejoin his helicopter. Wheeling round at the aircraft steps he gazed across at me, thirty yards away, and raised his left hand to his chin. Even at that distance I could see his signet ring on his little finger, trapping the last glint from the sun on the seaboard horizon.

I stood at the lab door as the lights rose and disappeared, hearing the rotor's hammer and feeling the wind on my cheeks when the aircraft was no longer there. Then, in case the old sod wanted it double-checked later on, I placed Lawrence's serum sample in a hermetically sealed dish. It went into the deep-cool locker of the security cabinet and I spun the combination lock. Knackered after a long day and the stress of the last twenty minutes I tore off my gloves, closed the lab down for the night and headed for bed.

The Search went ahead orchestrated nationwide by a hyper-active Marcus. Hundreds of thousands lined up at the mobile clinics of the AIDS Campaign to be screened for HIV. The numbers had quadrupled thanks to all the publicity. One in eighteen male screenees was checking the box for the weeping gene test. Marcus's gamble had paid off financially. The Rostrum was raising new millions by public appeal.

I realized now that apart from Tillman the nearest thing I had to a real friend inside those cloistered walls was Polly Ann. Out of a mixture of curiosity, prudence and welling bravado I checked her and confirmed she was negative for HIV. She primped her nose when I gave her the news and told me not to use that word 'negative' again in case someone was eavesdropping and got the wrong idea.

'What about you?' she joshed. 'Have you got any diseases?' She framed her question in that tone we used when we asked a new bedmate if they were on the pill: serious, but joky to cover our embarrassment.

'I've got plenty,' I called back. 'They're all in little glass dishes. I was checked years ago. God's truth. I haven't been good since then but I've always been careful.' That, I knew, was a lie. Take Amelia for instance.

I'd cleared Polly Ann with Cunliffe-Jones and with everything set up he was instructing her, alongside our eager technicians, how to batch-process Shakespeare hopefuls through the computypers. Meanwhile I'd taught her how to run the easy-to-use Cambridge BioScience test. I was surprised when she insisted on taking a sample of *my* blood for practice. 'Not positive for HIV,' she called out to me from the path lab shortly afterwards. 'Like to try the gene machine?'

The gene machine was C-J's name for the computyper. 'Do I look like Shakespeare to you?' I called back. 'I am more lovely and more temperate.'

'But thy eternal summer shall not fade,' she replied, astonishing me. I'd have expected little learning and less literature. She was certainly not the airhead I'd first taken her for. She walked into the room where I was standing removing my gloves. 'How do I know what Shakespeare looks like?' As she spoke I caught that feral glint in her irises that never failed to stir my domesticated English blood. 'You're the one who knows what he looks like,' she said, 'so do you resemble him? What does he look like?'

I thought back to the sight of that monstrous corpse and tried not to shudder. 'He doesn't look very happy,' was all I said.

'Neither do you,' came her reply. 'So you do look like him.' She made for the door, wiggling her arse at me. The tempo of her buttocks, first one then the other, was irresistible. I followed her to the gene machine room where C-J usually operated. No one else was there. Polly Ann whipped round and with a command of 'no looking!' ordered me out. The cheeky smile that went with it brought me to my senses. After a moment's reflection I gave her a sheepish smile. As I retreated to my own lab I heard her shut the door behind me.

It was not long before she joined me. 'Take a look.' She'd filled in one of the reports we used for gene machine candidates. The Shakespeare logo looked up at me from the top and the Bard gave me a slow wink. So it seemed. I glanced at the report on my own genes. *Negative*. Not related.

'Disappointed?' Polly Ann asked, taking the paper from me.

I looked her in the eye. 'Nope. If I'm going to be famous one day, it'll be for something I've achieved, not something I inherited.'

'Did you ever run the test on yourself?'

For the first time it struck me how jumpy she was. Really on edge. 'Nope,' I said. 'No point really.'

She seemed to accept that and was already flinging her own gloves in the trash can. Without a further word we went out to the patio, side by side, each still wearing a white lab coat. She unbuttoned hers as we entered the midday glare, revealing a 'sunset' shirt and jeans.

'Let's talk over there.' I indicated two deckchairs where I took anyone I wanted to talk to in confidence. Cunliffe-Jones had discovered half a dozen transmitter-receiver bugs built into the walls of Lao-Tzu House. These, along with the wiretap on our telephones, had been removed. Nothing was said to Baba when he paid us a visit the day after and I wondered at the time if he knew about the bugging. Polly Ann had intimated that Savita and her Witches had made a number of decisions recently, mostly to do with security and public relations, that were thought not to have received the guru's imprimatur.

I leaned back and put my hands behind my head, closing my eyes to the sharp sun. 'It's like a little totalitarian state here, run by the thought police.'

At that she grew defensive. 'People come here freely. They want to be deprogramed from all the garbage and stuff that's been running their lives.'

'I'll go crazy if I have to eat any more alfalfa sprouts and sisal ryebread. Call that freedom? I may see the funny side but no one else in there does.' I missed the booze but the whole ashram was strictly an alcohol-free zone. It wouldn't do any harm to cut back for a bit. I could live without it, though right then I'd have paid a bomb for a swift Heineken. In the meantime Polly Ann kept me plied with orange juice. I nodded in the direction of the lab. 'Real freedom's about caring for others, not brainwashing people.'

'Are you free?'

I considered my answer carefully. 'I was before I came to America. Some scientists mooch around in their ivory towers, hobnobbing with each other and getting worked up over their reputations. Scientific hubris can make you lose sight of the real meaning of scientific freedom. The problem is to see the illusions behind the things that go fucking up our lives.'

'Is your life fucked up?'

'In a way. I've been through a pretty bad patch since my marriage fell apart.'

'Baba says we don't just choose the good things that happen to us. Like without knowing it we also choose the bad things. Without both kinds of choice there wouldn't be any freedom.'

It struck me again how she was not just a pretty arse. She seemed to be summing me up from where she sat sideways on her chair with her legs drawn up, one hand fiddling with her buttons. 'I feel isolated here,' I said. 'Out of touch with real people.'

'There's no need for you to be that way.' She twirled a strand of blond hair round one finger. 'What was your wife like?'

She looked quickly away as I turned toward her. I tilted my face to the sky. 'Lucy, oh, you know, we marry someone we think we understand, but it's all a mirage. When we wake up and see who we really married, everything falls apart. Lucy was like that. It took three years to wake up.'

'Have you got a girlfriend?'

I answered with a nod that said 'yes', adding 'sort of'.

'What's she like?'

I took a deep breath. 'The trouble is you remind me of her.'

She smiled wanly. 'I think she's a very lucky lady.' The next moment she jumped to her feet.

I watched her heading for the clifftop path. What was it about her? I was reaching out for something, something that I'd thought at first I'd found in Amelia: an end to isolation in a fractured world. But if I followed temptation, wasn't there a risk everything would collapse? How solid was my relationship with Amelia anyway? Sometimes from the way she acted oh so independent and uncommitted it hardly seemed to be there. I was aware there was no way of knowing for sure.

I'd already run the Cambridge BioScience test on a handful of long-faced *sannyasins* who came to Lao-Tzu House anxious to check whether they might be infected. Each of them had received the all-clear.

Some of those who'd checked into the AIDS Campaign mobile unit that called on Mendocino hadn't been so lucky. Polly Ann gave me a full report. Looking more like a silver recreational vehicle than a medical lab, the trailer had stationed itself in Mendosa's parking lot on the corner of Lansing and Little Lake. Two of the Witches had put in extra time stamping passes as demand for screenings grew inside the ashram. According to Polly Ann, by mid-afternoon an orange line writhed halfway round the block. The Mendocino locals steered clear of Mendosa's store, aware they were outnumbered. It was the first time the *sannyasins* had invaded the place *en masse*, apart from the festival the year before when thousands came from Baba's overseas communities to attend a week of dancing and singing. Many shops closed their doors throughout the visit of the mobile unit.

The next day Polly Ann brought me more news. She was saying four *sannyasins* were infected with the virus. One was her friend Simant. 'She's in a real pissy mood. Like she won't let anyone come near her. I left her to cool out for a while.'

'If you like I can talk to her. The others too,' I suggested.

'Too late. The Witches've already declared them negative. They'll be gone by tonight.'

'Where to?'

'Wherever. It's their problem. Only Simant's got nowhere to go, like she could develop full-blown AIDS. Then what happens to her?'

'She's only asymptomatic. Hopefully she won't develop anything.'

'But what if everyone infected develops AIDS?'

I turned to face her. 'Since that's a strong possibility, that's why we've got to find a working antiviral . . . fast.'

Polly Ann wasn't pacified. 'When I tried to talk to her she said: "Go away." She just lay there howling her head off.'

'Doesn't Baba have a responsibility?'

'That doesn't count for shit. He says they should've been more careful. It's everyone's responsibility to take care of themselves.'

The following morning I learnt that Simant had left before sunset, taking a bus down the coast. In her pocket in Polly Ann's writing she carried the address of a house in Berkeley where she'd be sure of a mattress.

John Fryer was a graduate of Marcus's Rostrum Training and took *sannyas* two weeks after he arrived. In the lab he was called John, but the *sannyasins* knew him as Videh. He wore a *mala* with a blue quarantine bead. He was a lanky man with the air of an amiable wolf: almost good-looking. It hadn't taken him long to find a girlfriend, a curvy brunette with almond eyes and a carnivorous smile. She was called Ma Prem Deva and had been with Baba once upon a time in India, at the Ramapuri ashram in Goa. The blue bead on John Fryer's *mala* advertised he was involved in a regular sexual relationship. The team put up with his ways good-humoredly. The two male lab assistants Gary and Damian had quickly found themselves *sannyasin* girlfriends without the need to take *sannyas*. But the four girl technicians Donna, Frankie, Eileen and Sharon all remained religiously single, untempted by the never-ending offers from the ashram's inmates.

Most of my scientific team were not overjoyed to be stuck in the purgatory of an ashram, but so far they were getting on with the job in hand. From time to time there were complaints about the absence of meat in Siddhartha House. The food we ate was generally wholesome and tasty, but patience in that department was showing signs of wearing thin after a month of the same dishes over and over.

To make matters worse each of the team had been body-searched on arrival. I was the only one who'd been spared. That had left the Witches on the wrong foot from the beginning. The situation grew worse when they realized they would need a pass each time they wanted to exit the ashram. I was refused one on the couple of occasions I tried. All of the team drew the line, in spite of pressure from the Sparkies, at wearing their ID bracelets. All except John Fryer.

Mostly, though, morale was high. Cunliffe-Jones kept us in fits of laughter, the laureate of the lavatorial joke. Not that relations with the *sannyasins* were bad either ... or even with Baba, who never listened to anything anyone said, but guffawed at everything when he visited Lao-Tzu House. The problem was always Ma Anand Savita and her all-female cohort.

As I watched John Fryer talking to Carol Hill the senior lab technician I wondered if his orange jeans would soon turn into meditation pants. A poster stared out of the wall behind them: an AIDS Campaign advertisement encouraging young unmarrieds to use condoms. It showed a pouting teenage girl.

It was no secret that Fryer's affair had reached a torrid stage. He worked long hours like everyone else and still managed to wage lust with the passionate Deva at all hours of the night. I reckoned he was looking a bit pasty-faced. Deva shared an A-frame with another girl just beyond Krishnamurti Grove. Every night at ten Fryer headed over there. I wondered how much longer he could go on taking the pace.

As I dismissed the thought that he might burn out – I'd seen it happen a couple of times in Oxford – Cunliffe-Jones walked in from next door with a smile plastered all over his oafish face. If you hadn't known, you'd never have believed the guy was a genius. 'Anyone for a spot of rape and pillage?' He beamed round the lab and we all knew he was off to his second – and probably not last – group therapy. As well as court jester he was also our resident sex maniac, quietly letting me off that hook.

It was Polly Ann who showed me the editorial in the *San*

Francisco Chronicle: Dr David Tarzief from the Université Pierre et Marie Curie had inoculated himself about five years ago with an AIDS vaccine modified from another existing vaccine. His antiviral, which had seemed to work at first, had failed following a second booster inoculation. As an HIV carrier with lowered immunity he'd succumbed to a rare lymphoma and was in the final stages of physical and mental disintegration. I reckoned he'd been completely off the wall to begin with. The writer pointed out the enormous difficulties that still blocked the path to a successful vaccine. Already at least a dozen had reached the testing stage. For me and the team there was no need to be reminded of our competition or the technical problems we faced.

I went over to show the article to a disheveled Roderick Tillman who was sitting at a Formica benchtop squinting at the screen of our scanning tunneling microscope, Hitachi's latest, with one million times magnification of DNA. I took a look at what had just elicited a grunt of disbelief from my old colleague, a short man with a full beard. It was the familiar sight of a cluster of CD-4 receptors under threat from a platoon of HIV surface proteins.

'I don't get it.' Tillman held up his hands and shrugged his shoulders in mock helplessness. 'The suppressor T-cell ratio is already below one, but the antibody picture just doesn't add up.'

'I don't get it either.' I was tapping my pencil on the workbench. Straightening up and addressing no one in particular I muttered, 'It's got to be the core or nothing. A surface peptide's too risky.' John Fryer caught my eye from across the lab and I could see what was going round inside that superbrain of his. He knew that after a vaccine it was a green lamplighter that I wanted more than anything else in the world and he'd probably guessed that Amelia had something to do with it. Four days ago our relationship had surfaced mysteriously in the *National Enquirer*, embellished with disinformation that plumbed new heights of suggestiveness. As if I didn't have enough on my plate without the sleaze factor to hobble me as well. Though I didn't know it yet, the story would disappear from the press just as mysteriously the following week. Fryer's personal priority right then was a vaccine. A green lamplighter would not save lives.

*   *   *

150

My standing in the world of AIDS research wasn't wasted on Polly Ann. I could see plain as day that in her eyes I was almost as much a guru as Baba. She and I were alone one night, as frequently we were, with Deveraj in the lab. It was Guru Poornima, the guru's full moon, and the rest of the team had gone to join a marshmallow roast round a campfire by the lake. Baba had promised to be there.

While I couldn't fault the Rostrum's avowed objectives I realized Baba and Marcus were charlatans both. Where did that leave Lawrence? One sodding thing after another. I couldn't find concrete evidence but I reckoned someone unauthorized had been poking round in the lab where they shouldn't have been. Maybe Baba had spies checking up on me. Worse, it could have been spies in the ashram reporting to the competition. I abandoned Polly Ann and Deveraj in the den, glued to a rerun of *I Love Lucy* on our precious TV, and slipped out to get a breath of fresh air.

The lab was in darkness when I returned just after eleven. I went in and was about to switch the main light on when I heard a noise. Groping my way to the nearest of the two computypers, I flicked the on/off switch, felt for the button marked 'Light Test' and pressed it. Seconds later the balloon on top of the machine glowed eerily green. There was a faint swishing noise behind my back. I whirled round. I was barely able to discern the figure standing in the doorway. As my eyes settled to the semi-light I made out Polly Ann. She'd changed into a short cerise tunic. 'I forgot my shawl,' she said matter-of-factly. I'd never seen her scantily dressed before. She always wore baggy meditation pants.

She sashayed past me with Deveraj scampering behind. It was over a month since I'd been with Amelia. When Polly Ann came traipsing back I stepped out and blocked her way. In the poor light I could only sense her apprehension as she made to go round me. I grabbed her hand and pressing against her I tried to kiss her, but she tugged away from me and averted her face. I pulled her roughly to me and forced my mouth to hers. She held out against me for half a minute, then yielded with a gasp. Her shawl fell from her hand.

Deveraj had climbed onto a bench and crouched there tugging at his scalp while he grinned foolishly and made smacking sounds with his lips.

Polly Ann stood on tip-toe, her lips brushing my ear as I forced her fingers into my trousers and grabbed her wrist to stop her withdrawing.

'I thought you really liked me,' she said in a smothered voice.

'I do.' I could feel the computyper pressing against my buttocks as I released my hold. Her hand didn't withdraw. It lingered and began to stroke me.

She made no protest as I quested under her tunic and hitched it up round her waist. She wore nothing underneath. When I brushed the defile welling up between her thighs she found the voice to object: 'No, please don't, please.' No sooner had she spoken than she was taking my hand, guiding my moist fingers to her lips and sucking off the fresh secretion. I saw it as a sign. Then she stood away from me and stripped off the only garment she wore. I looked down at her breasts. From between them in the green light beamed the face of the guru. Seconds later she was scrabbling to undress me.

Unbidden she wriggled to a sitting position on the edge of the computyper. Her hands roved over my skin. Deveraj squatted on the bench nodding his head and simpering as his mistress spread herself open with one hand and guided me straight inside her with the other. At my ear she whispered my name over and over under her breath, her lips wet against my skin. Hot and cold ran tingling up my spine as her gimbal thighs roiled around me.

The next morning my first regret was that in my excitement I'd come too soon. When I'd finished shaving and wiped away the last specks of foam I looked at myself hard in the mirror. The shadows under my eyes told me I should be sleeping more, not making love. The date was 28 March. Amelia's arrival was still over two months away.

Intellectually Polly Ann couldn't hold a candle to Amelia, but physically I'd have had my work cut out to tell them apart in the dark, though probably Amelia's heavier breasts would have given her away. What concerned me was there I was indulging in unprotected sex. For all I knew, everything but the train had been that way before me. I should have checked her out for other nasties. And my conscience for once in my life was playing silly buggers. In between Lucy and Amelia I'd been sort of in love with a woman who only appeared in my dreams, as if she were a substitute for life – only better. Was that why one woman had been much like another? Don Giovanni was condemned to hellfire for less and his list probably wasn't as long as mine.

The next night Polly Ann gave me the first of many full body massages, showing me intimate techniques she'd picked up in her Tantric massage group. When she'd finished she roused me from my lethargy and guided me over her own body, giggling to herself as I pulled and pummeled and kneaded like a total beginner.

After a week of potlatch pogging I was beginning to see her in a new light. By then I was heavily racked with guilt. When I made love to her I found I still fantasized about Amelia, but Amelia's image was growing paler from one night to the next. Earthy Polly Ann or intuitive Amelia? What if Amelia found us out? Something that wouldn't go away was the feeling that I was a married man out on the sneak, but I reminded myself of a wise Arab proverb: 'one fruit, then another fruit' and I wasn't thinking of Cunliffe-Jones.

I made love repeatedly to Polly Ann, mostly in the lab late at night, playing Irish roulette with her monthly curse. Still no condom. She screamed all right, but she didn't have a lot to say in the sack except things like 'harder, harder' and 'oh it's so good', which she burbled in my ear, between screams, with such monotony that it sounded like a mantra and left me feeling spacy.

Before, I'd called Amelia almost daily. Now we spoke infrequently and I found our conversations inhibited. I asked if her play had been a success. Apparently it had. She didn't elaborate. *Found the Dark Lady yet?* No, not yet. There was a short silence then she said she wondered if she'd discover the proof she needed in time for her Dark Lady lecture. I inquired how analysis was going. 'Fine,' she said. 'I've told Katie about you and me.'

A pause. No explanation. Agreement broken. After the article in the *National Enquirer* did it matter anyway? We avoided that subject too. Maybe, telepathically, she'd cottoned on to me and Polly Ann.

———— ● ————

Polly Ann lay naked in bed beside me. I was sure she resented my phone calls to Amelia. I was always distant afterward and that made sex perfunctory. When she insisted, I showed her the photo of Amelia, which had long since gone to join my *mala*. She looked at it, saying nothing. The next day she slipped out of my room at dawn and reappeared a few minutes later.

She was holding a photograph out to me. I sat up in bed and looked at its matt surface. It showed her lying naked as a nymph.

'Have it as a keepsake,' she said, 'and don't hide it.'

'Where's it taken?'

'By the lake. D'you like it?'

'It's gorgeous. Who took it?'

'Just a friend.'

'Someone's been tampering with the gene machine . . . number two.'

With one eye on Cunliffe-Jones I let go of Polly Ann's hand and took a step away from her. Our relationship wasn't the world's best-kept secret, but we tried not to flaunt it. 'How d'you know?' I asked him.

'Someone's flicked the alternative program switch.' He was looking angry.

Polly Ann said, 'Must go wash my hair. See you later.' She brushed past C-J without looking at him.

'Anyone could've flicked it by accident.' I didn't know much about the computyper next door. It was an update on the one we had in Oxford. That didn't have an alternative program mode.

C-J was saying, 'You can't flick it by accident. You have to depress the key next to it and turn it while you're still depressing, before the switch can be flicked. Whoever flicked it knew how to do that, but they didn't know to turn the key in the opposite direction to flick it back.'

'Baba's spies?'

'Maybe.' He looked doubtful.

'Our crew?'

'Unlikely but possible. I'll check with them this afternoon.'

'Let me know if anything else has been tampered with. I got a feeling last week someone had been poking round. Nothing specific. Everything was in place but not *right* in place.'

That evening C-J took me out on the grass to tell me he'd quizzed everybody and nobody had confessed to touching the switch.

I woke up early the following day and lay in bed trying to grasp the remnants of a dream that featured Mannering, Drake and Amelia. It wasn't the first time I'd had the weird feeling I was tuned into Amelia and vice versa. The first time had been in January when I called to let her know we'd made it into Shakespeare's grave and she more or less said she knew already. Not: *Did you make it?* No. She said: *I knew you'd make it* before I got a chance to tell her anything. No reason not to believe in telepathy. It had happened to me a bit before, but nothing like this bizarre thing with Amelia.

9

When in disgrace with Fortune and men's eyes,
I all alone beweep my outcast state,
And trouble deaf heaven with my bootless cries,
And look upon myself, and curse my fate,
Wishing me like to one more rich in hope . . .

Sonnets, 29
William Shakespeare

With a brisk step Amelia walked from her office in the English Department annexe on Kirkland over to departmental head-quarters on Prescott. She had a tingling feeling that told her Bob Carr wanted to talk to her about more than just her teaching schedule in the fall. She had a strong impression that someone else was there.

She mounted the steps to the veranda of the elegant building that was Warren House, passed the reading room and went up the stairs. Beyond the secretaries' office and the Placement Office on the second floor she came to the Chairman's mahogany door and paused to get her breath before she knocked.

'Come in.' She knew that voice so well. 'Good morning, Amelia.' Professor Bob Carr rose from a high-backed chair and gestured in the direction of a seated figure. 'I think you know Reverend Adrian Mannering.'

She found herself facing a man she knew well by reputation and had noticed on a couple of occasions at Shakespeare conferences. The anodyne Adrian Mannering was in his early sixties with dense silver hair. Gray eyes gazed through half-moon spectacles crimped on the tip of his nose. Around his neck was the collar of an English parson. He had an eccentric chin and seemed angular and paunchy at the same time. As Amelia walked across the floor he rose and mumbled something civil about the last time their paths crossed. Swords was more like it, she thought, weighing up the severity of his expression. She could not forget their bitter variance over Shakespeare.

She shook his hand, which was surprisingly warm, almost electric, and took the chair indicated by Bob Carr. The erudite chairman of the English Department was one of her staunchest supporters. She spotted his malacca cane and brown fedora slung on a hatstand in the corner of the book-filled room. There was some truth in the rumor that her presence in Professor Carr's department had put a strain on the bookish academic's self-control. It was fortunate for his blood pressure that he was not her advisor.

Bob Carr was in his mid-sixties and wore his habitual paisley bowtie. Amelia had a soft spot for his unkempt style, his chalky corduroy jackets, even the smell of the briar pipe he invariably smoked. He waved it now in the air in his accustomed manner when he was about to make a point. None of his lectures on William Blake would have been the same without the gesticulations of his pipe.

'Amelia,' he said, jabbing the short stem at her in a manner that would have put a twinkle in the eye of Katie Barber, 'as you rightly say, is something of an expert on Shakespearian biography.' Mechanically his other hand repositioned the few extant hairs on his head.

Reverend Adrian Mannering sat stiffly with his hands on his knees. 'As you know, Miss Hungerford,' he said, twisting to face her while peering through his spectacles, 'the Birthplace Trust takes a great interest in maintaining the Bard's good name. We receive large numbers of visitors in Stratford – many from here in the United States. A part of the money they bring rubs off on Holy Trinity.'

'From what I hear,' Bob Carr put in, 'you can't get a seat anymore, it's so packed after all the stories in the press.' Nursing his pipe in his hand he absent-mindedly coaxed it into flame.

'That indeed is a problem,' Adrian Mannering went on in the elegiac voice he usually reserved for his sermons. 'Since Bosworth's desecration of the Bard's final resting place, the number of visitors to Holy Trinity has reached almost unmanageable levels. The result is growing pressure on the Trust and the church now that bardolatry has reached an all-time high. Many people want me to arrange an official opening of the tomb this time. To make matters

157

worse I'm being pushed from within the Trust itself. It's like 1964 all over again . . . I was just as opposed at the Quatercentenary as I am now.'

Christ, you're full of piffle, Amelia thought. Her vision skipped to an unquiet grave. She had an inkling of what was to come.

Mannering threw her a look between disdain and indifference as he continued. 'Then there's the question of Shakespeare's curse. The tomb has been violated by Bosworth and visited by me, so I feel if the curse is going to have any force it may already be too late. I'm not superstitious, believe you me, but I think if I were in Bosworth's shoes I'd be fairly uncomfortable about it.' Then he added: 'I'll be frank. I have no time for genetic engineers and all this tomfoolery with chromosomes. If man wants to arrogate to himself the right to play God, he's in for a bigger fall than he ever got in the Garden of Eden.'

As if he hadn't got enough problems thanks to Bosworth, Mannering went on, the Trust had to answer hundreds of letters each week, mostly from Shakespeare supporters – and he certainly counted himself one – defending the Bard's good name. He was not at all happy about the accusation of adultery and suggestions that Shakespeare frequented whores and fathered children outside his marriage. Or that he was some kind of religious heretic. And that brought him to why he was in America. It was well known that Miss Hungerford was an eminent scholar of Shakespeare's life and times. He understood that in the past few weeks her father has come to be connected with Bosworth.

'Your father's new colleague is wanted by our police for questioning about his invasion of my church. It's possible that our Director of Public Prosecutions will see fit to bring charges against him, depending largely on my advice. Should they choose not to, Holy Trinity is left the option of prosecuting privately. Again that's largely up to me.'

'What are you trying to tell me?'

Bob Carr drew on his pipe and through an eddy of blue smoke took stock of her nails scratching at the varnish of the armrest.

'Simply this,' Mannering replied with a testy undertone. 'We cannot extradite Bosworth to England for grave-robbing. We have no way of knowing for certain, but it seems possible he took a valuable artefact from the tomb. Now I understand he's continuing his research in California in a quasi-religious community noted for its armed guards and hostility to visitors.' He added: 'A place I don't think I'd be very welcome.'

'If you're suggesting . . .' She couldn't help sounding sniffy. Her voice trailed away. She was looking at what appeared to be an egg stain on the front of Mannering's shirt: a sure sign of the elderly bachelor. Bob Carr's unironed shirt told the same story. Two men of a kind.

Interrupting before she could speak again, Mannering came out with: 'Local Stratford legend holds that Shakespeare was buried with a cross in his hands.'

You liar, she thought. *There never was such a legend. How do you know about the cross?* She wondered if he knew what kind of a cross. *Heretical Tau cross or conventional Christian cross?* How had he found out? It had come like a bolt from the blue when Daniel had phoned her from England and mentioned the cross he'd taken.

'I've been conducting one or two inquiries. It would seem to be public knowledge,' he looked at her closely, 'that you and Bosworth know each other extremely well.'

She flushed. The remains of her nails clawed at her seat.

'That's a bit strong,' Bob Carr protested. The minister's supercilious approach was beginning to grate on his nerves. He could not deny the truth of the statement. The gossipmongering press had discovered the connection between Daniel and Amelia and had had a field day two weeks earlier with smutty suggestiveness. He was not aware why they had suddenly lost interest: that Lawrence Hungerford had quietly pulled a few strings behind the scenes.

Mannering sat back in his chair with a smug look which was at least, to Amelia's mind, better than the unflinching stare it replaced. He didn't wish to offend anyone, but he did want to get his point across, he emphasized. He was prepared to make a deal with Bosworth. If he handed over the cross, which was a part of England's national heritage, he thought he could guarantee there would be no prosecution if and when Bosworth returned to England; some questions, probably, but no prosecution. He scrutinized Amelia's face.

What kind of a cross does he think it is? Her thoughts were racing. Mannering had attacked her repeatedly in his amateur but widely read articles on Shakespeare. If he knew it was a Tau cross, was he trying to get it quietly returned to save face? The Tau proved once and for all Shakespeare hadn't just been a sober family man, an orthodox believer or even a closet recusant like his father. She eyed Mannering for a fraction of a second, but he looked to Carr, giving nothing away. She felt sure Mannering was not what he appeared to be. His need to whitewash Shakespeare's name was too extreme. Had he not just come all the way to America? For what? To restore Shakespeare's grave to the way it was? Maybe just that. Maybe he was sincere, even if he was mistaken about what kind of cross it was. But why the fabrication about the Stratford legend? She could not ask him what kind of a cross in front of Bob Carr.

'I don't see how I'm in a position to answer on Dr Bosworth's behalf,' she replied to his question. Mannering was flustered. She had already gone onto another tack. 'What if there's a further opening of the tomb as you suggested? Aren't only a limited number of people going to be present?'

'Undoubtedly.'

'I'd like to be one of that limited number.'

'I suppose it could be arranged.' Adrian Mannering stroked his chin. 'However I can't give you any guarantee the tomb will be opened again. I'm strongly opposed to the idea and my voice carries a lot of weight in such matters.'

'I'm sure it does,' Bob Carr said.

It was Mannering's turn to look hostile. 'I can make no promises but if Bosworth has cooperated and there's a reopening to reinstate the cross I will try to make sure you're invited.'

'What if Dr Bosworth doesn't wish to cooperate? And what if he didn't remove a cross from the tomb?'

'I'm sure, Miss Hungerford, that you have influence where Bosworth is concerned. As to whether a cross was removed, let's just say I have a hunch, shall we?'

Another possibility entered her head from nowhere. What if something more sinister lay behind Mannering's mission and his obvious need to make sure that the cross didn't become public? What about the exaggerated interest Scotland Yard was showing in the incident? Could Mannering belong to a secret society that had links with one of Freemasonry's higher orders, with their web of influence, especially among senior police officers and politicians and more heterodox elements in his own Anglican Church? Her mind raced back to her discussion with Daniel about early Christian sects. Did Mannering belong to some secret order that was so ancient that they still revered the Tau cross as a sacred symbol? Then perhaps all the time Mannering secretly agreed with her theories on Shakespeare and didn't want them proved publicly, especially if Shakespeare really was some kind of surviving Gnostic. The cross seemed to confirm that he was. Maybe Mannering was trying to perform a cover-up. Confused by so many possibilities she felt slightly dazed for a moment. The next thing she knew she was shaking her left arm. Another attack . . . over in seconds. Bob Carr appeared to have noticed nothing, but the look from Mannering was very strange. This time it was almost lecherous.

She dragged her mind back to Mannering's proposal. 'All right, I'll do what I can.'

Bob Carr was taken aback by her compliance.

'Don't take too long,' Mannering said. He looked more normal suddenly, almost kind.

'I'm sure Miss Hungerford will do her best.' Bob Carr gave his visitor a look of displeasure. 'And I'm sure what has been said between these walls will stay confidential.'

'Fine.' Mannering looked across to Amelia.

'Okay by me,' she said. 'I've got my lecture on Shakespeare in twenty minutes. Gentlemen, you'll have to excuse me.'

The two men stood.

'Miss Hungerford, I'd like to attend your lecture if I may,' Mannering suggested.

She found herself agreeing and admitted to herself he had something about him she found alluring. It occurred to her that Englishmen were an acquired taste.

Two minutes later they were crossing Quincy in the direction of Sever Hall. To her astonishment more of Mannering's iciness dissipated in the spring sunshine. She took his arm as they reached the other side, surprising herself.

She glanced sideways, catching his eye. He simpered back at her, much to her amazement. The transformation was total. Gone was the pontificating tone.

'Don't look so alarmed,' he said. 'The disappearance of the cross won't be divulged if it's put back safely where it belongs.'

'It wouldn't be a good idea if it were to become known,' she said, trying, despite her growing appreciation of this man, to sound threatening. At least they agreed on that. Though the

161

hermetic cross would have proved one theory about Shakespeare, something she could not explain to herself let alone to Daniel forced her to admit that the cross must stay a secret. She even agreed with the minister, though she was careful not to say so, that the cross must be returned to Shakespeare and shouldn't have been taken from him in the first place. But just what kind of a cross did Mannering really think it was? Perhaps she'd misjudged him, but the stuff he wrote about Shakespeare *was* so damn sanctimonious . . . as if Shakespeare had led the blameless life of a saint. Her arm still clung to his.

Finally she came out with it. 'What kind of a cross d'you think Dr Bosworth took?'

'What do you mean?'

'Y'know, what kind of cross? Maltese, Celtic, Tau, Christian, Egyptian?'

'Christian, of course.'

We'll see about that. But she kept the thought to herself.

Adrian Mannering went on disarmingly: 'You and I may disagree about Shakespeare, Amelia . . .'

His tone was so familiar she blushed and caught her breath. Did he *really* think it was a Christian cross?

———— • ————

The number rang and rang. I let the phone dangle and smoothed my bed. That was my fifth fruitless attempt to reach Amelia in two days. Life in the ashram was so circumscribed I was ready to explode. No vaccine breakthrough, though things looked promising; no green lamplighter, except for a false alarm caused by a circuit malfunction; no Amelia.

And to make matters worse my relationship with Amelia had been splashed all over the tabloids three weeks earlier, after that piece in the *National Enquirer*. The only good thing about that was the way it had made Polly Ann more passionate. But the last thing I needed was the sexual guilt I was going through.

In the short break from work I made up my mind to call Matthew in London. I'd never had anyone really close to turn to. Matthew was always the closest and I needed to touch down in my own familiar world before I became unglued completely.

'You secretive old so-and-so,' he said when I got through. 'We read in the papers you've joined a commune. You can not be serious?'

I tried to explain, giving him a concertina update on my relationship with Amelia. But I found I could open up when it came to Polly Ann, even laugh about her in the crudely sexist way that men would always laugh about relationships that were – so they liked to say – nothing but physical.

'What's she like?' Matthew was asking. 'Y'know, is she a good lay?'

'Oh, we have incredible sex together. I bonk her two or three every night. She blew me in the shower this morning.' I felt bad as soon as I'd said it.

A hand appeared over my shoulder and cut off the phone.

'You bastard!'

I swung round and stared at Polly Ann. 'What in hell did you do that for? That was my brother.'

'I don't give a flying fuck who it was!'

'What're you doing nosing round when you're meant to be in that bloody intensive? Spying for Big Daddy, I suppose.'

'It's canceled, ding-dong,' she jibed at me, 'until Babaji gets back from Frankfurt. Why don't *you* go to the next bloody intensive? You might just wake up for a change.'

'You can stuff your intensives and all the other crap that fatass rams down your throat.' My voice was brutal. 'Why don't *you* wake up?'

'Big fucking deal.' Her face was bilious. Then without warning she began to wail. With her palms pressed to her face she took one step toward the bed and plonked herself down. 'You don't care about me,' she sobbed. 'All you think about is your goddamned work, work, work and *that* woman. If she means so much to you, why didn't you stay with her in the first place?'

'I bloody well wish I had. At least she didn't carry on as if she owned me. You went into this thing with your eyes open' – I stopped myself from saying 'legs' – '*you* like to fuck. *I* like to fuck. Why don't we just leave it that way without complications?'

'You don't *fuck* women, you fuck them over.' The next moment she softened. 'Is there something wrong with our relationship?' she asked in a crumpled voice.

'You're the only thing wrong with it. The rest is great.'

'All you do is take me for granted.' Her voice sniffled. 'Don't you feel *anything* at all for me?'

'How am I supposed to know what I feel?' I sniped back.

'Words, fucking words.'

I sat down on the bedspread and put one arm round her. 'I do care about you.'

She shrugged my arm away and stood, swabbing her face with her sleeve, then weaved in the direction of the glass door to the patio.

I followed and touched her shoulder as she leaned in the doorway looking toward the ocean. Everything was gray. She made no attempt to move when I put my arms round her waist, but her snivels subsided.

I led her unprotesting back inside and made her lie on the bed. I closed the door and hurriedly pulled the curtains. Her face that was usually so perky was streaked with tears. I settled myself beside her. She pulled back to look at me, then coiled one arm round my neck and drew my head down against her shoulder, saying, 'I'm sorry if I bitched you out.' I moved so that her lips were against my ear. Being careful not to move my head she wriggled her free arm underneath me and hugged me in a bosomy clinch.

———— • ————

I glanced at the time. We'd slept five hours, fully dressed. I removed my own clothing, then hers, trying not to wake her. She sprawled on her belly, one leg hooked over mine, one hand not quite touching my thigh. I snuggled close beside her and she opened her eyes, startled for a moment. I moved down her side and took a snuffling bite of her buttocks. She tittered and squirmed on to her back. I stretched an arm out and cupped the tip of one full breast.

At her bidding I rolled on to my back and teased her by telling her she had more arms than an octopus and a tongue like the whiplash of a butterfly's wings. My hands curved round her buttocks. I was all tensed up. 'Want you,' she was saying. 'I like your shoulders and your brown eyes. Most of all I like your butt.' I watched her through a haze as her fingers worked into her perfumed truffle. Then she was anointing my member with a lather of her intimate oil and mounting me where I lay. Twenty minutes later I sank back toward sleep with half a view of her delta swallowing my dying sword.

164

*   *   *

'There's a call for you.' Polly Ann, who'd been strutting her stuff lubriciously all morning in C-J's lab, popped her head round the office door and held out the phone. She sent a roguish look in my direction as I took in her short shorts and orange T-shirt with a deliberate grunt of appreciation. I knew she never wore knickers now.

It was Marcus, calling for the first time in a week. 'How's progress?' he asked me.

'Steady,' I said. Polly Ann was leaning over, planting a quick kiss on my mouth. 'Shakespeare hopefuls are running close to capacity and not a green lamplighter in sight.'

'We've got something interesting on them from our market research people. Over half of them can trace descent from an English immigrant in the seventeenth century. We're getting the most likely candidates, the way we hoped. Lots of them have taken the AIDS screening just for the Shakespeare test.'

The samples we worked with on my side of the lab were identified only by Red Cross numbers, but I guessed if we could check actual names on both sides of the lab we'd find a much lower incidence of HIV among the men with traditional English surnames. I put it to Marcus that he might like to look into the theory, then I asked how the screenings were going.

The Rostrum's latest projection from their resident seroepidemiologist showed there were just over one million HIV carriers in the US. That was in line with CDC figures. Marcus sounded jubilant about it. 'Boy do we have a profile of these people!'

Marcus *wanted* large numbers of carriers. It dawned on me for the first time and I felt revolted. I tried not to let my feelings show. 'And the fundraising?'

'Gift flows are up, mostly through appeals on local TV and the network concert with CBS. We're sixteen million dollars ahead, after costs.' Marcus could afford to boast. The AIDS Campaign was more than just back on its feet. It was on a roller.

Polly Ann had gone to her desk across the room. I put one hand to the phone and blew her a kiss.

'. . . and get this. The computer's saying four million will be screened in the US this year – over half of them by us.'

Numbers. That's all you bloody care about. Numbers and money. What about people? With Marcus it was always the same song-and-dance

165

routine. I wondered why he bothered to tell me anything. Hadn't he got what he wanted: millions of dollars worth of free publicity? I'd long since realized this self-made shit didn't care one way or the other whether a green lamplighter was found. Even an AIDS vaccine had only limited value for the Rostrum so long as they had no stake in the royalties a vaccine would bring. It would just be worth a little more media glitz: that was all.

Polly Ann caught my eye and held up a paper cup from the water cooler. I gave her a signal that put her on hold then changed my mind. She brought me water and I hoovered it down.

'Lawrence sends you his best, Daniel; says he hopes Baba's keeping you out of harm's way.'

I sucked in my breath. 'What about the two journalists those zombie enforcers caught sneaking in here? They beat the poor buggers till they nearly died. Now one's in hospital.'

Marcus took a worryingly long time before saying anything. 'We're onto it. They weren't journos, Daniel. One was a federal agent from their undercover cult squad. The other's a detective' ... pause ... 'from Scotland Yard. Name of Frank Hillaby. He's the one in hospital with the busted collarbone.'

Almighty Christ. Could this be happening to me? What did those people want from me? Blood? I only broke into a grave without permission. I waited for Marcus to explain, but he pointed out maybe they were spying on Baba, not me; that the FBI always got heavy with Baba when they couldn't crack the Moonies or the Rajneeshies. He was refusing to give more details about the incident. My imagination went into overdrive. If it was Scotland Yard, it was me they were out to get: not Baba.

'Listen, if the Peace Force didn't adopt a tough line half the reporters in America would be trying to gate-crash the place ... not just the FBI and English bobbies.'

'Bloody hell, I've been here a month and a half and I still haven't been outside the fucking gates. When I ask about it I always get "no" for an answer. There's a bloody great electric fence round the place. To keep me in or people out?' I might as well have asked a brick wall.

'Do you like parties?'

I was caught off-guard. 'How d'you mean?'

Marcus went on, saying he'd organized a party at his place Saturday night. Some journalists would stop by, most all of whom he knew personally, all highly respected. It wasn't going to turn into a press conference. It would just be a party. A few Rostrum people involved in the Search would be there. Naturally some of the guests would want to ask me one or two questions.

'I'd rather do a stint in the Buddhafield prison.' Polly Ann gave me a winsome eye. 'How can I be sure I won't get mobbed?'

'Put it this way, my house isn't exactly open to the public. By the way, you'll need overnight things. You'll be back Sunday.'

'How do I get there?'

'A chopper'll come by the lab at five Saturday afternoon. Dress low-key. Everything'll be fine. Okay? Take it easy now.'

Polly Ann looked at me as I put down the phone. 'Are you going someplace?'

I noticed her crestfallen look. 'Just for one night. Marcus is giving a party.'

'Can I come too? I like parties.'

'Sorry, it's strictly to meet the press. They might get the wrong idea.' I zapped a kiss on the end of her nose. For all his showmanship, Marcus was a dark horse . . .

Baba flew back from Frankfurt the following evening. He came sweeping into the lab office and greeted me like some incarnation of Kali in a black robe. It was shortly after nine. I was working late as usual. 'How are things?' he asked, putting an avuncular arm round my shoulder and patting it before taking the seat across the desk.

I squirmed in my executive chair and catching sight of unnaturally perfect teeth I thought of piranhas. The guru's smile vanished from one moment to the next.

'Swami Ramamurti,' Baba began, 'you are a scientist. I am a spiritual man.' He made a theatrical gesture. Usually when he visited the lab it was to nose around, laughing and poking things and posing questions without waiting for answers. This was a double first. He'd never entered the office before or visited when I was alone. His arm drew a paternalistic arc in the air. 'Don't think I go round with my eyes shut.' The eyes were twinkling. 'I've provided you with a peaceful place to work and a pretty girl to help you make it through the long hours.' A small movement caught my eye. I noticed Polly Ann was standing in the open doorway. Baba had his back to her. Deveraj was in her arms.

'You probably think that in business I don't know my ass from my elbow,' Baba said. 'Well the Dayananda Investment Corporation is a well-run organization and I do most of the running. It looks after investments from its headquarters at my German ashram. It finances this Buddhafield and my communities in other countries.'

'So what's your reason for telling me this?'

'We have many ways of channeling funds offshore. This ashram is funded through a Cayman conduit.'

The guru wore a flat look. I studied his face opposite while I felt my blood pressure rising. 'Don't you think you're talking to the wrong person?'

The guru was sniffing the air with nostrils that went in and out in syncopation. I noticed small tufts of white hair sprouting from his ears.

'As one man of the world to another,' Baba said, 'I want to make you a deal. It concerns this vaccine we all think you're going to come up with soon . . .'

I might have guessed: the royalties gambit again. Marcus had tried to leech that one out of me and walked away empty-handed. What if Baba and Marcus were in cahoots? The royalties if the breakthrough came would go to medical genetics at Oxford. I was hyperconscious that after the clinical trials on Retrovir – to give protection from AIDS to HIV carriers – had turned up trumps, Wellcome's stock had put on two billion dollars overnight.

When Baba had finished his lengthy sales pitch I exploded. 'Why don't you go back to India instead of fucking up a bunch of sycophantic adults with more money than brains.' I stopped myself from calling them 'seekers serving a life sentence'.

Baba ignored my reaction but there was a sudden whimper from Deveraj. I expected Baba to turn round. Instead his nostrils flared again. Deveraj was cooing and pouting in Polly Ann's embrace, covering his head and eyes with his hands as if trying to hide.

Baba addressed Polly Ann without moving his head to look at her. 'What do you think, Gopi? You heard what Swami Ramamurti said. Do you think he's right to refuse?'

She caught my eye for a second. Baba spun round in the revolving chair. Polly Ann looked helplessly at each of us. I could see the conflict and willed her to tell the old humbug where he could put his proposition.

Her lower lip was trembling. She looked back to me for support, but outwardly I gave her none. 'I think Daniel's right.' It came blurting out.

Baba leapt up and strode over to her. He seized her by the wrist. I thought I heard him say: 'Goody fucking twoshoes.' Deveraj howled and jumped to the ground, cowering. Polly Ann struggled unsuccessfully to free herself. I was already hurtling from my chair, vaulting the desk. At the same moment the giant Rishi appeared through the doorway behind Polly Ann.

I stopped. 'Fucking pigs,' I yelled at guru and bodyguard in a blitz of anger. Baba gave Polly Ann's arm a twist. She screamed.

An impassive Rishi was staring at me, hairy arms folded across his chest. Polly Ann made a sudden movement and twisted loose from Baba's grasp. She tried to bolt past Rishi, but Deveraj clung to her ankles, anchoring her escape. Rishi thrust one arm sideways and seized her by the collar, ripping her shirt open. Her breasts tumbled out.

I moved forward by instinct then stopped again. I was no match for Rishi, armed or otherwise. The bodyguard carried a revolver tucked plainly into his orange waistband. I watched helplessly as Rishi and the guru dragged Polly Ann, kicking and hollering, out into the night.

God, you make a Wall Street arbitrager look like Mother Teresa. I was hissing. There hadn't been a spiritual blandishment in the whole effing package. I'd had a gutfull of that place.

It was almost eleven. The sky had turned clear after the squalls that had brought rain sluicing down in the early evening. I stopped myself again from going to look for her. She usually came by after *satsang*, around ten. *If it weren't for that giant moron Rishi . . .*

I must have dozed off again. I found it was twenty after one. I still had my clothes on. I went to the glass door that was splattered with raindrops and pulled it to. Moisture in the air had already blotted out the scent of the bug candles on the patio. I returned to bed shivering in my sweater and counted the seconds between each flash from the lighthouse.

There was a tapping sound on the door and I went over. A rain-soaked Polly Ann hovered there, fidgeting with her fingers. I caught sight of bruises on her arms and legs, and one naked breast jutting from her torn shirt. I fumbled with the door and slid it open, expecting her to come in, but she gestured me to join her outside. She was shivering. I went back inside, threw on an old oilskin and rummaged in the closet for my leather bomber jacket and a pair of corduroys. Back out on the patio I helped her into my oversize clothes. When she spoke I realized she was more afraid than cold.

'Put your arms round me,' she wailed. 'Rub my back.'

I rubbed her shoulders as we walked away from the A-frame. The wind had freshened and it looked as if it would soon be blowing a gale. By the time we reached the edge of the cliff she was trembling again. The smell of the sea was in the sky. The beam from the lighthouse punctuated the dark.

'Tell me what happened.'

She was standing there looking out to sea as if she were invoking the elements. A wave burst against the cliff-face sending spindrift into the air. I pulled her back as salt water rained down. 'He held me,' she moaned. The wind whipped her words away.

'I don't follow,' I shouted into the gusting rain. My spray-drenched hair hung over my eyebrows, half covering my line of vision.

'Rishi . . . he made me watch.' She raised her voice against the waves below. 'Baba just sat there staring at me. Savita walked in and started screaming at him. When she cursed him I got away.' More spume rained down. She was talking about movies, the video movies that Baba was supposed to watch, lying on his bed, blissed out.

'Slow down.' I tried to sound calm. 'What were they making you watch?' I wiped my hair out of my eyes.

'They're not old movies like we thought. Not all of them.' Between sobs she was shouting. 'He's got an infra-red camera in your ceiling. Some of the movies . . .' A few words were drowned out '. . . you and me making love. Rishi was forcing me to watch them. He kept hitting me if I shut my eyes or looked away.' A long wail. She was still shivering. 'Please take me to the party. I knew I should have told you about Baba and Savita before.'

I stiffened.

170

'Until you came I had this relationship with him . . . and with Savita before that.'

I noticed how moonlight came and went between the clouds and bounced off the broken water. 'I'll talk to Marcus, sweetie.' My mouth was jammed into her ear. 'You'll be okay till then if Savita's on your side. Marcus and I will get you away from that fucking bastard.' Just saying it half satisfied the killer instinct.

'No,' she pleaded, twisting to face me, 'you've *got to* take me tomorrow. You don't understand.'

10

BEROWNE: A whitely wanton with a velvet brow,
With two pitch-balls stuck in her face for eyes;
Ay, and, by heaven, one that will do the deed,
Though Argus were her eunuch and her guard.

Love's Labour's Lost, Act III, Scene 1
William Shakespeare

Sunyata Ku lay hidden from view at the end of Cliffside Drive, an expensive cul-de-sac at Little Dume, five miles north of the Colony in Malibu. Behind a stone wall stretched three acres of garden. The Japanese-style house with its curling tiles stood center, surrounded by a criss-cross of paths, bridges and waterways swarming with carp.

To some visitors Marcus Freeman's house with a ceramic fishtail at every gable must have conjured up images of Japanese Samurai in their ancient strongholds. The moat at the front gave the place the appearance of a castle keep. On summer evenings a local Buddhist group, I'd been told, came to sit *zazen* before a shrine in the grounds, where a variety of trees and shrubs flourished, never so profusely on the seaward side that they blocked the view of the ocean. A cedar that grew close to the north-west corner of the house held a solid balcony in its branches.

Indoors the house melded Japanese and luxury Californian, with floors and walls crafted from burnished redwood. Apart from the bonsai garden on the roof, dwarf trees grew everywhere, even, apparently, in the library with its showcase of books on oriental philosophy, few of which, if any, Marcus had read, if Amelia was to be believed.

I looked out the window of the executive helicopter that had brought me from Mendocino. The deck of the helipad came up to meet us and we touched down in a circle of light-studs. I

172

straightened my tie and strained my hair with one hand. The memory of Polly Ann would not leave me.

As the blades came to a standstill a Japanese valet appeared and opened the door, releasing the folding steps. Marcus, elegant as ever, stepped forward to grip my hand while the valet bowed and relieved me of my bag. 'Good to see you, Daniel. Welcome to Sunyata Ku.' The landing lights went off and I saw a rooftop lit by particolored lanterns, red and green. A figure emerged to my right.

'I've got a surprise for you. We wanted to keep it a secret,' Marcus announced. I looked into Amelia's shining eyes. She stood there in a sleeveless white dress. I stepped forward and wrapped my arms round her.

'I'll leave you two alone for a minute.' Marcus was already disappearing down a flight of stairs. 'Feel free to come and join the party – separately. The papers may have linked you both together but it still isn't official.'

'I'm only here for the weekend. I've got to be back Monday,' she said quietly.

I took a step back. Looking at her against the soft backdrop of the Pacific I felt the urge to ask her to marry me there and then. 'I'd better go and meet the media,' I said awkwardly.

'I'll follow later.' She dropped her gaze.

I gave her another hug and whispered 'angel' in her ear.

Down the stairs I found myself on a terrace between two streams. Marcus appeared from the shadows and, touching my arm, guided me over a willow-pattern bridge in the direction of the sea.

'I thought you deserved a surprise so I asked Amelia to fly out for the party. Take my advice and stick to her like glue. They don't come any closer to perfection.'

I wondered if this was a hint or a warning. I wanted to bring up the subject of Polly Ann. Now I hesitated. Marcus was rehearsing me in the impressive list of journalists who were there. After some minutes I caught the aroma of chicken yakitori on the breeze. Marcus nodded in the direction of the house.

Steam rose from the pools of an indoor cascade and disappeared through a suction vent hidden in foliage. In the atrium that surrounded the pool at the bottom guests dressed casual-smart schmoozed around drinking and nibbling sushi against the drone of cocktail flummery.

Amelia was talking over her glass. She glanced in my direction and returned her attention to this pint-size dork who was trying to bury his nose in her bosom. No one noticed my arrival. I was aware that no recent photos of me – so far as I knew – had been published. Marcus introduced me to Jody Javitts of the *San Francisco Chronicle*. A few heads turned and from the heightened ripple of conversation I knew I'd been identified.

In the next half-hour I was presented to each of the guests, many of them staff from the two arms of Marcus's empire. On meeting the third Rostrum employee from the Santa Monica office, a Wharton MBA, I realized why the Shakespeare Search had taken off so smoothly in so short a space of time. This one was Belgian Eurotrash and wore all the airs and graces of a smarmy investment banker.

People had begun to drift outside to the hibachi barbecues and I followed, talking to a woman who had buttonholed me and introduced herself as Debbie Armitage, a medical reporter from ABC Television. She had her question well polished and she came right out with it. 'Are the rumors true about you and Lawrence Hungerford's daughter? I see she's here tonight.'

'Of course. You're not suggesting I'd make them up, are you?' I squinted down my noise at her pokey face and glowered contentedly.

She stormed away.

Immediately I found myself in the firing line of four more journalists. The questions ranged from trivial to searching, but mostly they were aimed at my personal tastes or the contents of Shakespeare's grave. I sidestepped on both.

Some time later Marcus found me beleaguered by a group of his guests and took me off in search of a drink. 'How's it going?'

'For a bunch of medical reporters they seem to want to know a lot about my private life.'

'That's journalism.'

'Marcus, I'd like to talk to Amelia at some point. D'you mind?'

'So long as it's in private, feel free. I've put you in adjoining rooms. One word of caution, though. My advice is to stay here where the security's good. There's a lot of muscle

174

round Sunyata Ku, but I can't guarantee your safety outside these walls.'

'You always talk about security as though my life depended on it.'

Marcus looked into his glass of Aqua Libra and swizzled the ice cubes with one casual finger. 'Daniel, this isn't England. Y'see those reporters in there: they're the civilized ones.' He wagged his chin toward the house to underline his point. 'If they can get your hackles up, what d'you think the guys from the other end of the media world might do to you? God only knows who else might like a word with you in private apart from the FBI and Scotland Yard. The Russians? The big biotech corporations? Some sicko with AIDS? D'you think you can be as famous as you are and walk down Main Street like Joe Blow?' This time there was no mistaking his warning. He waited for it to sink home.

I gulped down the remains of my drink and lifted a glass of champagne from a passing tray. The picture behind the patter might be blurred, but I was beginning to see where Marcus was headed. 'Okay, I get the message. What you're saying is: stay quietly locked away and everything will go smoothly; step outside and I could upset the Rostrum's money-making applecart. Y'know, Marcus, you're not stupid, but you won't scare me with half-truths. I'm going to find that vaccine and I'll find it without your help if I have to.'

'Jesus Christ thought he'd save the world and look how he spent his Easter vacation.'

Was this a quicksilver reply or some kind of a Jewish joke? I was about to laugh when I realized it was Easter Saturday.

'Listen, Daniel, Lawrence agrees with me it's better if you don't take any chances. We can look after you, truly, but only so far . . .'

'I'm glad to know Lawrence is still alive.' I wished straight away that I hadn't said it. *Don't get drunk*, I ordered myself. Again when I tried to bring up Polly Ann I couldn't find the words. My head was reeling. Everything was falling in on me at once: Polly Ann pleading to come with me before the verdict of negativity was pronounced . . . the shock of seeing Amelia . . . the relentless babble of questions. We'd reached a statue of a dragon that stood guarding the end of the path and I steadied myself against its tail. The heavy scent of mimosa filled the air and choked me up with some childhood memory that I couldn't lay hold of.

'Your safety is *our* problem,' Marcus was saying. 'You just get on with finding a vaccine while the rest of us take care of the details.'

It was a short distance back to the atrium. My hand was trembling, spilling a little of the remaining champagne. Inside, the first person to catch my attention was Amelia. I screwed up my eyes. I could hardly miss her. She was standing on a staircase that seemed to sway beside the top of the cascade, a glass in each outstretched hand. Her hair was a mess.

'Jesus, she's pisseder than I am.' The sight made me squirm. I turned back but it was too late. Marcus had already taken my elbow. *So help me God.*

At first she eyed me blearily, then she recognized me and waved. I made as if to go toward the stairs.

'Hold on.' Marcus kept a restraining hand on my sleeve. 'Leave her to herself for a while. Remember you're not supposed to be with her. If you do anything it'll bollix the party.'

Amelia tossed her empty glasses into the waterfall and blew a double-handed kiss in my direction. A few guests glanced at her in embarrassment. A woman laughed nervously.

I stood rocking back and forth looking helplessly at Marcus. Arrive the dispensary of oblivion: the champagne tray. I switched my empty glass for a full one. I caught snatches of small talk. Amelia's white dress was dirty with liquor stains. The staircase had no banister and she looked as if she might trip into the water at any moment.

'Stop her, Marcus.' My voice was slurred.

'Let her do her number. It'll burn out. I've seen it before.'

'The woman's mad.' The words came oddly from the back of my throat.

'Not necessarily.' Marcus's casual attitude amazed me. 'Just mad enough about something to get really drunk. Leave her to me. You go outside and talk to people. I'll get her to her room. Give her some time to sober up.'

With a last look at Amelia sitting legs parted on the top step with her dress waist-high to reveal pubic hair sprouting from almost invisible string panties I angled for the open air, miserably

176

drunk. A woman in a kimono passed with a tray of champagne and I helped myself to another.

'How does it feel to be a wanted man?' The owner of the voice sidled up.

I found myself looking at a cute-faced brunette in jeans and a white sweatshirt on which, emblazoned in red, were the words *Honi soit qui Malibu*. 'Are you one of the journalists?'

'No, I'm on staff at the Rostrum office. I liaise with the Sparkies at the ashram on public relations. My name's Charlene. My friends call me Charlie. I feel as though I know you already, my work connects so much with yours. D'you mind if I call you Daniel?'

'Why not?'

'I like you, Daniel, so I'm going to do you a favor. I let Amelia know about Polly Ann.'

I choked over my drink.

'Savita called me today and asked me to do it. She and I talk on the phone most every day.'

Charlie disappeared in the direction of the tree balcony. I stumbled after her and caught up with her, ten feet above ground, leaning on the railing in full view of the moon. Spangles danced a slow minuet on the water. The mellow fog in my head was dissolving slowly. 'Why the hell should Savita want Amelia to know?'

'Listen, Daniel, if you don't understand women better than that by now, you're never going to understand them. I like you. I thought I'd tell you and give you time to think things over before your fine lady tells you herself.' She gave me an impromptu smile from halfway down the ladder and called: 'Marcus knows. He understands these things. Oh, by the way, I was a *sannyasin* once.' She vanished into darkness.

I lurched along the path to the atrium as I tried to work it out. My head wasn't so furred with alcohol I didn't know Marcus must have set me up. Maybe Marcus had even set up Polly Ann to get me laid in Mendocino. Did Marcus fancy Amelia and want to break up our relationship? Wasn't that what I'd been afraid to admit all along? Jealousy had always been my problem: sexual jealousy. It made me want to puke. Christ, what a shit heap I'd landed myself in. Time to bail out.

I seized the arm of a valet. People drifting by looked like actors

177

in a Thirties Technicolor movie. Seen pie-eyed the colors were not quite right. *Quit drinking or you'll start seeing parrots again.* The elderly Japanese showed me to my room. I found my bag on a stand. The door through to Amelia's room was unlocked. She lay naked on top of the bed, out for the count. A sprig of pink cherry blossom adorned the table. I picked up the matching card. On one side was written neatly in black ink:

> *Tare ka Shiru tōki enrō ni*
> *Betsu ni koshiryō dru Koto o?*
>
> *Who can know that far off in the misty waves*
> *Another more excellent realm of thought exists?*

On the reverse were the words:

> *The Gates of Dharma are manifest*

More of Marcus's mystic bullshitting? I dropped the card.

'Amelia, wake up.' My voice alone didn't work. I shook her by the shoulders. 'Jesus, woman, wake up, will you!' She groaned and half-opened her eyes. As they focused near-sightedly they opened fully.

'You cheating bastard.' The effort to speak made her cough.

'Get up.' I grabbed her dress from a chair and threw it on the bed.

'What're you doing?' she said and hiccupped.

'Don't ask,' I snapped back. 'Just get up and get your clothes on.' I helped her unsteadily into her dress. No knickers. Her shoes she managed for herself. 'Quick. I want to get out of this place. How did you get here?'

'Rented a car at the airport.'

'Where is it?'

'Outside, I guess.'

'Got the keys?'

She managed a gesture that connected her hand with her overnight bag. She opened it, rummaged inside and nodded.

I paused only to pick up my bag before heading through the French windows to the balcony. Amelia weaved after me.

The noise of the party came from round the corner of the house. I leaned against a rail to get my bearings and, taking her free hand, guided her down the spiral staircase to the garden. Angling in and out between shrubs and along a flagstoned path I half led, half dragged her in the direction of the wall.

The climb looked impossible until I found a tree. 'This is an asshole thing to be doing in the middle of the night,' she mumbled from a distance of two inches, lying face to face with me along the top of the wall.

'Shhhhh.' I pointed in the direction of a guard in a black jacket following a German Shepherd. When man and dog disappeared I breathed freely again. Amelia was already lowering herself to the ground.

'You drive, you lying slob.' She delved into her bag and tossed me a key attached to a Hertz tag.

I threw the bags into the back of the Mercedes and sank into the driver's seat. Amelia was already bundled in. Her dress was filthy.

'Where to?' she said. 'I just wanna sleep.'

'Mendocino.' I revved the engine. 'Then England.' It was the voice of mutiny. Something was out of synch, a bit, and I was totally rat-arsed.

'Have you lost your lunch?'

I took the first left, passed Big Dume and gunned the car down the twisting hill to join Pacific Coast Highway at Zuma Beach.

'God,' she muttered, 'I haven't gotten so shit-faced since the Americas Cup party.' She looked at me and seemed to reach a decision. She adjusted her seat backwards until she was almost horizontal, settled herself comfortably and had yawned off to sleep by the time we crossed into what a sign told me was Ventura County.

I checked the clock. The alcohol was wearing off but I still had to fight to stay awake at the wheel. By the time we reached Oxnard I was getting some perspective on what had happened. That didn't solve the problem of how to handle a confrontation between Polly Ann and Amelia. Would they scratch each other's eyes out? I was sick and tired of the ashram. I wanted out. The effort of thinking was giving me a headache. Already I was hungover. It felt like a troupe of scorpions was picnicking inside my head.

When we got to Santa Barbara the headache was fading but I had a taste like porridge oats in my mouth. I pulled into an all-night station and filled the tank. The radio remained silent and Amelia slept on, twisting round fitfully in her seat from time to time. *Where are your deities now? Where's Black Jenny?*

The only noise was the rumble of tires and the hum of the engine. The dials in front of me focused more easily. The clock said twenty-eight of midnight. A car coming the other way blinded me, sending a stabbing pain to my head. What did I have in common with Lawrence, Marcus and Baba? Chutzpah maybe: that and an articulate sense of my own destiny. I wiped my lips and rechecked the mirror. Never mind William bloody Shakespeare. If I could just get out of this thing in one piece.

She hadn't found our Dark Lady yet. That much I'd gathered on the phone the week before. I conjured up a beautiful woman with penetrating black eyes . . . an aristocrat if Amelia was on the right track. Who was the Friend in the *Sonnets* who stole the Dark Lady from Shakespeare and screwed the arse off her? Who was the Rival Poet who competed in verse for her favors? Who was Mr W.H. in the *Sonnets'* weird dedication if he wasn't Henry Wriothesley, Earl of Southampton with his initials reversed? These thoughts flashed by like the odd car heading the other way. Why did Amelia always make me think of a woman who'd been dead for hundreds of years?

Santa Barbara was receding into the distance and there was no sign of pursuit. The speedo read seventy. Poor sweet Polly Ann. Maybe I could get into the ashram over the wall, but I knew at heart that if I wasn't to flub everything the only way was to brazen it out.

Amelia was still asleep when we reached San Luis Obispo at five after one. I checked the mirror and swung off to the right, following the signs for Morro Bay where surely the coast road had to lie. A car was in my blind spot in the slow lane. Its horn blared when I cut in front of it. *Got to get a grip on yourself.*

A sign said 'San Simeon'. The road had been following the coast for some miles. Lights to the left identified a Holiday Inn among a group of weekend motels. From one minute to the next the highway was climbing, enshrouding us in mist. I slowed down. Everything was ghostly. Eyes loomed out of the fog, coming straight for me. I pulled the wheel over. The other car swerved and was gone, but the Mercedes fishtailed and I had to fight for control.

I struggled to master the serpentine chicanes of the road linking San Luis Obispo with Monterey. Amelia slept on unaroused by the highway that unwound over the hour that followed.

At twenty after two the fog cleared abruptly. I gasped at the moonlit view of rock walls tumbling into the sea, sheer from the lip of the highway.

The mists closed in again. I kept the speedo down. It was getting chilly and I switched on the heater. With the touch of warm air Amelia stirred and opened her eyes.

'Where are we?'

'Monterey's coming up next.' I lifted my eyes off the highway.

'That's dumb. You've taken the slow way.'

'Why don't you drive, then?' Another tailspin. The car shimmied and slewed and almost ended up crashing against the steep bank on my right.

I blenched and concentrated on my driving. I knew why I hated to see her drunk. It brought out something of Lawrence in her, something nasty I didn't like. Forget her multiple personalities. As far as I was concerned she had just two sides to her: soft and sweet on the one hand, and tough and unpleasant, almost masculine – yes, that was it – uncaring and masculine on the other. I'd caught a glimpse of that demanding masculine side too many times before – as if she were entitled to anything she wanted by some kind of divine right.

I asked myself whether I could spend the rest of my life with this woman. With soft Amelia, yes. With hard unfeeling Amelia it was a categorical no, unless I wanted to end up ball-broken in defeat or forever battling for her commitment in a war that couldn't be won.

A sign showed out of the mist on the left: 'Esalen Institute'.

She was sitting up. 'Marcus picked up a lot of his ideas there,' she said, rubbing her eyes and yawning.

'When was that?' Anything to try and repair the broken bridge.

'Way back after he threw in Scientology. Alan Watts rescued him and turned him on to Zen.' Then casually she added, 'I had a relationship with Marcus, in case you're interested.'

Wasn't it what I've suspected all along? All I could say was: 'Is it over?'

She hesitated. 'Yes.'

181

'Who ended it?'

'I did. Maybe,' she mused, 'it fulfilled his need for rejection. No one ever seemed to reject him.'

'Was he a good lover?'

'That's classified.'

'You've got to tell me.' I shut my eyes for two seconds, gripping the wheel harder. I tried to sound as if I didn't care. 'Isn't he supposed to have a reputation as a lover?'

'The performance is even better.'

'I'm totally underwhelmed,' I managed to say in a stifled voice as I swerved across the road.

'Why don't you shut the fuck up.'

From that moment I had no more qualms about hurting her. That woman Charlie *was* trying to bust us up for Marcus.

'Maybe Marcus still likes me,' she was saying.

'Look, I don't give a tupenny ha'penny damn who Marcus likes anymore,' I told her.

'Listen, dog brain, where do you think we're driving to right now?'

'To see my friend the guru.' No mention of Polly Ann.

'You and whose army?' she said tartly.

There was no answer to that. We both knew it.

'I probably know Baba as well as you do – or better,' she said.

'You didn't tell me you knew him.' I was going hoarse.

'Do I have to tell you everything?'

'How do you know him?' I hunched forward against the wheel.

There was a pause. 'Marcus took me there last summer. What's good enough for some bimbo from Berkeley . . .'

'After you met me?'

'What is this . . . the Spanish Inquisition?'

'Why didn't you tell me?'

'You didn't ask.'

Her voice had softened. Was this the woman with balls of a moment earlier? First a ring-ding fight, then a hint of armistice. In one respect nothing had changed. She was as unpredictable as ever. As if she could read my thoughts she laid a hand on my knee.

Advantage Amelia. My shoulders were slumped over the wheel. As I straightened up I caught sight of lights and a sign off to the right: 'Deetjen's Big Sur Inn'. The car had already passed the redwood cabins lurking in the mist. There was nowhere else to pull over. I suddenly felt too zonked to go any further. I drove on and found a place to turn at a sweeping bend and the car crunched to a halt facing a board at the side of the road. I peered at the inscription:

NEPENTHE

LUNCH COCKTAILS DINNER

THE PHOENIX SHOP

Backing up a few yards I completed my turn.

'Going somewhere?' She took her hand from my knee.

I glanced over. 'I'm damned if I'm going any further tonight.' I drove back to the Big Sur Inn and parked out of sight of the highway behind a one-light cabin that looked like the reception.

A girl with fuzzy auburn hair, a latterday hippie, stirred in an armchair behind the desk. She blinked without rising. 'Hi, I'm Lisa. Are you checking in?'

She looked about Amelia's age.

'Had a no-show last night. You can have the Antique Room. Ninety-four dollars . . . cash . . . no cards . . . checkout time's noon.'

Amelia was huddled against the car wearing a sweater on top of her dress. At the sight of me and the girl she straightened and followed to what looked like a cabin left over from the California Gold Rush.

I took in the Scandinavian-style interior. Above a double bed was a book-filled shelf. The girl held open the door to a second bedroom. Amelia hovered in the outside doorway as the girl went to crouch at a wood-burning stove ready laid with kindling and struck a match. In half a minute the flicker of fire brightened the room. Amelia entered and switched on a brass lamp. With the words 'May your fire burn forever' the girl was gone.

I went to the car and retrieved our baggage. When I returned Amelia's shoes were scattered across the floor. She lay sprawled over the double bed as if staking claim to sole occupancy for what was left of the night. She wasn't asleep. I could hear her humming quietly to herself the way she did when she was really

183

hyper. There seemed little choice but to take the single bed next door. Pinned above my bedhead was a picture of Blanchard, the French balloonist. Half the cramped room was filled by a standing-room-only bathroom that could only have been added as a guilty afterthought.

I woke first next morning, my throat parched from the sweltering stove, feeling like death warmed up. No regrets: no retractions. I pulled on clean underpants and wondered if Marcus knew about her different personalities. They sounded psycho to me. She'd once said something about Othello. Was that how I felt . . . bloody jealous? Whose voice was it in my head goading me to feel that way? Aside from the dykish Cissy, did I have my own private Iago telling me tales of Cassio? First Cissy had warned me of the possessive Lawrence. Who else but me had my sweet fucking Desdemona screwed since she met me? A voice had warned me of that travesty of a Jewish gigolo, hadn't it, right at the beginning? Maybe the people we hated most were those who reminded us of the side of ourselves we'd rather not admit to. Marcus Freeman: my nemesis, but a smooth operator.

It was just after sun-up and my head was thick as fur. I went through and shook Amelia and opened the back window to let in fresh air. She rolled over with a groan as I disappeared to take what turned out to be a gnat's piss of a shower.

Ten minutes later I was back in clean clothes feeling sluggish but tolerably alive. Amelia sat head in hands. She looked haggard, uncooperative. I was about to ask if she'd like some of the make-your-own coffee by the stove when I noted her eyelid, red-rimmed and drooping. Somehow I'd come to think of her as impervious to hangovers. She looked diabolical, her hair a lifeless mop. Her eyes were lusterless. I forgot about coffee and wiped a fleck of dirt from her cheek.

She made a listless gesture as if trying to stand. I went to the front window and peeped from behind the curtains. A red Chevy Blazer was parked next to the Mercedes. It hadn't been there when we arrived. Not a human being in sight. Five minutes later I was still there when there was a movement behind me and I felt something hot at my shoulder. Amelia urged a cup of thick black coffee into my hands like a peace offering while she squeered at me over the top of another.

'Let's take a walk,' she said. 'The air will clear our heads. Maybe then we can sit down and make a rational decision how to get out of this mess.' So our relationship hadn't gone down the tubes.

She sipped away at her coffee, then put it down for a minute to go and plant her contact lenses back in her eyes. I was wondering how I'd had the hair to leave the party like that as I swallowed the scalding brew.

She changed out of the remains of her dress into a khaki shirt and slacks and pulled on a crimson sweatshirt. In a gesture of peace I helped her get into a pair of Reeboks she pulled from her bag.

A few minutes later she joined me outside. Ahead lay a broad trail up into the redwoods. Amelia hesitated as if she'd had second thoughts. I looked at her. Finally she followed. I thought I understood. She'd come so long as there were no questions about her exhibitionist behavior or Marcus. In return there'd be no questions about Polly Ann.

A stream trickled past the trail. After a hundred yards we stopped and looked round and Amelia explained the geography of Big Sur as if to remind me she'd been in the area before. If anyone was after us, despatched by Marcus, there was no sign of them. I trekked on with Amelia a few paces behind. Whenever I glanced back I could see she was trying to avoid my eyes. The drooping lid had gone. We halted at a sign that said: 'Drawe Canyon Trail'. The way was already steeper. Against the bird calls and running water the only sound was our footsteps solid on the morning earth. We zig-zagged through the redwoods that filled both sides of the canyon. I was already covered in a film of sweat. Amelia had fallen back. She caught up with me beside a sign marked: 'Trail Happy'.

When we reached a redwood that lay fallen over the gully I went first and turned on the far side to watch her cross. Almost to me, she slipped. My arm shot out to grab her and she slid on to her knees, clutching my sweater.

The other side was a scramble up a gradient of damp earth coated with rotting leaves. Beyond the redwoods at the outer edge of the canyon grew bay laurels and tanbarks. From somewhere came a rasping sound: the staccato call of a pair of black-crested stellar jays. The trees were thinning out but the undergrowth, wet with dewfall, made the going slow. Amelia was some yards behind, covered in dirt. While I waited for her I tugged off my sweater and tied it by the sleeves around my waist. The air had an aromatic texture that came not just from the trees but from clumps of gray-green sagebrush that began where the treeline petered out. It was a rich scent that grew stronger as we climbed. In front a barbed-wire fence leading uphill blocked our way. I held two strands apart for her to wriggle through and followed unaided. As I scrambled under the wire she turned and hostility evaporated. She laughed till she coughed at the sight of me strung out horizontal. I caught my arm and the barbed wire tore my shirt-sleeve. With an oath I freed myself and hurried after her.

By the time I caught up I was wheezing. Behind us the hazy ocean filled the horizon beyond the trees and the invisible highway. I felt exhilarated. My watch showed we'd been on the move forty minutes. Ahead lay a scrubby hillside patched with sagebrush and here and there, rocky outcrops. One hand waved her on, indicating the ridge a few hundred yards above.

She spoke for the first time in twenty minutes. 'You go ahead. I'm going to stop for a wizz.'

'I'll wait for you at the top.'

I pushed on, grappling with gnarled sagebrush, using it as handhold or foothold. There was no trace of Amelia further down. She could have been in one of the clefts in the hillside. I examined myself. I was soaking with dew and sweat. I traversed to make the going easier, panting toward a ridge that never seemed to arrive. When I looked behind I lost my footing and stumbled. One palsied hand grabbed a clump of sagebrush. I spun on its axis and my head hit a spur of rock.

Slightly stunned, I waited to catch my breath before picking myself up. Then I was moving again. I knew when I was out of shape.

Still no sign of Amelia. It was an effort just to look round. *You're losing, Daniel. Don't fall flat on your gezonker.* There were more outcrops of rock, lichen-covered, to get a hold of. I dropped to all fours, clawing my way. Those last yards to the ridge that staggered against the sky . . . my chest knotted. All the while I prayed for my guardian angel to keep me going and make everything alright.

There was a spell when I thought I was going to black out, then the finishing line was just ahead and I managed a spurt. My breath echoed in my head. I spat out the gathering sputum and mustered a final effort to stumble forward. But a stone tripped me and I sprawled on my belly.

When I raised my face from the grass I heard the chirping of a cricket and the plangent cries of birds. I could taste the smell of the sagebrush and the trees, even the ocean air.

I pulled myself to a sitting position and struggled to unknot my sweater. The sun was high. Mirages shimmered in the heat. I had the impression that Amelia put an arm round my neck and laid a drowsy head on my shoulder, her hair redolent with the smell of the shampoo I could never name. I looked down at my earth-stained shoes and fancied my feet belonged to someone else. I tethered myself to the grass with stiff fingers in case I floated away.

The rush of adrenaline and the clean air were exhilarating. I felt swoony with the excitement of something that transcended the ho-hum things in life.

There was no sign of the real Amelia. A cabin stood off to the right along the ridge and a tree-filled valley stretched beyond where I sat with what had to be the Ventana Wilderness for a backcloth. Further off still rose hills, probably the hills of the Santa Lucia range of Big Sur. From the far valley came the babble of water. I crawled back a few yards the way I'd come. No sight or sound of Amelia. My forearms turned to goosebumps. I recalled Marcus's words: 'This isn't England.'

From a distance came the sound of a branch breaking. My head spun round. Nothing: only stillness disturbed by the cries of two jays again, playing their ritual games.

I rose to my knees, breathing hard, then to my feet and advanced on buckling legs toward a solitary tree. With a groan I flopped down at the foot of the trunk and rolled on to my back.

Where in God's name was she? I stared up at the sun streaming overhead between the leaves and my vision danced in a blur. When I raised my right hand to blot out the flickering light my fingers were crawling with red ants. Without dropping my hand I flicked it backwards and forwards to shake them off. Was I spinning round or was it the sun?

Truly, wasn't that what Janey my angel had been warning me all my life? That someone was trying to eat into my head and suck out all my thoughts; someone with eyes that screwed into my back.

11

I oft have seen the western part
And therein many a pretty elf
but found not any in my heart,
I like so well as of yourself.

Willobie his Avisa, Canto XXXIV
Henry Willoughby [Anonymous]

A web covered with dew catches the sunlight and glistens like gemstones on a string. The gossamer filaments soft-focus and come back sharp against the background of a whitewashed ceiling. You grope for your last memories, but nothing will come. Your head is a lump of lead.

You take in the source of light, a small glassless window with two crossed bars that throw their shadow on a floor no more than twelve foot square. The only sound a cicada's burr. A suggestion of some sweet-smelling plant hangs in the air. The floor is stone.

With an effort you move your head, then summon the energy to move your body and push yourself to a sitting position. You lift a hand to your eyes and rub. This gesture makes you yawn and a pain shoots up the side of your face.

Underneath you is a rush mat, but the cell is featureless except for a dark hole in the floor.

You call out 'hello' – once quietly, then a second and a third time in a louder voice, but no reply comes. Wincing, you flex your arm muscles and stretch your legs before rising and shuffling to the window where you grasp the mullion.

Sunny hills spread into the distance, covered with vines sprouting tendrils from their cutback stumps. An olive grove fills the foreground.

At the black hole in the floor you look down. Wooden steps disappear into darkness. Your shirt is torn and the left sleeve is missing. You touch your face and find the stubble of a three-day beard.

For a few minutes you move your arms and legs to unstiffen them. The hole in the floor seems to invite exploration so you put a foot on the first rung and find it firm. A minute later the only light is a pale square the way you have come.

Reaching bottom you go down on your knees and feel around in solid darkness. Underneath and to either side is stone. You stand and move away from the steps. With outstretched arms you can touch both walls at once: rough like the floor sloping downhill.

Your foot comes into contact with a slick surface and you fall, sliding several yards before the floor levels off and you come to a halt. The only sound is the tympany of your heart. You grabble and find the walls trickling with a slimy growth. When you roll over and try to stand you slip again and land awkwardly on your side, banging your head. When you come to, a will-o'-the-wisp dances in the blackness overhead – a bluish light. You shut your eyes, only the light is still there, but when you open them again, it vanishes. As you inch forward on hands and knees something slithers between your fingers.

The floor slopes gently upward, dry again. You sink onto your back, then struggle to your feet and go on. There is a glimmer of light ahead, the tremor of fire. You make out a rounded ceiling. Features emerge: hieroglyphic graffiti painted on walls cut from limestone.

You look through an archway to your left and find an oil lamp sputtering on the wall in an iron sconce. The chamber is small. A stone sarcophagus with a wooden lid fills most of the floor. When you lift the lid it shrieks – there are no hinges – and violates the stillness. The sarcophagus is empty. An amber stone set in the wall beneath the lamp catches your eye.

You have to lean over the empty grave, supporting yourself with both hands, to make out the head of a dog. The stone under your palms scratches your skin. You pull away, but not before you have taken the lamp from its bracket.

With this light held aloft you forge ahead, the passageway sloping downhill again before leveling out at the top of a flight of steps. You descend and reach water lapping at the bottom. A rowing boat is moored to a spike. You lose your footing on the algae-covered step, crashing into the side of the boat and sliding with the lamp into the water, which snuffs out the fire. Your feet kick in the depths as you cling to the gunwales. With an effort you heave yourself up and roll over the side into the boat.

There is no need to cast off. The samson post is broken, the warp gone. You lie shivering on your back, abandoned to the mercy of the waters. Above you pinprick lights illumine the vault of a glow-worm ceiling where polyps of green hang like flaccid gargoyles.

From one moment to the next the lights are gone. The boat moves quickly with an unseen current. You hear the sound of rushing water and feel the boat tilt and hurtle downward. It hits flat water sending spray flying and emerges into a subterranean lake. Light emanates from dozens of oil lamps around the wall of a natural vault over a hundred feet high at the dome.

The current fades away. Around the edge is a strip of sand with a limestone ledge beyond. There are archways in the wall of the grotto, their shape irregular, but they appear to be evenly spaced around the lake's circumference. The one opposite is much larger than the rest. There is no sound except the plashing of water.

The boat bumps to a stop on the far side from the tunnel mouth. You climb out, puddle the last few feet through the squelching water and step onto the ledge in front of the great opening. Without hesitation you enter. Your clothes are already drying in the warm air.

Every few yards a lamp burns in a bracket. In the walls are triangle-shaped alcoves with a pilaster at either side. The first holds a statuette of a pelican. On the opposite wall is an effigy of a phoenix, followed further along by a whole motherlode of figures: a swan painted black, an eagle, a quail and a lion. Then the head of a dove, made of jade, and another dog's head.

One niche displays a concave silver mirror. When you look at yourself in it, caked in grime, you fail to recognize your blowzy features. Opposite is a musical instrument made of metal. It has some kind of clockwork mechanism and a key. You wind it a few times and a silvery toccata erupts carrying all the gaiety of a dirge in double time.

The next recess holds a skull. Traced in black on the forehead like a capital M with an extra flourish is the astrological sign of Virgo. You reach out and touch it with one finger and from its maw comes a terrible screech like the cry of a harpie. You pull your hand back and the infernal racket stops. You hurry on to another niche with a showstone perched on a stand of yellowed ivory. You glance into it but all you see is your own tatterdemalion reflection.

In the middle of the passage stands a table like an altar. The top is painted in symbols, some of them faded beyond deciphering. Under a six-point star, in archaic script, you read the words:

IGNE NATURA RESURGET INTEGRA

In the center of the table is a pyramid with the point lopped off. The impress of an arcane sigil shows faintly on the top. You pick it up. It is heavy, seemingly made of gold. You put it back in its original position.

You trudge on until your way is blocked by massive double doors decorated with a network of circles interconnected by lines. In each circle is a pictograph. On a bronze pediment in ancient letters stand the words:

IAM REDIT ET VIRGO

Bronze pillars flank the doors. You strain to make out the inscription on the capital of each. One bears the astrological symbol of Venus. Opposite is the sign of Mercury.

On one:

IN VITA MORTE RESURGAM

On the other:

TRES TESTIMONIUM DANT

You look behind. A mist is creeping up the passage. From it comes a baying like hounds. You whirl round to face the doors, seeking escape. A rope hanging to the right catches your eye. You step toward it and pull. Behind the right-hand door a bell rings twice followed by the sound of trudging footsteps. A key turns on the other side and a small door within the larger opens with a groan.

You step over the threshold and the door slams behind you. You swing round and start at the sight of the apparition standing there: a figure slightly shorter than yourself, dressed in a floor-length white robe with a red Tau cross woven into the chest. The figure's head is covered in a pointed white hood. Two eyes are cut in the fabric and a slit at mouth level. The headcover is held in place by a drawcord around the neck. The figure gestures with one arm and you follow.

Here the vault is less dimly lit. It has dozens of niches filled with a grimoire of figurines. At the far end a wall blocks the passageway. The figure leads the way to this and, taking a stave from two supports, bangs on a door cut in the center. A port slides open and eyes look out. The port closes. Again a key turns. The door creaks open to reveal a second figure dressed like the first.

'*Quis patebit?*' The second figure looks you up and down and seems satisfied. A hand appears from the folds of his gown and he makes a beckoning sign.

At a horseshoe table in a great hall sit nine further figures, similarly garbed. On a dais beyond them is a chair more grandiose than the rest. There, wearing a plain black robe without a hood, sits a young woman who looks uncannily like someone you know, with a bump to her nose and tawny blond hair and eyes that could be dark. In the lugubrious light there is no way of telling for sure.

With a sphinx-like expression she stares through you.

You stand at the open end of the table. There is no place for a twelfth. Shadowed eyes watch as you turn your attention on them. The table supports a delicate phoenix, its wings outstretched. The smell of sandalwood wafts in the air from unseen thuribles. There is incense too, burning sweetly in censers on top of tripods.

The hall's ancient appearance is accentuated by flickering lamps. Beams and buttresses joist the ceiling. Beyond the woman steps lead to a raised floor level filling the back of the chamber like an apron stage. Here ten seats are ranged against the stanchions of either wall.

At the rear of the platform you can make out two shapes, taller than a man, flanking a smaller devise between them. The right-hand structure is a wooden Tau, the other an Egyptian cross. The focal point at the top of the central devise is a concave dish. Its gleaming surface traps the light. From this dish something silver protrudes shaped like a six-point star or a rose with strangely looping petals. You are reminded of a child's whirligig but this is more ornate. The dish and its star are mounted on an upright that rises from a wheeled plinth supporting a lamp.

Your two ushers take their seats and the figure at the apex of the horseshoe rises. You walk back to an empty circle carved in the floor, plant your feet in the center and pivot round.

The figure at the table speaks out: 'Glory be to Netzach. The path of *neshamah* is long. Such is the Trial of the Supreme Master. Will you meet the subtle challenge of Mercury, Lord of the Shadow?'

You sense the question begs no response.

'Blessed are the Lights that are the Sacred Names of God.'

You reply: 'I stand for those who will follow as I ascend the Path. I am ready to learn the way of Heaven's Wind that I may join the Chosen.'

The hierophant turns to face the blonde woman. How familiar her features are. She comes down from her dais, ascends the steps behind her chair and crosses the platform. The two ushers walk a respectful distance behind her, followed by the nine remaining figures. Eight split off to the sides and take their seats. The hierophant stands alone in the center.

Meek as the Paschal Lamb you go to take your place with your back to the Tau.

The woman sheds her robe beside the Egyptian cross. Underneath she wears only a black loincloth. The ushers strap her wrists to the *patibulum* of the cross with leather bands. A foot support projects from the *stipes* and takes her weight. The wooden circle of the cross crowns her head like a giant halo.

When her ankles are firmly secured the ushers turn to you and you step back onto the wooden block protruding from the upright of the Tau. You stretch out your arms. Standing on stools the two figures reach to secure your wrists, but they remain inches short of the cuffs fixed to the crossbeam.

The hierophant removes a broadsword from where it lies on a credence table beside one wall. A red ribbon flutters from the pommel. Brandishing the weapon in both hands he advances on you, followed by an usher bearing a lance. There is a cry of 'Geburah'. The sword is raised in his left hand. You launch yourself from your cross straight at the hierophant. The weapon glints in the lamplight. You spin sideways and the blade flashes past your groin. You shoot out one hand, seize the sword by the quillon and twist it from your opponent's grasp. Gripping the backpiece with both hands you swing the weapon and thrust the point straight at where the hierophant's own manhood lies. With the grace of a t'ai Chi expert the figure steps to one side to avoid the blow. You are faster. The hierophant's arm catches the edge of the blade. It scythes through his sleeve into his arm and he screams. Blood spurts from a severed vein. The sword clatters to the floor.

Then oblivion.

You come round in a sitting position on the floor in the grip of two adepts. A voice pronounces: 'The Chalice of Venus.' You drink down a pleasant-tasting philter in a gold bowl . . . *'in nomine filii.'* You see yourself soaring above the earth with arms outstretched. The wind roars past your ears. You are invisible.

The vision fades and you are hanging on the cross. They have raised the foot support, but not far enough. You inhale laboriously and strain to support your weight on tip-toe.

With a painful effort you turn to look at the woman on her cross. The hierophant stands in front of her, his arms extended to the side. The lower half of his left sleeve is missing. A blood-soaked bandage swathes his forearm. Around his neck he wears a gold chain with a rubicund stone. Behind him the adepts kneel as an invocation follows.

'Rex Divinissimus, True Redeemer,
Who givest the Divine Dew in the Crucible,
Who rulest the Ram,
We hail Thee in the name of the Holy Conjunction.'

He continues in Latin: *'Aperiatur terra et germinet salvator . . . Corpus Salutare accipiamus . . . Fortuna Minor quae Collegium tegit . . . Tibi utriusque capaci servimus.'*

The woman's breasts jut and fall with her breathing. The star gadget has been wheeled in front of her. The lamp at the base is burning strongly, its beam of heat directed upward by a glass funnel. There is a flutter of light. The silver rose begins to turn. As the rising heat rotates the petals they catch the light from the flame underneath in their curious angles. The star whirls faster,

194

the dish reflecting a vorticose light into her eyes. One moment she is staring at its strobe fire, the next she screams. Her body goes into a convulsion, taut against the straps. The veins in her neck stand out. Saliva dribbles from her mouth, followed by a rivulet of blood as she bites her tongue. The hand you can see on the end of the crossbeam is clenched in a fist.

The adepts have risen and gathered round her cross in a semi-circle. The ushers step forward, extinguish the lamp and trundle the whirling device away. When they rejoin the group all except the hierophant prostrate themselves in front of the woman.

Her body twitches and blood and saliva form a steady trickle down her chin and drip to the floor.

The hierophant's body stiffens. He moves forward and kneels at the foot of the cross, his head bowed. The woman's head lolls to one side, rocking slightly. Her eyes are closed.

The hierophant stands, takes three paces back and begins to sing. The adepts rise and join with him. The sound is pleasant like a Gregorian chant and you feel drowsy. All pain has gone. An aureole envelops the woman. The assembled figures fade. Your body is charged with a warm current. You feel your penis swell and rise up before your eyes and a voice is crying: 'By the power of the sword am I stronger and mightier than those who are mighty.' You float over the scene and witness yourself hanging on the cross below.

As you drift back into your body you hear a solemn canticle:

'Rough hymns shall be my chant and woven songs,
For Thou art all for which my spirit longs;
To walk within the shadow of Thy Hand
And all Thy Mystery understand.'

With the chant that follows, the adepts' voices reach wailing pitch and their words are no longer clear. They quake and sway in possession by their beloved Trismegistus. Then gradually their orisons ebb and rapture subsides.

The hierophant addresses the woman in a stentorian voice: 'Lift up our bodies and rejoice in our seed. Bring down the Spirit of Light into our hearts like a rain from the Firmament. In the name of Hod and Netzach show us the Supernal Triangle. In

195

the chariots of Tiphereth the *shinanim* will lead us. Geburah is mighty.'

She responds in a haunting voice: 'Give me the Cross of Life but if thy seed be barren there will be no increase. I shall come with Diana's jackal and the horse of Mars. Geburah wilt thou hold in dread.'

The hierophant plunges both hands into a pocket in the front of his habit: 'From here I give thee my seed which is mighty as the Tree of Life is mighty.' He holds a silver T-cross in the flat of his right hand, the left hand supporting it underneath like a host of the Eucharist.

A cry of *'Ecce salutiferum signum Thau nobile lignum'* goes up from the assembly.

From the hierophant comes the visceral response: *'Ve Hod, Ve Netzach'*. At the name of each *sephirah* he raises the cross in the air.

'I embrace thee with my body,' she intones, her voice a husky monotone. 'Enter me and fill me with thy longing.'

The hierophant steps forward, kneels and places the Tau on a silver paten at the foot of her cross. From the *stipes* he detaches a Caduceus some eighteen inches long. Around it are entwined two hooded serpents. The adept picks up the T-cross and clips it into the end of the silver rod, upside down, the crossbar held between the mouths of the serpents. An usher comes forward bearing an earthenware cruse and the Tau is dipped in a warm chrism.

The hierophant holds the Caduceus and passes the upturned cross under the front of the woman's modest garment. She strains against the *stipes* to separate her thighs and receive the sign of fertility into her comb. Her body shudders for several minutes before she gives a long-drawn sigh. The hierophant's chest swells as he breathes deeply to absorb her aroma.

With a cry of *asherah* he withdraws the Tau and touches it to his mouth-slit before placing the Caduceus across the paten. He rises, takes two steps back and extends his arms out front, thumbs and index fingers joined to form a triangle, the apex at the top.

You hear the words *stella rorata*. Their sacrament over, the eleven figures now gather in front of your cross.

A rhapsodic voice wells up inside you: *Seed of thy Father's seed, out of the Third cometh the One as the Fourth; out of Death cometh new Life.*

The hierophant turns and extends his arms from his sides to form a cross. An adept steps up to him and raises a silver *ankh* to the mouth-slit of his hood.

The other adepts cry: '*Shekinah*' in unison.

Two ushers come forward. One kneels at the base of your cross and lowers the footrest until your body takes all your weight and your feet fail to find support. Your ribs crush your lungs and you cannot inhale. Pain racks your shoulders. With a wax taper the second adept has relit the lamp under the *stella* and trundles the contraption round.

The eleven figures prostrate themselves in front of you. The twisted petals stab your sight. You turn your head in the woman's direction. Where her face should be, you see the face of your mother, through a fog of incense, carrying a look of desperate appeal. As you watch, her breasts swell up larger and larger. Your voice is drowned in tears and the blood rushing in your temples.

You can feel many eyes upon you as you see through the *stella* into the distance to the circle beyond the empty horseshoe table. A form is rising there in blue-white penumbra. When you shut your eyes it is still there . . . growing taller. You are moving through space toward it. It is faceless and featureless . . . too tall to be a man . . . an ectoplasm specter . . . tall enough to be a god. For a moment you are two . . . then one. You are ten feet tall. You are thrice-great Mercury.

You open your eyes and confront the starfire. Its rhythmic pulse matches your heartbeat. You grow conscious of breathing so deep one breath will last for an age. Your thoughts turn elastic.

The voice of your mother calls you. The light becomes the sun. In the middle is a black point. It swells and turns into a man on a gallows, upside down. Yourself. Choking.

When the scream comes you bite your tongue. Your blood is sweet to taste. Beyond the wind you hear harmonies like a spinet's notes.

You witness the veil lifting.

12

ROSALIND: Then to have seen much and to
have nothing is to have rich eyes
and poor hands.

As You Like It, Act IV, Scene 1
William Shakespeare

A fuzzy sound . . . the voice of a man, a pause, a man's voice,
a silence, the man's voice again. Half my belly had been torn
out. My head was floating in a tub of acid. Somewhere outside
me was a dull ache that would not go away. The voice again.
I made out 'goodbye' and the click of a phone. Then a woman's
voice . . . Amelia's voice. I lay still for some time trying to force
my eyes to open.

'Daniel. It's me, Daniel darling. Wake up.'

Nothing focussed when I got my lids halfway apart, but the
glare was blinding. Then the white hair of a man came into
perspective. I winced as the man bent forward. 'You're going to
survive, Dr Bosworth.'

'Daniel, this is Dr Bendix.' It was Amelia's voice. Despite an
excruciating pain I twisted my head and her face appeared.
'You're going to be just fine,' she said. 'Dr Bendix has checked
you over.'

I noticed the doctor's bag in the corner with an oxygen bottle
and a mask. On the bedside table – Amelia's bed in Hungerford
House – lay an empty syringe on a pad. I raised one arm stiffly
and touched my face to make sure I was real.

I took in the kindly eyes of her family doctor; his veiny hands.
Amelia kept calling him Uncle David. 'You've taken quite a shock
to your system,' he was saying, 'partly from exposure and partly
from the drugs they pumped into you. Couldn't find any wounds,
though. Not a scratch: just bruises and plenty of dirt. You were
thrashing around again so I gave you a shot last night.'

They? Who's pumped drugs into me? I tried to speak, but a coughing convulsion seized me and I couldn't say anything.

'You must have been unconscious for some time, certainly the last two days,' Dr Bendix went on. 'If you like I can arrange for the Medical Center to check you over, but I don't see anything seriously wrong. That's your decision.' He put his stethoscope into his bag. 'Pleased to have met you, Dr Bosworth. Can't say I understand the first thing about genetics – a bit before my time, y'know – but I hear you're doing a great job on AIDS.'

I feebly shook Dr Bendix's hand and the old man departed. My head felt ready to split. The taste in my mouth was worse.

It came back to me, patchily at first. With an effort I recalled my struggle to climb the hillside at Big Sur. I remembered going on ahead and reaching the ridge, exhausted. Then nothing. My memory was blank from that point on, though something was tugging at the fringes like the after-image of a dream. Something that refused to filter through.

Amelia's eyes shone as she spoke. Gone was the acrimony. 'You look just dandy with stubble.' With a wet towel she dabbed at my forehead. Her words were joky but her tone was serious. She bent and pressed her nose to mine – the tip, not the Bump.

I felt my face with the palm of one hand. 'What happened to Polly Ann?'

Her face turned somber. 'I've been trying to work out the best way to tell you,' she said in a whisper. 'Polly Ann's dead.'

Silence. Then I tried to sit up, ignoring the pounding in my head and the scream of a muscle in the small of my back. I didn't want to believe it.

'Marcus called four days ago to tell me. They found her body in the sea off Mendocino. A drowned chimpanzee was still clinging to it.' Her eyes were covered in a watery sheen. 'They'd both died of hypothermia.'

'Jeezers Christ, couldn't somebody save her?' *Why didn't I take her with me when she begged me to?*

'They're not sure whether to treat it as suicide.' Her eyes turned hard and I slumped back on the bed when she looked down at me like that. I could have cried my heart out, if I'd tried. 'It happened two nights after Marcus's party. Fishermen found her body close to the shore at the western end of a place called Big River Beach, under the Mendocino headland. What caught the fishermen's attention was her orange pants and the chimpanzee's.'

'Oh God, I don't believe it . . . Has there been a funeral?'

'Not yet. The Ukia Police Department have decided they don't want to handle it. They thought there should be an inquest. They sent her body to Oakland for a police pathologist's report. You might be called to attend the inquest.'

She vanished and reappeared with a cutting from the *San Francisco Chronicle*. Two days old. The date confirmed I had 'lost' a week of my life. 'Marcus had it sent over.'

I read it word for word:

DEVOTEE AND CHIMP DROWN IN MENDOCINO

The Ukia Police Department have revealed the name of a Dayananda devotee apparently drowned with her pet chimpanzee on Monday. The partly clothed body of blonde 20-year-old Polly Ann Janowitz was found near Mendocino by local fishermen Jack and Brent Tubman as they put out to sea at dawn. 'They couldn't have survived more than twenty minutes in that freezing water,' Brent Tubman told our local correspondent. 'The chimpanzee was dead, but it was hanging on to her like a babe in arms. It took a long time to get their bodies on board.'

This is not the first time there have been bizarre goings-on at the religious community of the self-styled guru of peace and safe sex. The bodies were found only a quarter of a mile from the cliff at the sea edge of Dayanandpuram, and the police are said to be keeping an open mind on whether it was suicide. The guru and his followers, who dress in the same orange garb that clothed the victim and her chimp, are believed to be cooperating with the police investigation. One rumor circulating is that the girl, whose parents have not yet been traced, was linked to Dr Daniel Bosworth, the English scientist known to have been masterminding the Shakespeare Search from the ashram. He is believed to have disappeared and the police are not ruling out the possibility of foul play involving the controversial Bard hunter.

At the morgue in Oakland, a police pathologist is today

200

examining the bodies of the victim and her cuddly primate,
a young male, for signs of drugs or violence.

I looked up in stunned silence.

'Lawrence has gotten you off the suspect list,' Amelia said.

I couldn't hear her. I was far away on the edge of a windy cliff,
feeling my face salt-whipped by spray as I hugged another blonde
to my own body, absorbing her warmth against the cold. Seeing
those laughing eyes that defied the very idea of death. Hearing
her voice again, pleading for me to take her away. How could she
have simply jumped from the cliff? I saw Rishi's powerful arms
grasping her from behind, groping her breasts, as she kicked out
in vain. Deveraj clinging to her for dear life and being carried
with her as, with a long scream, she vanished into blackness.

Again that look in Amelia's eyes. I closed my own. What
mourning I would do for poor sweet Polly Ann I would have
to do alone, in a place inside me where not even Amelia could
go. Least of all Amelia. Without opening my eyes I asked her
how long I'd been at her place.

'Two days.'

There had been dreams – a long sequence of shadows – but I
couldn't get hold of them. There had been a struggle. It hovered at
the dark rim of my mind as I tried to excavate it for memories.

'How did I get here? You lost me on the hill.' Polly Ann's face
wouldn't leave me.

'You mean you lost me. You just vanished.' She sat on the side
of the bed and took my hand. 'When I couldn't find you I drove
back to Marcus's and apologized for everything. What else could
I do? Marcus promised to find you. He knew you weren't at the
ashram. I caught a plane back here.'

She explained how Marcus sent his security people into the
hills. They'd found me three days ago, staggering round in the
Ventana Wilderness in a kind of trance – about two miles from
where she'd last seen me. I'd got dirt all over me and dry blood
down the front of my shirt.

'What happened then?' Still I saw the face of Polly Ann.

'Marcus said you went berserk when they tried to bring you
out. You ran completely amok. They had to give you strong
tranquilizers to knock you out. Marcus had you flown from
Oakland to Boston yesterday on a stretcher. An ambulance

picked you up and drove you here. You've been in a kind of coma. Uncle David's been by twice. He gave you a shot of Valium or something and listened to your heart. He said you'd be fine; just needed some time in bed.'

'Did you miss me?'

'Worried sick.' She leaned over and kissed me lightly on the mouth. 'I've hardly left your side since you got here. You should see your face. You look like an escaped convict. You've still got some ugly bruises.'

'Where's Lawrence?'

'He's been in Palm Beach for the World Cup polo.'

'How long is it since we were in California?'

'Eight days.'

'What's the date?' This was pretty intense. I was thinking: *Over a week of my life squiffed away?* I couldn't believe it. And poor Polly Ann.

'Shakespeare's supposed birthday . . . April twenty-third.'

I turned my head to the window. Dust motes drifted in the sunlight's shafts. On the table, behind the syringe, was a vase of fresh anemones and jonquils.

'Where's Maria?'

'She's gone home to Guatemala for a vacation. I think the house was starting to get to her. Falstaff's gone too. He goes to our summer cottage when the weather warms up.' She drew a sharp breath and sneezed. 'It's just hay fever. I get it round now every year. Katie says it's psychosomatic.' She fished in a drawer for a tissue. 'Not a lot's happening there. I still get my gods. Or they still get me, but it's you not me we've got to worry about for a change. I got a friend to cover my classes yesterday and this morning. I've got class this afternoon but I'll blow it off unless you think you'll be fine. I've got Katie at four.'

'I'll survive,' I said with a grunt. 'I feel like I want to throw up and my head keeps banging away. Like I've had a branding iron planted in the middle of my forehead. It's like I've been on a long journey and no one except you can save me. D'you understand me?'

'I think so. You still need lots of sleep.' There was a short pause.

More fleetingly now I saw Polly Ann's bright-eyed face. 'I just

202

wish I didn't feel so weird. All my things are at that bloody ashram.'

'You mustn't worry your head about anything. Marcus isn't out to get you just because you left his party without telling him. He wouldn't have found you and brought you here if he'd felt like that.'

I struggled to sit but keep falling back on the pillow. 'What about all my data?'

'Right here in the cellar. Everything important at the ashram' – she gave me a quizzical look – 'came with you on the flight. All your clothes and stuff too.'

Was I supposed to feel grateful or something; what with Polly Ann dead? All I did was ask: 'And Roderick and Alistair and the others?'

'Everyone's gone home. The search for Shakespeare's cancelled – unilaterally. Marcus figured it was running out of steam. He thought the effect would start to get negative if it went too long without finding someone. Basically you've blown it.'

'Is he calling it quits because of everything that's happened?'

'He said he was going to anyway. The AIDS Campaign will keep on going. It's still got loads of life. I'm the one who should be disappointed about no green lamplighter.' She added: 'Nor a Dark Lady to wow the world.'

I managed to make it to a sitting position. Amelia was stacking pillows behind me. 'Where's Cissy these days?' I tried to take my thoughts off Polly Ann.

Her reply was measured. 'She's quit GSAS. Twyla Tharp finally took her.'

So the born-again virgin had finally downed tools and upped and awayed to brighter lights. I hoped I'd seen the last of the ambiguous Cissy. I wondered when I'd run into Marcus again. 'I didn't think Marcus could do without me quite so easily.'

'You don't know Marcus.'

The memory came back. Amelia and Marcus. Hadn't she said it was over?

I asked: 'How about something to drink?'

'Sorry, baby. Uncle David says nothing to eat or drink before tonight except water.' She nodded in the direction of a china pitcher beside the bed. 'What's it to be? Do I nurse you this afternoon or can you look after yourself?'

My hand groped to find hers and give it a squeeze. 'I'll get by.' Then I added, in case she'd forgotten: 'I still want to go back to Oxford. That much hasn't changed.' I was tired of slumming it in America but I didn't say so.

When she'd gone for the afternoon I lay basking in the warmth of the sun streaming in the open window, nursing the hurt inside me. Wisteria shoots hung across the top of the glass, spreading a shadow over the foot of the bed. The pain in my temples persisted. When a wave of nausea swept over me again I rolled out of bed and staggered to the bathroom to examine myself in the mirror. Gaunt eyes stared from a haggard face. I wanted to spew my guts out but on an empty stomach churned to a knot I could only stand over the loo and retch.

I sat on the bidet and covered my face with my hands. My head was throbbing. I got up and shambled far enough to get a Tylenol from the cabinet and wash it down with a handful of water. What the hell had I been doing for a week? What had happened to Polly Ann? She surely hadn't killed herself over me. My cotton sweater was gone. My Rolex too. I sat down on the bidet again and put out a hand to steady myself as a new spasm wrenched my stomach. My fingers touched the dirty linen basket. On top lay my scrofulous jeans beside a torn and crumpled shirt.

I inspected the once clean shirt, feeling every grain of its weave. It smelled of stale sweat. The left sleeve was missing: bloody patches covered most of the front. There were dirt marks everywhere. I looked at the bloodstains carefully before touching them. The shirt felt thick where the blood had hardened. For no particular reason I wondered if the strongbox at the safe deposit firm in St James's was untampered with.

I re-examined the dark patches on the shirt then checked my own upper body, but there were no cuts or scratches, just some yellowish bruises. An idea was beginning to gel.

The only syringe to hand was the one Bendix had left by the bed. If not sterile it should be clean. I washed it out and ran the needle under the hot tap. Taking the dirty shirt I tore off the remaining sleeve and tied it round my left arm as a tourniquet. Even then a vein was hard to find, but eventually I got the needle into my forearm and pressed the plunger. Withdrawing it was more difficult with only one hand. When the chamber was full I bent and held it firm with my chin while I withdrew the plunger, then the needle, which I detached and threw in the wastebasket, and the vial of blood was buried neatly in a box of cotton balls I found on the bathroom shelf. My briefcase, which I'd last seen in my office in the ashram, lay by the wicker chair. I opened it using the combination and stuffed the box into it.

I hobbled to the window. Gone was the tundra landscape. Among the wisteria roses threaded a spiny course. Shrubs in the garden were already green. Ragweed grew at the edge of the flagstones that formed the mossy terrace. An elm was in leaf and beyond, screening the house from the view of neighbors, stood a small copse of maple and high-crowned beech. Forsythia planters guarded the corners of the flower beds. Behind a stone statue of a nymph, two gray squirrels were feeding busily, threatened by the shadow of a flowering cherry. In the light spring sunshine Hungerford House had shaken off its doomsday air. Even the thought of the cellar no longer sent my pulse accelerating.

Dr Bendix had said stay in bed. I managed to smile to myself, despite the thought of Polly Ann. Nothing would keep me in bed for long. One afternoon at the most.

I flicked through the phone directory and found what I was looking for: the Whitehead Institute for Biomedical Research – possibly the best outfit of its kind in the world. I noted their number down beside the number of the limo service that Amelia had given me. A few feet away on a chair eyes were glaring in my direction. Amelia's rag Rosaline. On impulse I seized the doll by the feet, swung it overhead and smashed its doleful face down on the vanity bench.

Sweet Polly Ann. But hadn't I been growing tired of her demands on me? I saw her again, flashing her teeth at me and jerking one hip, the way she did, so cute and sexy that I always felt like a pervert just watching her.

When I went to meet him the following day, Ben Talbot, Director of the Whitehead Institute, thrust his paw into mine and shook it vigorously. 'Glad you survived the ruckus outside.' I knew Talbot's published work better than I knew Talbot himself – as someone whose research in genetic marker identification led ultimately to the pinpointing of the gene cluster responsible for cystic fibrosis in the midsection of chromosome seven. In fact he was one of the best immunologists in America.

I liked the jovial tone. Till now we'd been only one rung past nodding acquaintances at conferences. Ben Talbot had the buff body of a twelve-meter racing grinder. His hair was dun-colored. A pair of steel-rimmed glasses enhanced the warmth in his eyes and I put him at no more than forty-five, seriously underestimating his age, and took at once to his easy-going manner.

'I've been hearing a lot about your work in California,' said Ben.

'That was nice work you did on enzyme blockers with the Fox Chase people.' I tried to sound alert but after only one day's rest my head still felt like it had been through the wringer. 'What're you working on right now?'

'We've got a big push on to sequence and map all the base pairs in the human genome by the year 2005. We decided if Wally Gilbert's grail of human genetics was good enough for the Department of Energy and the NIH it was good enough for the Whitehead Institute to join their initiative. How's the hunt for your green lamplighter?'

I shrugged and showed two palms. 'Sixteen thousand tested without a direct hit. Maybe a few more months at the same rate and we'd have found someone.'

'Pity. It would have been interesting to find him, just for sentimental reasons.'

'It would certainly mean a lot to Amelia's research.' I didn't elaborate.

'Miss Hungerford? I read about you two in the paper some time ago,' Ben said with a jocund grimace.

I smiled. That reminded me of something. At seven I'd dragged myself from bed feeling rotten and called the limo service. The media had tailed me all the way from Hungerford House. Outside the shiny chrome and glass doors of the Whitehead they'd launched their attack: at least thirty newshounds and cameramen begging for interviews and photographs. Only the limo driver – he'd been a bodyguard – had saved me from being mauled as I ran the gauntlet.

Ben was apologizing, saying he had to be at a meeting with some members of the Human Genome Advisory Committee, but he hoped the path report wouldn't take too long. I should feel free to use any of the Whitehead's facilities. He'd be back at two. Before Talbot disappeared I asked one more favor: any information he could get on Dr David Bendix.

I found myself alone in the Director's private lab. I crossed the floor on legs that were still wobbly and pressed my head to the window. A score of media people were staked out on the tidy forecourt. A mobile TV van announced the presence of NBC Television. Its stout cables trailed across the pavement to a group of three men encumbered with halogen lights and video equipment. A reporter was pointing up. I stared down at the scurrying figures aiming cameras toward me and pulled back.

——— • ———

'Here's the results of the toxic screen.' A lab assistant handed me an envelope.

I tore it open and scanned the path report on my blood. At the top, neatly typed on the Institute's official notepaper, was the date followed by my name in capital letters. I went over the figures then read the summary a second time.

My blood pathology was far from the way it should be. The neurotransmitter serotonin was over the top. The secretion from the pineal gland called melatonin and the stress hormone nor-adrenaline showed abnormal levels. The toxicologist had found traces of three extraneous substances: an opium derivative that resembled morphine, droperidol and a very small amount of diazepam. The report was signed 'J.S. Ficino'.

There were a few words scribbled at the bottom: 'Maybe you'd like me to get a forensic chemist to run some tests. This one looks serious.' I immediately got hold of Ficino on the internal phone. 'I'd say someone slipped you one helluva Mickey Finn,' the toxicologist replied to my final question.

I hung up with Ficino's words ringing alarm bells. No wonder I couldn't remember a thing. Droperidol was mind-boggling. Wasn't it a dangerous behavior-altering drug used to control Tourette's syndrome? An overdose could kill you. The effect of droperidol combined with morphine was unimaginable. An older man might have been finished off. If that was Marcus's 'tranquilizer' what in hell had his security people been trying to do to me? As if I needed Valium on top of that lot anyway.

I glanced through the report one more time. It explained how I'd felt on waking the day before: utterly exhausted. I didn't feel that much more together now. For one thing my joints still ached.

I thought of Marcus and his fancy footwork the night of the party. I had my doubts I'd ever get an answer out of him . . . even if we met or spoke again. As for the notion that I'd spent a whole week yomping round the hills of California in some kind of a trance . . . I woke up to the fact I hadn't eaten anything all day except for the toast and coffee that Amelia had let me have at breakfast. I was ravenous. I called the limo service and prepared myself mentally for a quick getaway by the rear entrance through to the parking lot.

Amelia was surely full of surprises: 'Baby, I had a visitor from England two weeks ago. Adrian Mannering came by here, y'know, the guy from the Birthplace Trust. He seems to know somehow you took the cross from Shakespeare's grave. He said he wanted it back. He said if you comply he'll make sure you don't get prosecuted when you get back to England.' She wriggled to get comfortable, lying naked on top of me, and pressed her breasts down on my chest like semi-solid sponges.

'Couldn't you have told me this sooner?' I was thinking back. An inkling of something that had crossed my mind in Mendocino.

'Please understand, baby,' she whispered moistly in my ear. 'I thought if I told you you'd accept and I might never see you again.'

'Does the offer still stand?'

'I guess so. He left me his card with a number to phone if you agree.'

'He came all the way from England just for this?'

'Mmmmm. He even knew all about you and me.'

'Who doesn't know all about you and me?' I said bitterly. 'Let's talk about it later, okay?'

'Baby, are you worried about Mannering?'

'Not really.'

'He called yesterday . . . wanted to know how you were and if you agreed to his terms.'

Something was tugging at my memory. The man's – Bendix's – voice on the phone as I'd come round the day before. 'Was that him talking to the doctor on the phone?' It was coming back. It had seemed like a long conversation.

'Don't be silly.' She pulled back and in the moonlight I could see her frown.

'Just wondered if they knew each other.'

'You must be kidding.'

I was only half mollified. I'd already had a chance to phone Dunkley in London. He'd confirmed the pressure was still on from Drake and the file on my mother's murder over thirty years ago was still open. Why, he still didn't know. He had one good piece of news, though. My blueprint of the weeping gene was now registered officially with GenBank at the Los Alamos National Laboratory.

'Just leave Mannering to me,' Amelia was saying.

'D'you want to stay here? I'm going back to face the music.'

'No, will you take me with you?' She slid off me and ran her fingers down to my navel. 'I'm sick of being hassled by a load of pooh-pooh critics and that harridan of an advisor.' Then, sweetly: 'I just want to be with you, baby.'

I caught the soft camber of her cheeks between my fingers and slowly drew her lips to my mouth where they lingered playfully.

Then we were separating. I was saying: 'I'll take you anywhere you want to go, angel . . . on one condition.'

'What's that?'

'That you marry me.'

When I had breathing space to think about it later it still seemed like the right question. I was crazy about her, at least one side of her, but at the time when she said 'yes I will' I felt Janey, dear guardian Janey, threatening to resign. I was well aware that the Hungerfords were a family you could marry into, but never belong to, without the blood. But proposing to Amelia unexpectedly like that was always on the cards. Something you might do. You just didn't talk about it first. The fact that she accepted the idea of commitment and coupledom struck me as equally unexpected. Coming from her independent masculine side it would have been unthinkable. Instinctively I'd caught the feminine side of her.

Something else I kept thinking about. Any day I'd get subpoenaed to show up at Polly Ann's inquest and I visualized her naked body as I used to know it. Back in England I'd be able to wriggle out of that one.

13

'Look at it this way,' Katie Barber was saying, 'since Bosworth came into her life a lot of things have happened to her.'

The man absorbing Amelia's case history was George Frost, Hanford Professor of Neurology at the Harvard Medical School. As they crossed over to the river Katie concluded she had been right to call him. They had been through Harvard together and George had gone on to study under the great William Lennox, becoming an authority on epilepsy.

The day was a scorcher and house crews were out on the river. The grassy bank was filling fast. Katie never wore a bra and her breasts lolloped in counterpoint to her hips beneath a cheesecloth dress that eddied in the breeze.

The previous day Amelia had told Katie of her secret engagement, only three weeks after she'd admitted from the couch that she and the famous geneticist were having a relationship. Katie had been surprised by the news of the engagement: less surprised than Rosie.

'Let's sit over there.' George Frost ran a twitchy hand through his crop of carrot hair. Katie looked where he was pointing, a little back from the water. A few yards from the spot a girl in cut-off jeans sat in thrall to a man reading a book. It didn't look likely they'd be overheard by the couple.

Katie asked: 'D'you mind if I smoke?' as she lowered her adipose shape to the ground.

'Go right ahead.' George hated smoking with a passion, but his hatred did not extend to smokers. In fact he was fond of Katie.

They had kept in touch over the years and he was pleased when she dropped in on him, as she had that afternoon, and dragged him off to consult him on something that was bugging her.

Not that Katie's view of Amelia's illness had changed with the revelation about Daniel Bosworth. She was more concerned about the probability Amelia would quit analysis to go with him to England.

George's gaze strayed to the passing boats. 'Let's go back over the details. You've explained about her brief absences, even in your office, but you also mentioned a more generalized seizure. Does that ever happen *outside* your office?'

'Not so far as I can make out. But there's a lot of memory deficit there. Who knows how much she's forgotten that she can't face consciously.'

'Tell me about her seizure.'

'Well, before it began her eyes were on the ceiling fan. It was the first really hot day, as hot as today. The fan had been off during all her previous visits.'

'Tell me carefully what you saw.'

'She'd been talking normally then there was silence for maybe a minute. I leaned over to see her better. Her eyes seemed to be glued to the fan. Her pupils had grown wider and she blinked a couple of times.'

'The stroboscopic effect of the fan produced a reflex epilepsy. Did you hear anything?'

'She made a swallowing noise. She stiffened for maybe twenty seconds and stopped breathing. I stood against the edge of the couch to make sure she didn't fall off. Her body jerked several times, but instead of coming round as I expected she stopped breathing again. She was in a cataleptic state. She'd turned almost blue.'

George looked at the cigarette that clung to the corner of her mouth.

'She looked for all the world like a corpse, then she started trembling and after a couple of minutes the color came back to her skin in a flush. She was sweating buckets too. She looked terrible. I tried to make light of it. I didn't tell her it was more than just one of her partial seizures. She seemed confused. After a quiet period where she was in a twilight state she complained she felt feverish and wanted to vomit.' Katie paused. 'She had absolutely no recall of missing time afterward. It was as if that time just didn't exist. What d'you make of it?'

George was careful not to comment too hastily. He had not become a full professor at thirty-six without an overweening curiosity and the ability to channel hypomanic brio into original if non-conformist avenues of research. The bank of the Charles was getting more crowded as the temperature rose.

'Catalepsy is one of the psychomotor . . .'

'Just keep it untechnical, okay? and don't patronize me.'

'Okay,' he replied a shade testily. 'Let me explain a few things about catalepsy and other xenophrenic states. Catalepsy's better known as suspended animation, since it mimics death. I've been studying a group of advanced meditators. A few of them have worked with John Lilly at the Institute of Mental Health. They can bring on the euphoria some epileptics get as an aura. They hold it in a kind of ecstatic trance. We can see this from monitoring the magnetic field round the brain using a micro-miniaturized squid. Catalepsy is just a particular kind of trance.'

Katie turned on to her back to catch the sun on her face.

'Some brain waves can produce out-of-the-body sensations, like a feeling of levitation – even the subjective power to see visions. All that sixth-sense stuff – telepathy, things like that – in almost every case of charismatic gifts that we look at, we find strong alpha or theta. In Tibet it's linked to the *siddhis* of Tantric tradition – magical powers.'

'Like spiritualists?' Katie suggested.

'A lot of trance mediums and channelers show symptoms of epilepsy like one sagging eyelid – even one whole side of their face that tends to sag. There are usually signs of automatism. These are the people who claim they can read your mind or see distant events. And often they can, after a fashion. In a trance their senses are all heightened – what I call "exalted".'

He described how one benefit of deep meditation was that you got increased synchronization of the waves produced by each of the brain's hemispheres, the so-called male and female brains. He called this the Androgyny Effect.

Katie's cigarette had gone out. 'That's some theory.' She looked around as she spoke. 'Come on, let's walk as far as Eliot Bridge. If we're going to talk about Amelia we need to be out of everyone's hearing.'

'From what you've told me Amelia's got a low convulsive threshold. What I'm not convinced about is the possibility there are psychological triggers at work as you've suggested. Remember that hysteria can mimic epilepsy.'

Katie got to her feet and looked at him. 'A hysterical-depressive syndrome like multiple personality disorder is a borderline problem and epilepsy is epilepsy. But we both know that the link between low level borderline pathology and abnormal temporal lobe discharges is an undisputed fact. The question in Amelia's case is not the link and it's certainly not a question of mimicry. It's whether a trigger that's psychological and not organic can set her off.'

'Has she got a family history of epilepsy?'

'Great-great-grandfather and great-grandfather both epileptic. One had polio too.'

George looked perplexed. 'For the last hundred years medical science has been busy tearing mind and body apart.' He hesitated. 'But y'know it's just possible I'll swallow the idea that epilepsy and multiple personality disorder might sometimes be connected psychologically. Though her high sex drive doesn't fit. It's unusual with any epilepsy.'

'Maybe not with her high testosterone level. I checked out her hormone profile. She has enough male hormones to give her the sex drive of . . .' she struggled for a comparison . . . 'of a Catherine the Great.'

'But why does it have to be epilepsy – and not an imitation?'

'Aren't we all epileptic if we're pushed far enough?'

'This is true.' He could see that Katie would not be dissuaded. 'Listen, don't get too carried away. I was thinking about the paper you said you were working on. Maybe I could meet with Amelia and run some tests. Then we could write it together if we found there was a non-organic connection between her epilepsy and her personality disorder.'

Katie protested, putting a hand on his sleeve. 'Are you asking me to share the glory? The theory's mine, remember. So is Amelia. I just wanted to see if you agree with me.'

'Perhaps you're onto something. I'd just like a share in it, that's all.' He was smiling. 'By the way, I do know of epileptics who are triggered off psychologically – only all of them are men, and they're all fetishists.'

She caught the look that went with this piece of information, and smiled back. 'Maybe with enough male hormones a woman can be a fetishist too. There are times when Amelia *does* seem very masculine; rather like her father in fact.'

———— • ————

A week and a half remained to Reading Period. When I suggested Amelia should wait until after Commencement before coming to England, she refused, saying she wasn't going to let me go on my own. She'd have a word with Bob Carr and see if she could cancel her last lecture the following week. Anyway there was still no news on the Dark Lady front. Maybe she'd return in the fall to give the lecture: a special one if she'd solved the mystery of the *Sonnets* by then. Either way she'd have to resign from the English Department. I was glad to realize nothing – not even Lawrence – had the power to stop her from coming with me.

She'd planned to find someone to rent the house, but when she called Lawrence in Washington to tell him of her impromptu engagement he congratulated her coldly without asking to speak to me and insisted she leave the house untenanted. Maria would be back to look after the place the day after we left. Falstaff would have to stay in America. English quarantine laws were too strict.

There was the question of my own relocation to see to. I talked on the phone to Erik Sigurdsson back at my immunochemistry unit, then Godfrey Shanks, Professor of Genetics. With more trepidation I called Sir Leon Fitzpatrick, the Warden of All Souls, to prepare the final ground for my return. Having disturbed the donnish old advocate in the middle of lunch I was surprised at the welcome I got over the phone instead of the expected carpeting. I wouldn't be stripped of my All Souls Fellowship for what happened in Stratford. In fact I learnt that no one seemed to care. In a cautiously optimistic frame of mind I phoned Dunkley again and he confirmed what I already thought. I'd not be infringing my agreement with the Rostrum if I pulled out now.

I toyed with the idea of calling Santa Monica. Marcus had 'saved' me at Big Sur – or had he almost killed me? True, he'd brought me back to Cambridge with my database – hopefully complete. It was hard to call that a slap in the face. In the end I decided not to phone. As for that fucking old fox the guru . . .

I would be carrying the pain of Polly Ann's death around inside me for a long time to come.

Amelia left me to make calls undisturbed. 'I've got a bunch of panting Seniors to hold hands with till eleven,' she called as she disappeared out the bedroom door.

Almost two hours later I banged down the phone with a stiff arm and went downstairs. I sauntered through the screen door to the porch and tripped over something at my feet. It was only a forsythia planter. I sat by the loggia on a garden bench and drew a lungful of air. An old man with his back to me was pruning back Virginia creeper over by the patio wall.

The media people would be lurking in wait at the Whitehead again, apart from half a dozen who usually laid siege to the house in daylight hours. I'd been surprised not to see them on Brattle Street when I'd looked outside first thing that morning. Since my whereabouts were public knowledge, why stay caged in Hungerford House? I felt something egging me on to take my chances.

I opened the screen door to the kitchen. It was twenty after eleven. I almost ran to the phone.

'Something happened?' Amelia asked when I got through to her.

'I just decided I'd like to meet you someplace for coffee.'

'D' you realize what that'd mean? You might get mobbed.'

'I think we can handle it. Where d'you suggest?'

'I've got a window at one. We'll meet in the Coffee Connection at a quarter after. It's a coffee shop in the mall on the corner of Dunster and Mt Auburn.' There was a catch in her voice.

Before I headed off to meet her I plucked up the courage to go down into the cellar and check on all the stuff that had come from Mendocino. For no obvious reason I couldn't explain why I felt different about the cellar now, but as I raised the trapdoor in the floor I knew I wasn't afraid to go down there this time. In fact it was almost as if I belonged to the house, as if it were home, even the cellar.

I'd brought a strong torch, which was just as well as the red bulkhead light seemed even fainter than before. It didn't take long to locate my stuff and it looked as though it had all been professionally packed. The two containers had even been covered in heat-shrunk plastic. I imagined Marcus's pugmark on everything as I tore open the larger one, turning the security cabinet's combination lock from memory, and breathed deeply when, inside, I found the file on my mother. The cooling cabinet was there too, stuffed with dry ice. The disks were in the adjacent container. Before we left I'd fix to get everything air-freighted to London.

Just as well there was plastic round everything. The cellar hadn't seemed so dirty on the last occasion. I was nosing around a bit and this time I took a good look at the wine bottles. It was unbelievable how priceless some of them were. It was virtually *all* vintage. In fact it could almost have been the All Souls cellar.

Despite the fact that I was trying to walk carefully my feet were stirring up quite a bit of dust. I breathed shallow to swallow as little as possible and approached the snug in the fireplace. This time with a torch I could see right inside the baker's oven. It was about eight feet deep. A few ancient ashes still covered some of the blackened brickwork.

Red wax lay in a dried puddle on top of the old stove in the fireplace. I broke off a piece that hung on the edge like an icicle and crumbled it into fragments between my fingers. The candle wick lay like a black worm in a frozen caldera. The temperature down here was pleasantly cool, the air totally odorless. No hint of the nauseating smell that I'd felt so strongly the other time.

I took a last sweep round with the torch and climbed back up to get changed for my unprotected foray into the world at large.

On the way, I tried the door to the master bedroom one more time. Still locked. The keyhole was blocked by a key on the inside, but armed with a screwdriver from downstairs, it took only seconds to push it out. I looked again. There was not much light, but I could make out part of a fireplace in the opposite wall, and a leather armchair. The gap at the foot of the door was too narrow to try to hook the fallen key and drag it out. It struck me as odd that the key should be on the *inside* of the door if no one was in the room. There was no obvious alternative way in.

———— • ————

The day was hot and I walked self-consciously. No one seemed to be following though a few heads turned my way, or so it seemed. This time there were no dark glasses.

I passed through the crowd in Harvard Square. The Coffee

216

Connection was filled with the aroma of fresh coffee beans. Amelia was already at a table in the far corner.

'What'll you have?' she asked, rising to greet me with a buss on both cheeks and a third for good measure.

'I'll have a cappuccino,' I said when the waitress came. So far so good. Not a reporter in sight. It was almost like being paroled. For a second I thought of Mannering's offer and what stood between me and a possible crown sentence.

Amelia ordered another *chocolat liégeois* and danish and asked for more Chantilly cream this time. She wore a cashmere sweater and a figure-hugger of a miniskirt. For once tweediness has been thrown to the winds.

My coffee arrived and I savored the aroma before tasting it. The place was half full. A couple came in. Amelia nodded in their direction and they waved back effusively. 'Friends on the faculty,' she whispered in response to my look.

She was asking about the phone calls. I explained that as far as Oxford was concerned I'd go back as if nothing had happened. Since I'd taken six months sabbatical leave, I'd actually be returning three months early. Roderick Tillman would be there. I wondered to myself what awkward questions Tillman would ask: Cunliffe-Jones too. I'd found out from my calls that he'd resigned from Caltech and would be joining British Biotechnology. As for John Fryer, his old department in San Diego had given him a second chance. I'd managed to speak to him yesterday evening. Fryer was going to get married to Ma Prem Deva and start work on a re-engineered retrovirus vectors project.

With a cry of 'My God, what's the time?' Amelia looked at her watch. 'I've got to see Bob Carr at two,' she said with relief in her voice. I gulped down the rest of my coffee and rose to take the bill to the desk.

I walked back over. 'Are you coming?'

'Sit down. There's one thing we haven't talked about. I've got a couple of minutes.'

I sat down on the edge of the chair.

'If we're going to London at the end of the week, what about Mannering?'

'I'll go along with him.' I dropped my voice. 'I'll phone him myself and tell him the cross is safe and sound. He can come with me to collect it. I think he'll accept if I put it back where

217

it came from myself. In his presence of course. I think that's how Shakespeare would want it to be.'

'You've got other ways of placating Shakespeare's shade,' she suggested quietly. 'You've turned him from a run-of-the-mill saint into a megastar.'

'Maybe he'll withdraw his curse out of gratitude.'

'If he wants peace as much as you do, maybe he'll double it,' she quipped. 'Did I tell you the Radcliffe Seminars have asked me to run a study tour of Stratford in June? They'll meet me in Oxford. You can come too if you're not still working your butt off.' She leaned over and gave me a lip-smacking kiss.

'You're going to be late.'

'Oh, Bob won't mind.' She looked at me expectantly. 'Well?' she said.

I looked puzzled.

'Haven't you noticed? Look round. See anything?'

Along the walls were nearabout a dozen of her paintings, each with a white sticker bearing a letter.

'They're the ones the gallery didn't sell,' she said. 'They've sold two here so far . . . on commission. Katie says I should work at it seriously. It's therapeutic.'

I was about to jest that it ought to bring in a useful income, then I thought better of it. A month earlier *Newsweek* had labeled her 'one of the last old-style heiresses in America'. Lucre was something I tried not to think about. Amelia was pig-rich, but after paying Jake and Roy five thousand quid each to become accomplices in my Stratford crime I was getting close to broke.

She gathered her bag off the table. 'I'll see you back home at six.'

'Would Bob Carr mind if I came with you?' I followed her to the door.

'I guess not. He might even be pleased to meet you. Only if the press are after your blood, well, y'know, be it on your head.'

For no particular reason I recalled the old man working in the garden before I left the house and I asked Amelia about him.

She gave me a peculiar look and asked: 'What old man?'

When I tried to describe him I found I couldn't remember anything about him. 'I only saw him briefly, from behind, from a distance.'

'Two girls do the gardening . . . and they come on Fridays. Today is Tuesday.'

She was looking a bit sallow and seemed anxious to change the subject. So I dropped it.

I wanted to go by Nini's Corner on the way to Bob Carr's office. When we got there I'd no sooner stopped to glance at the foreign newspapers than an antsy Amelia was nudging my arm. 'I'm coming,' I said.

'We're being followed,' she replied. A photographer and three journalists I recognized from the Whitehead stood a few yards away, ready to pounce. The photographer's camera was raised.

'Christ Almighty,' I groaned under my breath. I raised one hand to shield my face. At the same time I felt something of the thrill of the chase: the kind of excitement that had been missing at the ashram and which I'd savored climbing the hill at Big Sur.

We crossed quickly and entered the Yard. As we approached Sever I spotted the ambush but it was already too late. The motley platoon of newsmen launched its onslaught from a stand of trees. I cursed fluently. Either someone had tipped off the press while we were in the Coffee Connection, or worse, the phone in Hungerford House was bugged.

A salvo of questions shot from all flanks. There was a battery of cameras. 'You go without me,' I shouted after Amelia who was already yards ahead. If she heard, she paid no heed. She hurled her shoulders at the jostling crowd to get back to me and paddled to my side in safety, trembling with rage.

There were some twenty of them. A man brandishing a microphone and looking more aggressive than the rest advanced with his TV cameraman behind. I stepped forward to beard him and the reporter from NBC's *Today* show backed off. An NBC sound recordist wearing headphones swung a boom in front of my nose. I trapped the eye of the man holding the other end and yelled 'Bugger off' into the mike. The boom jerked away.

A shove at my elbow made me turn to my other side where the phalanx was being bulldozed from behind by a squad of students. 'Amelia,' I shouted. We were separated again and she was mouthing something. It was me, not her they wanted. I picked up her message in garbled pieces.

She'd go on to Bob Carr alone. I watched as she burst clear of the throng. This time she did attract attention – from the student mob. They were hooting and yelling at the unusual sight of her thus scantily clad, her curvy shape bursting from her blouse and what little skirt she had on. To hand in her resignation to Bob Carr she hadn't dressed in her usual sober garb, that was for sure.

The gentlemen of the fourth estate were still upon me: the bastards. With a last yell and wave at Amelia I began the long fight to retrace my course across the Yard, ignoring cameras, questions, microphones. When it was clear I wouldn't cooperate, a path opened up but the last pestering reporter didn't give up on me until I was back on Brattle Street.

———— • ————

Amelia felt a burst of energy as she reached the steps leading up to the front colonnade of the library. Everything had gone swimmingly with Bob Carr. Inside Widener, buoyed up with anticipation, she headed upstairs to the Periodicals Room where a woman attendant gave her a glance and a nod of recognition.

Someone had got to Case 48 before her: Nancy Bretton. *The Shakespeare Quarterly* was out that afternoon and the library's copy always arrived before departmental copies. As Amelia and Nancy both knew, its arrival could be timed not just to the day but to the hour. Amelia's advisor looked up as if this encounter was not unexpected. Each knew why the other was there. It was a joyous grin like that of a small boy with a new bicycle that Nancy Bretton found writ large over Amelia's face: a grin of triumph. It was too late to hide the pages the journal was open at. People were looking across the broad oak table.

'Congratulations.' The sarcasm in the older woman's tone needed no interpretation. 'So Mabel Sutherland' – she was referring to the editor of *The Shakespeare Quarterly* – 'was sufficiently convinced Shakespeare had syphilis to print your paper.'

Amelia knew she had the upper hand. Caught unprepared, Nancy was plainly trying to put on a brave face. Amelia could not resist the temptation to ask: 'I suppose he caught the pox from the seat of his privy?'

There was a flash of revulsion, a snarl from Nancy Bretton. She slammed the journal shut.

Unfazed, Amelia sat down opposite and dropping her voice added deliberate insult to injury with her next question: 'D'you think, dear Nancy, his penis maybe dropped off early in his life and that's why the Shakespeare Search hasn't been able to find any little bastards?'

Another snarl, disguised as a splutter, from Nancy.

'I see that *is* what you've been asking yourself,' Amelia pursued in full hue and cry after her quarry. 'You obviously haven't got to the end of my paper. Shakespeare's body, dear Nancy, was almost as intact in the grave as the mortal remains of Christian Rosenkreutz; even his dick – as immortal as his genius, if a little scarred.'

Words came to Nancy at last. 'You're a sex-crazed charlatan,' she hissed, glancing away only to encounter the acrid gaze of the foreign-looking woman at the inquiry desk.

Amelia was already on her feet. 'You can find yourself someone else to advise,' she declared. 'I'm moving to Oxford to finish my doctorate there.'

At this parting shot Nancy's lower jaw fell and she sat staring after Amelia's provocative figure.

———— • ————

'So what's going to happen with Daniel Bosworth?' Rosie asked.

'Clearly he's an issue for her and we have to take him into account. After all he's the crisis that brought her into analysis in the first place. There's no doubt about it.'

'Would you like some coffee? I'm fixing some anyway: strictly not decaf.'

Katie followed Rosie to the kitchen and helped herself to a slice of cake. 'You know something, Rosie, I've been thinking about Amelia's father; how she confuses him with Shakespeare in her phallocentric fantasies. It's pure guesswork but I think what she unconsciously saw in Bosworth was a figure who would rescue her from her father, a kind of knight in shining armor. He was someone on whom she could safely displace her incestuous feelings for her father.'

'Sure. We're out of skim milk. How about half-and-half?'

'Just this once.'

'If I follow your argument, you're going to say the white knight may turn out to be a false rescuer.'

'Not exactly, Rosie. In her mind Bosworth's associated with Shakespeare too through what he did going into that crypt. But we haven't met him,' Katie said as they returned to the living room, 'except through Amelia, and here we are talking about him so familiarly.'

'What does her father think about them getting married?'

'If he sees Bosworth as a serious rival and he's as pathologically jealous as I think he is it could turn nasty.' She added darkly: 'Lives could be at risk.'

'She's got to escape from that ogre somehow. Going to England with Bosworth may actually help.' Rosie shifted her meager weight around in her chair. 'Also I'm sure Bosworth's given her the excuse she was looking for to get away from that envious advisor of hers.'

'I can't comment on her advisor,' Katie said stuffily, 'but I'll comment till the cows come home if it'll help me get to the bottom of her relationship with her father. Y'see Rosie, I suspect Lawrence Hungerford is suffering from full-blown pathological narcissism. I've checked with one or two people and discovered the Hungerford family has a history of mental dysfunction . . . but because they were rich and powerful nobody locked them away. Lawrence Hungerford has the classic symptoms of manic grandiosity. You often see it exhibited in powerful males over the age of fifty. Men like that believe they have a right to command others and make obscene sums of money. Unconsciously they think they'll live forever in a universe with self as center. Society, sadly, tends to look up to people like that.'

'D'you think there's a connection between his relationship with Amelia and the fact he's not remarried?'

'That's more than probable. Lawrence Hungerford wields as much power in his daughter's inner world as he does in the outside world. You could say he's psychologically married to her, and she to him. That tells me women have the power to scare the hell out of Lawrence Hungerford. He's probably locked into an unconscious war with women in general. But there's more to the syndrome in his case. From what I've learnt about him there are signs of the complex psychopath. It could be dangerous for male rivals, or for women too, including Amelia.'

'A psychosexual pathology?'

'Without doubt; one that Amelia's heavily involved in. Did it occur to you he doesn't have a son and heir?'

'I didn't think about it.'

222

'Did you ever hear of a megalomaniac who didn't want a son and heir?'

'No. Are all megalomaniacs male?'

'Mostly. Lawrence had a son once. He was born prematurely and though a whole hospital of medics fought to save him he died the next day. His wife died a few months afterward.'

'That's kind of weird. You're not suggesting he wants to get Amelia pregnant, are you?'

Katie burst out laughing. 'Dear Rosie, you get the wildest ideas. You'll be telling me next only the power of the Holy Spirit can heal Amelia.'

Rosie was not amused. 'I prayed to God for a word of knowledge about Amelia and he spoke to me powerfully. The word was "son".'

———— ● ————

When my limousine pulled up in front of the Whitehead around midday it was surrounded by a score of hectoring reporters, photographers and TV cameramen. I recognized most of the faces by now. Many of them had been in the Harvard Yard attack.

I stalked to the front door, shouldering off attention with the limo driver's assistance. The cute receptionist gave me a smile. When I got to Ben Talbot's lab on the fourth floor I found the Director on a call.

'Got a problem?' Ben asked, putting down the phone.

'Those bastards from the media.'

'We caught two people snooping round inside this morning. Anything I can do to help, like I said, just yell.'

'Did you get anything on Bendix?'

'Not a lot. I talked to a doctor friend. Bendix is the Hungerfords' doctor like his father before him. Bachelor all his life. Well respected. Harvard Med School then pharmacology, but he opted for general practice in the neighborhood. Worked with his father till the old man died. People say Bendix is Lawrence Hungerford's closest friend.' Talbot held up his right hand to illustrate his point. The first two fingers were wrapped round each other. 'Some people say he's Lawrence Hungerford's only friend: almost his shadow. That's about it.'

'Thanks, Ben. That'll do fine.'

'Meeting in half an hour with Chuck Morrell – I guess you don't know him – to talk about a new vectors project. Chuck's from the Massachusetts General Hospital. Would you like to come? It's only in Boston.'

'I can't, Ben. Thanks all the same. Got to pack.'

Ben Talbot and I exchanged promises to keep in touch and Ben excused himself, leaving me alone in the lab.

Before I left I sat down at Talbot's desk, pulled a piece of paper from my pocket and dialed a number in Warwickshire on the desktop phone. It rang at least a dozen times before Mannering himself answered.

14

My tongue-tied Muse in manners holds her still,
While comments of your praise, richly compil'd,
Reserve their character with golden quill,
And precious phrase by all the Muses fil'd.

Sonnets, 85
William Shakespeare

The haze of a spring day lay over the English countryside north
of the Channel and the South Downs as the plane alighted eleven
weeks and six days after my clandestine departure for Boston. In
the Immigration Hall I split from Amelia. The duty officer gave
me a brief glance and I was through. I felt in good shape as I
pocketed my passport. Almost too hot for a coat but I kept my
Burberry on.

With Amelia behind and a baggage trolley in front I made for
the Green Channel. All I had to get through Customs were the
same suitcases I'd taken to America. Talbot had agreed to arrange
air-freighting my security cabinet over a few days later along with
the database. At the doors that were all that separated us from the
outside world I waited for Amelia to come alongside. This was it:
home territory.

The doors opened and we walked straight into a ratpack of
newspaper hacks and scribes. I took in the crowded faces. *Bloody
gutter press: not again.* There were cameras and questions. I pushed
the trolly expecting bodies to make way but our path remained
blocked. In the background travelers stopped to gawk.

'Will you look for a green lamplighter in England?'

'Do you think Shakespeare was homosexual?'

'Do you always swim half nude?' The question fired at Amelia
came from a woman reporter, alluding to an old *paparazzo* shot
taken in the Virgin Islands. The picture had appeared in the
issue of the *National Enquirer* that divulged her relationship with

225

me. To her disgust as much as mine they'd titled her my 'heiress protector'. There had been no denying the minimalist nature of the swimsuit.

A reporter stumbled against Amelia, shoved from the rear. His hand went out to save him and encountered Amelia's bosom. He pulled back muttering in his embarrassment and turned angrily on the man behind him who replied by making a demotic gesture with two fingers.

'Dr Bosworth! Dr Bosworth!'

I ignored the call until its distinct tone registered and I craned over the heads of the mob to glimpse a figure wearing a dog-collar. The parson gesticulated from behind a BBC cameraman, pointing in the direction he wanted us to go.

I gave the trolly a heave and with Amelia clinging to my arm we barged our way clear. The pressure from behind subsided as Adrian Mannering raised his right arm like Moses parting the Red Sea. The pack pulled back.

Mannering was surprisingly low-voltage considering the circumstances. I thought I saw a twinkle around his eyes, even if it did seem to be directed at Amelia. In his Volvo estate heading into London on the M4 there was time to talk. I sat alone in the back seat.

'It will take a good deal of digging to open your tunnel,' Mannering was saying. 'We refilled it some weeks ago. I was going to ask you to pay for the cost of all the work but you'll be pleased to know donations to Holy Trinity have quadrupled since February so I think we'll let the matter drop.' Amelia twisted round in her seat and placed a hand on my knee.

'It took us twenty-four freezing nights to dig it in the first place,' I replied.

'I'm surprised it didn't cave in on you. Only we three and Inspector Drake and Dr Gillespie the archeologist will be going into the crypt in two weeks time. Again the public will be disappointed but the media and other interested parties will get in there over my dead body.' Obviously he knew I knew who Inspector Drake was; that or I was meant to ask him. I did no such thing and he prattled on.

Opposite the Sheraton Park Tower in Knightsbridge I started at the sudden threnody of a police siren. I watched the flashing light woffing off into the Hyde Park Corner underpass. Mannering was reminded of something. 'As you're aware, in view of your gesture, Holy Trinity has decided not to pursue the matter of criminal charges. For that matter neither will the police. However as I told you on the phone they'd like a short word with you just to tie the ends of the red tape together.'

When the car emerged into Piccadilly we stammered to a crawl in sclerotic traffic beside Green Park. Some things about London never changed. 'I'll let you out here,' Mannering said near the corner of Albemarle Street, 'and wait for you outside the door.' I sprang from the car and weaved my way to the top of St James's Street where I vaulted the railing.

The London Security Company had been recommended by Dunkley, whose office was next door. It took two minutes for me to announce myself and be shown to a windowless room with a green baize table. Here I'd no sooner taken a seat than one of the managers came in. He produced a paper for signature and checked it against a file facsimile before asking me to repeat my password. My nerves were perfectly calm but the manager's seemed on edge. He looked at the clock on the wall and completed the time on a form.

'This way, Dr Bosworth. I hope you've got your key?'

The elevator was embarrassingly small and it was impossible to tell how many floors we'd gone below ground when the Victorian cage came to a halt. The grille and the outer door opened and we came face to face with an attendant stationed on the other side of six steel bars. The manager showed an ID.

The door opened and clanged shut, leaving the three of us in a cramped area facing a second door. The attendant pressed a button. There was no sign of whoever looked out through the fisheye lens in the wall, but a moment later the door swung open. I could see it was almost half a foot thick.

Along one wall were several hundred safe deposit boxes in rows of varying sizes. I headed for box C194 and put my key in the left-hand lock. The manager produced a flat key from his pocket and, reaching across my arm, inserted it in the lock on the right of the first. The two keys rotated clockwise through one hundred and eighty degrees.

The manager indicated the table with its solitary chair and went to a room off the main vault to join the attendant. I jerked the box from its slot and placed it on the table. The air was cool and dry. There was no sign of monitor cameras but I was taking no chances. I turned my back on the anteroom door.

I lifted the green metal lid and stared in.

My treasure was there.

Unsullied.

———— • ————

Mannering drove back along Piccadilly, crawled round Hyde Park Corner and headed down Grosvenor Place toward Victoria Street.

'Here, let me straighten your tie,' Amelia said. We were outside the elevator on the eighth floor of New Scotland Yard. I leaned forward. Mannering waited. After half a minute he coughed politely.

When we went in, Detective Chief Inspector Tom Drake of the Criminal Investigation Department, in plain clothes, rose slowly from his chair and introduced another man with the rank of Detective Constable: Frank Hillaby, an intense-looking man in his twenties, more features than face. His name hit me like a hammer. So this was the cop with the busted collarbone caught trying to get into the ashram with an officer of the FBI. No wonder he was giving me that look. It wasn't hostile but it was no pal's act either.

Drake, who looked taller than on a TV screen and much older than when I'd met him seven years earlier, waved us to seats, ignoring my outstretched hand, and sat down behind an oak-veneer desk. Here in London after so many years he was still a Yorkshireman with a Yorkshire way of putting things that left no room for maneuver. I placed him around fifty-eight, maybe sixty. His hair was short and gray. He was flicking through a sheaf of notes in front of him.

When Drake looked up I caught the sharp eye of Hillaby sitting off to one side with a notebook on his lap. 'I won't keep you long, Dr Bosworth,' said Drake. 'Let me point out straight away, if it weren't for the research you're doing you wouldn't be walking away scot-free from your little digging expedition.' Mannering nodded and coughed politely as if to signal his agreement.

'There's one little matter,' Drake went on. 'How did your two Stratford associates come by the sum of five thousand pounds each?'

I looked at my fingertips at the mention of money and Jake and Roy. 'I had to pay them or they wouldn't have done it. No one was going to do it for nothing. Except me,' I added, meeting Amelia's gaze for half a second. She looked away.

Drake was sifting his notes when a Scotland Yard tea lady came in with an urn on a trolly and started handing out cups.

'I assume you're not going to charge them with anything?' I asked, taking a cup.

'Don't assume anything, Dr Bosworth. In a case like this I'm the one who's entitled to make assumptions. When we checked up on your friends we found they'd been having a grand old time armed with your money and a little black book that contained the name and phone number of every prostitute known to the police from Slough to Swindon . . . and a few more besides.'

I exploded. 'That book's confidential and it's strictly for professional purposes! I never dipped into it myself. I've never needed to *pay* for sex. The women – and the men – get paid out of university funds for volunteering for research into sexually transmitted diseases.' This was the first I knew of my duplicate black book – what I called my Filofucks – being stolen from my room at Forest Spring. Jake and Roy were in for one hell of a bollocking.

'Calm down, Dr Bosworth. No one's accusing you of anything. But if your two accomplices didn't have AIDS before they set off on their brothel tour I'm sure they must have caught a dose by now.' He opened a desk drawer and pulled out my address book. 'I'm giving this back to you. Lock it up safely in future. And next time you want to poke around in a grave, do what you've done in the past and get an official authorization.'

Just when I was thinking: *That's it, we're finished*, Drake said: 'There's the little matter of a girl called Polly Ann in California.'

I gulped. I'd been trying not to think about her. Again I saw her sweet smile and for a moment I wanted to die.

'We have good liaison with our opposite numbers over there. You'll be relieved to know your ex-girlfriend' – at this point he looked carefully at Amelia – 'is thought to have committed suicide. Motive unknown. The postmortem showed no evidence of skulduggery.' He was looking back at me now from small eyes that struggled to escape between shaggy brows and puffy pouches. I tried not to blink. 'There won't be an inquest for you to attend.'

I suddenly found myself wondering if chimpanzees could swim.

I hadn't a clue and made a mental note to find out. Despite the relief, I was left wondering what else Drake knew about me. Maybe my private thoughts were on the New Scotland Yard computer. I was about to ask when Drake leapt to his feet and said, 'Thank you for coming in.'

Amelia was still cradling her cup on her knees. Dumbly I thought her tea must be growing cold. Drake looked to Frank Hillaby, who replied by shaking his head as he stood up.

The interview was over.

I was about to ask Drake to explain why he'd reopened the file on my mother, then decided it wasn't the moment: not in front of Mannering. Like Drake he already knew too much about me.

This time Drake shook hands, but Amelia made no attempt to offer hers. I caught a keen look in the eye of the taciturn Hillaby and picked my black book off the desk. When I asked with half a voice how his shoulder was, the constable gave me a nod of acknowledgement and said: 'Just twinges.' Then as if regretting his reply he wiped any sign of comprehension off his features. I turned back to Drake and buried the book in my jacket pocket next to the bulge in my raincoat. Something about the way Drake was looking at me made me feel transparent, as if he could see right through to the cross. I made a mental note to tackle him on his own. I knew I'd got to find my mother . . . and the vaccine. I was doing it for her, in a funny kind of way. *Easy, Daniel.*

Outside in the corridor I loosened my tie.

Mannering turned off at Exit 15 in the direction of Ramsbury near the Wiltshire–Berkshire border and soon we drove in through the stone gates of Forest Spring. The Colonel's estate butted against the Elizabethan manor of Littlecote.

The russet-brick farmhouse was big but not grand enough to be called stately. Fully restored, the sixteenth-century structure was a Grade Two star listed building. It stood at the edge of the estate with woodland and paddocks on one side and farmland, separated from view by outbuildings, on the other. On the side away from the drive was a formal eighteenth-century Italian garden walled at the far extremity with brick and flintstone.

Matthew appeared as the station wagon rolled up at the front door with its canopy of spring honeysuckle. The Colonel, a good few inches shorter, was behind him. In spite of his Norfolk jacket, perhaps thanks to his categorical mustache, the Colonel looked more like a soldier than a clubbable country landowner. Though he'd been out of the army for years he still had the exaggerated posture of a soldier. When he came forward he limped. Another exaggeration to justify tales of Rommel and the Western Desert. One that had earned him the nickname 'Stiffy'. That or something else.

I glanced over in response to a cry of 'Yooee'. Sue, looking a bit on the porky side since I saw her last but as Sloany pony as ever, appeared in green Hunters and a headscarf from the vicinity of the loose boxes. A string of pearls hung round her neck under a navy puffa. A moment later an unprepossessing Hattie Bosworth was standing beside her in a decrepit Barbour.

Maybe Hattie was screwing the vicar: maybe she wasn't. He was certainly giving her something more substantial than tea and sympathy while the old goat looked obligingly the other way. Hattie had typecast herself as the long-suffering gentlewoman to whom every good thing in life was due by virtue of a congenital hyperlectic twang that could – and often did – make itself heard from Harvey Nicks to Peter Jones.

'You could have written,' she scolded. I looked at the mucky hands my adoptive mother held out to her sides as she proffered her cheek for a mid-air kiss. I obliged her and gave Sue a hug before turning to introduce Amelia, and Mannering who stood scuffing his feet on the gravel. Amelia was immediately the center of attention. As we made our way to the drawing room Hattie as usual was wittering on and Amelia was fielding the polite questions that probed indirectly to get the measure of her. There weren't many people who weren't cowed by Hattie the first time they met her. She could be pretty overpowering, but Amelia could handle her, no problem. Amelia wasn't at all the way my family expected an American heiress to be: she might almost have been English but for the lilt of that Bostonian accent. I could tell at once that Matthew liked her.

When Adrian Mannering said he had to be going, Hattie informed him the kettle was just coming to the boil and insisted he stay. Mannering acquiesced and Hattie rang her diddy little silver bell to summon Mrs Patridge, her ancient daily who doubled as lackey and just about everything that would once have been called a servant.

I was leaning back against the stone fireplace when Matthew caught my eye and I looked away to where the Colonel sat in his blue chintz armchair. He was glaring at Mrs Patridge as she unloaded the tea things from a pewter tray. I knew the old boy would want to conduct his own court martial in the smoking room afterwards. There would be some explaining to do about the Stratford business. He was already looking huffy, planning his attack. Though I did have a soft spot for him, Matthew was the closest thing I had to a confessor.

Dancer, our old black labrador, shambled in front of us. As we came to the end of the withy walk at the ha-ha that skirted one side of the weed-choked lake Matthew flung a stone out into the water, narrowly missing one of the Colonel's prized ducks. I visualized a hand appearing from among the lilies, trailing a wet sleeve, catching the stone, but it plopped and was gone and the duck had second thoughts about taking off. We each carried a glass of Pimm's Number Six Cup jam-full of mint from the vegetable garden.

'What's she really like,' Matthew demanded, 'now that you know her better?'

'Like I explained before, she's kind of neurotic.'

'Can you imagine anyone like that being sane?'

'Yes, but not Amelia.'

'Money for old rope if you marry her.'

'Believe me, I won't feel a penny richer.'

'What about the one you were rogering day and night who was into all that guru caper?'

'Dead . . . suicide.'

He didn't ask for details. It was hard to face the fact Polly Ann was really dead and without thinking how stupid it sounded I tried to make light of it as I drove her drowned face, Ophelia-like, from my mind's eye. 'You know the type she was. Pheromone fuzzbox. Tantric sex. Y'know, they worship the Great Donger, things like that. God, the things I do for England.'

Matthew glanced across at me with a wide smile. That was the best thing about Matthew. He was never seriously envious. He just pretended to be, sometimes. I'd placed my glass on the ground and stood throwing pebbles into the water. What was left of the palladian folly faced us across the water. In front of it was a

232

cast lead statue of Minerva. 'Are you doing the right thing, getting married?' he asked. 'Is she worth the candle?'

'That's what worries the hell out of me,' I said fretfully.

We walked round the lake and sat down on the mossy bank with the ivy-covered folly behind us, half-hidden in rhododendrons. The only sound was the song of the blackbirds on the other side of the spinney and the twitter of a tomtit from beneath the dilapidated roof. I explained everything.

'Does this Zen crackpot Marcus Freeman make you jealous?' Matthew asked when he could get a word in.

'I guess so.'

'And her father's possessive about her too?'

I nodded assent.

'You always did go for the ones who'd end up hurting you. Think of Lucy.'

'I can't help it, believe me. If my nerves hadn't been so ragged what with Lucy and years of divorce on top of everything else, then the whole Stratford thing, maybe I'd not have asked her to marry me. She said "yes" just a bit too quickly. Sometimes I think I'm going stark raving.'

If Matthew had a reply to that he was careful not to voice it. There were some things in my past even he wouldn't talk about. He was looking soddenly into the mint at the bottom of his glass and asking: 'And *her* problem you told me about?' I'd not given him the details; just told him she had this neurosis and went to this analyst. 'Isn't that really what's bugging you more than her father being jealous of you?'

'I suppose it's both really. And Polly Ann. No one will come out with it and say so, not even Amelia, but they all think it's my fault she killed herself as if I left her with a broken heart.'

'Didn't you?'

'Oh she was upset alright, but not *that* upset. She'd been beaten up at the ashram and she begged me not to leave her there with that sonofabitch guru. But she didn't look the sort to die for the love of anyone, let alone me.'

'You think maybe it wasn't suicide?'

There was a flurry on the water and the regular batting of wings as the duck did a perfect take-off. 'Uhuh, maybe. Someone could have pushed her off the cliff. She wouldn't have lasted long in that freezing water – not in the middle of the night.'

233

'Is there anything you can do about it?'

'Not a lot except keep on fighting for control . . . of me, my life. Sometimes I think I'm losing. There are things I want to say to Amelia, but they won't come out. Something stops me.'

'Trust?'

'Lack of it. I don't have anyone to say that to apart from you. You know the shit I've been through like the whole world's ganging up on me. I just don't want to lose because if I do, this time I might not pull through.' I stopped myself from telling him about the eight days of my life that had gone missing at Big Sur.

'Have you told Amelia about y'know?' This time he dared to hint at it.

'No. How could I? She's got her own problems without having to handle mine. Jeezers, Matthew, what a pair, her and me, fighting to keep our heads above water. The last thing I need is to marry someone else like that . . .'

He seemed perplexed as he glanced at his watch and suggested we complete our tour of the lake following the woodland walk as far as the ancient mulberry tree that we used to build huts in when we were kids. Tailed by Dancer, we set off and five minutes later we were taking one of the paths that criss-crossed the lawn at the rear of the cob-walled coach house.

After an early supper I picked a blue hyacinth from the east side of the house and set off for the churchyard to visit my mother's grave, thinking about Jake and Roy. They'd worked for the Colonel for years, but when he'd got wind of their sexual exploits after Drake told him about my little black book, he'd fired them on the spot and they'd disappeared from the village from one day to the next. I wasn't looking forward to being carpeted that evening and I slowed my pace.

———— • ————

My rooms at All Souls were bachelor quarters, so for a week we took a suite at the Randolph while Amelia hunted up and down the Victorian houses of North Oxford with a copy of the *Oxford Evening News* and an agent from Andrews real estate office at Carfax.

Through her contacts it took her two days to arrange matriculation. However, it turned out to be more difficult to get an exemption from 'keeping terms' for the minimum two years required for an Oxford D. Phil. In the end they granted her, exceptionally, three terms cross-credited from Harvard, which would enable her to complete her doctorate after one more year of research.

Nancy Bretton, Amelia told me with a grin, had looked flabbergasted when she'd learnt of her plan to abscond from Harvard, but Bob Carr had been full of understanding when she'd visited him contritely, and more soberly dressed than the first time, the day before her departure. His call to Elizabeth Chambers, her new supervisor at Lady Margaret Hall, had worked miracles in short-cutting the Oxford system. Amelia, I knew without asking, would always have a soft spot for Bob Carr. He'd agreed to rescind her teaching contract on condition she returned at a later date to give a special lecture if she finally uncovered the real Dark Lady. He must have known what a riot he'd have to deal with when her Senior groupies learnt they'd been abandoned.

I was aware there were Harvard faculty – not just Nancy Bretton – who would not be sorry to see the back of Bob Carr's departmental whiz. Amelia's pronouncements on Shakespeare had been rumored to be getting outlandish of late and there had been growing pressure not to extend her teaching appointment.

With the house agent Amelia found us a comfortable furnished flat on the second floor of a redbrick house up the Banbury Road and the following day she helped direct the men who came to move everything from my rooms in college. The building, with its view from our bedroom over the tree-filled lawns and herbaceous borders of middle-class Oxford, was owned by St John's. The agent warned we would have to put up with a group of undergraduates on the floor below. I noticed the sitting room had one of those kitsch artificial gas fires. But it also had a piano, which was the main reason Amelia liked the place.

The silver T-cross was securely lodged in a cashbox in the bursar's safe at All Souls.

Forty yards from the rope two policemen stood guarding a makeshift shack on the west bank of the Avon. Yesterday under Mannering's watchful eye students from the archeology department at Exeter University had all but finished digging and shoring up the tunnel. Dr Clive Gillespie from the Oxford University

Laboratory for Archaeology had joined the excavation toward the end.

The temperature was closing on seventy-five degrees when Amelia and I walked into Holy Trinity through the main door in the north wall of the nave. The church, like the churchyard, was closed to the public. Adrian Mannering waited inside, his clerical collar emerging from the top of black overalls. He gave me a more tepid reception than at Heathrow. 'You'll find it shadier in here,' he said shaking hands dismissively. When he turned to Amelia his features relaxed. 'It's all ready.' He pointed in the direction of the north transept. 'The sexton's arranged suitable clothing. You'll find it on the bench in the vestry. I hope it fits.'

Mannering handed Amelia the earthenware vessel which we found him holding when we returned in overalls and wellingtons. 'Holy water?' she asked in a jumpy voice. The receptacle looked ancient. She turned it round, taking care not to dislodge the stopper.

'Yes do be careful with it, my dear. It's probably as old as the church itself, perhaps older. We don't have many relics in Holy Trinity. This one was used for requiem mass before the Reformation.'

'I'm just going to take another look at Shakespeare above ground,' Amelia said. 'It's four years since the last time I was here. I'm supposed to be showing some people round Stratford at the end of the month.' Cradling the chalice in both hands, she passed it back.

Mannering and I followed her up the aisle past Clopton Chapel, the vestry, the old carved pews of the quiristers and the font in which Shakespeare was baptized in 1564, to the roped-off area of the chancel.

Shakespeare – a plump Shakespeare – gazed down from the wall on the left: the Shakespeare sculpted by Gheerart Janssen, the bourgeois Bard whom scholars couldn't reconcile with the genius of his work. My heart drumming, I stared at the gravestone with its malediction.

Amelia drew my attention to the T-shaped spade of Priapus at top left of the bust. 'Fertility, regeneration, immortality – and the mystic enlightenment of sex,' she said in a distinct voice. 'Priapus was the son of Venus and androgynous Dionysus.'

Mannering coughed behind us and checked his watch. 'I think

it's time to go; almost two o'clock.' He proceeded to frogmarch us, so to speak, back down the aisle.

Outside the shack one of the policemen made a saluting gesture. Almost hidden from view trailed the mud-covered figures of the final shift behind a hillock of soil. Unlike me, they hadn't used the river to get rid of their diggings.

I turned on the rubber-coated torch Mannering had given me and stepped inside the makeshift shack that leaned out over the bank. I squinted down the steps. Amelia followed, grasping two torches to shine the way for Mannering, who balanced the chalice in one hand and held onto a rope handrail with the other. She slowed for him. Crouching, I continued down the joisted conduit. At least the air was less revolting this time round. The ground sloped at first but the last twenty yards were flat, covered in a layer of sludge which made a soft sucking underfoot. The passage had only been damp before: now water from the river was seeping through.

I made out a light ahead and in the aperture in the vault's wall met Gillespie for the first time. The archeologist transferred his torch and held out a blackened hand: 'Clive Gillespie, Balliol.' He looked a worried man.

'Daniel Bosworth, All Souls.'

My hands were clean despite the passage I'd just navigated. Gillespie saw the look and withdrew his hand. The aperture was completely open. Inside the vault the ground had a glutinous consistency. I scraped at the surface with my foot.

'Terracotta tiles,' Gillespie said. 'Twelfth century. This crypt predates the one directly above it, which means there was probably an early-medieval church on this site. This is the original crypt. There are bones here going back seven or eight hundred years, maybe more. Are the others coming?'

'They're just behind.' I stared into the gloom and almost jumped. A dark shape glided out from behind an oaken upright. As it stepped into the pool from my torch I recognized Tom Drake. He nodded in my direction as if he was reluctant to acknowledge me at all. I could only nod back. I heaved my shoulders and returned my attention to Gillespie, aware that Drake's eyes were watching every move I made.

'Pity Reverend Mannering won't authorize a proper excavation,' Gillespie said. 'I've had the last hour to snoop around. Over there,' he shone his torch across the top of the sarcophagi, 'there's an archway with a groined roof. Beyond it there's a cavity in the wall containing a reliquary with four lead boxes that probably hold bones of local saints. One has an ivory fish in the top.'

'Daniel, give me a hand.' Amelia's voice was squeaky with nerves. I took her torch while she helped Mannering as he shuffled forward holding the chalice at arm's length. Drake nodded at each in turn.

Gillespie stood on the other side of Shakespeare's sarcophagus. Amelia stared at it, then shone her torch round the chamber, awed by the neat tiers of bones. There was a pungent smell that made me hold my breath. I turned to find Mannering genuflecting at the foot of the grave. The chalice lay on top of the one next to it. 'Let us remove the slab,' Mannering pronounced, assuming the mournful intonation of the Anglican pulpit.

Amelia took care of the torches. Gillespie gave the orders. Resentfully I noticed that Drake was only going to be a spectator. What the hell was he playing at? The rest of us got into position and heaved. It took several minutes before the stone lay round at right angles. Mannering, breathing hard, crossed himself.

'It's hotter down here than you'd expect,' Gillespie pointed out unnecessarily as he ducked out of sight. When he resurfaced he carried a battery pack connected to a needle-thin cutting blade.

As Gillespie worked on the lead for the next half hour I found I was mesmerized by the casket lid. Amelia too kept gazing at it while off to one side her fingers worked distractedly up and down the furrows of the poet's rough coat of arms in the top of the slab, as if trying to clean it with her chewed fingernails. Or was she getting a sense of something by touch, like a clairvoyant who needed to feel something belonging to a departed loved one in order to make contact with the spirit world? Twice, as if perhaps to prove she wasn't imagining things, she ran her hands all over the lead surface inside the sarcophagus. Each time she did so Gillespie straightened up and switched off the cutter. The second time his task was done.

Mannering's eyes were shut as he murmured a prayer. Just as I was beginning to wonder if the mumbo-jumbo would ever end the clergyman dropped to his knees and recited a short supplication: 'Our Poet asked that his bones remain undisturbed through the ages. We who are likewise subject to the mutability of our mortal coils are here today to keep faith with him and ensure that his last wish is respected . . .'

With a glance toward Amelia Mannering took from his pocket what looked like a gold eggcup. Amelia put the torches down and picked up the chalice. She took out the stopper and poured Holy Water into the gold vessel.

'. . . *et spiritus sancti.*' Mannering had on his most precious look, that I'd noticed he wore like a uniform whenever he was sermonizing, which was virtually every time he spoke. He sprinkled dashes of water on the casket and delivered an orotund blessing before signaling Amelia to refill the cup.

It was time to open the casket and put an end to this mummery. Mannering picked up a torch in his free hand. I used the small crowbar Gillespie had passed me to prise up the lid. Gillespie got his fingers under the edge on the opposite side and the two of us lifted together.

Amelia's thin scream went reverberating round the walls of the chamber. Her hands went up to cover her face and the chalice crashed to the ground, breaking into half a dozen fragments. But my first thought was for Shakespeare. I shone my torch straight into the coffin. My face fell. As I'd expected, fresh bacteria had got in when I'd opened the coffin in January and they'd been multiplying, playing havoc with the corpse, once so perfectly hearsed, ever since. Even though the lead had been resealed within a month. Now the body was ravaged. Already the moldering head had begun to resemble a skull. The trumpet nose had turned into a hole. The lower jaw had loosened and moved, exaggerating the frightful mouth that echoed Amelia in a silent scream. Parts of the winding shroud had turned to shreds. A fungus had taken hold of the ghoulish hands that clutched a sere pelvis like the talons of a hawk.

Mannering, still holding the gold cup, moved one foot toward Amelia and slipped, lurching against the slab. His spectacles clattered on the ground. The cup tilted, spilling holy water across the Bard's midriff. Gillespie and I looked at each other in consternation and quickly dropped the coffin lid sideways over the top of the slab.

I stared in shock as Amelia sank to the floor, her arms stiff at her sides, her body rigid. Mannering had replaced his spectacles and was making a sign over her. Drake emerged out of the darkness holding a torch and he and Mannering appeared to communicate without speaking. I was rooted to where I stood, fearfully aware that Amelia was having some kind of an epileptic fit. I leaned over and picked up my torch.

Her eyes twisted up into the top of her head so that only the whites showed . . . ghoulishly. Only seconds had elapsed since her first scream. It felt like minutes. I waved my light at Mannering and Drake and finally there were words: 'Help her.' I heard my hoarse whisper. Mannering was already on his knees beside her. Drake was bending over her from the other side. She was gurgling and saliva ran down the side of her face. Her body was twisting this way and that on the dirty floor as if she were bound with cords and an immensely powerful but invisible creature had hold of her and was flicking her body around. *Help her*, I shouted. Gillespie was still standing rigid with a slack jaw.

Amelia's back curved into an arch, like a bow taut to breaking. At that instant Mannering, so calmly I thought, seized hold of her shoulders and bending right down, pressed his mouth close to her ear. Drake seemed untroubled. I was shouting something I couldn't even understand. Drake was kneeling on the ground pushing down on her ankles with what looked like incredible strength. Even so the two men were only just able to hold her. For a moment it looked like the force of her convulsion would throw them off and she'd rise into the air. But Mannering was saying something in a low voice. I strained to hear but it was well nigh impossible against the slurry of sound erupting from Amelia's throat. I caught only the Latin: *in nomine filii* . . .

Amelia's body relaxed. Mannering glanced at Drake for a second then from me to Gillespie and, relinquishing his hold on her, straightened up, leaving her huddled there, panting. Her eyes were flickering this way and that, but were back in the part of her head where they belonged. She had a congested look to her. In fact she looked a pathetic spectacle, but at least the attack was over. The whole thing had only lasted a couple of minutes. At last I was able to move and I went to help her, first to a sitting position, then to her feet.

She stood whimpering, covered in filth. Her hands were over her face again. Drake had drawn back into the shadows. Mannering seemed to be leaving center stage to me. Gillespie produced a calorgas blowlamp and a small hammer.

'Hold it,' I cautioned. 'We still have something to do.' My words were directed at the clergyman.

Mannering loomed so tall I felt I had shrunk.

Amelia lowered one hand from her eyes, crossed herself hurriedly and covered her face again. Up to then she'd seemed about as religious as a praying mantis. I could see her lips moving in silence. Her face looked dreadful.

I put one hand into my overalls and brought out the silver T-cross. It glinted, sending an arc across the back of Amelia's raised hand. I fondled the amulet for several seconds, noticing again the small grooves at the ends of the crosspiece.

I held the symbol of fertility out to Mannering, who stared stolidly back at me. What sort of cross had he expected? I knew Amelia hadn't told him to expect a Tau . . . or any kind of cross in particular. Had he got *any* emotions?

Peeping between her fingers Amelia caught sight of the cross and the Bard's corpse again. She let out a second nerve-shattering scream which Mannering ignored as he mumbled something in Latin in a solemn voice. The shards of the broken vessel lay scattered around his feet.

I raised the T-cross to my lips. Amelia watched between fingers still fanned across her face as I fumbled to reinstate the artefact between Shakespeare's hands, *patibulum* toward the head, *stipes* pointing at something the size of an inch-worm, the tiny mortified penis that had still been surprisingly substantial back in January. The Bard's decrepit fingers were now so stiff that I had to use force to get the cross back into its original position. As I pulled them apart the whole corpse seemed to sink a fraction and the last remnants of the calico top-knot round the head gave way. The effect was horrific to watch. The lower jaw, already stretched open to create an inch gap between what remained of the upper and lower teeth, suddenly widened another couple of inches when the support of the cloth band was removed from under the chin. The mouth was now gaping wide. The thin lips that had been pulled back on my last visit had vanished completely, but skin still adhered to parts of the cheekbones in dried patches. I forced the cross into place and stood back before letting out a deep breath.

As the lead was resealed Mannering watched stiffly, lips moving in tacit prayer. Amelia was in tears. I passed her a torch. She took it numbly and shone it at the grave. When I

241

looked to where Drake was standing, I could just make out his shadowy form.

Mannering's self-control was impressive. He picked up the pieces of the broken pot and joined with Gillespie and me to work the slab back into place. Amelia was swaying backwards and forwards. Mannering looked her way. 'Are you going to be alright?' he asked.

'She's fine,' I answered for her. I took her by the hand and she followed limply. I still wanted to interrogate Drake about my mother but this was hardly the time and place.

———— • ————

I gunned the car in the direction of Stratford's town center, the roundabout and the road to Oxford. A sidelong check told me Amelia was going to be fine in spite of the fact she looked washed out. With her dirty hands and hair she was a total mess. She managed a smile. I said nothing yet, leaving her to think things out before I put my questions. Christ Almighty, what a fiasco.

'You had a terrible convulsion, sweetie. Can you remember anything?'

With the top down Amelia's hair flew in the wind. I told her I thought she might have had an epileptic fit and she almost seemed relieved by that, as if any kind of fit was better than turning into Black Jenny again . . . in front of people. She had only vague recall of going down into the crypt and nothing after that until we emerged into the sunlight above. She was still shaken and didn't want to talk about it. Her head was throbbing and she felt like she wanted to be sick, she told me, sounding awfully subdued.

'Did you put the cross back?' Her voice faltered. 'What did he look like . . . Shakespeare?' A pause. A sniff. 'Was Mannering jarred when he saw the cross?'

'"When I in earth am rotten . . ." Basically he looked pretty ill.' I tried to make light of what had happened. 'The cross is back where it came from. Mannering didn't seem surprised . . . not happy or dismayed. He was totally unmoved. Drake too. God, what a weirdo that guy is.' I tried to explain exactly what had happened; how Mannering and Drake had held her, but all she wanted to talk about was the cross, almost as if she didn't want to think about her attack.

'Did Mannering expect a *crux capita*, y'know, the regular Christian cross?' she asked, 'or the *crux commissa*?' She was looking terribly pale still, under the dirt smudged over her face, when I glanced at her.

'The *crux* what, sweetie?'

'The *crux commissa*, the Tau that proves Shakespeare was a heterodox Christian.'

'I don't know what he expected, but if he has any sense he'll stop criticizing your theories from now on.' I mentioned the broken chalice and she seemed upset. 'You've broken a priceless relic.'

'Just don't go on bugging me.' She pulled her head away from me. A snippy voice. 'Anyway, why did you take the cross from Shakespeare in the first place? No one said to.'

'I told you before, it seemed like the right thing to do at the time. I mean it wasn't just a souvenir or something. It felt *right*, like something was really pressing me to do it. A voice said "Take it" and I took it.' She'd only asked once before why I'd taken it . . . the day afterwards when I'd phoned her to tell her everything had gone alright on the night. I'd given her the same explanation then. Come to think of it she'd sounded a bit upset on the phone, but after that she'd never asked again. Not till now.

But she wasn't listening. My answer must have broken another line of thought. Whatever had been coming next had vanished. Her voice softened. 'I still don't understand what happened back there. Did he look awful?'

'Shakespeare?'

'Uhuh.'

I glanced at her as I slowed to go through a picture-postcard village. 'You screamed enough when you saw him.'

'I'm sorry, baby. It's just that . . .' Her words tailed off. She snuggled her head up against my shoulder and dropped off to sleep.

I decided to skip that year's International Conference on AIDS and instead of going to Milan at the beginning of June, Amelia and I were married quietly in the chapel of All Souls by John Thompson, the college chaplain. My immediate family came and Lawrence sailed across from America on the *QE2*, taking rooms at the Randolph for a night. Cissy was to have flown over. A week before, she phoned and begged off with a bad attack of

ME, then she turned up anyway, ME temporarily in remission, and surprised us all.

When Amelia signed the register she noticed I was unusually tense. It made me look older, vaguely distinguished, she told me later. At the same moment I was looking toward Lawrence, who had just taken out his pen. It was there again – the tic under his left eye. It was so small it was barely visible. There was a look on the old demon's face that I hadn't glimpsed before: a tranquility verging on sadness as if his mind were somewhere else.

Nuptials over we all shot across to the Common Room for a quick reception and a toast from Roderick Tillman who'd been hauled in at the last moment to act as best man. Strained wasn't the word for it. I avoided Lawrence and Lawrence avoided Cissy, so it was inevitable that Cissy and I would end up forced to glower at each other over a glass of a very expensive Krug that Lawrence had had sent over from the Randolph. Amelia, Tillman, Matthew and Sue were engaged in a lengthy conversation while the Colonel held forth to Lawrence, and Hattie did her seductive best to corner the chaplain.

Amelia must have told Cissy that I knew about her affair with Marcus because that was all the cow wanted to talk about. At least that made a change from not-so-subtle hints about Amelia and Lawrence. Cissy and I, to my relief, had not run into each other since that day in the gym. It wasn't much comfort, however, when she assailed me now and told me – as if that was what I wanted to hear straight after tying the knot – that Lawrence never approved of Marcus getting involved with his daughter. Obviously it was taken as read that he didn't approve of me either. As if I needed any reminding. Apart from a nod before the ceremony Lawrence hadn't acknowledged my existence since he flew in and out of the ashram. I almost wished he had AIDS. It would have served the bastard right.

Cissy was first to leave. She hugged Amelia and told me she was surprised Lawrence had bothered to come, before flourishing out to go and stay with friends in London. The departure of one became the signal for mass exodus and Lawrence was next to beat a hasty retreat, explaining he was having tea across Radcliffe Square with surviving dons from the Fifties at his old college: Brasenose.

My family drove straight home to Forest Spring. We newlyweds said a quick goodbye to Tillman and Thompson and hurried up the Banbury Road in an attempt to beat the rain that hung in a thundery sky.

As we reached Summertown a few drops fell. We ran. With less than four hundred yards to go the deluge came.

We raced up the stairs totally soused. Amelia was still laughing a minute later when she stepped out of the bathroom and threw a towel at me. 'C'mon, baby,' she said, smirking in my ear, 'consummate our marriage.'

When she was naked she sank on to the duvet. Wriggling to the side of the bed she drew me down beside her and I kissed the Bump. She removed my wet clothes. 'Mmmm,' she murmured and snuggled up to my chest. It was the first time, it struck me, that we were making love in daylight. She was still very hairy down there; and I loved her armpits completely unshaved, but she seemed different: lighter.

Such a tortured expression spread over her as she built to orgasm. For the first time I could watch her face. Tiny lines appeared round her eyes; her skin turned mottled pink; her mouth opened by slow degrees and her lips pulled back in a rictus that could be pain, but I knew was pleasure. She screwed up her eyes and tiny beads of perspiration sprinkled her forehead, catching the light. I could feel it coming in her when she gripped me in corrugated waves and forced the rhythm faster. When her agonized cry began I suddenly saw Marcus and I wanted to strangle her. I plunged viciously hard, which only doubled her cry, and I was helpless to resist the flow as she sucked me up inside her. As I vanished the last sound I made out was her screaming: 'I want to die.'

We did not see Lawrence again. According to Amelia he checked out of the Randolph and a chauffeured limousine drove him to Windsor to play a friendly game at the Guards Polo Club with some of the older members. He phoned Amelia from the Speedwing Lounge at Heathrow.

'Who was that?' I asked as she hung up.

'Just Lawrence. He's acting kind of weird.'

'What d'you expect? Did you think he'd give you away willingly?'

'It's like I'm kind of dead for him all of a sudden. There's no emotion there anymore.'

I tore open a Heineken. 'What's he going to do now?'

'Going back for the Opera Ball at the end of the month.'

'D'you think he'll ever slow down and just relax?'

'Look who's talking. He'll be in Newport for the Onion Patch Series. That usually unwinds him.'

I swigged my lager.

I knew from news reports that although the Shakespeare Search was officially over, the Rostrum's fund-raising for the AIDS Campaign was as buoyant as ever. For Marcus Freeman, according to *The Economist*, the Search had been a huge success. It had failed only in its failure to find a descendant of Shakespeare. For all my dislike of the man in particular and charismatic cults in general I suppose I felt a grudging respect for the way Marcus had taken the Search and turned it into a marketing strategy for the Rostrum.

For the first time I had the feeling Amelia could live without Shakespeare. The day after our visit to Stratford she'd phoned the Radcliffe Seminars office to resign as tour guide.

Since early May I'd been going to work six days a week at my lab in South Parks Road. Roderick Tillman had been back on the job a week before me.

In the second week of June on a sweltering night Amelia told me she was pregnant. I put my arms round her and held her tight. The news was not unexpected. If the pregnancy had not been planned, neither had its prevention. She had given up taking the pill in March. What I called a no-fault pregnancy. I knew a baby was what she wanted. For me too it meant a lot. After Lucy and the miscarriage there had always been that need.

I'd noticed another change in her since our visit to Stratford. Her fingernails were growing again. Maybe her 'problem' had died down.

Amelia continued her research through the summer vac, regularly visiting Elizabeth Chambers. She still painted but her style had changed. Gone were the tropical vistas. Instead she took my car twice a week and drove out to Cotswold villages to paint rural settings. A dozen of these were to decorate the flat by the end of August: not a Virgin Islander in sight I pointed out ruefully one Sunday as I hung a watercolor of a buff-tinted Bibury church.

She and I talked a lot. She loved Oxford; she loved the Bodleian Library with its creaky floors and painted ceilings; but most of all she loved being pregnant. For a short time Lawrence phoned her almost daily but by July his calls had ceased. From time to time she checked in by phone with Katie Barber. Katie must have been worried about her departure from analysis in mid-stream. But the tone of a pregnant Amelia on the phone assured her all was well, so Amelia told me afterwards.

For the last few days Amelia had been acting pretty strangely, like not sleeping much and getting up in the early hours to raid the fridge. Aside from morning sickness, pregnancy could do strange things to your metabolism, but that didn't seem to be the whole story. She admitted she'd never felt so nervous before, as if something was happening to her and she had no control over it. Something much bigger, even, than a baby: a feeling that affected both of us that she couldn't put a name to. It was like her sixth sense had gone haywire. Sometimes when she woke up in the night I could feel her wet with perspiration. But whatever the feeling was she just couldn't describe it to me.

One evening, a cool one, something happened again. We were cuddled together on the floor by the artificial fire, rocking a little, with no clothes on. Like the other time, she must have been staring too hard at the flames. She was frozen there.

I knew her at once from the voice: Black Jenny. 'I prithee, my lord' was all she said. She turned her head to look up at me. The raunchy glint I remembered so well was back.

'Who are you?' I stammered in my excitement. I had a hard-on already. My hand was between her thighs and from the feel there I knew what she wanted.

It was hard to say what way it was different making love to Black Jenny. Not better or worse, but so different that I felt adulterous. Only one thing reminded me she was also Amelia. Thanks to pregnancy her waist was thicker. She said nothing as we undulated face to face on our sides. Maybe it was the way she seemed so submissive, after Amelia. Like a small child who would do anything in the world to please an unloving parent: total capitulation to the will of a man. That excited me more and I found myself making love faster than I wanted to.

Black Jenny responded by gripping my leg with hers as if trying to draw me impossibly deep inside her. This way she managed to slow my pace. Her belly rocked against mine and I began to lose track of time. Later I realized we must have made love like that, her so tenderly, for close to an hour.

I wanted Black Jenny desperately. Hadn't I been waiting since her first appearance for another chance?

When she came there was a deep moan that seemed to go on and on. It rose to a peak then tailed away. The sound triggered me off and within seconds I was beyond redemption, groaning as her contractions forced me out of myself. I ran with the ebb, transformed in seconds from her milord to her abject slave.

She was stroking my hair as I came back to consciousness and she whispered something. I missed it the first time and she repeated it, in her strangely accented voice: 'Yet if you know a bird so base, in this devise she hath no place.'

Silence.

I pulled away to look at her eyes in the firelight. They were closed and I felt a surge of disappointment at losing her.

When I squeezed her hand and she opened her eyes slowly, Amelia was back. This time there were no physical after-effects.

She guessed again at what had happened. She had no recall. I explained, repeating the words Black Jenny had said before I forgot them.

That made her have a long think and she wouldn't look at me. Or the fire. She sat huddled in a ball, her feet tucked under her pretty arse.

Then the scream. This one was different. It was a Eureka scream. The atmosphere crackled and she bounced to her feet and disappeared into the study. When she emerged she rushed at me with her nakedness, bowling me over, lassooing my head with her arms, dragging me down on the sofa beside her.

With an effort I struggled to get to the bottom of her enthusiasm. She held a book I'd seen in her hands many times before, a modern reprint of Willoughby's curious *Avisa*, the poem from 1594 that seemed to be related to Shakespeare's *Sonnets*.

'Baby, baby, she's broken it.'

'Broken what?'

'The Dark Lady. Black Jenny's got her. It was hidden in a single word. This is the clincher. I just *knew* it had to be her, but before I could never find the absolute clue.'

I felt a thrill of anticipation. I'd got half a hard-on again, rolling around on the sofa. We were all arms and legs and somewhere in there was the book opened at two pages of a poem that was added to the *Avisa* in the 1596 edition: *The Victory of English Chastity under the Feigned Name of Avisa*. She was jabbing her finger at two lines repeatedly. I managed to take a look: it was the same two lines Black Jenny had spoken.

I was confused. Amelia was breathing in my ear in her eagerness. Who was this Avisa bird? Amelia and I had discussed it again and again. I was no authority, unlike her, which was probably why those lines didn't give me a clue, though I'd read them before.

'*Devise*, baby, *devise*,' she was saying. 'What's a *devise*?'

'I suppose it could mean a poem.'

'Of course it does but it also means something else.'

I looked blank.

'It also means a motto.'

'So?'

'*Devise* . . . base: the clue that's *proof* who the Dark Lady was is "base": a motto beginning with base.'

'Is there one?'

'Of course there is, baby: *Basis Virtutum Constantia*.'

'Translate.'

'*The basis of virtue is constancy.*'

'Whose motto?'

She gave me a tantalizing look to keep me on tenterhooks. 'Secret,' she said. 'You'll have to wait till I've double-checked the other parts of the picture to see if they correspond . . . but it's her, it's her. I just *knew* it all the time. Only I had to be totally sure . . . and now Black Jenny's cracked it.'

We talked about how Black Jenny could have pointed to those lines like that. Amelia felt sure it had to do with her psychic gift.

I had my own reasons for desperately wanting to be with Black Jenny again, but I kept them, as always, to myself.

Most days I came home for lunch but it was special the day after our Dark Lady came to light. We'd made love most of the night and afterwards she'd pretended to be too dog-tired to tell me the Dark Lady's name. So I only learnt the secret over breakfast. Amelia was very jumpy.

I was hovering around for our celebratory lunch, having only been in two minutes, when the phone rang. Amelia started and stared at it, willing it away, but it went on and on ringing. She gave me a look so crestfallen I wanted to rush to her, but she waved me away and walked unsteadily over.

I tip-toed to the bedroom and picked up the other phone just as she took the call. I'd been doing that a lot lately. Just checking. It was David Bendix. 'I'm sorry to tell you this,' he said to Amelia. 'Lawrence died last night.'

There was no outward emotion from Amelia.

Bendix continued, 'I'm really sorry. It was heart failure. You know how he drank. I'm only surprised it wasn't his liver. Don't be upset. He was out of it very quickly. As his next of kin I need your go-ahead for autopsy.'

'Okay.' Bendix seemed to be waiting for her to say something else. 'Was there no warning? Couldn't he have been saved? Was he with anybody?'

'Let's just say he died happy. Your father was a stand-up guy, Amelia. He did a lot of good in the world.' There was a pause. 'I'll call again about the arrangements. I'll be calling everyone to let them know.'

Still no tears. She hadn't spoken to Lawrence for three weeks. I put the other phone down quietly and slipped back to the sitting room.

Sinking into an armchair she repeated everything in a flat voice. I touched her belly, faintly swollen under a cotton blouse, and leaned over to kiss her on the forehead. My reaction was: good riddance, but I kept it to myself. Then she went to the kitchen, switched off the oven and poured herself a whiskey-rocks. For the time being the Dark Lady and our lunch were forgotten.

That night Amelia curled up alone on her side of the bed. No tears. She said nothing when I spoke. I couldn't tell whether she was awake or asleep.

The next afternoon Bendix called again to tell her Lawrence would be cremated without any service or ceremony. He'd look after the urn until Amelia wanted to collect it. The will made Bendix executor. One half of the well-sheltered estate, mainly Old Masters from his Georgetown collection, Lawrence had bequeathed to the Met. The other half once probate was granted and assets were realized would be held in trust for her unborn son: William Bosworth. The details were contained in a codicil signed only days before he died.

I was listening in again, guiltily. *Her unborn son?* Was it legal to leave a legacy to a fetus, even in trust, even if it had a name? Two weeks after finding out she was pregnant she'd decided it was going to be a boy, a conviction which I'd been unable to shake, any more than I was apparently going to be able to stop her from calling him William. Her assertive side had seen to that. After she'd told me the baby's hypothetical sex and name she'd called Lawrence. That phone call at the end of June had been the last she'd had with her father.

'He's being cremated tomorrow, Amelia, but I know from a remark he once made that he didn't want anyone to be there. I guess he just didn't want to make you sad. Just tell me if you want me to organize anything, like say an inscription on the urn.'

'Just put his initials. That'll do fine.'

She showed no sign of regret that there wouldn't be a funeral; no mourning to purge a sense of loss. Nor curiosity about the details of her father's death, as if things like that were not important. Or maybe it was just that she knew the form anyway when it came to a death in the Hungerford family.

For two days she said almost nothing, hanging around the flat listlessly. She ate nothing but drank one *citron pressé* heavily loaded with sugar after another. I took time off to be with her, going out only to get fresh supplies of lemons from the corner Indian. On the third day she was normal again as if nothing had happened. I set off for the lab feeling relieved.

I didn't have time to read the papers much; nor did Tillman, usually, but he'd spotted the *obit* on Lawrence in *The Times*. Even a flattering photo taken yonx ago. Flattery wasn't the word for all the ballyhoo about his contribution to museums and art. Not being much up in that particular world, it came as a bit of a surprise to learn how highly he was thought of. The writer obviously couldn't see the man for the trees.

The bit that really got me was how he'd had a PR man, the way Howard Hughes did, apparently, to keep his name *out* of the media. That was news to me. The writer said he'd been one of the richest men in America, thanks to his art collection, and mentioned Amelia with that obscene word 'heiress' again. Not that I'd realized he was quite *that* rich, despite what *Newsweek* had said in the summer. Loads of wonga, that had been obvious. But they were talking about him as the 'billionaire art historian'. They'd even thrown in a token negative: *thousands of acquaintances, but few if any real friends*. That figured.

As I handed the paper back to Tillman, I felt a strange pang, just for a moment, as if I actually missed the old bastard. I wiped this sadness away and threw myself back into work. There were better things to do than grieve over someone who had shown me no personal kindness. And Amelia looked as if she was going to survive.

As for the Dark Lady, Amelia and I held back from discussing her. It just didn't seem like the right time.

On a September evening when I was sitting watching the news Amelia stuck her head through the doorway. From the kitchen came the aroma of a walnut pie. 'I'm going back to America,' she announced in a dead-serious voice.

I spun round.

'It's okay, I'm just going back to give my lecture, the one I missed in the spring. It's time to tell the world who the Dark Lady was. I'm hacked off with letters saying who *was* she and who *were* the *Sonnets* dedicated to? I spoke to Bob Carr three weeks ago. It's all fixed for the day after tomorrow. I didn't want to tell you sooner in case you tried to stop me.' She patted her womb. She was nineteen weeks pregnant.

'You've certainly given me loads of warning.'

'If I don't go now I'll be too far gone and if I wait till afterward I'll be too busy. Bob's fixed Sanders Theater. It was to be Harvard Hall but so many invitations got accepted he had to switch it. I thought I'd have a last session or two with Katie, just for a check-up. Also there's dozens of papers to sign to sort out the estate.'

'What does Joblove say?' Philip Joblove was her much respected obstetrician. Twice I'd been with her to visit him at the Radcliffe.

'He says take it easy. I'll be fine and dandy . . . and William.'

'Do you have a ticket?'

'No, but I'm sure there's a flight every day.'

I felt guilty sitting down while she stood there moving around to keep the weight of pregnancy off her feet. I pulled a gold card from my jacket pocket and went to the study to call my London travel agents. As I attacked a slice of her walnut pie ten minutes later the phone rang.

'It's WEXAS,' I called across with one hand over the mouthpiece, thinking: *efficient as ever*. 'They're phoning back to say everything's fixed. First Class tomorrow. Tickets will be waiting for you at the British Airways sales desk at Terminal Four.' I finished the call and hung up. 'You'll miss my birthday.'

'I know, baby. I'll make up for it when I get back, promise.'

The next morning I drove her to Heathrow. There was no crowd this time. She cut an ultra-conservative figure in a brown tweed suit, the jacket let out at the waist to make way for her baby. Her normally rebellious hair was tied back in a severe but elegant barrette. Outside Passport Control I gave her a quick hug. She put a hand to my ear and whispered: 'Luvya. We both do.' Her other hand went to her distended belly and I noticed the Moorish-looking gold bracelet.

15

LAFEU: . . . He lost a wife
Whose beauty did astonish the survey
Of richest eyes; whose words all ears took captive;
Whose dear perfection hearts that scorn'd to serve
Humbly called mistress.

All's Well That Ends Well, Act V, Scene 3
William Shakespeare

'Look over there.' Rosie Kahn took one hand from the wheel of the Toyota pick-up. A church tower stood on the promontory at the side of a small bay where thunderclouds made a mezzo-tint draped over deep ultramarine. A pencil of light hit the tower, throwing it into relief.

It was the end of September and Katie had flown to Oahu to spend a week with Rosie who had left her for good that summer to live with her mother. Katie's symposium in Fort Lauderdale was off, so Hawaii made a pleasant alternative. They had driven from the airport, taking the long way round by the south-western shore. After a brief stop at Makaha they had pushed on over the hilly road that led to the island's center and the North Shore where pineapple fields stretched away to the township of Haleiwa, and Kam Highway that ribboned round the coast. On the way they had been through two rainstorms and it looked as if they were facing a third. Rosie pulled into the parking lot at Waimea Bay.

Katie's instinct was usually on target. She felt that her former partner had done the right thing by getting into the group of Christian therapists who had formed the Kahala Pastoral Center. Rosie needed to stand on her own two feet and Katie knew she herself had often been difficult if not downright domineering: intolerant too, evangelically speaking.

They could make out a huddle of surfers on the water a hundred yards off Waimea Point. The previous day the first big swell of winter had arrived pushing down from Aleutian storms thousands of miles to the north.

By the church they clambered over the sea wall and picked their way across the lava rock to sit down on a boulder.

'I'm going ahead with the paper,' Katie said, 'even though Amelia pulled out without finishing. Only it'll be for the *Journal of Abnormal Psychology* again.'

'You think you've got enough to go on?'

'Not until last week. Then she came three times and a lot happened.'

Rosie noticed Katie kept fidgeting with her hands. She knew she was trying to quit smoking. 'Is she fucking her father?' She coughed as she spoke.

'He died last month.'

'I'm sorry.'

'She's well rid of him. Now she's super-rich just to add to her hang-ups.' Katie added hastily: 'Not that she came back to see me unhappy. A lecture she'd just given had made a big splash and she was bursting with pregnancy.'

The edges of Rosie's skirt blew in the offshore air that funneled down Waimea Valley.

Katie went on: 'Maybe she's let out all her suppressed rage at what happened years ago.'

'Aren't you jumping the gun?'

'Hold on. We're coming to something really big now.'

'She *was* fucking her father.'

'Now look who's jumping the gun. No, it's something different. Amelia and her husband attended a small official opening of Shakespeare's grave. More came up under hypnosis this time. She was beginning to open up.'

'Completely?'

'Well, some things were still vague and other stuff she held back. When it got to where they saw the body of Shakespeare she started to sweat and clench her fists. Then she screamed right there on the couch. George Frost should have been there to see it.'

'Possession?'

'The minister probably thought so by the grave. But *grand mal* epilepsy is still a better word for what happened in the crypt. Only it wasn't epilepsy on the couch in my office. Heavens, that scream sounded like all the devils in hell going out of her. When

255

she stopped screaming she was curled up on her side in a fetal position, sucking her thumb. I brought her back to a waking state very slowly. She seemed perfectly normal afterwards.'

'Primal scream?' Rosie asked, adding hastily: 'She was anointed with the Gift of the Spirit and all her memories of trauma were being drawn out of her.'

'The first. Even under hypnosis I couldn't find out precisely why, but the point is she screamed. I never thought I'd see catharsis take the shape of a scream quite so literally. I would guess her other personalities left for good with that scream. For the first time she seemed to have access to real emotions.'

'It makes years of analysis look like a waste of time, doesn't it, if emotional blocks can be removed in a few seconds? To be born in the Spirit you only . . .'

'Don't make the mistake of assuming she's cured,' Katie answered back. 'Her multiple personalities may be gone, but she's still a borderline with a dominant and a submissive self, though I think the split between them is closing.'

'I didn't say she was cured,' Rosie retorted. Some things between the two women never changed. 'What about incest?'

'I think it's less of an issue for her but it's too soon to say. Maybe it's finished business, maybe it isn't.'

'How d'you mean?'

'Well she can't admit it to anyone, even to herself, but under hypnosis I found she's lost a lot of her interest in Shakespeare. It's no longer personal. She's not obsessed with him. Also I found out she doesn't fake her orgasms with her husband anymore. They're real now. That's one reason I think her splitting behavior is less severe. There seems to be real empathy at last, less of the constant backwards-and-forwards from her larger-than-life self to her regressive self.

'The unconscious male and female in her?'

'That's right. She doesn't feel so empty now. Less like a desert.'

The wind had shifted. When the next wave broke they got drenched in spray. They retreated to the safety of the wall and sat on it. The rain that had threatened had held off. There was a blazing cobalt sky.

Katie made herself comfortable. 'If she's cured she might even swap Shakespeare for the much-maligned joys of motherhood. I think she buried Shakespeare's ghost when she saw his body.'

'What about all her critics?' Rosie recalled the many enemies Amelia had in academic circles.

'I gather there's going to be a lot more of them after her latest lecture, including her old advisor. Amelia's stirred up a whole hornets' nest of opposition – and support – worldwide. But she can handle that, no problem. It's her emotional difficulties she's got to worry about.'

'And her gods? Are they really gone for good?'

'From now on I doubt she'll have so much as a whiff of them.' Katie surveyed the yellow mu-mu she'd bought specially for Hawaii. It was sodden. She hoped the colors wouldn't run. 'Look at it this way, maybe she's gotten rid of her father at just the right moment. With further analysis in due course the poor dear will have a chance of leading a more normal life.'

'Incest,' Rosie said. 'Did she or didn't she?'

'In the third hour a lot more stuff came up under hypnosis about her childhood. Her father very much wanted a son, but the mother seems to have had difficulties conceiving and her severe problem with alcohol didn't help.' The sun was hot. Katie was thankful for the wet dress.

'Tell me about her mother.'

'Amelia was brought up attending the Episcopalian Church. Her mother was seemingly quite religious. When Amelia was twelve she was confirmed.' Katie stared into space as if she conjured up a vision of a twelve-year-old in an immaculate white dress. 'I could never talk to Amelia about this, I don't think. A lot of it's too conjectural. Some things are best left repressed forever.'

'What? Tell me.'

'On the day Amelia was confirmed her mother got too drunk to go to church. A few months before that she'd been pregnant. By then she was forty-six and Lawrence Hungerford must have thought it was a miracle. The child was born prematurely in the eighth month. They tried to save it, but it died soon after birth. It was the boy that Lawrence with his dynastic view of the Hungerfords had surely prayed for.'

'Except he probably never prayed in his life.'

Katie ignored the interruption and shook back her bushy hair. 'Lawrence Hungerford had the baby's remains baptized. Amelia remembered the name, such is the power of hypnosis. It was

William Randal Lawrence Hungerford. Then it was cremated and together Lawrence and Amelia scattered the ashes in the sea off Nantucket. Amelia can't remember any of it consciously. It was the closest her father got to producing a son and heir. But imagine the state the mother was in: pregnant at forty-six, a dependent but controlling figure who in her own sad way manipulated Amelia's life every bit as much as the father did.'

'And to him Amelia was son and daughter.'

'The son he never had. Now do you see why there's a strong hint of the lesbian in her? It partly explains why she had a relationship with that woman friend of hers. Added to which, gender confusion is very common in women with borderline problems. It's basically an arrest at the oral stage.'

'Aren't we all a bit that way?'

'Some more than others . . . Amelia was very attached to her manipulative mother. Alcoholic or not she was all she had as a female role model. And Amelia must have been very upset about her baby brother. Then a few months later she and her father come back from the confirmation. Amelia's wearing her pretty dress and holding a rose the bishop has given her.'

'Ravishing even then,' Rosie mused.

'. . . And they get back to find the mother dead, asphyxiated on her own vomit. It happens more often with drugs than alcohol, like Jimi Hendrix and Janis Joplin.'

'So Amelia was traumatized.'

'That's an understatement.' Katie folded her arms. 'They called David Bendix and he brought in the Police Department. They took the body to the morgue at Mt Auburn Hospital. The pathologist concluded she'd been unhappy and had choked on her vomit: kind of suicide if you like to call it that. Amelia was told she'd died of cancer, but she'd seen for herself. She wasn't fooled . . .' Katie's voice faltered. 'But her mother did have cervical cancer and she would have died of it anyhow.'

'And Amelia calmly told you all this under hypnosis?' Rosie's skepticism was leaking out.

'Yes . . . oh she was having a fair old cry. All to the good. Without catharsis I don't think any of it would have gotten out.'

'What's your diagnosis?'

'You've got to imagine Amelia, twelve years old in the grip of puberty, as a capsule raging with infantile conflicts. She was

258

ripe for the trauma and repression that followed. One part of her idealized her mother while another part was in bondage to her father: conflictual loyalties. Who could she identify with? Not the alcoholic mother. Not the narcissistic father. The side of her that loved her mother hated her father. And the part of her that worshipped her father felt ashamed of her mother.'

'It's no wonder she felt alone and unloved and became promiscuous.'

'If she hadn't been an only child it would have been less difficult for her to open up and develop a real "good" self that could achieve emotional autonomy – not just an artificial "good" self – her masculine side. Her multiple personality disorder is simply one step beyond the splitting of the personality common to all low-level borderlines. Come on, let's walk. My legs are going to sleep.' Katie staggered to her feet. 'Amelia felt deep down she was responsible for her mother's death. As an infant she'd never separated from her mother emotionally, so her sense of guilt was overwhelming.' She picked a path back the way they had come.

'She can't own her feelings of hatred for her father and blame him for her mother's problems,' Rosie was saying, 'because she's besotted with him. Perhaps only God can heal the underlying memory.'

'Was besotted,' Katie corrected. 'He's dead, remember. But it's true she did play the masochist to the sadist in him. She needed the recognition of an idealized figure or she ceased to exist.'

'Maybe she's still besotted with the internalized father in her.'

'I don't think so, not anymore.'

'And Shakespeare?'

'I'm coming to that.'

They had reached the parking lot. Two surfers were leaning against the pick-up truck, scanning the sea. They moved away with a quick 'Howzit'.

Katie opened her window as the engine started. 'Amelia's a very unconscious person. A lot of stuff will stay repressed and a lot of insights will happen in their own good time.'

'So can she be healed?'

'That's the sixty-four-thousand-dollar question.'

Katie stopped talking to take in the scenery as they drove along 'the Kam' toward Sunset Beach. At Ehukai Beach they pulled off the highway and got out for a walk. Again the parking lot was full of surfers and more cars with boards seemed to arrive by the minute, while just as many seemed to be departing. When they walked through the trees and looked out they saw why the surfers were not in the water. Huge but shapeless waves were bursting on the inside reef. The wind had turned onshore in the last half-hour.

'What's really hanging you up about Amelia?' They were walking toward the sandspit in the distance. Rosie knew Katie only too well. She could tell when she was holding back.

'A lot of vague stuff that came up to do with the day her mother died. The connection between death and sex is a powerful one.'

'You're losing me.' Rosie knew when Katie was off on one of her tangents.

'It's certainly no photograph. In fact it's a very impressionistic picture. Maybe the incest was Amelia's fantasy and wish fulfillment. You know my hunches, Rosie. They're usually right.'

'So what's this one?' She wondered if Katie still had power to shock her. It turned out she did. It left Rosie completely out of her depth.

'Multiple personality disorder can draw on the defense mechanism we call denial. Amelia may have tried unconsciously to bring her mother back to life. Not literally. It's just possible she tried to *become* her mother by becoming her father's wife. The parts of her that split off from her core personality denied that her mother was dead. In a way, if she *was* her mother, then her mother was still alive. And normal husbands and wives have a sexual relationship.'

Rosie raced to follow Katie's logic. 'But her other personalities didn't include her mother.'

'Correct. They took the form of her gods. But one in particular, the Black Jenny prostitute, could be her mother in disguise.'

'And one of the male personalities could be the father that she'd internalized?' Rosie suggested, smiling to herself.

'Yes, in the shape of her fifth god.'

'I thought there were four.'

'We made a breakthrough. Y'see there are five of them. The fifth could be her father, but he comes to her disguised as Shakespeare disguised as Othello. Remember how I said she tended to confuse her father and Shakespeare?'

'So what's her relationship to the fifth one?'

'As Black Jenny she has sex of a kind with him in a sado-masochistic scenario where she's dressed in black French lingerie

– all that frou-frou kind of thing – and she gets suffocated like Desdemona in the murder scene in *Othello*.'

Rosie's tone showed utter disbelief. 'Are you saying she does this for real?'

'That's what I can't figure out. We know how easily she goes into a fugue. It could be real where she's acting out in a hypnoidal state that her father induces. In time, with repeated post-hypnotic suggestion, it would be relatively easy to turn her into some sort of obedient automaton . . . and to make her forget everything afterwards, at least consciously. We know how *obedient* she is to her father.'

'What about her mother?'

'Like I said, Amelia's original motivation at the deepest level would be to bring her mother back to life.'

'As a prostitute called Black Jenny?' Rosie stopped and took off her sandals. Katie had gone over the top this time.

'Maybe. There has to be a connection with Amelia's mother. It can't all be her fantasy.'

'I think we should be getting back. Mom's expecting us by six. She's really looking forward to meeting you. She's fixing something very Hawaiian.'

'What?' Katie's ears pricked up at the mention of food.

'Secret. I hope you still like pork.'

'I haven't changed that much.' Katie's laugh came like a giggle that evaporated. Her tone was immediately serious again. 'There's something else I'm determined to get to the bottom of, not just to get it into the journal. Amelia's mother didn't just choke on her vomit. Someone stifled her to death. I'm almost certain. Amelia witnessed her own mother's murder. Her funeral too. Lawrence cremated her in the baker's oven in the cellar of Hungerford House.'

16

And yet this time remov'd was summer's time,
The teeming autumn big with rich increase,
Bearing the wanton burden of the prime,
Like widowed wombs after their lord's decease.

Sonnets, 97
William Shakespeare

I swore softly as I left the lab. The pavement was wet from a shower that made the air muggy. I took off my jacket as I ambled past Keble. I'd always made an issue out of my birthday. I knew she'd said she was sorry not being there, that Bob Carr could only fit her impromptu lecture in on the second day of the new semester and Katie Barber was going on vacation a few days later. I still felt let down. I stopped to look at a TV that was on in a shop window in Summertown. A program on AIDS in Africa. Those oh-so-familiar eyes: a child haunted by death. I scuffed the pavement with my toes.

I'd doled out sixteen hundred pounds that week for a new Rolex. The one that had vanished at Big Sur hadn't been insured. Tightwad Amelia kept all her money to herself and I was paying for the flat. If that kept on I'd need to sell the boat and mortgage my old DB6. My wheels and I had been together since before Lucy even. Maybe I should be charging stud fees.

If I'd been feeling more on top of everything I'd have accepted the invitation to speak at the Union. They'd wanted me to oppose the motion that prostitutes should be registered and compulsorily checked for AIDS. Obviously I agreed the idea was totally fascist. They'd got another speaker now and all I got was to feel guilty for saying 'no'.

I'd been putting in long hours at the lab. The only interlude had been half a day in the Bod. At least it had been quiet in the summer vac. I'd pored over the library's priceless copy of the 1594

262

edition of *Willobie his Avisa* while an attendant breathed down my neck. Now that I knew who the Dark Lady was I saw her more and more clearly in various clues.

The vaccine was coming along nicely: that was something, but I had to make a conscious effort to hoist my shoulders. The people I passed belonged to the world: I didn't. Never had. But I'd get by. I was a survivor. If I wasn't barking up the wrong tree I could be there with a vaccine in under a year. Then the world would have to admit me to its ranks. If you couldn't belong by being outstandingly ordinary you had to be outstandingly different. I'd kept progress close to my chest. Only a handful of colleagues knew where I stood. Roderick Tillman was working the same long hours, grabbing meals on the trot. In fact working round the clock we had more than a fighting chance of coming first: what Amelia called 'blowing the rest of the field away'. I hoped she was right. I no longer had the same range of HIV samples, but my time in Mendocino had taken care of that.

I was wondering about Marcus. The light was fading. Marcus had made no attempt to stop me returning to the UK with a copy of the master database ... much more valuable than the one I'd brought to Mendocino. At the end of Lonsdale Road I puzzled over whether Lawrence had had a hand in making it so easy for me. I was none the wiser about what had made the old bastard tick. Love of power? Love for Amelia? Then why had he stayed away as soon as we'd married; virtually severed contact when he'd heard she was pregnant? The bugger had gone and croaked without even saying goodbye.

I'd got Drake on the phone that morning; told him point-blank I knew he'd reopened the file on my mother; asked him why he'd done so and got a very peculiar answer. Basically he said he'd never be satisfied until he'd worked out all the answers to my mother's murder: who she was and who had killed her. *Neither would I*, I told him. *Why the interest in Shakespeare's grave?* To which he said he thought it might have something to do with the murder. *Did it?* I asked. *Maybe*, he said. *How?* I demanded to know. I must have raised my voice a bit. Anyway he hung up on me and when I called back he was 'in conference'. I swore at the sergeant on the other end of the line and slammed the phone down again.

I reached the front door and headed upstairs in time to catch the early news on BBC2.

263

The issue that crossed my mind repeatedly was how, if I trusted Amelia, could I have let myself get involved with Polly Ann? Trusting Amelia and Shakespeare's cross were wrapped together in this. Amelia was admitting she never wanted to publish the cross's existence even though it would have been powerful evidence for her theory about Shakespeare and an ancient hermetic society.

She'd kept wondering aloud how Mannering had known there was a cross in the grave and if he'd really known all along that it was a Tau. He was seemingly as keen as Amelia *not* to publicize the cross and we'd heard he'd started writing about Shakespeare again in the same old vein: Shakespeare the pillar of Holy Trinity Church, as if the cross had never existed in the first place.

I'd promised Amelia I wouldn't talk to anyone about the cross, but I felt my promise didn't extend to Gillespie, since he'd seen it too.

When I called him at college the porter said he was at the hospital, but my phone rang soon afterward and a very different Gillespie was on the line. We hadn't made contact since our bizarre encounter in the crypt. I quickly broached the topic of the Tau. He seemed reluctant to talk about it, but I wasn't going to let him off the hook so easily.

'Undoubtedly it's a very early Christian symbol,' he said. 'One that the Christians borrowed from the pagan world, much the way Easter was a pagan rite that passed into Christendom.'

He was opening up despite himself and I prodded harder: 'Is it something you would write about?' I now knew enough about his work to know his field was the spread of Christianity up to the Middle Ages.

'I'd like to bring it into an update of one of my papers, but when Reverend Mannering got me involved in February I promised not to reveal anything that was found in the grave.' Then he added: 'He made me promise again last time after we refilled the tunnel.'

'Why d'you think he wants it kept secret?'

'It would make headlines if it got into the news, just as a Shakespearian descendant would if you found one.'

'Unlikely now that we've stopped looking.'

'My theory,' he was saying, 'is that Reverend Mannering doesn't want much of his life's work made to look ridiculous, which of course it would be.'

'In what way?'

There was a deep pause at Gillespie's end of the line before he continued. He sounded depressed. 'Shakespeare the Hermetic and Shakespeare the Good Christian are two very different people. Your wife will know as well as anyone what that could mean to the Shakespeare business.' His voice was very tired all of a sudden. 'As a symbol appearing from a grave dated 1616 the Tau may have enormous significance to the historians of secret societies.'

Excited, I was demanding to know: 'Like the Freemasons or Rosicrucians?'

'Possibly something much older.'

'The Templars?'

'Maybe older still.'

'The Gnostics?'

'There were many Gnostic sects,' he was saying. 'In spite of what historians pretend, we don't really know very much about them. But if they were around today – and I don't mean the modern Gnostics – they would be the *real* Christians, directly descended from Christ. The Roman and Orthodox Churches were schismatic. They were early breakaways from the mainstream. The Gnostics weren't another breakaway. They *were* the mainstream.'

'Gnosis,' I was saying, talking half to myself. 'The direct knowledge of God.' Something was trying to percolate through my head that I couldn't put a name to. Too vague to be an idea. Too weak to be a feeling. 'Listen, I'd like to talk more about Shakespeare's cross and the Gnostics. Could we meet tomorrow?'

There was exhaustion in his voice this time. 'I can't meet, Dr Bosworth. I shouldn't even be talking on the phone. Doctor's orders. I've got to take it easy and I'm liable to get too excited if we discuss the cross anymore.'

I felt as if the curtain was falling before the climax. 'What's the problem?'

'Lucky if I live till Christmas . . . a brain tumor . . . thought it was benign . . . migraine and nausea . . . brain scan in the spring . . . shouldn't have been heaving stone slabs around, really. Too tempting, though.'

'You're getting the best treatment alright?'

'They're doing what they can, X-rays and chemotherapy. Most

days I go into the John Radcliffe Hospital. In two more weeks I'm moving in there to live . . . and die.'

There was little I could say to that. In my awkwardness I expressed the hope that there would be a miracle and he would recover.

When I put down the phone I felt very mortal myself.

At Hungerford House I'd looked at a few books on the history of Freemasonry in America: how it had started in Boston. Paul Revere had been a Freemason and he was supposed to have stayed with the patriot Hungerfords in 1775. But did that make Lawrence Hungerford a Freemason, let alone a Gnostic?

I was working harder than ever at my lab in South Parks Road. Other things could have been distracting me from my vaccine, but I felt as if my vaccine and the puzzle of my life were the same thing and while I worked on one I tried to put together the pieces of the other.

What *had* happened at Big Sur? Something was struggling to filter through but couldn't make it, notwithstanding my prayers to Janey, my angel on high. How had Polly Ann really died? Why did Amelia and Mannering not want the Tau cross made public? How had Amelia and Lawrence been so sure our baby was going to be a boy? I knew I'd got as many answers out of Amelia as I could. She thought I'd spent my time at Big Sur wandering round in a trance; that Polly Ann had flung herself off the cliff for love of me; that Mannering didn't want the Tau made known for the reason that Gillespie had just suggested; that she didn't want it publicized for reasons she'd simply refused to tell me on the two occasions I'd asked. And she had this sixth sense that told her the baby would be a boy and Lawrence believed her because he believed in her sixth sense and anyway he had the same gift himself. She'd always liked the name William. There had been a William in her family once.

Even Lawrence's death had something odd about it. He'd never looked that healthy to me . . . the pills, for example. But Amelia had been very agitated just before he died . . . either pregnancy or the oncoming discovery of the Dark Lady or she'd known – he'd known – he was going to die. Hadn't Bendix said he'd changed his will a few days before he died?

Was it any wonder I felt less able to confide in Amelia. What kind of a relationship was it that wasn't based on trust?

*   *   *

She came back on the second-to-last day of September.

'I wanted to give you a surprise.' She flew into my arms. 'Happy birthday from me and William.' She disappeared. 'Have you eaten?' she called through to me.

'I've been starving without you.' I had on my old whipcord pants and a navy shirt worn threadbare at the elbows.

I could hear her talking on the bedroom phone. She bounced back into the sitting room. 'Birthday treat,' she said, giggling like a child with a sweeping grin. 'We're going to eat at the Quat' Saisons tomorrow night.' Unkempt, I look more darkly handsome if slightly more manic, she told me. 'Any food in the kitchen?'

'No. I've had nothing to eat since you left. Seriously, I've been living on poached eggs . . . the ones I didn't manage to cremate.'

'You'll have to make do with me for tonight,' she said in that voice she knew would excite me.

She came and floated in the bathroom doorway as I removed shaving suds with my cut-throat. I was watching her reflection in the mirror. 'How did the Dark Lady go down?' I waited for her reply but she disappeared through to the bedroom. When I'd wiped my face I found her lying on the bed staring at the ceiling. I asked my question again as I changed into a clean shirt.

'The place was packed. Saul Lindenbaum came. He sat with Bob Carr.'

A day-old copy of *The Times* lay beside the bed. The Dark Lady was already a feature at the bottom of the front page: *Shakespeare's Dark Lady Uncovered*. There'd be many more column inches in the days and weeks to come. 'I've got one more birthday surprise for you,' she added.

'What's that?'

'Wait and see. Tomorrow we're going to Wiltshire. You don't get your birthday dinner till afterward.'

A private road stretching two miles between tall ornamental trees and mature shrubs brought us into an Eden of a parkland where black-faced sheep looked up. We stopped the car to get a good look at the palatial pile in the distance: Longleat House, home of the entrepreneurial sixth Marquess of Bath.

As we drove slowly on down the hill toward the weather-mellowed house the surrounding landscape that Capability Brown engineered gathered up around me from its chill-soaked ground and steered me along. The sky was flat and wet with drizzle, giving the building the sorrowful appearance of one of those places that was more museum than home.

I'd given up trying to guess the reason for this secret mission that I had to undergo to qualify for my supper that evening at the Quat' Saisons. Amelia spoke at last to remind me of something she'd told me back in February.

'Henry Willoughby lived over at West Knoyle, seven miles from here. Charles Blunt's manor Brook House was eight miles from Longleat. Another piece in the Wiltshire enigma.'

I parked to one side of the forecourt and we bundled out. The place looked desolate – maybe half a dozen cars – but winter was coming on and the season for visiting stately homes was winding down. Behind us another drive led almost a mile in a straight line from the front door to the original gateway. Amelia hadn't been there before but she seemed to know the place by instinct. While she was mounting the stone steps I was gazing up at the statues along the roofline that were peering down at me. It was getting dark early.

Amelia was having a problem with the heavy front door till I got there and added my weight. The lobby inside was unlit but there was no mistaking the smile of the woman behind the desk or the welcome of her Airedale puppy which darted between my legs and almost sent me flying. We were clearly expected and Jill Bentley, Lord Bath's archivist, would be down in a minute.

While we waited I wandered round the Great Hall behind the receptionist, leaving Amelia to chat about the house. When I got back to the desk a woman looking studious in gold-rimmed glasses was waiting. Jill Bentley took care of Longleat's fabled collections of books, manuscripts and works of art. She was expressing her condolences on Lawrence's death. She'd known him fairly well. She looked at me carefully and turned to introduce us to someone else who'd just arrived, a woman in her thirties who smiled from head to toe. Alice was one of the house's regular guides. She was dressed in a navy skirt and shetland with an elegant gold brooch pinned to the scarf round her neck.

The first portrait we came to, at the foot of the grand staircase that Wyatville designed, was Robert Devereux, second Earl of Essex. The thing that struck me about him was that his head with its bushy beard looked too small. I couldn't help imagining the blood dripping all over his fancy white outfit, if that was what he wore for his beheading in the Tower. He'd got his left hand on his sword and a blue ribbon round his neck with a kind of medallion showing the insignia of the Order of the Garter. And in case we missed the point the garter itself was round his left leg just under his knee. Showing on it were the words 'Y Pense'.

Jill and Alice led us through a door to the right into the so-called Red Library, a long room with bookshelves that almost reached the ceiling. Alice was saying how this room was haunted by an old man in black who'd been seen standing in the north-west corner. 'I've seen another ghost in here that no one else has seen,' she added mysteriously. 'A King Charles spaniel stretching in front of the fire.' She was pointing to the spot a few feet away. I looked up from the floor to the mantel shelf supporting two statues, each holding a six-branch candelabrum that must have been switched from flame to electricity in the not too distant past.

Jill was explaining to Amelia that the painting over the mantel, a Resurrection, was by Johann Rottenhammer with flower surrounds added by one of the Brueghels. Alice went on to point out – these two really had their routine down to a fine art – that the three-dimensional effect of the floral cameos in the ceiling was an illusion: they were painted flat. We craned necks to see and I got a crick in mine.

At the far end of the library close to where the ghost of the old man had been seen was a tall Italianate door dating from the 1870s, made of walnut with boxwood inlays. Above it at a height of about nine feet was what we had come all this way to inspect. This was where Jill really came into her own. Amelia hadn't seen the original before but she'd seen copies. Jill was saying the real authority on pictures of this period was Sir Roy Strong and she was thinking of getting his views on it.

It was only about two and a half feet square and would have been hard to see from where we were standing, but Jill had a torch that did the trick. We all stood gazing in silence for at least a minute. To my ignorant eye it looked technically outstanding.

Jill broke the silence, saying an Elizabethan double portrait was a great rarity. It had come into the Longleat collection some time in the seventeenth century.

I sucked in my breath and wondered which of these two Elizabethan women was the Dark Lady. I knew which one I preferred. They both had eyes like jet and dark-gold hair and eyebrows. Amelia was saying nothing.

As if she'd anticipated my next question Jill said: 'You can't see it from here, but there's a fine gold inscription at the top – one that was obviously added later. It reads on the right: "Dorothy D'Evereux Countesse of Northumberland", and on the other side: "The Ladys Penelope Counteese of Warwick".' She spelt it out for us, mistakes and all. 'Of course,' she went on, 'Penelope Devereux, who married Robert Rich and became Lady Rich, was never Countess of Warwick. She was long since dead when Robert Rich became Earl of Warwick.'

I was staring at the woman on the right. She *had* to be our Dark Lady. But Amelia had come up with Penelope Rich as her final answer to the enigma and the inscription said Penelope was on the left if the order was anything to go by. Jill was just saying what a dilemma it had been deciding which was which and then with all the phone calls since the Dark Lady's identity had been splashed across the news two days ago . . . Longleat's phone number, unlike ours, was not ex-directory.

But it was easy to see Jill Bentley was over the moon about the significance of the portrait. Previously it had been an object of interest as a picture of Sir Philip Sidney's Stella. Only now as Shakespeare's Dark Lady . . . I had to agree with her it made the painting very significant.

I tried to make a mental photograph of all the details. Both women were wearing necklaces studded with pearls. The woman on the right, by far the prettier of the two, had a flower and pearl garland in her hair with a baroque pearl hanging at the summit of her brow. She was wearing an embroidered velvet bodice of claret red and white slashed sleeves with ruffle wrists. Her hair was the same tawny color as Robert Devereux's beard in the painting by the staircase.

When Alice repeated the question: which was the Dark Lady Penelope and which was her sister Dorothy? Amelia spoke for the first time, with an authority that took our two guides and even me by surprise. 'The inscription starts with "Ladys" so the elder,

Penelope, had to take precedence and be written first. As the elder of the two sisters she also had to be painted slightly in front of the younger. Apart from the Countess of Warwick mistake there's no confusion. The Dark Lady is the woman on the right.'

I breathed free again and took a step backward. Jill Bentley shone the torch away from the portrait for a few seconds as she turned to look at Amelia, then she seemed to change her mind about something and aimed the light back again.

'The costumes would suggest a date around the early fifteen-eighties,' Amelia was saying. 'Penelope left the Earl of Hunting-don's home to get married to Lord Rich in fifteen-eighty-one. She was eighteen at the time. Her sister Dorothy was sixteen. The portrait was probably a pre-nuptial one made in fifteen-eighty-one to celebrate the occasion. There's little doubt Penelope was the prettier of the two women. That's clear from the portrait as well as the literary record. If we look hard it's not difficult to see the figure on the right is the elder and more confident of the two. I don't see any problem with identifying which is which.'

The woman on the right was drawing me into her, with her kiss-and-tell smile, like a Mona Lisa with bedroom eyes and a body designed for the pleasure of men.

Amelia was reciting the litany of Penelope Rich's courtly relatives – perhaps to make her relationship with a bourgeois Stratford glover's son all the more dramatic. Alice was standing with her hands clasped in front of her in a pose that suggested silent rapture. By the time Amelia had finished even I would feel I had to whisper when I pronounced the Dark Lady's name, the way you whispered in churches. Here, after all, were the famous dark eyes that Shakespeare and Sidney had gone overboard for. Given the standards of the sixteenth century it was little wonder everyone had raved about her beauty in the 1580s and 1590s.

Amelia's list of her relations was almost endless: 'She was the elder daughter of the first Earl of Essex, the elder sister of the second Earl of Essex out in the hallway, first cousin twice removed of Queen Elizabeth, ward of the Earl of Huntingdon, putative lover of Sir Philip Sidney, wife of Lord Robert Rich, lover and husband of Charles Blunt who was eighth Lord Mountjoy and Earl of Devon, stepdaughter of the great Robert Dudley who was Earl of Leicester, cousin of Elizabeth Vernon who married the third Earl of Southampton, godmother to their daughter who was Lady Penelope Wriothesley, sister-in-law of Sir Thomas Perrot and later Henry Percy alias the "wizard" Earl of Northumberland, sister-in-law of Frances Walsingham whose first husband was Philip Sidney, and friend of Sidney's sister Mary Herbert who was Countess of Pembroke. The Elizabethan aristocracy were horribly calculating and incestuous when it came to marriage.'

It was no wonder the likes of Nancy Bretton were up in arms, claiming there was no way Shakespeare could have had a relationship with that exalted court beauty.

Amelia was reading my mind again. Jill turned the torch off and we all faced Amelia to listen. 'Penelope,' she was telling us, 'was first spotted as a Dark Lady candidate as far back as the eighteen-sixties, thanks to all the puns in the *Sonnets* on her married name: Rich. But critics came along at once and poured ridicule on the idea. They pointed out that the puns were the stock-in-trade of a dozen Elizabethan poets who were trying to ingratiate themselves with her. Constable's a prime example.'

'They might have a point.' Jill Bentley raised an eyebrow that suggested she didn't want to offend Amelia, but she just might need a little more convincing.

'Long ago I looked at Penelope as one of the Dark Lady possibles,' Amelia snapped back, 'and ruled her out for exactly the same reasons as everyone else did. Later on I began to change my mind, but I needed more concrete evidence. Now that we've identified Avisa, I don't see how there's still room for doubt. Besides, Penelope was thirty-one – positively ancient in those days – and had undergone six pregnancies by the time Shakespeare came along. She was a good year older than Shakespeare.'

I got my oar in to defend Amelia. After all I was pretty well informed by now. 'Let's not forget Shakespeare was the upcoming poet to know in 1593 after *Venus and Adonis* turned into a blockbuster. Why shouldn't she fancy him for his reputation as a poet? *Love's Labour's Lost* shows how intimately Shakespeare was involved with Southampton's and Essex's circle and anyway the English aristocracy have always been the first to break the rules of propriety.' Jill coughed awkwardly and shot me an intense look over the top of her glasses as if to remind me that we might be overheard by Lord Bath or his son, Viscount Weymouth.

Amelia rallied to my side. 'Penelope's mother Lettice Knollys made her reputation by flouting convention. She usually got pregnant first and asked questions afterward.'

Trying to steer the conversation back on course Alice reminded us that the best-known portrait of Penelope's mother was in the house. That seemed to be a hint that it was time to leave the Dark Lady, so I cast a last glance at her portrait and we carried on to take the tourist circuit.

Despite what I'd just been saying I could see for myself what it was that got Nancy Bretton's back up. It was as if I wanted to switch sides suddenly and join the fight *against* Amelia. It was that hard masculine streak in her again that made her a Lawrence look-alike. It was the one side of her I'd really got no appetite for, though admittedly I'd seen less and less of it since we left America. But I could tell when Jill Bentley was backing off. With difficulty I stopped myself saying anything and tried to concentrate on Longleat House, which turned out to be riveting quite apart from the Devereux sisters.

In the Lower Dining Room Alice pointed out the portrait of Louisa Carteret the second Viscountess Weymouth. We learnt that she'd taken a lover; that he'd been found out by the husband and done to death. Louisa had died five days after giving birth to her third child which her husband had suspected of being her lover's.

Now, Alice told us, Louisa Carteret was known as the Grey Lady and her ghost had been seen by Lord Bath's mother and Mrs Trump the housekeeper stalking the second-floor corridor known as the Grey Lady Walk.

We went on through one lavish room after another, but each was more unlived-in than the next as if there were more substance to Longleat's ghosts than to the idea that this was a real place in which real people led their lives. I told Alice what I was thinking and she replied that the Thynne family – that was Lord Bath's family name – had lived in virtually the whole house until recently.

In the music room we stopped for an extra-hard look at another important portrait: Sir Philip Sidney. He'd been an arrogant man in life and standing there with his white ruff and his hand on his hip it showed. Take away the Elizabethan clothes and with his short haircut and clean-cut jaw I could see him on the cover of *GQ* magazine. No wonder girls went wild. Only Byron was fit, amongst English *literati*, to hold the candle to him in that department.

There was the sound of ducks quacking from somewhere outside. I went over to a window and looked out. We were on the first floor. All I could see was the long avenue with formal ponds on either side that looked as if they had fountains in summer.

Ten minutes later, tour completed, we stood at the foot of the Grand Staircase saying our thanks to Jill and Alice, and then I was steering Amelia toward the front door. After tripping over the Airedale puppy again it was out to the car and back to Oxford to change for dinner.

17

TO. THE. ONLIE.BEGETTER. OF.
THESE. INSUING. SONNETS
MR. W.H. ALL. HAPPINESSE.
AND. THAT. ETERNITIE.
PROMISED.
BY.
OUR. EVER-LIVING. POET.
WISHETH.
THE. WELL-WISHING.
ADVENTURER. IN.
SETTING.
FORTH.
T.T.

Dedication, *Sonnets*
William Shakespeare

It was dark when we arrived at the fifteenth-century manor of the Quat' Saisons in Great Milton. As we drove through the gates the stone façade emerged from the autumn mist. I parked beside a Jaguar. Swaths of late flowers decked the edges of the house: chrysanthemums and asters. The front entrance was a haven of light.

In the drawing room as we sat by a fire over champagne and canapés a waiter took our orders. From the wine list I ordered a rare Batailley Pauillac. From the napery to the choice of pictures pink was everywhere in the dining room, relieved by lily-of-the-valley in the center of each table. As soon as we sat down Amelia delved into her bag and with a small cry pulled out a parcel wrapped in green silk. 'Happy belated birthday,' she said, 'from a Scorpio to a Virgo, even if you are a crypto-Cancer.' She'd always insisted my real birthday was in July. More of her sixth sense.

There was no card. I gave her an embarrassed smile and

untied the red ribbon. If my life could only have come wrapped so daintily. Guests at a nearby table were glancing over.

'Go on,' she said, 'hurry up.' I opened the bundle. I was looking at two Elizabethan miniatures limned on vellum, mounted in gilt frames. One depicted a man in green doublet with fancy points. On a background of midnight blue was the emblem of the Order of the Garter. The woman in the other was good-looking by twentieth-century tastes and dazzling, I thought, by the standards of the sixteenth. Now I saw why we'd gone to Longleat first. I recognized Penelope Rich, only here she really *was* a stunner.

'Lawrence left them to me. I want you to have them. He left me his whole collection of Elizabethan portraits, instead of the Met, including one of Southampton and another of Frances Walsingham. There were eight Hilliard miniatures, including these two.'

I looked at her, amazed. Of course Lawrence had a vast art collection, so why not? They had to be worth a king's ransom – petty cash to Lawrence. I could feel her boring into my head, reading my thoughts again. I studied Penelope, who was wearing a dress quite unlike her delicate Longleat costume. At that moment my *confit de canard* and Amelia's *coeurs de palmier* arrived and we tackled the food like some kind of gastronomic foreplay.

'That's Robert Devereux again . . . her slightly wacky brother,' she continued, breaking the long silence. 'You know something, I was getting unbelievable criticism over Penelope almost before my lecture finished.' She nodded at the miniatures. 'They're definitely by Nicholas Hilliard. Neither of them's cataloged. The one of Penelope was thought to have disappeared centuries ago. Apart from the Longleat portrait it's the only authentic picture of her that's still around. This one of Essex isn't known to have existed in the first place. Don't you think he's loitering appropriately . . . or is it palely? Lawrence had a flair for unearthing things like that.'

They were less than two inches across. I turned over the picture of Penelope Rich, handling it as if it might break at any moment. Here too her hair was tawny-fair to burnt gold, the eyes dark. There was the ghost of a smile in her lips and a suspicion of teeth, unheard of in an Elizabethan miniature. With a little imagination her look was sexy. The picture bore Hilliard's monogram. On the back were words in a spidery hand: '*Guarde la Foy*'.

'Keep faith,' I mumbled to myself.

'Take this.' She passed me a magnifying glass from her bag. I examined the faded paper stuck to the back under the Rich motto. It read in microscopic letters: *To Mr Hilliard upon occasion of a picture he made of my Lady Rich.*

Tiny lines of verse followed. She was watching me as I strained to read through the glass. 'Henry Constable,' she said, then she whispered:

> 'But think not yet you did that art devise
> Nay think my lady that such skills you have
> For often sprinkling her black sparkling eyes.'

I looked at the portrait again. 'I could fall for her right this minute.' Since Longleat we hadn't talked about her again.

'Lots of men did. After Sidney's *Astrophel and Stella* came out in 1591 poets didn't just allude to her by punning on her name; lots of them dedicated their work to her. The difference with Shakespeare was the lengths he took her name to. He started off using it as the standard quibble, but in the end it became personal. I haven't decided at what point yet. It depends what order you think the *Sonnets* were written in.'

I signaled the waiter for a second bottle. 'I did find her name in the *Sonnets*, but it didn't look too personal – at least not in the early ones.'

'The whole sequence was written over at least a couple of years. Shakespeare's early quibbles on "rich" and "blunt" were standard for the poetry of the day. At that stage he wasn't involved with Penelope. She was still Charles Blunt's mistress then and his alone. But, mark ye well, the Rival Poet sonnets are addressed to Penelope, not Willoughby. Of course Henry Willoughby's the Friend and Fair Youth to whom, as Mr W.H., the *Sonnets* are dedicated. By the time the Dark Lady sonnets were written Shakespeare's relationship with Penelope was very personal.' She dropped her voice. 'It probably didn't last long, but while it was on it was heavy sex all the way.'

'I still find it hard to believe she had an affair with Shakespeare,' I said, recalling the conversation at Longleat that almost became an argument.

277

'I've found something else,' she said, 'apart from the motto, to show it was Penelope. From the same fifteen-ninety-six poem:

> Thou princely judge here mayst thou see
>   what force in error doth remain,
> In envious pride what fruits there be
> To write the paths that lie so plain;
>   A double darkness drowns the mind,
> Whom self will make so willful blind.

Apart from the obvious pun in "willful" there are several allusions to the *Sonnets*, and Penelope, starting with "envious pride" – Penelope's other motto: "*Virtutis Comes Invidia*". Then there's a quibble on Shakespeare's "lying" sonnets: in both it's telling lies and getting laid.'

I managed to get a word in. 'Penelope's two dark eyes – the double darkness, followed by an allusion to the "self" image that Shakespeare develops in one part of the *Sonnets*.'

'You got it, baby,' she said, 'apart from the "blindness" theme,' and she sat back and looked round the room. Nearby something *flambé* was attracting attention. 'It's going to always be the biggest problem,' she said. 'But why shouldn't we believe a woman out of society's top drawer would have stooped to a cross-class dalliance with a common burgher? Another point people are missing is that she wasn't marrying him. She was a very fickle lady. He was a quick fling, one of several to judge by the *Avisa*.'

'Who were the others, besides Willoughby?'

'I don't know about the nobleman or the Frenchman,' she said, referring to the first two of Avisa's six suitors, 'but I'd put my money on Sidney for the Caveleiro, and Sir Charles Blunt for Dydimus-Harco, the Anglo-German. The Blunts were descended from German nobility.'

'Didn't Blunt's affair with her start in fifteen-ninety?' I'd found time to check the facts on Penelope Rich while I was in the Bod. Apart from the cuckolded Lord Robert Rich and Sir Philip Sidney, Blunt was the man she was always associated with.

Amelia helped herself to a fresh roll from the basket. 'She had a love-child with Blunt in fifteen-ninety-two. But in fifteen-ninety-three he was overseas on military service. Enter Shakespeare and

Willoughby, stage left. Penelope was a lot like her blue-blooded mother . . . a hot-blooded vamp who relished her reputation as a courtesan.'

'That *still* doesn't explain why she'd jump into bed with Shakespeare.' I held the two miniatures side by side.

'Rough trade, baby, as Victorian gentlemen used to call it.'

'And Willoughby? Wasn't he too downmarket for her?'

'Still socially inferior' – she pursed her lips – 'but a good cut above the Bard. Willoughby had other things going for him like a sexy young body . . . eighteen to Penelope's thirty-one. Her sex life with Robert Rich died a death in fifteen-ninety-one. In fifteen-ninety-three she was hot after the poet and his friend and had a quick thing with them to keep in shape till Blunt got back from Brittany.'

'What year did he become Lord Mountjoy?'

'Fifteen-ninety-four when his brother died. The name was a gift. Look at the puns on "joy" and "mounting" and the "mounting phoenix" which I've suddenly woken up to in the *Avisa*. They're so obvious now that I don't know how I missed them.'

'Were the Elizabethans that crude?'

'You bet they were.' She lowered her voice again. 'Penelope fucked her way to fame . . . apart from being beautiful and the sister of Essex. Anyhow there must have been good reason why King James called her "a fair woman with a black soul". She wasn't really dark. You've seen for yourself she was fair apart from her famous dark eyes.'

'Poor Penelope Rich. Maybe Shakespeare called her "dark" to disguise her identity.' I was looking through my wineglass at the flame of our single candle.

'Vindictive irony more likely. In the Renaissance dark eyebrows were a poetic conceit that signified a woman who enjoyed sex outside marriage. Fair eyebrows were the sign of a faithful wife or a virgin. Shakespeare made Penelope's eyebrows dark to suggest infidelity, but being the innovator he was he extended the metaphor to the color of her hair and skin. It wasn't meant to be taken literally.'

'He admits in one sonnet that she's really fair.' I pushed my seat back expectantly.

She smiled across at me. She'd finished her first course. 'Dark Lady sleuths who look for a swarthy woman are wasting their time,' she said. 'Look, I'll tell you something sexy. See how her eyebrows are fair.' I examined them under the magnifying glass. 'There's an esoteric tradition that you can tell the color and texture of a woman's pubic hair from her eyebrows.'

She caught the direction of my eyes as they moved for a second. My thoughts were on the tuft of pubic hair she'd given me. I couldn't remember where I'd put it. The wine was beginning to go to my head. We were halfway through the second bottle and the main course hadn't even begun. Nor, with her epilepsy and her pregnancy, should Amelia have been drinking alcohol at all. I turned my attention to the Earl of Essex and read out the only words written on the back of his miniature, the now familiar Devereux motto: '*Basis Virtutum Constantia*'.

'They had another motto,' Amelia said, 'the one I mentioned: "*Virtutis Comes Invidia*" . . . "Envious pride is virtue's mate". The English translation for every word in Penelope's three mottos is found in the few stanzas of *The Victory of English Chastity under the Feigned Name of Avisa*.'

'I'm surprised she managed to fit Shakespeare in between all her noble lords,' I said.

'She fitted him in all right. He tells us so in Sonnet a hundred thirty-five:

> So thou being rich in Will, add to thy Will
> One will of mine to make thy large will more.'

'The willing conceits on William and Willoughby again?'
'Not quite there.'
I frowned. 'Isn't Shakespeare talking about himself sharing Penelope's . . .' I glanced round, '. . . pussy with Willoughby? "Will" is a pun for "sexual part", isn't it?'

She giggled and clapped her hand to her mouth. 'I meant you missed Sidney. His pet-name was Willy. If he's the Caveleiro in the *Avisa* then he probably did get laid by Penelope.'

I noticed how attractive she was looking despite the flight and pregnancy.

She continued, ignoring heads that had turned our way. 'One nickname of Lettice Knollys her mother was "the little western flower". Oberon even uses it in *A Midsummer Night's Dream*. On the face of it, that was an allusion to the diminutive Floscula and Lettice's Staffordshire origins, which Penelope shared. But "western" was bawdy shorthand for "anal-genital" and "flower"' was obviously . . .' It was Amelia's turn to glance round. A couple looked hurriedly away. 'Well I'll leave you to guess. Remember, Willoughby's phoenix bird Avisa came from the "wester side of Albion's isle", and the Anglo-German had often seen "the western part".'

'But why compare Penelope with a phoenix if that implied she was faithful?'

She took a sip of wine and said her throat was getting dry from talking too much. 'In the *Avisa, contraria contrariis*, it was for comic effect to highlight all the hypocrisy by depicting her as the opposite of what she was. Poets kept calling her a phoenix to flatter her: Gwinne and Constable for example. Thomas Campion dubbed her "*Stella Britanna*". In the *Avisa* she's "this Britain bird", so the "wester side of Albion's isle" could be bawdy for Penelope's lissom little ass.'

Amelia had raised her voice as if she needed to convince others too. This time half a dozen heads turned. I glanced at the next table then grinned thievishly at my wife. 'Shakespeare didn't stand a chance.'

She returned my look. 'It's no wonder the upper classes noticed him. People knew their station in the sixteenth century. Not many got to rise above it. Shakespeare was in a hurry to arrive socially, so he took a shortcut via Penelope's bed. The *Avisa* succeeded in embarrassing everyone involved. It cost Shakespeare the patronage of the Earl of Southampton, who was one of Penelope's closest friends. After all Shakespeare had gotten laid by the sister of the Court's darling. Essex was one of the most powerful men in England. Blunt was luckier. He and Essex were buddies.'

'I'd like to think he screwed his way up the social ladder.'

'He certainly tried . . . and got the pox for his pains.'

'D'you think he gave it to Penelope?' My question was half-serious.

'He may have gotten it from her. It's on record she had smallpox, but it left her face unmarked . . . at least so they say. For all we know she could have had syphilis as well.'

'Don't you think it's still possible Shakespeare's attention to her was no different from all her other admirers?'

'No, I'm certain he went farther than the other poets who

idolized her. The *Avisa* pokes fun at all the men at her beck and call . . . labels them "Venus idolaters". Penelope liked to dress up as Venus when she went to costume parties. Which reminds me. Penelope was always being compared with Venus, the "pearl" of the ocean. Think of the droplet pearl in the Longleat portrait. A perfect pearl, like a piece of coral, was another symbol of the philosopher's stone. Shakespeare uses "rich" and "pearl" together in umpteen places.'

'She may have fooled around, but in the end though she went back to Blunt,' I pointed out. Our candle had started to die. It was snuffed and conjured away and a new one took its place.

'They got back together some time in fifteen-ninety-four and stayed together until he died in sixteen hundred and six. Penelope died the year after. She had five children by Rich of whom one died, and six bastards by Blunt and one of them died also. There was another too, born early in May fifteen-ninety-four at Leighs Priory. It wasn't her husband's. Nor was it Blunt's. He'd been on the Continent nine months earlier. The child wasn't stillborn as she made out to people after it was whisked away.'

'Whose was it?'

'You're as bad as everyone else. Always more questions.'

'D'you think once your thesis is published critics will accept your Dark Lady theory?' I asked between mouthfuls of Norfolk squab. If the wine was good, Raymond Blanc's food was in another world.

'Maybe but not before. Only I don't think Nancy ever will. For her it's a matter of principle regardless of evidence.'

'Until then your critics will vilify you, I suppose.'

'Vilifying's a bit strong. Most of them are a bunch of pifflers and band-wagoners. Some are on my side though. Like Lindenbaum.' She stretched a hand out to me. Her sleeve knocked over her glass and wine spilled across the tablecloth, just missing Penelope's face-up miniature.

I seized the pictures and rewrapped them. Two waiters descended and covered the wet table with a half-cloth of pink linen and Amelia returned the miniatures to the safety of her bag. We ate in silence for some minutes, making the most of the food. The boyish Raymond Blanc himself came by and in French exchanged a few words flirtatiously with Amelia.

Finally I came out with it again. 'Penelope's child that was whisked away . . . I'm meant to have guessed it was Shakespeare's or Willoughby's, right?'

'Right. The child was called William Willoughby. He was raised by Willoughby's family. I'd be inclined to say no one knew at the time whether Henry Willoughby or Shakespeare was the boy's father. Maybe they didn't know themselves. The *Sonnets* suggest there was a time when they were both boffing Penelope. But there was someone else who had inside information . . . Thomas Thorpe, the *Sonnets*' publisher. It comes back to that word "begetter" in the dedication again. Henry Willoughby set forth for Virginia in sixteen hundred and nine as an "adventurer of person" with the Virginia Company. Young William went with him. Henry procured the *Sonnets* for Thorpe. He was also their main inspiration. But Thorpe knew a thing or two and fancied he'd write a dedication in cipher to prove how clever he was . . . and to protect himself.'

I ran the dedication through my mind. I'd read it so often I knew it by heart.

'Is "begetter" the creator of the *Sonnets*? If not,' she continued, 'it could mean "father" . . . in this case William Willoughby's father. Rearrange Thorpe's word order and if you put "begetter" with "Mr W.H.", Henry Willoughby becomes William's father. But put "begetter" with "our ever-living poet" and it's Shakespeare who's the father. Thorpe probably didn't know which of the two of them it was, but I'll bet he knew who the mother was. It wasn't for nothing the *Avisa* was reissued in sixteen hundred and five when Blunt became the Earl of Devon and married the recently divorced Penelope, or in sixteen hundred and nine when Thorpe brought out the *Sonnets* quarto.'

'If William Willoughby sailed to America in sixteen hundred and nine what happened to him then?' I was still keeping my voice low. We'd passed up the cheeseboard. As I attacked fresh loquat and starfruit sorbet a plateful of *petits fours* arrived.

'Henry Willoughby was drowned on the voyage to Virginia. William died a few years later having fathered a son. I don't know the name of the mother. In fact all we have to go on are two documents. One refers to the death of "Henry his father Wm Wilobie".' She spelt it for me. 'It's dated sixteen-twenty-two.'

*   *   *

283

Most of Amelia's research for her doctorate was complete before we left America, so writing it up as a dissertation occupied much of her time at home. She was quite open with me about the way her interest in Shakespeare had palled, but she said Elizabeth Chambers was sure from the chapters she'd already seen of *The Hermetic Tradition in Elizabethan Literature* that it would impress the two gowned and capped examiners she would face for her *viva* in the Examination Schools. Bill Arden, a commissioning editor at Oxford University Press, had met her at a dinner party – another I'd missed – and voiced an interest in the book that would follow her thesis.

At Harvard Amelia had always had her detractors. As Michaelmas Term progressed the revelations of her special lecture and the lack of published evidence for back-up caused a groundswell of interest on both sides of the Atlantic, particularly in academic quarters. Most reactions were negative, especially at Harvard. Three weeks after the lecture Nancy Bretton had flown into print to denounce her. Scholars at Oxford were more receptive. She'd anticipated criticism. She knew that as time went on opinion would swing in her favor and there would be a lot of red faces. I watched the Dark Lady debate from a distance as the groundswell turned to a floodtide by late October when Lindenbaum finally spoke out and plumped in Amelia's favor. But it was clear that the controversy would not be settled once and for all until Amelia's thesis was published. Meantime she was a celebrity in her own right. For a couple of weeks so many journalists dogged her footsteps instead of mine that I began to feel jealous. A phone call from Marcus to congratulate her did little to help, seeing that our phone number was ex-directory and she admitted she'd phoned him soon after we'd taken over the flat.

It was ironical that Amelia's interest in Shakespeare was declining. The divide that had long separated her from the rest of the field was closing fast. I heard through faculty channels that Elizabeth Chambers put it down to pregnancy at first, but never having been pregnant herself, felt she was in no position to judge. She must have wondered if her protégée was approaching burn-out. From these signals and rumors and from what Amelia had to say about it I decided it was just as well for William – even I was calling him William now – if she didn't overdo things. What was positive too was that Katie had told her she thought she

284

was cured of the worst of her 'problem' – her gods. Getting rid of them had begun from the moment she'd screamed at the sight of Shakespeare's body, then continued with her father's death and been completed with her cathartic scream on the couch two months later. Despite my secret longing for Black Jenny I hoped she was right. There'd been no more Black Jenny since the second time and none of her bouts of glazed eyes and shaky arm.

In mid-November, with Philip Joblove's agreement, I decided to carry out one of the new safe antenatal screenings. No amniocentesis was necessary. It was a technique developed by an Australian group with George Glover, an acquaintance of mine in the Department of Biochemistry. He isolated a cluster of fetal cells from Amelia's blood and after I'd set up a culture to clone some more of these cells for later tests, I had my pathologist analyze our baby's DNA. That night I brought home the news that it was a boy. Amelia had been right. William was finally official. She gave me the best grizzly bear hug she could manage with a pregnant belly.

Rarely in my life had I walked as much as I did on those mild evenings that were so clear and starlit. I walked for miles after the final shift in the lab was over, coming home in the small hours long after Amelia had gone to bed. Research was making progress much faster than expected thanks to the wide range of samples from California, and we were reaching a critical phase. It was only around this time that I became aware of my depression, but I couldn't explain it to myself or dispel the gathering cloud which grew darker the closer my vaccine came. With these black moods came a feeling that I'd been abandoned by my guardian angel. Instead there were not just eyes and voices. There were footsteps that dogged my own on my long nocturnal jaunts. I was being reminded by all kinds of trivial things that I still needed to find my mother.

With Amelia's attention directed toward her body I was feeling increasingly detached from the outside world. The vaccine race was on in earnest and there were bullish noises over the grapevine from a group seriously in the running at George Washington University, not to mention another closer to home at Westminster Hospital.

Daily I was tearing myself away from the lab, sometimes before dark, to be with Amelia. After dinner I went back to work to make up lost time. We hardly saw each other at weekends when

Amelia went to visit my family and I pushed myself doubly hard in the lab. I could tell Amelia noticed that I was tired and twitchy though she never said anything in case it discouraged me. She thought she should be working more on her thesis but pregnancy imposed limits. She tried hard to discipline herself, making time each day for a spell in the Bod or the Radcliffe Camera. Three hours a week were allocated to tough antenatal classes in Somerville with other pregnant students.

Amelia loved the traditional round of North Oxford hospitality and would have preferred to go out more, but my work was growing even more demanding by the end of November. Now she often went out anyway, alone.

She'd already bought a carry cot, a high chair and a dark-green bassinet and filled three drawers with Babygros from Mothercare and a cupboard with Pampers nappies. For Christmas we'd penciled in four days for Amelia at Forest Spring, and one for me.

Amelia shared my feelings about the importance of my work, but though I was always home for dinner it wasn't enough to her way of thinking. When she told me – which she did more than once – all it did was make me feel guilty. I couldn't explain the feeling to myself, let alone talk about it. She didn't even smile when I did my Mick Jagger impression the other day. It was a real killer that used to have Lucy in stitches. She just walked away and I was left wondering what had happened to the woman who'd once been able to harmonize the warring elements inside me.

Could I admit that now and again I thought wistfully of Lucy, the way she used to cradle my head between her breasts if I was feeling low? Hadn't Lucy been my other self once? I'd been devoted to her at the outset. I'd been lame since I left her. If only Lucy could have fed the inner man. There were also times when I wanted Black Jenny to appear again and in making love to Amelia I sometimes fantasized that the whore was back. But if anything Amelia seemed more stable now, more her feminine self; less and less the playmate with balls who'd once driven me to distraction with her air of uncaring independence.

When we left America Amelia talked constantly of Falstaff and when she'd see him again. Now with her baby growing into a person inside her she never mentioned Falstaff.

Nor Marcus.

Maybe it was finding out the gold bracelet was a present from Marcus. Maybe it was the things Cissy said and left unsaid at the wedding. Amelia's relationship with Marcus hadn't been touched on since our row in the car. We'd both carefully stepped around it, even when Marcus's name had come up on other fronts. But I had no evidence their relationship was dead.

Amelia must have known I was listening in on the phone, on and off. The time that Marcus phoned, it was me who took the call. It would have been too obvious if I'd gone and picked up the bedroom phone, so I hung around the sitting room and only got Amelia's end of their conversation.

It didn't go down too well when I came into the Faustian world of the Bod and crept up behind her sitting in the Upper Reading Room engrossed in a sixteenth-century tome. The leatherbound folio was almost too big for the reading stand where it was propped. When she asked me what I was doing there I gave her a sharp look and said: 'Just checking to see you're all right, sweetie.' That must have rankled with her. She asked did I imagine I needed to check up on her? Didn't I trust my own wife, one who was five months pregnant? At times like that when she was dismissive and volatile she was completely unreachable.

If I thought going for long walks would drive away Marcus's ghost I was wrong.

18

My struggle to damp down my possessiveness often foundered and when I was by myself in the flat I occasionally hunted through Amelia's drawers, hoping to find some indication that she'd been unfaithful – a phone number, a letter, another present she couldn't explain – something that would lead back to Marcus and prove her treachery, turning her into a Carmen, a faithless harlot that no man could ever trust to be his alone. My quest, which eventually became a daily ritual, failed to turn up anything.

Then in December her trunks, eight of them, arrived from the States by sea. Our flat was roomy by Oxford standards but there weren't enough cupboards and drawers to house all the stuff. Five of them were stacked unpacked in the spare bedroom next to the loo, waiting for my inspection the night Amelia went off to a dinner party in Henley. I'd told her to go without me. Too much work. Which was true except that I crept home early, allowing myself a good three hours for the job.

I pushed the top trunk to the middle of the floor. It was all books. The second looked more interesting when I finally got it open. Even with the right key the iron locks were too rusty to want to come easily. This one was full of clothes, lots of them, all neatly folded. Near the bottom I found handfuls of her underwear: even a black corselet which I pressed into my face, snuffling it up. There were dozens of unopened packets of black stockings, Amelia's favorite brand, and several pairs of satin cammie knickers. Something unusual caught my eye. I picked up the delicate black flower, made of lace. It was attached to a black elastic garter. I'd come across Amelia in black stockings before, but never underwear like this. I piled it all on the floor before I got too excited by it. The fusty smell of the leather trunk blended oddly with Amelia's own scent that permeated her knickers. The heady combination of the two sent me dizzy for a while and filled me with need for her as I grubbed deeper.

Further down my fingers found something firm that wasn't the bottom of the trunk. I hauled all the remaining garments to the floor and uncovered academic journals, Amelia's neatly bound collection – the ones in which she'd had papers published. Most of them I'd read. I was about to put everything back when I noticed something different among them. Moving two copies of *The Shakespeare Quarterly* I unearthed a flat leather case about eight inches square, like one of those jewel boxes, only larger. Its surface was shiny hard and it had a snap-shut lid. It wasn't locked.

It didn't contain jewelry, just a few pieces of paper that I delved carefully into. The top three sheets looked very old – a letter of some description, foxed and damp-stained and covered in words in faded ink that hardly looked like English at first glance. The sheets were not flimsy but were frayed at the edges and I took them out one at a time, careful not to damage them, and laid them out on the dressing table. The fourth sheet was a piece of modern paper written in Amelia's clear hand.

I switched the table lamp on to get a better look, starting with the three old sheets. The odd word – it was English – was decipherable here and there. Elizabethan or not long after. There was a signature with an ostentatious flourish at the bottom of the third sheet and after staring at it till I couldn't stop blinking I decided it read: William Willobie. In February Amelia had mentioned that she had a document referring to a member of Henry Willoughby's family. I hadn't seen it at the time. Then I remembered she'd mentioned something else, at the French restaurant: two documents with his name, one of which, dated 1622, referred to 'Henry his father Wm Wilobie'. She'd spelt it out. The spelling here was slightly different.

Marcus was forgotten as I found myself caught up in the

Shakespeare enigma again, wondering whether the Bard or Henry Willoughby really fathered the person who appeared to have signed this letter.

I picked up the sheet of paper in Amelia's writing and studied it under the lamp, clutching at the corners of the dressing table and feeling my knuckles grow tighter as I read down the page.

The bombshell finally hit me. Ideas were flying everywhere. The page drifted in and out of focus turning my head in circles. I didn't know which way to look. I wanted to scream. *You've been betrayed, Daniel*. No, I whispered. *Betrayed* a voice echoed. There it was in her own handwriting.

It must have been several minutes before I got a grip on the situation. I tried to read the script in the old letter but it was wasted effort. It would need an expert. An expert like Amelia.

I checked my watch. It was getting on for nine. She wasn't due back much before midnight. There was one way to find out if it was true.

I abandoned everything where it lay on the carpet, stumbling on the pile of clothes as I ran for the door. Grabbing my jacket from the peg in the hallway and checking my keys were in the pocket I bolted down the stairs. Normally I would have walked the mile to the lab in South Parks Road. This time I ran, trying to choke off the anger. Amelia must have known all the time. Or had we both been cynically manipulated? Marcus too.

Maybe all the time Lawrence had been pulling Amelia's strings. She'd once said he knew almost as much about Shakespeare as she did. He just didn't talk about it. But why the subterfuge?

Panting, I opened the inner door to the lab, locked it again from the inside and turned up the heating. Cold air stuck to everything.

That evening at the ashram I'd put her father's serum in the coolbox inside the security cabinet in case Lawrence wanted it double-checked later. Since then I hadn't given it a second thought. It had come to Oxford via Hungerford House along with everything else important to me in Lao-Tzu House.

When I'd got my breath back I rotated the combination dial and the door swung open. The coolbox door inside was stiff but I wrenched it open and inside on the second shelf exactly where I'd left it nine months earlier I found Lawrence's ichor in a frosty dish I'd marked with his name.

There was so much hurt ripping through my stomach I had trouble donning a pair of latex gloves and preparing a fresh solution from the dry blood. Under my breath I swore *you fucking bastard* – over and over.

From a drawer I took a hard copy of a genetic blueprint attached to a sheaf of continuous stationery. Baba had described the gray and black pattern that looked more like a bar code as 'genetic spaghetti' on one of his visits to Lao-Tzu House. I glanced over the summary data page to make sure I'd got the protocols right and turned all systems on.

I grappled to get a hold on my feelings. *You fucking bitch* I said under my breath and took a tiny steel vial from a cabinet. With my thumb on the bulb of a pipette I sucked up a quantity of the solution in the dish and released it into the vial. The computer was on standby in 'Active' mode, warming up. When the master disk had been loaded in I inserted a catheter into the tiny orifice in one end of the vial and its male shape slid into the receptive female slot in the analysis chamber of the computyper. At that moment C-J would have been an asset. I was still far from comfortable not doing it manually, but that would have taken forever and a day. I hadn't used the machine too often in Mendocino and then mostly with C-J's beaky face squinting over my shoulder. I'd only used it a couple of times since then. I switched it on.

I thought I had it set right and swore again for good measure – *bastards*. The current would force Lawrence's genes through the typing gel, enabling the correct stuttered regions of DNA to be matched to the corresponding radioactive probes in accordance with the program.

I keyed a series of figures. There was a knock at the pebbled-glass door and someone tried the handle. I was feverish to the point where I blocked out sight and sound, everything except the job in hand. The knocking grew more insistent. I went on not hearing it or seeing the vague male shape looming through the glass. Footsteps retreated down the corridor outside.

Shifting back in my chair I held my breath and flicked the 'Read' key. For a few seconds there was a whining sound as the computyper went through the critical scan of millions of molecules reacting to the electrically charged gel, searching for the critical labels to match the master probes.

There was an endless pause. I noticed how my hand still shook.

When the green light on top of the machine flashed on lit by Lawrence's weeping gene in its Shakespeare format I blinked numbly and fought off the urge to pick up the chair and smash it down on the light.

Lawrence was the green lamplighter. Desperately I repeated the words as I returned the remainder of his serum to the coolbox and slammed shut the cabinet door. Mechanically I switched the equipment off.

Twenty minutes later I was back at the flat. It wasn't eleven o'clock. Amelia was still not there.

I looked at the mess strewn across the floor and knew I had to leave it that way for her to see. I wanted her to know that I'd found her out, the moment she walked in, and realize that I felt betrayed because she hadn't shared her knowledge with me. Why had she and Lawrence gone to such lengths to set up the Shakespeare Search? I'd been duped all along, maybe even into marrying her.

Grasping a Heineken I went into the bedroom, shivering uncontrollably. As I pulled a navy sweater over my head and forced the hand holding the can through the sleeve I returned to the spare room and stared down at the genealogy lying in the lamplight. I put down my lager and laid the sheet of paper alongside the pages of the antique letter. The family tree appeared to cover the Willoughby connections Amelia had described to me at the restaurant. Only here was more – in her own handwriting.

Here William Willoughby's father was Henry Willoughby or William Shakespeare, just as she'd said. There was a big question mark by Shakespeare's name. But the genealogy didn't stop at William Willoughby or *his* son Henry. It went on right down a further eleven generations and the name at the bottom was Lawrence Hungerford. *The green fucking lamplighter*.

Had she, had both of them really known all along? A thought came back to me: Amelia's *let's find out if Shakespeare fathered any little bastards*. I pictured her. Apart from the blond hair and the inviting smile I couldn't see the resemblance to Penelope Rich. On the other hand if I visualized her with Lawrence's dark eyes instead of Sarah Hungerford's perhaps I could see the similarity after all.

Back in our bedroom – 'our' sounded funny now, as if we were

292

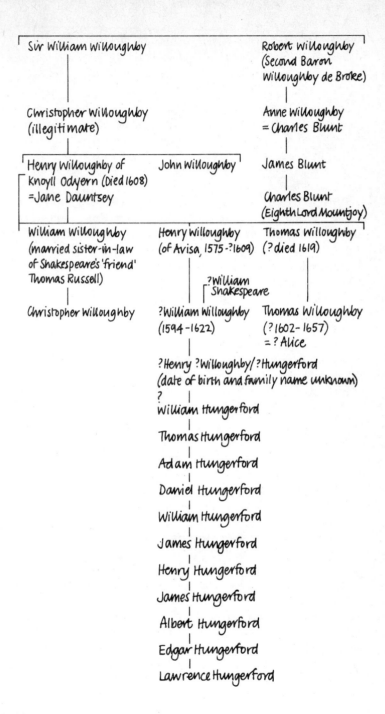

Sir William Willoughby — Robert Willoughby (Second Baron Willoughby de Broke)

Christopher Willoughby (illegitimate) — Anne Willoughby = Charles Blunt

Henry Willoughby of Knoyll Odyern (Died 1608) = Jane Dauntsey — John Willoughby — James Blunt

Charles Blunt (Eighth Lord Mountjoy)

William Willoughby (married sister-in-law of Shakespeare's 'friend' Thomas Russell) — Henry Willoughby (of Avisa, 1575-?1609) — Thomas Willoughby (? died 1619)

?William Shakespeare

Christopher Willoughby — ?William Willoughby (1594-1622) — Thomas Willoughby (?1602-1657) = ? Alice

?Henry ?Willoughby/?Hungerford (date of birth and family name unknown)
?
William Hungerford
Thomas Hungerford
Adam Hungerford
Daniel Hungerford
William Hungerford
James Hungerford
Henry Hungerford
James Hungerford
Albert Hungerford
Edgar Hungerford
Lawrence Hungerford

instantly divorced – I caught Amelia's rag Rosaline sizing me up from on top of the piano. In the kitchen I found what I was looking for – a meat skewer from the cutlery carousel. I tiptoed back into the bedroom, rechristened the doll 'Amelia' with a wave of my Heineken and stabbed her through the heart, twisting the skewer a few times before withdrawing it, then carried her remains to the sitting room and threw them into the gas fire that burned low in the grate. I watched her turn brown and curl from the toes up without really catching fire. I didn't turn my back on her till her aspic irises finally popped.

Typical Amelia when she got in soon after midnight to know about the doll already, though not from a stabbing pain in her heart as I'd hoped, or a cardiac arrhythmia over the after-dinner mints. My psychic wife just stood there jiggling from one foot to another, seven months pregnant and itching to run for a pee. The funny thing was I felt sorry for her and William, so sorry that I tried to put my arms round her, but she pushed me away and after a glare at the hearth she marched first to the loo then to the spare bedroom.

When she came back she was holding the leather case. She put it on the mantelpiece and a long silence followed as we hurled invisible daggers back and forth. She'd gone terribly white.

Who's pulling your strings now, Daniel? I was wrestling with the voice and pushing myself back against the window to look at her better. *Get out, get out* I heard myself screaming. My face was on fire with tiny needles. Visions were skipping by.

Amelia was shooting me with her round green eyes and then flying for the door, but I was faster and I was slamming it shut in front of her. I was leaning over whispering in her ear: 'Not you' and she recoiled, panicky, those eyes so frightened where I expected hatred. *Scream, Daniel, scream. You've just been cheated of your freedom.* Amelia's head was swiveling under the grip of someone's hands. *What have you been up to all these years, Daniel?* The voices never taunted so viciously before. A spider crawled up the wall to the side of her head. *Janey, save me, please.*

My face jerked round. I took my hands from her throat and stood over her where she'd fallen in a heap. She was gaping at me with her jaw curiously slack, feeling her throat which was bright pink.

'I'm sorry,' was all I found to say. 'I just wanted an explanation.'

The voices had gone but I was scared stiff at what I might have done. I nodded in the direction of the two armchairs in front of the fire and with a quick glance at the door she stumbled to her feet and sank down in her usual place.

There were days and days. This wasn't one of my lucky ones. I slumped into my seat to get a better view and waited.

When it was clear she wasn't going to say anything unless I asked the questions I made an effort to control my rage and asked her if Lawrence knew he was descended from Shakespeare.

With her eyes so watery with the tears she was holding back she nodded at that and said: 'Lawrence always thought he was Shakespeare's descendant in the direct male line – a bastard line. He used Baba to get Polly Ann to test his blood – the blood he left behind at the ashram – against your program. She did it. She got the green light.'

Jeezers, Lawrence's blood was sitting round in the cabinet at the ashram for several weeks . . . the computer switch that someone had tampered with. Polly Ann knew how to run the weeping gene test if everything was all set up . . . which it always was. Polly Ann in the lab on her own late at night without the lights on, looking guilty. Before we got involved with each other. But she was dead now. A guilty suicide after all? Pushed off the cliff to silence her? My thoughts came out aloud.

Amelia was saying, looking me straight in the eye, that I must be out of my mind to put this last suggestion to her. She was crying softly as she spoke, but she kept her chin up and eyes wide. Polly Ann had deceived me. I didn't have to feel guilty about her anymore.

'You *knew* about Polly Ann,' I said.

'I went along with it. It didn't feel right.'

'To use me and her?'

'Right.'

'What about the girl at the party . . . Charlene . . . and Marcus?'

When it came, her reply was: 'He just thought you were involved with Polly Ann . . . that I ought to know about it.'

'Jealous?'

'Uhuh, yeah, I was jealous. Marcus didn't know why Polly Ann was doing it, getting involved with you, truly.'

'I meant was Marcus jealous of me and you. But you really were jealous. You did care, didn't you?'

'Yeah, I didn't need to hear about you and her. Not just then. I'm sorry, baby.'

Why should I believe her? She'd deceived me too. 'How could Lawrence have known I wouldn't throw his serum away after I'd checked it out?'

A long sniffle. 'When Lawrence wanted something to happen it usually did. He knew you wouldn't try him for a green lamplighter at the ashram.'

'But I have tried it, haven't I? I've just checked the bloody thing in the lab and it panned out fine. Your old man was the green lamplighter and you bloody well knew all along. I suppose that was intentional too.'

'Baby, I swear I was going to tell you anyway. Only Lawrence wouldn't let me while he was alive. Listen, I was waiting for the right time, that's all. I was afraid of what you might do to me. The letter and our family thing about Shakespeare's line didn't add up to proof, but that was all we had to go on before your test. Lawrence was always convinced about it, but I couldn't prove it for him with the letter and the family tree. He was more and more desperate. That's why your gene meant such a lot to him. It gave him the idea . . . the chance for absolute proof.' Then she added: 'You know what I was like where Lawrence was concerned.'

That statement alone raised a thousand questions. 'Why in hell couldn't Lawrence simply have asked me to do it? Why all the bloody rigmarole?'

She came back at me with a brittle reply. 'Would you have gone breaking into Shakespeare's grave just because some American asked you to do it? Of course you wouldn't. Not even for money. You'd only do it if it would help your research.'

And a little bit for love of you, I thought. 'But why couldn't he have asked me when he came to the ashram?'

'And admit he'd maneuvered you into the Search in the first place? Lawrence might have had a . . . warped way of doing things, but he also had his pride. You've got to see he was *driven* to know if his descent was real. If you'd run that test he couldn't have faced you when the light turned green, not after the way he'd manipulated you.'

'*You'd* manipulated me,' I shouted back. 'You fucking liar.'

'Daniel, baby, please, please, please forgive me.' She half rose from her seat to come to me until she saw my look. 'Believe me, I was going to tell you soon. Lawrence stuck to his side of the bargain – you got all your samples and look what that's done for your work. He went on supporting the Search long after he'd gotten the green light.'

'Bully for him. I still haven't found the vaccine, remember.' She really *was* looking pregnant ballooning out of her armchair. 'I suppose now Lawrence is dead you're going to tell the world . . . now that I've found out.'

She was shaking her head. 'I promised him I never would.'

'Not even for the sake of your goddamned research?'

'Not even. And it isn't relevant anyway. It would have destroyed Lawrence's privacy and it would destroy mine now and yours if I went round for the rest of my life being Shakespeare's great-granddaughter to the nth degree. Anyway, if you marry into the Hungerfords you just have to accept our weirdo ways, Lawrence's Byzantine schemes, everything.'

Liars and cheats, I muttered to myself. A lot of things were beginning to clear in my head. It all explained why Amelia's interest in Shakespeare was so incestuous. Here was I with a wife who was descended from Shakespeare, and through her, a baby son. But betrayal, disloyalty, deceit were the words sailing inside me. Our relationship had taken a quantum leap after this little scene . . . backwards. No wonder the old sod had been cagey about taking the weeping gene test.

As always she saw my next question coming. 'Don't start on about Marcus,' she said. 'He never knew. He still doesn't. In the beginning I went along with Lawrence's plan for the Search for Lawrence's sake. Also I wanted to know too. There might have been others besides Lawrence. He needn't be the only descendant.' She was hesitating. 'Also I did it for Marcus and the Rostrum.' Another pause. She was fidgeting wildly. 'You've got to remember I'd been involved with Marcus up to then. When I put the plan to him he was keen to jump on board and get us off the ground.'

I spared her a lewd reflection on this remark. I was already steeled after what I'd been through so far.

'I was in love with Marcus,' she was saying while I sank lower. 'Or at least I thought I was. After you and I were together the first time I wasn't sure. When you went into that grave I knew it was you I wanted. Believe me, baby.'

Some consolation if she'd been fucking me while she dreamed of Marcus. 'Is it over?' I asked.

'Yes.' She trotted it out again as she ferreted round with her empty hands. Her tears had dried.

Why should I believe her now? She and Marcus had been in touch while I'd been conveniently out of the way for eight days at Big Sur or wherever. She'd still been fucking him then for all I knew. And maybe on her visit to the States in September. Carmen wasn't a patch on this one.

She still had a soft spot for Marcus, she was telling me. 'Sometimes he can be so considerate and gentle.'

'Gentle' was a euphemism for something else as far as I was concerned. Women could be such cunts. I thought of the Dark Lady's duplicity, the way she cheated on Shakespeare with his friend Henry Willoughby. Some friend.

'Did Lawrence know who the Dark Lady was?' I asked.

She took her time to answer that one. 'He knew who my hunch was and he agreed with it, but he never said why. I don't think he had any more evidence than I did. We still don't have *absolute* proof about her, the way the weeping gene's absolute proof about Shakespeare.'

The thought struck me. 'What about the miniatures?'

'They were just part of his collection. Edgar Hungerford found them years ago along with others.'

'If Lawrence was such a schemer maybe it was more than coincidence that he left them to you.'

'Along with lots more,' she reminded me. The barrier between us seemed to be lifting. 'There's one thing, though. It seems bizarre the way Black Jenny appeared and led me to the Dark Lady the same night Lawrence died.'

'It crossed my mind too. Supposing I revealed Lawrence's descent from Shakespeare?'

'I promised him that when you knew I'd make you keep it to yourself. After all, you're one of the family now and it's always been a family secret.'

I got out the question that had been tugging at my mind. 'If Shakespeare was a member of an ancient sect and descent passed in the direct male line, where did that leave Lawrence?'

She shuffled her feet before answering that. 'With Lawrence anything was possible. You'll just have to take my word there was a lot I never knew about him. He wasn't around much when I was a kid. He was a very secretive person and he belonged to all kinds of societies.'

'Secret ones?'

'If they were secret how would I know?'

'Don't you think for your research into that Elizabethan sect it would be interesting to know? What about the Tau?'

'Of course it would, but he never talked about things like that . . . not in terms of himself. We talked about Shakespeare a lot. He always wanted to know everything I'd found, as if he was always hoping I'd uncover clues to complete the record.' Her tone was not convincing.

I grew insistent. 'Maybe Lawrence belonged to a secret sect that Shakespeare once belonged to. Maybe Lawrence had to prove direct descent in the male line to strengthen his right to membership or his position in the sect. Maybe *that's* why he needed to prove his descent.'

I could see my frankness had shaken her. Her voice was edged, surprisingly, with bitterness. 'The thought had occurred to me.'

'Did you ever put it to Lawrence?'

'No. I knew it would be pointless. He wouldn't have told me. You'd understand that if you'd been around Lawrence all your life. There was so much he never said . . . I was his daughter and he never once told me he loved me.' The bitterness spread to the corners of her mouth.

'Why not?'

'I was a woman and as far as he was concerned women were subhuman.'

Though we'd rarely talked about Lawrence in such terms the picture fell into place. I reckoned she'd been his slave all her life because she'd been waiting for him to say he loved her.

'Will you read me William Willoughby's letter?' I asked quietly.

She rose uneasily and went to get it from the mantelpiece. When she'd taken her seat again she said she thought it was a rough draft of a letter sent from Virginia, probably to someone in England, possibly Shakespeare. The letter wasn't all there, just the last part of it. It contained no clues to the Dark Lady, but if it was addressed

299

to Shakespeare and the clean version got to him it was probably a third source document for *The Tempest*. Probably Shakespeare would not have been on speaking terms with Henry Willoughby in 1609 after the *Sonnets* were published without his authorization, but that would not have stopped him feeling affection for a youth who might be his own flesh and blood – someone who perhaps saw him as an uncle.

She read the script as easily as I could read the nutrients on a packet of muesli. She knew it virtually off by heart.

'Touching this misfortune it being of about two hours after noon a great rain and much wind came upon the sea and our little pinnace was shaken up by the waves until we came abeam of the Sea Venture whereupon to vouchsafe our lives Captain Gates did take myself and three other youths on board with such expedition that we could scarce protest and were nearly cast into the water I having first taken leave with much sadness of my dear father who remained to face such ill hap as should beset all able-bodied souls aboard the smaller vessel. Sad it is to relate that I never thereafter saw him who took leave of me professing much love to me and truly in mine eye am I fortunate not to have met the same end for his mortal remains must now lie at the bottom of the sea. On the following day we were cast on to the edge of an Isle that is called Isle of Devils where God be praised we did all come to shore of one piece – *there's some words crossed out here. I can't read them* – Notwithstanding certain of the company did bewail in piteous sort such as I could scarcely brook we relics of Neptune's tempest were compelled to pass a year in this unfortunate refuge which time we did occupy in fashioning a new pinnace from the carcass of the Sea Venture and from hence by God's grace of which we were ever mindful we came to this strange land – *there's another line crossed out* – praising the Almighty for our salvation while we did make question all the while whether the savages in this place or a sickness which so many have here taken may not yet portend a fate more dire than that from which we have been delivered with so much fortitude. There is by the shore a small chapel which resembles rather a rude cottage built of wood than a place of holy worship for

300

there is no glass and not much else in this land and therein presently assembled diverse of our small knot to give thanks and pray for those notably my father Henry Wilobie gent. who went to God in the course of our voyage to Virginia. When next leisure serve me to bring further tidings of our sojourn in this land I shall write further if the savages God willing and hunger and sickness do not send us also to Paradise. I pray this letter may cross the seas and come at last to your eyes.

Wishing you all contentment I remain yours to command.

Wm Wilobie'

She looked up at the end and her face creased into an uncertain smile when she saw I was reasonably relaxed, sipping my flat lager, with my legs slung over the side of my armchair.

'Since this was always a Hungerford family heirloom,' she was saying, 'it strengthened the connection from the Willoughbys to the Hungerfords. Only the letter didn't prove Shakespeare not Henry Willoughby was William Willoughby's father ... nor, now we know who the Dark Lady was, that Penelope Rich was William Willoughby's mother. But with the evidence of Lawrence's weeping gene it's certain that Shakespeare was William Willoughby's natural father and highly probable that Penelope Rich was his mother. I'm sorry Lawrence never lived long enough to find out I'd confirmed my hunch about Penelope Rich.' Sadness had crept into her voice. 'Not that he was bothered about the Dark Lady. It was the male line, the Shakespeare side that obsessed him.'

'You still haven't explained how the Willoughbys turned into the Hungerfords.'

'William Willoughby, who wrote this letter, had a son Henry before he died in sixteen-twenty-two. Fifty years later my ancestor William Hungerford was living in Cambridge, Massachusetts.'

I let her explain.

'I've tried every genealogical record there is to connect this younger Henry with the William Hungerford who was in Cambridge in the sixteen-seventies. In sixteen-eighty-two William Hungerford built the original Hungerford House.'

'When's the earliest record of this William Hungerford?' Interest had swollen, but I was still having problems holding back my anger.

Amelia was looking anxiously for signs of my mood. *Jeezers, she must be feeling guilty.*

'William Hungerford,' she went on, 'witnessed a land transaction in sixteen-seventy-four. Maybe the Henry Willoughby born not long before sixteen-twenty-two was his father. Maybe this Henry Willoughby settled in New England, changing his name to Hungerford. Or at least his mother changed it for him when they left Virginia. Maybe if he was illegitimate, Hungerford was his mother's name and he was always Henry Hungerford.' Her voice brightened. 'Anyway, according to Hungerford tradition William Hungerford was definitely this Henry's son and Lawrence's green light would seem to prove it.'

'Did you tell Katie about Shakespeare and your missing link?'

'Nothing to do with Shakespeare . . . at least not the family connection. Lawrence wouldn't have agreed. It's too secret.' She threw me one of her disarming looks that she had down to a tee.

'Always bloody Lawrence. Are you going to change your mind and write about Shakespeare's Tau in your thesis?'

'No.'

'Why not?'

'I think you can go too far invading someone's privacy like that.'

'That didn't stop you deceiving me into desecrating his final resting place.'

There was no answer.

'If it weren't that I have so much trust in you,' I said sarcastically, 'I'd think you and Mannering were in this thing together. It's almost as if he knows he can go on preaching about an orthodox Shakespeare because he knows you won't come out with the facts about the cross.'

Fury erupted from Amelia. 'Okay, Saint Daniel, just let me remind you I promised Mannering I wouldn't publicize the cross – whatever cross he thought it was – in return for him letting you off the hook. You agreed to return it. For *your* sake I promised not to breathe a word about it. For godsakes give me credit for some integrity.'

'Did Mannering really not know it was a Tau cross before he saw it?'

'I have no idea,' she said, all hoity-toity. 'I certainly didn't tell him. What difference does it make now?'

I repeated her question to myself. At any rate she hadn't labored the point about what the Search had done for my vaccine. And Marcus, too, had been maneuvered into the Search, no matter how much money he'd made from it. I muttered something caustic about secret societies, but Amelia wasn't listening. She was smiling and rising to go and clear up the spare room as if smiles and explanations could make up for so much hurt. I could see how close I'd come to blowing a fuse. The voices had almost pushed me there.

Lawrence was the green lamplighter and the old bugger had known all the time. For a second I heard a voice again: a flash of someone else talking about me inside my head. Amelia's armchair was empty. Well, Amelia bloody Hungerford, your illustrious ancestor had at least one bastard who went on producing more of the species. You've proved *that* point. But your baby brother didn't survive. Lawrence was the end of the unbroken male line. *The weeping gene doesn't get passed on through daughters.* I chuckled grimly. Where was my guardian angel now?

The miniatures of Penelope Rich and Robin Devereux hung over our bed, side by side.

19

Then let Avisa's praise be spread
When rich and poor, when all are dead.

The Victory of English Chastity
under the Feigned Name of Avisa
Thomas Willoughby [Anonymous]

13 Farrar Street
Cambridge
MA 02138
8 December

Dear Rosie,

You told me to keep you updated on Amelia and my little investigation and there's so much to tell that I'll save all my other news for a second letter next week if I can find the time.

The *Journal of Abnormal Psychology* said they'd like to look at my paper, so you see why I'm anxious about validating everything. Amelia has no objection as long as there's no clues to her identity (no *double entendre* intended!). Let me explain.

When I started writing down the case history, I found my mind continually turning to Amelia's mother. That's why I thought it would be a good idea to call David Bendix. As you're aware, David and I have been professionally acquainted for years. I've always known he was a close friend of Lawrence Hungerford's, if you can speak of a megalomaniac having friends. He was more of a Hungerford family retainer really, besides being their doctor. I thought he'd be able to throw some light on poor Sarah Hungerford's death.

I certainly wasn't prepared for the reaction I got when I mentioned her name. He went very quiet, then excused himself and hung up on me, as if someone had put the fear

304

of God into him, which was probably not far off the mark as it turned out.

That evening I got a call from him. Could he come and talk to me right away? He sounded very flustered, I mean really distraught. Of course I said yes and agreed to his suggestion that our discussion should be treated as a professional one between doctors.

David must be all of sixty or so – the same age as Lawrence Hungerford. I hadn't realized just how well they knew each other. They were at Exeter together and contemporaries at Harvard. He was far from coherent as he sat down and answered my questions – some of them anyway. I think he'd taken a pill or two before he came over. This is more or less what I found out. Please keep all of it to yourself. You are *sworn* to confidentiality, my dear. Besides, I can't sleep unless I tell it to somebody and if that somebody is you, I'll feel less guilty about all my sleuthing around beyond the bounds of psychoanalytical duty.

While he was at Harvard, Amelia's father fell for an attractive Boston heiress called Sarah Carlton. They got engaged in 1953. He put her on a pedestal. No doubt it was the old thing about madonnas and whores that was prevalent in those days. According to Bendix she was a nice girl. I assumed by this he meant a virgin. It seems Lawrence Hungerford had fooled around with more than his share of bad girls by Senior Year. In 1953, after Harvard, he went to Oxford. In 1956 his father died and he came home for the funeral. He and Sarah were still engaged to be married. As Edgar Hungerford's only son (there was a daughter who died in some accident abroad), he would inherit every last dime of the Hungerford estate.

This is where it starts to get interesting. David Bendix probably knows more about Lawrence Hungerford than anyone. As I listened to him telling me all this I decided he could best be described as a confidant to Lawrence. You have to know someone pretty well for them to tell you they can only get an erection with prostitutes, even if the person you're telling it to is your doctor. But that's exactly what Lawrence disclosed to David Bendix – that and the fact that with Sarah he was impotent – or almost.

I suppose I was surprised at David telling me all this, but when all's said and done, Lawrence is dead, and even doctors like to unburden themselves to a sympathetic analyst once in a while.

Lawrence, it turns out, wasn't just impotent with 'nice' girls. He had another sexual problem. While he was at Oxford he caught syphilis. The secondary infection was treated with penicillin at the time and he was thought to be serofast. It was only later he found out his sperm count was very low as a result of the disease. Producing children was going to be more than a little difficult.

After his father's funeral, Lawrence went back to England to finish some research he was doing with an Oxford fellowship. It can't have been much of a torch that he carried for his fiancée while they were apart, but David said it wasn't Lawrence who wanted to postpone the wedding. Sarah Carlton had been strictly brought up and her parents kept blocking wedding plans on the grounds they wanted to see Lawrence settle down first and quit his legendary womanizing. The first signs of Sarah's drinking problem appeared during the years of her long engagement.

In the end Lawrence and Sarah did get married – in 1957, when he quit Oxford and came back to live in America. David was Lawrence's supporter at the wedding. The newlyweds went to Venice for their honeymoon, only it can't have been much of a vacation. David learnt afterwards that Lawrence had gone out on the town in the company of hookers, while Sarah stayed in the hotel and got plastered. That set the pattern for the rest of their marriage.

I got the feeling David didn't exactly approve, though he didn't say as much. His account confirmed the view I'd already formed, from things Amelia said, that Lawrence had a pathological thing about hookers. When I asked him to be more explicit, he hesitated. David's always been a bachelor, and I'm certain he isn't gay. Reading between the lines, I think he used to join with Lawrence in some of his whoring round, at least when he was younger.

He was getting more and more agitated while we talked. He seemed deaf to half my questions and kept mopping his face every other minute.

What David told me next came as no surprise. Lawrence apparently had another obsession, one that he shared with his father. He was manic about the Hungerford bloodstock. It was only when he decided it was time to have children – or perhaps I should say a son – that he discovered syphilis had left him less than up to snuff in that department. He wasn't sterile, but he wasn't far off it.

If Lawrence was impotent with his wife, what, I asked David, did he do to try and produce a family? I could see him weighing up whether to tell me. I left him to think about it while I went and made some of that strong bourbon Santos coffee that you and I used to drink endlessly. *Tant pis* for decaf! While I was away, I think he must have popped another pill. He certainly seemed more than a little high by now, though that sounds an odd way to describe a man his age.

Anyway, in the end he wouldn't volunteer what Lawrence did to solve his little problem, though Amelia's very existence made it clear he must have done something. By now I just *had* to know. We sat there drinking our coffee while my mind hunted for the answer. I suppose I was determined to get to the bottom of Amelia's Black Jenny personality that played the whore and had something to do with Sarah. In the end it struck me. Some of the things Amelia hinted about Black Jenny. I looked David in the eye as I asked him. It still seemed like a long shot at the time. I said did Lawrence turn Sarah into a whore to get an erection? Obviously he couldn't do much about his sperm count, but he had to have an answer to his impotence dilemma. David didn't answer my question. I wasn't sure what I was getting at myself, but I knew what I had to ask. My next question was: Did Lawrence get Sarah to dress up in sexy black female underwear – garters, stockings, French knickers, things like that? At first David gave nothing away. I wasn't sure if he knew the answer. Then very slowly he nodded – twice. He was obviously struggling not to look surprised. He must have thought I could read his mind.

Dear Rosie, Lawrence *did* have a fetish about black female underwear and suchlike! I was so excited by this time. I felt I was getting closer to the bottom of Amelia's problem, not to mention her poor mother's. Just imagine, Lawrence got an erection with his 'nice' wife by fantasizing she was a hooker! Of course that solved the erection problem, but Lawrence still couldn't get Sarah pregnant. In those days, there wasn't much medical science could do to help.

Over the years, Lawrence's need to have a legitimate male heir grew more and more manic. He kept trying and in the mid-Sixties the gods smiled on him. He got Sarah pregnant. He must have had a few good sperm left. In due course Amelia was born – not the son that he'd hoped for. To call him disappointed would be a terrible understatement. The more I think about it, the more I see Amelia went through some pretty bizarre stuff, living with a drunken mother and a fetishist father obsessed with producing a son.

David pointed out that Lawrence had this spellbinding power to attract women. It was something he never lost as he grew older and it accounted for his hold over Sarah. It's obvious he dominated her completely. In a masochistic way she must have relished being tormented by him, or she would surely have gotten out.

When Sarah Hungerford got pregnant for the second time she was in her mid-forties and must have been at the end of her childbearing days. David was amazed she got pregnant at all. As you and I are aware, dear Rosie, this child was male. Unfortunately it died a short while after being born prematurely. By this time David and Lawrence knew Sarah had cancer beyond curing. Sarah knew it. But wait till you hear this. Lawrence had neurosyphilis and didn't know it. The original infection in his student days was never completely cured as he thought. It was only latent. The dosage of benzathine penicillin he'd received in the Fifties must have been too low and therefore immunosuppressive, driving the infection into its latent phase and allowing the syphilitic treponemes to develop sufficient resistance for the disease to become incurable.

Syphilis of the central nervous system, as you and I know, can lie dormant in the cerebral cortex for fifty years or more. David had his suspicions when Lawrence died. At autopsy there were lesions on his shoulders, back and thighs which at first looked like Karposi's sarcoma, but turned out to be syphilitic. Lawrence's syphilis had gone into the tertiary phase. Lawrence doesn't appear to have consulted anyone about it, nor to have died of it, but he must have known what it was. David signed Lawrence's death certificate and requested a check on his spinal fluid as part of the postmortem and had that part done by an old buddy at the hospital. When the sample was tested, syphilitic spirochetes were detected. Then just to be sure he had them run a fluorescent treponemal antibody absorbed test. The result was also positive, but syphilis wasn't mentioned in the pathologist's autopsy report.

I talked later to someone I know at Mt Auburn Hospital – you remember Lloyd Wyatt? – and he sneaked a look at the autopsy report. It showed death from heart failure, which sounded to me like a total cop-out. However the report did show massive hemorrhaging of the adrenal glands and the pineal gland, which struck me as odd in the circumstances. George Frost is very keen on the pineal gland, the so-called seat of the human soul, but of course it's basically there to produce melatonin and control the body's rhythms around the clock. On the other hand the adrenal glands would rupture if he died from asphyxiation. When I tried George for an explanation of how Lawrence could have died, he was as baffled as I was.

As David Bendix had warned, there was no mention of syphilis in the report. A really cosmetic job, all in all, to keep the Hungerford name clean. But David did make it clear the syphilis was far from being advanced enough to be the cause of death. As far as he was concerned, the real cause of death had not been established.

I tried to get hold of the pathologist who'd done the autopsy – not the one who'd done the spinal tap – and found that he'd quit his job suddenly and moved out of the area. So I asked Lloyd Wyatt to check the autopsy report again to make absolutely sure he'd seen the original version and not a doctored copy. Imagine my surprise when I got the news that the report was now missing from the file. What's more the FBI had apparently requested a sample of Lawrence's blood from the pathologist – the one who'd moved – and been given it. That really got my curiosity aroused. Bendix showed surprise, real or feigned, and said he didn't have a copy of the report himself. Suspicion fell on the missing pathologist, a man called Bernard Koulack, and now he was untraceable. Even odder was the fact that he was the pathologist who did Sarah Hungerford's autopsy. Bendix said he'd met the man a few times over the years but had no idea where he'd moved to. Neither had the hospital, which struck me as bizarre.

So there you are. Lawrence Hungerford had a brain that latterly became impaired by syphilitic dementia, on top of his pathological narcissism and the Hungerfords' hereditary eccentricity. Before I knew it, I'd asked David what happened the day Amelia was confirmed. You should have seen the way he broke down at this point. I went and fixed us a snack while he pulled himself together. When I came back, he told me.

The day of the confirmation her mother was too drunk to attend the service. Lawrence and Amelia went without her. When they returned they found her in bed. She was dead, apparently asphyxiated on her own vomit, so the official version goes. Her body reeked of alcohol and she'd thrown up all over the pillow.

The first thing David knew about it was when Lawrence phoned him – surprisingly unruffled – and summoned him to Hungerford House. Apparently he was shocked to find Amelia was in the middle of what was going on, but Lawrence refused to send her to her room. David examined Sarah's body carefully. He knew he was meant to think she'd choked on her vomit. It was only when I said I thought she'd been murdered that he gave me that fearful look again and came out with the truth about her death. After he'd examined the pillow he came to the conclusion she'd choked to death with her head forced into it. You've got to remember David knew the three Hungerfords intimately, not just Lawrence. Sarah had cancer and would have died anyway within months. If Lawrence had helped her on her way, was he not putting her out of her misery? That was how David put it. If he'd said 'mercy killing' I'd have hit him. More like putting the poor thing out of her husband's cruelty was how I put it. David contrived to look blank, but

I could see what was going through his mind. Here was a doctor of medicine confessing he'd helped cover up a murder. Dear Rosie, is it any wonder Amelia was traumatized, or that so much has been deeply repressed?

Then David called the Police Department. They arrived with a pathologist – yes, Bernard Koulack – and took the body to Mt Auburn Hospital for autopsy. The report noted cervical cancer, which was quite advanced, and confirmed death by asphyxiation. There was no suggestion of foul play and no inquest was held. Could there have been a high-level cover-up? Sarah Hungerford's drinking binges were public knowledge. She'd almost choked to death on her vomit twice before.

When I suggested that perhaps Sarah was dressed up in her whore's outfit when she was murdered – I stressed *murdered* – he didn't try to hide his surprise this time. He looked positively frightened of me, as if I were a witch with uncanny powers or something. He said yes to my suggestion.

So I asked him outright if Lawrence ever had sexual relations with Amelia. He was wringing his hands. He looked like a corpse himself. You'd never have forgiven me if I hadn't asked. He said there was no question of them ever having an incestuous relationship – by which he obviously meant a physical incestuous relationship – however attached to each other they were. In fact he seemed shocked that it even occurred to me. Are we to conclude from that, dear Rosie, that Amelia's Black Jenny personality only made love to some patriarchal figure in her dreams and fantasies, which were vivid enough to have you and me almost fooled? Incest, if David was to be believed, was purely psychological. All the same, I was far from convinced.

I guess David had wanted to get all that stuff off his conscience for years, and now that Lawrence Hungerford was dead, he felt free to unload it. He even confirmed about Lawrence cremating his wife in the oven. The baby, too, that died as soon as it was born. The funny thing was he never asked me to explain how I knew so much. Maybe he figured I'd worked it out from treating Amelia.

311

And the motive for Lawrence to murder his wife? In his twisted mind I think he needed no more justification than Sarah's failure to produce a son after all those years. From the moment the infant male Hungerford died, Sarah's murder was a real possibility. Her cervical cancer was the excuse and her drunken bout was the opportunity he'd been looking for. Never mind that she may have been ready for suicide.

Enough certainly happened to account for Amelia's subsequent problems. The things she must have been forced to witness that day. When I think about it, it all seems to fit with what I learnt in the hours.

You'll remember from my visit with you that I thought maybe Lawrence murdered his wife. Even so, to hear David say it came as a shock. It really hit me a few minutes later and left me with a splitting headache. I tried to get more out of him, but between my nausea and his reticence it was a waste of time. I had other leads to follow up on and I could always get back to him later.

It was long past midnight and I drove David home. He was too shaken by this time to get behind the wheel of his car, and I wasn't in a much better state. I called him next day to be sure he was okay and he sounded fine. He didn't ask me not to repeat to anyone what he had told me. That went without saying.

I'll keep you posted on Amelia's case, and bounce a few ideas off you for my paper. Let me know what you think of it so far, and expect a big newsy letter next week – with luck – to let you know about all the other things going on here, even if they *are* a bit anticlimactic after Amelia.

Lots of hugs from me,
Katie.

20

For I have sworn deep oaths of thy deep kindness,
Oaths of thy love, thy truth, thy constancy;
And, to enlighten thee, gave eyes to blindness,
Or made them swear against the thing they see;
For I have sworn thee fair – more perjur'd I,
To swear against the truth so foul a lie!

Sonnets, 152
William Shakespeare

After our argument my days passed in the shadow of an elusive nightmare. I struggled to climb out of bed in the morning and I struggled to work, where my mood with each new progress turned increasingly black. Time rushed past like a freight train that wouldn't slow long enough for me to jump off. Yet Amelia and I still shared the same bed and she was trying oh so hard to make up for what happened. But I wanted to push her away and as I went to bed at all hours and usually woke up round four in the morning it wasn't surprising if our sex life had gone for a burton. I was trying to forgive her, but at that rate it could have taken forever. I felt as if she belonged to them – the haunting voices. All that I had left of my own were my mother, and Janey my angel. Even William, who was due to pop in a couple of months, hardly seemed to belong to me.

The idea of a secret society lingered with me in the days that followed our row. I needed to talk about it to someone I felt I could trust. I was sure that something was going on that I couldn't understand and that it had to do with Lawrence and the Tau cross. Amelia really had told me all she knew or she was a very competent liar. The sensation that gnawed at me was of being besieged by invisible forces that were programed to destroy me little by little; perhaps the same forces that had destroyed my mother . . . and even treacherous Polly Ann, maybe.

The closest I'd come to talking to anyone about secret societies,

313

besides Amelia, was Gillespie. When I called Balliol I had to identify myself this time, then they passed on the number of the John Radcliffe Hospital and Gillespie's extension. The hospital switchboard was reluctant to put me through and when they did I understood why. Gillespie was incoherent. His voice hardly sounded like him anymore, poor bugger. I got on to one of the consultants who explained there was nothing more they could do for him. He was completely gaga, his tumor was out of control and he'd probably die by early January – another three weeks. I asked gratuitously if there was anything I could do to help. They said 'no', but I got Gillespie on the line again anyway and said I'd be thinking about him, in case he understood. When I hung up Tillman was muttering to himself in the next room. I could see him through the open door, tambourining the top of a bench with his fingers and shuffling his feet noisily. Maybe all the tension was getting to him as we got closer to breakthrough. He'd never grumbled about going to California or coming back to Oxford. Work was work to him. The place didn't matter.

The other avenue that kept coming to mind was Freemasonry. There was Lucy's father. He belonged to the Isaac Newton lodge and had tried unsuccessfully to get me to join a few years before. But Maurice Humpherson was doddery now and I doubted whether his lodge had much in common with the kind of secret society I was after.

There was Dunkley. He was my own age and an active Freemason, but I had a nasty feeling – nothing I could pinpoint – that he wasn't to be trusted, especially where something like Freemasonry was concerned. After all they did take a vow of secrecy when they joined and the price of disclosure, it was rumored, was meant to be a cruel if symbolic death. In practice, though, I knew that many Freemasons had told part of the inside story or how else would the rest of us know they even existed? There were hundreds of books on Freemasonry and most of them were written by the Craft's own adepts. One of them that I delved into contained something interesting: Teddy Roosevelt was a very active Freemason. Hadn't Amelia said he went hunting with Albert, her great-grandfather?

I'd give Dunkley a miss but there was someone else I was willing to trust. Geoff Alton was now head of Genetics at Leicester University. He wasn't yet a Freemason as far as I knew, but we'd kept in fairly regular touch and I was aware he'd been pressed more than once to join. As the man credited with the discovery of genetic fingerprinting – my part in it was minor compared to his – he came into close contact with senior police officers and lectured regularly to police pathologists on the ins and outs of obtaining genetic bloodprints in the hunt for rapists. He'd told me he'd resisted the invitations to become a Mason because he didn't believe in all that 'hocus pocus'. I dialled his direct line and he answered it himself.

I could see a jaunty Geoff standing there with his short dark beard brushing his polo neck, smoking one of his Golden Virginia rollos, as unlikely a Fellow of the Royal Society as you could hope to meet. He was probably even more overloaded with work than I was, but that was the nice thing about Geoff: he always made you feel he had all day to spend talking to you. I checked and discovered he still wasn't a Mason and the pressure to join was now intense. He didn't go into details. It was clear when I asked him about it that he'd been looking into Freemasonry more seriously and knew a lot about it. The good thing was, he pointed out, he'd taken no oaths and as far as he was concerned he'd be happy to tell me what he knew or find out answers to any questions if he possibly could. He didn't seem curious to know why I was asking so I didn't tell him. Maybe he thought I was a candidate for Craft masonry myself.

I began by asking him if Freemasons were capable of having someone killed. He seemed surprised at that and said some of the things you were always reading about were a load of crap. The same old Geoff. He didn't mince his words.

So I told him about Drake. Said I wanted information on the guy that would link him to Freemansonry . . . or, I added darkly, any more sinister secret organization. Geoff said he had CID contacts in the Leicestershire Constabulary, in particular the county's Chief Constable, Derek Enderby, who he knew would agree to talk to him as Enderby was the man who'd been trying to recruit him.

Geoff couldn't have wasted much time because he rang me back the same afternoon. As it turned out he didn't have a lot of information, but the little was interesting. Detective Chief Inspector Drake *was* a Freemason, a member of lodge number 9179, one of the most powerful lodges in the United Kingdom.

Manor Lodge, as the Manor of St James's Lodge was known, was made up almost entirely of present and past high-ranking police officers. Most members, Geoff told me in a surprisingly restrained voice, had been Masters of other lodges, including Drake. He added that the CID was riddled with men 'on the square' and threw in the helpful statistic that 'at least one in every six cops in Britain is a Freemason'. Drake, it turned out, was a long-time personal friend of the Master of Manor Lodge and a drinking crony of the chairman of the London Superintendents' Association. I made a mental note that if Manor Lodge was based around St James's that was exactly where Dunkley had his offices . . . next door to the safe deposit company which had held the Tau cross for me.

Was it likely that Drake might belong to other similar organizations? I asked Geoff.

'More than likely. The higher you go up the ladder in this kind of thing the further the tentacles reach in all directions . . . and the more secretive it gets . . . and the more power-broking goes on.'

'So Drake could well belong to some ultra-secret society inside or outside the Craft?'

'Possibly, but that's one I don't think Derek Enderby would answer even if he could, even if I *were* to sign on. You know something, I think ninety-nine percent of Freemasons are used as a smokescreen by the other one percent. All the stuff that leaks out – bribery and corruption, secret passwords, hairy-knee initiations – a lot of it happens but mostly it's a load of old cobblers that's leaked deliberately to draw attention away from what the real insiders are up to at some more speculative level that the world doesn't even know exists.'

That was that. I thanked Geoff and went back to my vaccine, but concentration came grudgingly.

It was four days later that I got a call from the Colonel. After the meeting with Drake in London I'd tried a couple of times, half-heartedly, to get in touch with Jake and Roy. There hadn't seemed too much point after I'd found the Colonel had fired them, but old times were old times and we'd been friends of a kind. They could have got in touch with me, but I'd come to the conclusion they were probably too embarrassed after the incident of my little black book. Though I knew they'd left the village I'd assumed they'd stayed in the Newbury area. But now the Colonel was telling me he'd heard from Roy's mother and they were both in hospital. They were dying from *Pneumocystis carinii* – the Colonel said 'pneumonia cystitis' – and had been diagnosed HIV-positive. They were in St Stephen's Hospital in London.

Coming on top of Gillespie then Geoff Alton's information on Drake, I needed this like a hole in the head. Maybe I too had been singled out for some convenient elimination. Jake and Roy and Gillespie had all seen the Tau and been in Shakespeare's tomb. That only left Mannering and me and Amelia . . . and Drake. Or were Jake and Roy and I, the three original intruders, the only ones on Shakespeare's hit list?

Pneumocystis carinii was a rare kind of pneumonia, unless you happened to have HIV. Then it was common and almost always terminal. Hadn't Drake warned he'd be surprised if Jake and Roy hadn't picked up the virus after their brothel crawl round half the southern counties? But to my knowledge they didn't belong to any of the high-risk groups. The chances of a man catching HIV from a woman, even a prostitute, were slim. No one knew that better than me. The chances of them both picking up HIV then developing full-blown AIDS in such a short space of time were minimal. Just the development of HIV antibodies could sometimes take that long. I tried to call them at the hospital. Normally with my credentials it would have been easy to talk to somebody there, but everyone I spoke to acted like a halfwit zombie. I couldn't get to talk to anyone in charge, or Jake or Roy. The complete runaround. *Can you spell their names. Putting you through to Inquiries. Are you a relative? Dr Who? You'll have to talk to the Registrar, Mr Smallwood. Registrar's office. No he isn't here. Dr Who?*

Bruce Hazard was still testing his own HIV vaccine at St Stephen's. He and I had stopped talking to each other about eighteen months earlier. His decision. He obviously had the run of the HIV wards, for which St Stephen's was famous. Maybe he'd put two and two together after all the Shakespeare hoo-ha and figured I might come snooping round his territory on the QT. In fact, when all was said and done, if Bruce Hazard had an arch-rival it was me. Maybe he'd put the word around. *If Dr Daniel Bosworth starts sticking his nose into my cases – in particular two patients of his acquaintance in Ward C – do me a favor and give him a hard time.*

By some miracle I got through at last to the sister in command of Ward C. The little I got out of her hinted that Jake and Roy were pretty terminal and that absolutely no visitors were allowed besides their immediate family. It sounded as though Roy in particular might already be dead.

I told her I could see no reason why she wouldn't let me in as a respected AIDS researcher. It wasn't as if *Pneumocystis carinii* was infectious. The parasite for the disease was carried by most healthy people anyway. That was when she hung up on me.

I gave up on Jake and Roy after that, but I couldn't stop trying to figure out whether Drake was implicated or we were all being picked off to appease Shakespeare's shade. I ached to open up to Amelia, but something, my elusive angel maybe, stopped me.

Curst be he that moves my bones. Was I next after Jake and Roy? I felt like I was at the end of my rope. The curse wasn't so much hovering over me as ramming itself down my bloody throat.

I pushed the thought of it away and it rushed back at me stronger than ever. If and when the curse really came for me, what shape would it take?

I'd found out who Frieda Harris was, the woman who'd painted Amelia's Tarot cards. Not that Amelia had told me. It was as if someone wanted me to find out. It seemed like more than coincidence when the *New Scientist* fell open at a page about Frieda Harris's intimate friend whom she painted the occult cards for in the first place: Aleister Crowley. Even I had heard of the publicity-seeking magus who'd been a member of the Hermetic Order of the Golden Dawn. Was that bogus sect still around? The article said 'no'. If Edgar Hungerford knew Lady Frieda Harris, had he been buddy-buddies with Aleister Crowley too and been given the cards by the Beast himself? Amelia hadn't the foggiest.

Since my return to South Parks Road I'd been checking myself weekly for HIV. Now I stepped up to twice a week. I also had the telephones checked – office and home – by an Oxford security agency to see if they were bugged. They weren't.

I'd had little time and less reason to be with Amelia since the big showdown, but our relationship hadn't cooled completely, especially from her side. Put it this way, I didn't think our marriage was going to bust up over it. Christmas came and went and I took one day off for the holiday.

*　　*　　*

Oh Amelia, it wasn't just a false alarm.

February was already upon us when the call came through to me. They'd rushed her into hospital. She'd gone into labor two weeks early.

I dropped into my office armchair to watch TV. Was that me on the screen? I laughed loudly for the benefit of my absent Amelia as I raised a lager to myself.

She'd stood there that morning, so rotund in her latest smock, holding her tummy, and called me a workaholic. I'd tried to give her a hug and she'd snapped: 'go away'.

My exuberance drained and I rose and sloped off for another can.

I wasn't much use to anybody after that. There was the overseas call from something called the Cult Awareness Network. Did I know Baba Dayananda was fighting expulsion from the US by the Immigration and Naturalization Service? His main defense was that he had contributed to my great discovery. I didn't talk to the woman. They handled it without me. Ditto the call from the World Health Rostrum.

And so to bed.

Why are you lying on the lab sofa? It's cold in here and dawn is gathering you up in its arms. Was that a mouse running across the floor? Will she never move to the spare bedroom? Oh Amelia, maybe our marriage *was* just a false alarm. Beyond salvage. Who's the celebrity now?

In the second week of January everything had come in a rush and I'd done it, together with Tillman and our junior colleagues. I jumped in the air when the analysis of the prelim tests came through, punching the air like some scoring striker in a Cup Final and hugged Tillman until he hardly had air to breathe. The last few days had zipped by in an orgy of work. After so much effort we'd at last perfected a revolutionary approach to the antigen-coding genes common to all known strains of HIV-1 and engineered a prototype of the first vaccine that looked certain to stimulate the formation of cell-mediated immunity as well as sufficient antibodies without risk of harmful side effects. As I'd long suspected, the answer had lain in the body's natural immune system. A small minority of carriers just didn't seem able to develop full-blown AIDS, even after several years, thanks to a high natural concentration of neutralizing antibodies in their blood. The virus in these people lay permanently latent.

Clinical trials would last at least two years, even using San Diego mice at first, but the scientific world was instantly abuzz with approval. Publication of the full story in *Nature* would take me four months to prepare. But as far as the media were concerned the clinical trials were a foregone success, unlike other researchers' trials, in particular Technogen's HIVAC vaccine, which had come to grief in the recent past. On the eve of our worldbeating announcement the team held a private celebration. I was the only one who stayed sober. The next day tributes started pouring in.

I explained our success in layman's language to a group of journalists invited to the lab on the day the story broke: 'It's a one-shot subunit vaccine. The biggest problem we faced was antigenic drift.'

I had my back to the bench, the reporters facing me in a semi-circle. Tillman stood in the background. 'We've chemically synthesized the gene responsible for keeping AIDS latent indefinitely in a minority of carriers and we've built it into a safe HIV pseudo-virus. There are none of the risks of a live virus.' I coughed self-consciously. 'The gene will trick the immune system into producing effective antibodies to attack the real virus if it enters the bloodstream – and before,' I added, 'it gets a chance to move to safety *outside* the bloodstream. We've managed to fuse the two necessary ingredients: a gene with the code needed to produce the key Gc protein and a modified version of the instructions in HIV RNA. The resulting pseudo-virus can't reproduce. It's got none of the dangerous bits in the real virus and it covers a sufficiently broad spectrum.'

'So can you explain how it tackles the mutagenicity of the envelope?' The question came from a *Sunday Times* reporter.

'I'll try to put it simply. The pseudo-virus presents one protein that matches another in the core – not the outer coat – of the live virus. This is a highly stable protein that hardly varies between different HIV subtypes.' I slipped my hands into my lab coat. 'The problem with proteins in the outer coat – and most vaccines up to now – has been the variation between strains and the high rate of mutation. To flag our viral antigen to the immune system we've come up with a new adjuvant which we can't reveal the name of until patents are filed.' I raised an arm to emphasize my point. Had Tillman noticed that it was shaking?

'Do you own the intellectual property rights?' It was a reporter from one of the London tabloids.

'No, they now belong to Isis Innovation.' Then I added quickly: 'That way they're owned by the University. Like I said, worldwide patents for commercial exploitation are being filed right now.'

A woman from the *International Herald Tribune* asked about trials and how long it would take to get the vaccine on the market.

'Two years approximately. We're doing prelim testing using mice and a chimpanzee.' My thoughts flashed to Deveraj and Polly Ann.

'I thought chimpanzees can't develop AIDS?'

This one was smarter than the rest. 'They can't. They can only be infected with HIV, unless they've been made to carry cells of the human immune system, which is what we've done. Then they can develop AIDS. The mice too.' I couldn't wait to get this over with.

'And tests on humans?'

I was prepared for that one, the controversial one. Two female and two male prostitutes, all free of infection, had volunteered. They'd been inoculated and subjected two months later to a massive dose of the live virus. This experiment had been the final building block before the announcement. 'I've prepared a short hand-out. It answers that question and others. Dr Tillman will give you each a copy as you leave.'

I removed my lab coat as I escorted the journalists to the door and shook hands with them.

Tillman just stood there shaking his head with relief.

Mother, for you and I toasted her with a vial of my vaccine.

Didn't the *Sun* style me 'the thinking woman's crumpet'? The story of my career in *US News and World Report* was so full of plaudits it read like a hagiography. Was I not reading descriptions like 'an iconic figurehead' and 'a sunrise scientist'? Through the Communicable Diseases Surveillance Centre in London an offer was made of the directorship of the World Health Organization collaborating centers for AIDS. *Time* covered the vaccine in a major feature and although I refused to be interviewed they hailed me as 'the man with a messianic vision who would carry the banner of medical science into the next millennium'. The story called the new vaccine 'the greatest single advance in genetics since Crick and Watson unraveled the secrets of the double helix in the 1950s'.

After all the media palaver Princeton University invited me to deliver the Vanuxen Lecture the following year.

At the AIDS conference at the Pasteur Institute, one of my old stamping grounds – French girls are the greatest – Tillman and I are locked in together. The vaccine earned me a standing ovation, like a guarantee of professional apotheosis. Such a dinner afterwards. The bullshit flowing like milk and honey and Tillman killing me softly with his resignation. Something about Director of the Institute of Human Genetics at the University of Minnesota. Look into my eyes, Tillman. You're looking everywhere else. He's saying 'a paycheck pushing two hundred K'. Sterling or dollars, Tillman? You've sold out to the opposition. Is that why you wouldn't fly with me? You've betrayed me, Tillman, my closest disciple. *Stuff another Valium, Daniel, to go with the Mogadon.*

A child is born. A son. And the Messiah's name shall be William – two weeks early. Bouncing and burbling. *Leave him to sleep, he's exhausted.*

We're here, Daniel. We wouldn't leave you. White hooded figures are seated round your table. A phoenix swoops down and lands in the middle, wings outstretched. Something strong in the air is burning your eyes. The figure in the middle is removing his hood.

Now you see it: now you don't. His giant phallus. Sweet angel, what immortal hand or eye could frame thee? Feel the candle's pricket sharp. Down, boy, down. Voices whisper in the glimmer. Giant bodies fucking wet. *Run, Daniel, run, before he eats you.* Would you dare to steal the giant's woman? *Kill, kill, Daniel. Run before she swallows you.* You didn't see them in the candlelight. Fucking beasts. Did you?

A giant Lawrence Hungerford. His black eyes are laughing. Here in the maternity ward. The same eyes as William. Black eyes like Penelope Rich. Father and son. Father and fucking daughter. One by one they uncover themselves. They're all there laughing: Baba, Marcus, Drake, Mannering, Bendix, Dunkley. Someone is missing: your wife, the Black Madonna, the bride of Christ . . . Black Jenny.

You look up and she smiles down from her cross, parting her

322

thighs, inviting you into the darkness of her gaping sex that has given birth to this little Lawrence. Out of the Third cometh the One as the Fourth. A star burns your eyes. Open them again and Lawrence is stepping forward and ramming a gigantic Tau into the witch's cunt. The others gather round to watch in silence. *Amelia, don't scream.* You'll wake the baby. Too late. The baby is crying its head off in Lawrence's arms. *In nomine filii.* He passes you the baby. *You fucking bastard. Kill her, kill the baby. Kill William. Not now, Daniel. Later, Daniel.* Cry Shekinah and pop another Valium. *Hail True Redeemer.*

There's only you and darkness in the lab. Bedfellows again. A fair old alarum. Bats in the belfry. *Robbed of your freedom, Daniel.* Your door's unhinged. Better lock it.

Why is your hand so jittery as you draw your own blood? Safe and sound. Who killed Cock Robin? You, Thomas Drake?

Take the sample from the coolbox. Isn't that the culture from William's fetal cells? Still sticky after so long – thickened to a bistre hue. *Lay down your head, Daniel.* Cry your eyes out. Write to Geoff Alton care of Cellmark. You don't have their blood print program. Tuesday's his day there. Are these two samples the genes of father and son? Daniel and William? Am I William's father? I want to see the boy-child. Chance of error: one in two hundred and sixty-eight million, so help me God.

Pack the specimens, wrap them with a note to Geoff and leave the package sealed on your secretary's desk. *Courier this to Abingdon.* Wipe face, drop into chair and rest chin on hands. Ungarble your head. The weeping gene can't skip a generation through daughter to grandson. Lawrence had Shakespeare's weeping gene. That gene couldn't pass from him through Amelia. To William. Genetically impossible. It could only pass direct from father to son.

Easy, Daniel. Don't jump to conclusions.

Take William's culture again. How many minutes to concoct the right solution? Watch the preparation turn cloudy yellow. Fumble with the gene machine. *The fucking bastard.* Still loaded with the Shakespeare disk. *Press the pretty letters, Daniel. Press. Press.*

Lawrence's direct male line's extinct, isn't it? Since his baby boy died at birth. William's meant to be my baby, isn't it? So why the green light for William's blood? Why the green apple?

Bite it, Daniel. You fucking bastard. Scream, Daniel, scream. Let it all out. Lawrence fucked your wife. You too, Daniel. Lawrence did it. Lawrence William's father. Father and son. Lawrence and William. Who wants to kill you? *Scream, Daniel, scream. Smash the bright green apple.*

Kill, kill, kill, I say. *Fuck you all.* I don't need it. Don't need Amelia. Kill Amelia. Anymore. Kill the baby. Let the rain piss down. You're snug. You're invisible. No one can get you now. Janey will see to that, won't you?

Baby did it. Kill Amelia. Kill the baby. Kill Lawrence. Please angel, fallen angel.

Air heavy from a downpour. Drag yourself from the lab. Trek up the Banbury Road. Meander under a numinous sky. Dusk is falling. *Don't look behind.* Streets empty of passers-by. Surroundings dim into the distance. Traffic noise grows faint. There again. Eyes and footsteps. And voices. Together for the first time. *Don't look behind.* Cross the road at Park Town. The trees in the grounds of St Hugh's bend over the fence. St Claire's . . . shops . . . South Parade . . . green front door . . . flight of stairs.

Reach the landing and jam your battered key. Into the lock. Lucia Popp on the stereo. Amelia's favorite aria. From *Il Re Pastore.*

The room yaws.

Amelia's armchair empty. A movement. Catch your eye.

The phantasm rising. From where you sit. Smiling. Stretches out its left hand. Up the bare forearm. A snake wriggles no wider than a pencil. Gliding and swirling toward you. Turns into a livid crimson scar.

Half a second. Under the left eye. A tiny muscle twitching. *Scream, Daniel.* You hurl yourself.

At the epiphany of Lawrence Hungerford.

21

True chastity is sooner and oftener
found in the poorest than in the richest.

The Victory of English Chastity
under the Feigned Name of Avisa
Thomas Willoughby [Anonymous]

13 Farrar Street
Cambridge
MA 02138

16 May

Dear Rosie,

What can I say? I should have written weeks ago, but so
much has happened that I wanted to get it all sorted out
first. I expect you're bursting to know.

It's such a tragedy and there's so much to tell. How sad
Amelia looked when she came back to see me. I'd thought
I might not see her again. We just sat and talked the first
hour and I think I was able to comfort her a bit. Her
baby William – she's so pleased he's an Aquarius and not
a Pisces – sat in her lap like a small bundle of humanity. He
has a pugnacious chin that promises more than a grain of
determination. Amelia cooed over him and ruffled his fine
dark hair. By the way, she took her oral exam at Oxford
and passed.

You'll be wondering what happened to Daniel Bosworth.
The 'temperamental genius', as Amelia once called him,
developed an acute reactive psychosis the day he returned
from an AIDS conference in France. It was the same day
William was born, two weeks prematurely. He'd been to
the maternity hospital to see William and Amelia then gone
berserk in his laboratory before finding his way back to his
apartment. He had been under a lot of pressure to find a
vaccine for AIDS and the baby's birth was the straw that

broke his back. As he seemed dangerous he was committed – 'sectioned' was the word used in the report I saw – to the Warneford Hospital, an insane asylum in Oxford. Amelia's life and baby William's were thought to be at risk until they got him onto drugs.

I didn't press Amelia for information about him. That wouldn't have been kind in the circumstances. As it turned out later, I had a better way of finding out – Daniel himself. You see, dear Rosie, he is now recovering at Amelia's house and has become a client. So too has Amelia – again.

You'll ask what point there is in treating such severe dysfunction with psychoanalysis, and I will disagree with you. He's responding well to the latest drugs, which David Bendix is administering. My approach is interpretive, not confrontational, so I feel sure it can do him no harm to talk to me about the emotional side of his problems. He comes twice a week and we just talk. He doesn't even lie on the couch. He's totally self-involved and has the narcissist's illusory charm. I see now why Amelia fell head over heels for this pathetic little child who's spent his life in search of his mother.

I wrote to the consultant who'd been treating him at the Warneford. He not only sent me a copy of his notes and report, but also Daniel's complete medical history which he'd gotten from his family doctor. That file was a goldmine. The biggest nugget was a psychiatric report from when Daniel was fourteen. It recorded how he reacted when he was told he was an adopted child. The report gave a diagnosis of 'episodic bouts of undifferentiated paranoid schizophrenia characterized by intense periods of aliena-tion with auditory and visual delusions'. He apparently underwent complete withdrawal. There was full remission after several months of treatment with a variety of drugs. The report mentions 'an oral fixation involving his natural mother and a pathological fear of castration derived from deep-seated oedipal conflicts, overlaid with momentary but violent delusions of grandeur'. The psychiatrist also noted a pathological jealousy of rival males and a mildly hypomanic level of activity in all aspects of his life, adding that there appeared to be a deep underlying depression. A later report

326

showed that he had a relapse when his first wife miscarried. Up to that date, at school, at university and since, he'd spent a lot of time in his vacations morbidly exploring graveyards, trying to find a clue to his mother's identity.

The Warneford consultant's own report was an eye-opener. As soon as Daniel was admitted they put him in a room with padded floor and walls – he was still violent, remember. They tried him on clozapine, but it failed to bring him out of psychosis. He spent the first two days hunkering in a corner, babbling to himself about his mother – something to do with a cross. He also went on a lot about AIDS as if he'd actually discovered the AIDS vaccine he was looking for. In his rantings and ravings he saw himself as a saint who'd saved future generations from AIDS. He kept quoting how Tom Brokaw called him that – a saint – on *Nightly News* and he even thought he'd won the Nobel Prize. Sadly it was all pure delusion. It's now increasingly doubtful whether a successful antiviral for AIDS will be found before the end of the decade. All in all it's a classic picture of *folie de grandeur*.

The link between creative brilliance, even genius, and the diffuse personality is rarely hard to find. Just look at Lawrence and Amelia. In such cases there's almost always an inherited vulnerability to an abandonment depression that goes back to infancy. This depression is masked in the adult by a façade persona that shelters the infantile self underneath. It's ironical that those it happens to are often, like Daniel, really gifted people. They frequently end up as politicians or media celebrities or business superstars and few people, other than psychotherapists, see through their acting out to their low self-esteem underneath. Their false outer self is born out of fear of separation from an omnipotent parent. Real narcissists, like infants, have an astonishing sense of entitlement, as if the entire world owes them a living. They dread intimacy and when someone gets too close to them emotionally – usually a parent substitute – they back off in unconscious terror, for fear of being engulfed or abandoned; everything is white or black, good or bad. There's no gray. No tolerance of ambivalence.

After his afternoon medication Daniel was usually subdued enough to be left alone with Amelia, who came to visit with him every day with William once she came out of the maternity hospital. On the eighth day he'd just been heavily sedated and they were shown into his room. When the consultant came back an hour later to let them out he didn't go in to check on Daniel. He admits in his report he should have done so. It was two hours later when they found him unconscious with blood all over the place.

No, he hadn't tried to kill himself. He'd had an epileptic seizure and bitten deep into the side of his tongue. The blood was all down the front of his clothes and round his head in a patch on the floor. The report pointed out that they'd moved him on to chlorpromazine and this had probably triggered the convulsion if his threshold was low enough at the time. He may or may not be an epileptic in the normal sense.

You can imagine how distressed Amelia was by everything. Such an ordeal, and so soon after childbirth and all her own harrowing problems. She thinks that's why breastfeeding has been so difficult. She even had Scotland Yard on her back. They got her permission to take a sample of Daniel's blood while he was at the Warneford, and a photocopy of a picture of a woman they found in his pocket when they brought him in.

The combination of the epileptic attack, psychosis and the drugs was pretty serious so they moved Daniel to a room where they could monitor his condition round the clock. It was a couple of days before he regained consciousness, and when he did he was normal again. The psychotic phase had passed and he was discharged two weeks later with strict orders not to neglect his prescribed medication. I talked to him about epilepsy and he mentioned something similar had happened to him in the spring last year in California. I remembered Amelia saying something about it. Daniel and I concluded he must have had an epileptic attack at the time and gone into a fugue state lasting several days. He became quite nervous talking about it. He admitted it had been worrying him ever since.

Something else worried him too – something much bigger. It wasn't the fact that in reality he hadn't found a vaccine for AIDS. That he could accept, almost with relief. It didn't seem to worry him at all. It was something else that had been plaguing him most of his life. He must have been feeling he could trust me, because he brought a photo in to show me – probably the one Scotland Yard were interested in. It was his real mother. The few words on the back – 'Oxford October 1956' – were all he had to go on in the days when he tried to find out who she was. I looked at her. She had an attractive face, not unlike Daniel's. It was the kind of face you tend to remember. I thought I saw a sad look in her eyes.

It came as a shock when he told me she'd been murdered. He'd eventually traced her body, but not her identity. He seemed really distraught as he told me about it, and I hoped he wasn't going to relapse into psychosis. He said he'd had to accept a verbal summary of the homicide investigators' report which they'd written at the time – in 1959. It was still classified as an unsolved murder. Here he stopped to reconsider and added that it was still unsolved so far as he knew. Her body had been found in a cheap hotel bathroom in the town of Swindon in the county of Wiltshire. He'd been told – in 1985 – that the forensic lab's report dating from 1959 showed she had syphilis. The hotel was one of those ones with rooms you rented by the hour – no signatures, no questions asked.

But let me go back to David Bendix. It struck me that in the few months since I'd seen him he might have gotten to grips with his guilt and be more prepared to tell me what he knew about Lawrence Hungerford. This time I asked him over for a cup of coffee at the end of the day and on the phone he seemed quite pleased to get the chance to talk to me again. He'd seen Daniel a couple of times and he might have a fresh viewpoint on his case too.

We must have talked for hours, covering a lot of the same ground as last time, with me probing and him still trying to satisfy his conscience. You could see he was torn about how much to tell, but it turned out, if he was being honest, that he really didn't have much more to add this time. Eventually, though, I got a little more out of him.

He kept going back to the death of Sarah Hungerford and it took me some time to understand why. Because of the things I'd said, he was ransacking his brain for something that would exonerate Lawrence for helping his wife out of this world into the next. He found it in Lawrence's syphilis. If Lawrence had syphilitic dementia, he was mad and not responsible for his actions.

That sounded pretty lame to me. I didn't get a chance to point out that dementia would only have come years later with the tertiary phase of syphilis. He was rabbiting on making excuses for syphilis, so fast that I couldn't get a word in. He was saying Lawrence had picked up the disease from a prostitute – he said 'an Oxford prostitute' so disdainfully – one he'd gotten involved with in the mid-Fifties, a woman Lawrence had called Black Jenny.

I was flabbergasted. David saw my face freeze. I turned to hide my astonishment, but it was too late. He became extremely cagey after that. And no, he'd never met the woman, so he said.

I was thinking back feverishly to what Daniel had told me the week before when he'd shown me his mother's photograph. The police report on her death, which he'd known the details of since 1985, showed she'd died by suffocation. Her body had been dressed in very expensive black satin underwear. They hadn't been able – in 1959 – to identify her from any list of known Wiltshire prostitutes, but they'd had to conclude she was 'on the game'. I could still hear Daniel telling me in a voice that was breaking. In the end he managed to get it out and say 'prostitute'. Not easy to do when it's your own mother, but easier than the macabre way he first traced her – by digging up her body and genetic-fingerprinting her genes. It's too ghoulish for words.

Something clicked into place at that moment. Think laterally, I told myself. I had the copy of Daniel's psychiatric report in the top drawer of my desk. I excused myself and went to check it.

Sure enough, it said what I thought it said. Daniel had told the first consultant, when he was fourteen, that he'd had a guardian angel all his life – an imaginary female angel – one that he had a name for. That name was 'Janey'. I was too excited for words.

My head was reeling when I returned and faced David

Bendix across the table. Should I tell him my hunch? How much did he know? How much was he holding back? From the way he'd said 'an Oxford prostitute', and the look on his face as we sat there, I had to conclude he didn't know what seemed so probable to me – that Lawrence Hungerford murdered a woman called Black Jenny: Daniel's mother. The same woman Daniel had immortalized at the age of two as his guardian angel Janey. It had to be the same woman. Even the dates were right. You know me. I was so keyed up I had to go to the bathroom.

Did you see that movie *Rain Man* a few years ago, the one with Dustin Hoffman and Tom Cruise that won all the Oscars? Tom Cruise had an autistic brother called Raymond when he was very young. They were separated and Tom Cruise grew up without knowing he had this brother Raymond. But he had an invisible friend called Rain Man. That was how he'd heard 'Raymond' as a child and that was the way it had stuck in his preconscious. My hunch is that something similar happened to Daniel as a very small child. Jenny, the name he knew his mother by, became the angel Janey. Lawrence also knew her as Jenny or Black Jenny. She was Black Jenny to Amelia through Lawrence's fetishist scenarios and eventually she became one of Amelia's other personalities.

The prostitute had been asphyxiated with a pillow. If my speculations were correct, had Lawrence gone back to England in 1959 to murder her, and if so why? If he had, it looks as though he probably took her from Oxfordshire to Wiltshire to cover his tracks. Otherwise she'd probably have been identified and linked to Daniel. My guess is Daniel – remember he was only about two – was left for the day with another prostitute and when Black Jenny didn't return to Oxford, the woman panicked and abandoned him in the parking lot where he was found. The existence of the photograph suggests this woman wanted to leave a clue to Daniel's identity. She probably took it from Black Jenny's things. Maybe they were room-mates. She probably heard that an unidentified prostitute had been found murdered in a Wiltshire hotel, and she put two and two together.

331

Without voicing my suspicions about Lawrence, or admitting what I'd learnt from Daniel, I tried every ploy to get David to tell me more, in case he knew something I'd missed, but I got nowhere. I had the impression he'd decided his conscience was sufficiently cleansed with what he'd already admitted. I couldn't get anything else out of him, but I'm almost positive he didn't know about the prostitute's illegitimate child, or that Lawrence had murdered the woman who gave him syphilis, if in fact it was Lawrence who was the murderer. On the other hand David just might have been stonewalling. He's a damn good actor. Even I can remember seeing him in local amateur productions. But I still needed some piece of evidence that would amount to proof. There was no point in beating my head any farther, so I gave up on David and concentrated on Daniel.

I faced another predicament. How much, if anything at this stage, should I tell Daniel? After all, I was treating him for narcissistic personality disorder and I didn't want to make it worse. Should I tell him his prostitute mother was perhaps known as Black Jenny? That still didn't identify her. More to the point, did I give him the startling news that very possibly Lawrence Hungerford was his father?

I tried not to seem excited the next day when I asked him if I could borrow the photograph of his mother. It was worth a try. He refused, which I could understand, but on his next visit he brought me a photocopy of the front and back. I could hardly sleep at night for thinking about it. The words 'Oxford October 1956' weren't a lot to go on. They were printed, not written, in a clear hand. I called Mark Griffin at the Fogg to see if he had a copy of Lawrence Hungerford's signature. He went one better. He sent me a photocopy of a hand-written letter that Lawrence sent them for publication in their annual report many years ago – something about the tax treatment of art bequests to the Fogg. You may remember Frank Hartman, the so-called psychographologist on Tremont. I took him the photocopies of the two handwriting specimens, which didn't look much alike to me. He puffed away on his pipe and studied them under a magnifying glass while I sat there wishing I'd never quit smoking. He reported the writers were two different people – a man and a woman. No shadow of a doubt. So the writing on the photograph probably belonged to Daniel's mother.

By this time I was convinced that Lawrence was a double murderer. I actually felt quite cheated that he wasn't about to stand trial. It isn't fair that he got off scot-free by dying. In the end I decided there was no point in reporting anything to anybody – proof or no proof.

So there you have it, dear Rosie. The dates were strong circumstantial evidence, and black underwear and the names Janey and Jenny were the vital clues. I almost feel like some two-bit gumshoe private eye. Maybe I'm in the wrong business!

By this time I had some of Lawrence's psychopathic motivation figured out. One thing I'm sure about is that he had an *idée fixe*. His monomaniac obsession was to have a legitimate son. Who can be more devious and manipulative than a true narcissist? If my theory's right, Daniel the illegitimate son must have been watched and secretly manipulated by Lawrence all his life without being aware of it. Why else would Daniel have ended up researching sexually transmitted diseases? He was lucky not to have one himself. He could easily have picked up syphilis from his mother *in utero*.

Can you imagine, if I'm right, Amelia was steered by Lawrence into unwittingly marrying his illegitimate son Daniel! Lawrence's reasons for this I still can't figure out, but a psychopath's motives are usually beyond comprehension, so don't be surprised if I never come up with more than bits of the answer to the question why Lawrence should go to such incredible lengths.

I admit it's pretty shaky, without further evidence, but my guess is that to Lawrence Daniel represented the woman who'd given him syphilis, left him all but sterile and prevented him from having a legitimate male heir. We've got to remember illegitimacy still carried a stigma in the nineteen-fifties, especially for a family with the Hungerfords' social standing. I think that after he'd avenged himself by the murder of the original Black Jenny, Lawrence murdered her symbolically in every woman he had sex with. Heaven knows how many prostitutes were given that nickname and went through his Black Jenny act. With Sarah he finally took it to its original conclusion. He smothered her – this time for failure to produce a son. Now I see where Amelia must have gotten that stuff about Othello. Shakespeare's Moor of Venice smothered his wife with a pillow, like I suggested when I came to visit with you.

Of course Amelia was having sex with her father – over and over in the same Othello and Black Jenny playlet. It probably started with her defloration straight after he murdered her mother. God only knows, if he hadn't died he might have killed Amelia too. As things stand, I made her have a check-up for syphilis. I wouldn't tell her why. Mercifully, or should I say miraculously, she hasn't caught it. I can only assume Lawrence ended his affair with her the moment the disease came out of its latent phase. I can hardly suggest, in the circumstances, that it was conscience that made him stop.

Lawrence 'punished' Black Jenny and her surrogate successors. He turned the whole thing into a fetishist ritual with a nasty touch of sadism. It was the only way he could get an orgasm. On the day of her confirmation Amelia was forced to watch her mother being raped and suffocated. By falling into her mother's role and playing the masochist – a very controlling position – she unconsciously brought Sarah Hungerford back to life. She became the Sarah Hungerford who'd played Black Jenny for her father. Desdemona to his Othello. In a way Amelia did become her father's wife. I've come across some bizarre cases of sado-masochism before, but nothing like this. Here were two people in unconscious collusion getting what they wanted out of a pathological situation, but each for a different reason. Lawrence must have found out years ago that he had this Svengali power to hypnotize Amelia. No wonder I found it easy. He could induce loss of memory in her by post-hypnotic suggestion, and with traumatic repression on top, it's not surprising I found it hard to get the full picture out of her. Consciously she was totally unaware of what was going on.

Now that I've got more facts to go on, I'm less surprised about Amelia's multiple personality problem. I can see now that Black Jenny was a role that Lawrence trained her in under his hypnotic influence. Black Jenny became one of her gods and she turned Lawrence into another of them, the fifth, making him William Shakespeare, also known as Othello.

Given the timing of Daniel's conception around the date in the photograph – October 1956 – I think I can safely conclude that Lawrence *was* Daniel's father. Lawrence must have caught syphilis from Black Jenny around the same time.

Amelia and Daniel have no awareness they're related, except by marriage. I think their blood tie was one reason why she was so deeply attracted to him. She was besotted with Lawrence, however pathologically – he was her mother, father, lover and husband all rolled into one – so it was only a short step from there to falling in love with her half-brother. There would be psychological family resemblances, not so much physical ones, that she picked up on. The real reasons, dear Rosie, why people fall in love are often not apparent, but believe me they're there all right. They're usually very powerful where there are personality disorders on both sides and a hunger for infantile attachment – some would call it passionate or romantic love. These unconscious pulls have more than a little to do with parts of our parents we've internalized – or rejected.

I haven't told Amelia or Daniel any of the things I've put in this letter. I've decided that's totally out of the question. Amelia still seems to be cured of her multiple personality disorder, if I can use that terrible word 'cured'. Her pantheon of gods has not returned and it would be wrong to tempt them back with a lot of unnecessary revelations. Even her epilepsy seems to have gone, now that the psychological element in the trigger has been removed with Lawrence's death and Shakespeare taking a back seat in her life.

She's back in analysis full time now and we're concentrating on her splitting problem which is still there but much improved. She's less secretive and impulsive now and more willing to accept her femaleness. I've confronted her with her fear of deep emotional commitment and she seems to be taking on board the need to give her real self permission to take over, even at the risk of getting hurt.

Of course she knows that to do this she's going to have

to go through the guilt and depression that she's always avoided in the past. But I can see from the sadness and tears that it's happening. She has to let that pathetic little ego of her real self come out of hiding and grow. Otherwise her love life will continue to be chaotic. That would spell divorce and does she know it! She's going to have to cut down on liquor, too. It only makes her false self, her masculine side, even more uncaring and impossible for others to handle. Daniel found the switches impossible to keep up with.

The regressive personality has many options for avoiding the depression that often comes from flawed parenting. Multiple personality disorder, I think, is simply the most extreme option, short of psychosis.

When I saw Amelia yesterday she was on top of the world. Daniel and baby William are such a comfort. I told you motherhood would work for her, didn't I? Though much will depend on little William's own personality. And gone are Amelia's pastiche orgasms. Now they're real humdingers – dare I say it? – like the orgasms she used to have with Lawrence. I realize I haven't really interpreted this strange case, and knowing you, Rosie, you'll go crazy yourself if I don't. Here's what I think.

The triangular relationship between Lawrence, Daniel and Amelia hinged on the personality disorders of all three. Lawrence and Daniel were compulsive womanizers in search of their mothers, while Amelia's depleted real self was addictively and usually sexually looking for a surrogate father who would rescue her from her real father. Eventually she found a father figure, hardly by accident, in her mirror self – her own half-brother.

The mother Daniel carried around inside himself had the power of life and death over him. A mother substitute like Amelia could attract his infantile ego by promising survival through fusion with her own body. This symbiotic fusion takes place most obviously on a sexual level and reaches its peak at the moment of orgasm. The trouble was, Amelia wasn't just Daniel's idealized mother, she was also daughter, wife and even mother to Lawrence. In a way, she and Lawrence parented each other. A clash of the Titans was inevitable.

336

Narcissists are on first-name terms with death all their lives. To deny death they become compulsive and obsessive. Often it's substance abuse, like alcohol with Lawrence, or the fact that he never spent more than a few days in the same place and had to be surrounded by people constantly. With Daniel and Amelia it was sex, work and alcohol. They both had to be the best in the world at what they did, which is where Daniel went too far and tipped over the edge into insanity. He had to be the first with an AIDS vaccine. Even if his vaccine was only discovered in his troubled unconscious, he was highly successful in his field.

Given the facts of the case, I'm not surprised about Daniel's temporary loss of contact with reality. There is surely a hereditary factor as well in the Hungerfords that predisposes to mental illness: maybe there are genes for psychosis and the personality disorders.

In Lawrence Hungerford's case narcissism took the shape of megalomania and the effect was enhanced by neurosyphilis. What a twisted person it turned him into. Now the world has one less psychopathic killer to worry about.

In Daniel's case we shouldn't lose sight of the fact that he was a crusader out to save the world from AIDS. Pathological narcissism comes in many forms and has many ways of disguising itself in the gifted and famous. Look at the incredible power of some of the best-known charismatics – like Jesus Christ – and what happened to them. (Please take off your Christian hat and don't hold this one against me!)

In a strange way Daniel and Amelia each got what they wanted out of their relationship, so their marriage has gotten this far intact. Being addictive types, they had the potential to become highly dependent on each other. Both of them carried around the illusion that they were in control of the other. Amelia was able to transfer her devotion from Lawrence to Daniel because the two men, not surprisingly, were so similar. There was one major difference, though. Lawrence was a psychopath and Daniel wasn't. They may both have been narcissistic, but Daniel had some element of conscience. Lawrence had no capacity for feeling guilt at all.

Well, Rosie, life is full of surprises. Daniel has paid a heavy price for daring to risk the curse of Shakespeare. Now he and Amelia are living here in Cambridge with William. Their relationship went through a rough patch when he was working too hard in England, but since he's left others to carry on his research there, he's a lot more relaxed and I'm hopeful that with medication and a lot of analysis, he won't have a relapse. Amelia, too, has a lot of work and a lot of pain ahead of her on the couch. However, they've both got the makings of a very caring relationship. In fact instead of blowing hot and cold about marriage, Amelia dotes on Daniel as much as her baby.

Since most of her oddball ideas about Shakespeare are now accepted, Harvard have offered her a teaching job starting next semester. It's an associate professorship with good prospects of tenure. She could scarcely ask for more. However, she's lost all interest in Shakespeare and has already abandoned plans for her book. She asked what I felt she should do. Naturally I told her she should consult her inner voice, but I wouldn't mind betting she'll turn down the offer and perhaps go back to painting. While she makes her mind up, the three of them are going off to join the dog at their summer house on Nantucket.

Our quixotic Daniel has had an offer from Professor Walter Gilbert here at Harvard. You may remember him from that Med School lunch you came to a couple of years ago. They want Daniel to join a second group working on the human genome project – billions of units of genetic information to analyze. I hope he doesn't push himself too hard this time. I don't think Amelia would forgive him twice. He tells me he's accepted the job and starts next month – probably based at the Whitehead Institute.

I'm still not smoking, you'll be glad to hear, or over-eating, though I still get the urge. If only you could see me now! Do come and visit soon. I miss our long night-time talks. Do you remember when we were up all night discussing that guy who wanted to know where it was legal to marry your sister? I'm not sure where the law stands on half-siblings.

Well, that's all the details. No doubt you'll be as appalled by some of it as I was. If you can figure out anything further from what I've told you, let me know – like how Lawrence ever got interested in Shakespeare in the first place. It's the one thing I can't work out and it bugs the hell out of me. I'll send you the draft of my paper before it goes off to the journal.

Write soon. You know how much I love your rambling letters. Say Hi to your mom. And from me a big warm hug.

Affectionately,
Katie

P.S. There's something I forgot to mention that Daniel told me. He got a letter two days ago from a friend at some lab near Oxford. After mumbling something about a woman in California who'd 'rigged the results' and gotten murdered for her pains, he admitted that, like you, he'd suspected Lawrence of being William's father. In fact it was that suspicion – something genetic that I can't get to the bottom of – that struck him the day that William was born and pushed him over the edge into psychosis. I must admit that after figuring what Lawrence had been doing to Amelia, I'd come to the conclusion it was remotely possible. On the other hand it seemed unlikely if Lawrence's sperm count was so low, and he wasn't getting any younger. Anyhow about the time he had his psychotic bout, Daniel sent samples of his own blood and William's to this friend of his to have them genetic-fingerprinted. The good news was that Daniel was William's biological father. He seemed over the moon about that, but terribly anxious about something else he said he'd deduced from the results of the test. He wouldn't tell me what it was. I think the screw had turned and he'd worked out for himself who his father was, but I don't have the first clue when it comes to genetics, so I discreetly said nothing. If Daniel knows Lawrence was his father and he tells Amelia, that's up to him. I feel sure their relationship is tough enough now to withstand it.

22

Ah! But those tears are pearls which thy love sheds,
And they are rich, and ransom all ill deeds.

Sonnets, 34
William Shakespeare

'Here's what you wanted, sir.' Detective Sergeant Frank Hillaby
slapped down the report. 'Complete transcript from the FBI's
clandestine bugs and phone taps on the psychoanalyst's place.
We already sent ten DCs from the Mobile Reserve on door-to-door
inquiries to find if any old-timers remembered a Black Jenny in
Oxford thirty years ago. They covered almost four thousand
houses.'

Tom Drake ignored the report on his desk. He eyed the junior
detective intently before speaking. 'Get anything?'

'Bingo. They found an old boy name of John Tardew who was
a porter at Worcester College way back when . . . remembered
her name. He was in for a regular pint at a pub called The Bear
in those days. So was she. A woman with a foreign accent, so he
said. She stuck in his mind because she always wore black. Called
herself Jenny. He knew her the same way all the regulars did . . .
name of Black Jenny.'

The phlegmatic Superintendent Drake sat up straight.

'So then I fixed to show him the copy of the photo . . . the
high-resolution version. He said it was her all right. A regular
pro . . . a bit on the upmarket side. Stood out in a crowd. Too
smart. Round Oxford for a while . . . didn't remember any baby.
Then she disappeared. He said he couldn't forget her: she was too
good-looking; not the prostitute type. All her tricks were pretty
upmarket too. She was . . .'

Drake interrupted him: 'I've got the genetic profile through
from the rape department at the Forensic Science Service.
Everyone said I must be a nutcase when I froze the semen
deposit we found down the loo in 1959. They hadn't seen the

340

TV program about Francis Crick and James Watson: how genes would be better clues than fingerprints one day. Our friend should have checked after he tried to flush his condom away. Knotting it was not very clever either. It's almost as if, like Jack the Ripper, he wanted to let us know who'd done it. He can't seriously have believed we'd think she'd drowned herself. God knows what Bosworth would have done with the semen if he'd known about it and got hold of some . . . for research.' There was a faint sneer to this remark and he paused to put on a pair of spectacles. 'Might have gone round trying to genetic-fingerprint every male in the world.'

Not sure whether to laugh or not Hillaby laughed anyway. In response he got a shadow of a smile from his boss.

'That semen kept perfectly for over thirty years,' Drake said, 'waiting for the day when we got hold of the bastard's blood. Pity it was too late to nail him.'

'What's your conclusion?'

'You mean what do I think about Bosworth being the old boy's son?'

'That's right.'

'It's pretty weird stuff, all right. You heard as well as I did what the doctor and the psychoanalyst said to each other. You saw the transcript after the FBI intercepted her letter. The guy was a double murderer. Maybe he's behind other unsolved killings . . . over in the States or here . . . especially prostitutes.'

'The FBI said they were checking into that possibility, sir.'

Drake pulled a piece of paper from a folder in front of him and rubbed his chin with one hand as he studied it. 'She was certainly a good-looking woman.'

'Tell me something, sir. How important is it still to find out what her real name was?'

'Not very, Frank.'

'Any ideas, sir?'

'A few.'

'Who would that be?'

'Let's just say I'd like to work on it a little longer before I close the case.'

'Let me know when you get there, sir.' Hillaby rose and made for the door.

When he had gone Tom Drake went and turned the lock and

returned to his desk. He pulled a sheaf of papers from the folder in front of him: a photocopy of Dr Bosworth's hand-written findings on his mother's corpse, exhumed in October 1984, followed by pages and pages of DNA blueprints derived from her remains. The genetics people working for him at the Forensic Science Service had spotted something that Bosworth had missed, since he hadn't, to Drake's mind, been looking for it in the first place. *Synchronicity*, Drake said to himself.

They had constructed what they called a 'consanguinity paradigm' on the basis of the DNA fingerprints of Daniel Bosworth, Lawrence Hungerford and Black Jenny – a test which would show the blood ties, if any, between the three individuals.

Tom Drake picked up the folder from his desk and marched to the shredder. He turned it on and the machine whirred. A raw smile spread over his face as he fed in the contents of the entire dossier, even the old police file, recently reopened, on the death of the whore known to her clients as Black Jenny. Finally he held only the manilla folder. His own whimsical name for the case was inscribed in his neat hand across the top: *Death of the Just*. He chuckled as it disappeared into the shredder's maw.

As he switched the machine off and went to unlock the door he wondered whether Lawrence Hungerford's younger sister, the late Joanna Naresby Hungerford, had really had to die so brutally.

23

Full fathom five thy father lies;
Of his bones are coral made;
Those are pearls that were his eyes;
Nothing of him that doth fade
But doth suffer a sea-change
Into something rich and strange.

The Tempest, Act I, Scene 2
William Shakespeare

Moonlight covered Amelia's face. Her eyes glazed over as she hugged William against her inside her shawl. On the seat of the rowing boat lay her father's urn. Beyond the bluff the lights of Nantucket danced along the shore as far as the clapboard mansion where Amelia's Uncle David sat on the porch in a swing chair. Falstaff lay napping at his feet. The elderly man replied with a wave that said he was coming as Daniel leaned out of a nearby window and summoned him cheerily to the telephone.

The boat rocked gently on the eddies of the flood tide. In the last half-hour a breeze had sprung up from the northwest, scattering the sea-mist. Through the shadows a boat passed off to starboard making for harbor.

She raised the silver Tau to her lips. Holding William to her with one arm she reached down and replaced the cross. Hooking the bronze lid back on she lifted the urn with her hand and slid it gently into the sea.

Author's Postscript

Shakespeare peppered his works – not just the *Sonnets* – with clues to his Dark Lady's name. In the groves of Academe a whole industry revolves around her identity.

The Quarto of Shakespeare's *Sonnets* – all 154 of them – was peddled illicitly to a London public in 1609. Today it's simply the most famous collection of poems in the English language.

Who were these poems to and about? Here's my groat's worth of insight.

The first seventeen sonnets were written to the third Earl of Southampton, Henry Wriothesley. Though some of the next 109 are inspired by the Dark Lady, most find their muse through a man legions of Bardophiles have dubbed the Friend and the Fair Youth. He's young, he's beautiful, with the complexion of a maiden: the sort of man a girl looks twice at, and a few men too. That leaves twenty-six sonnets in another group, not counting the pastoral pair at the end. No surgeon ever dissected a cadaver like the exegesists have carved up these twenty-six: the so-called Dark Lady sonnets.

Are the *Sonnets* Shakespeare's autobiography, one in which the names of the cast are kept under wraps? Just who were these characters: 'Mr W.H.', the Friend, the Dark Lady? Was Shakespeare's Rival Poet Gervase Markham? As 'begetter' of the *Sonnets*, was 'Mr W.H.' their inspiration or perhaps the man who procured them for a grateful Thomas Thorpe the publisher? Were the dedication's 'Mr W.H.' and the Fair Youth one and the same?

The clue to the puzzle, I argue, lies buried in a lengthy poem that was registered in September 1594. It carried the title: *Willobie his Avisa* and the subtitle *The True Picture of a Modest Maid and of a Chaste and Constant Wife*. The poet lampoons an innkeeper's wife called Avisa. She is likened to a phoenix, a popular Elizabethan symbol of chastity.

Avisa is wooed unsuccessfully by six lecherous swains:

- a Nobleman
- a Caveleiro who is a military officer
- a Frenchman whose protestations of lust are signed D.B. (*Dudum Beatus* – happy until now)
- Dydimus Harco, Anglo-Germanus
- W.S.
- Henrico-Willobego, Italo-Hispalensis

A narrative passage in Willoughby's *Avisa* tells of Henrico-Willobego's 'familiar friend "W.S.", who not long before had tried the courtesy of the like passion, and was newly recovered of the like infection'. The author asks, referring to Henrico-Willobego's wooing of Avisa, 'whether it would sort to a happier end for this new actor than it did for the old player'.

No wonder that for over a hundred years scholars have argued excitedly that 'W.S.' is William Shakespeare; that behind the mask of the virtuous Avisa is the face of the far-from-virtuous Dark Lady who welcomed the Bard between the sheets before seducing the Fair Youth.

As if that isn't enough for Shakespeare aficionados to jump up and down over, events in the *Avisa* seem to parody Shakespeare's *Rape of Lucrece* which was registered four months earlier. A prefatory poem in the *Avisa* mentions *Lucrece* and gives the world its first printed reference to Shakespeare by his correct name:

> Yet Tarquin plucked his glistering grape
> And Shakespeare paints poor Lucrece' rape.

Lucrece is a tale of married virtue. The *Avisa* is a spoof on the same subject. The story of Avisa the taverner's constant spouse could have been another run-of-the-mill diversion for Elizabethan readers, quickly forgotten. But it wasn't. The *Avisa* sent up the adultery of one of the most prominent women in the English aristocracy.

About Willoughby we know a little. He was not the real poetaster who wrote the *Avisa*. He was only, as Henrico-Willobego, a participant in the Avisa story. The true author's name remains a mystery to this day. But there was a real-life Henry Willoughby. He was an Oxford undergraduate in the 1590s. Today his name would be just a literary footnote were it not for that enigmatic

'Mr W.H.' in Thorpe's cryptic dedication to the *Sonnets* where his initials have been reversed – a not uncommon practice – to obscure his identity.

If Henry Willoughby was the Fair Youth, the object of Shakespeare's lyrical devotion, what do we know about him?

Though they were a minor branch of the great Willoughby family (motto: *Vérité sans Peur*) the Willoughbys of Knoyll Odyern Manor in Wiltshire were well connected. Henry Willoughby's third cousin was Sir Charles Blount or Blunt, who was a close associate of Sir Philip Sidney and the Earls of Essex and Southampton. In 1593 Blunt inherited Brook House, fourteen miles from Knoyll Odyern.

Eight miles from Willoughby's home stood Wardour Castle, the seat of the Arundels, his kinsmen via the Willoughby family of Wollaton in Nottinghamshire. Mary Wriothesley, who married Thomas Arundel, was the sister of Shakespeare's brief patron the third Earl of Southampton to whom *Lucrece* was dedicated.

Eighteen miles from Knoyll Odyern lay the stately house of Wilton, the old house that was all but burnt to the ground in the seventeenth century. Wilton was and still is the home of one of the most prominent of Wiltshire's county families. Many of the leading talents of the Elizabethan age came to visit or live there for a time as the guests of Mary Herbert, Countess of Pembroke, Sir Philip Sidney's sister. Henry Willoughby's family tenanted Herbert land at South Burcombe.

In many ways Henry Willoughby was a fitting object for Shakespeare's quill: youthful (born 1575), armigerous and educated. For the socially ambitious Bard who overnighted in Oxford between London and Stratford he was eminently well connected.

The storyline of the *Sonnets* and the *Avisa* agree in the most crucial respect. If Avisa's suitor 'W.S.' is William Shakespeare then the Bard and Willoughby aspired to the same mistress one after the other. Every reader of the *Sonnets* is familiar with the lines in which Shakespeare chides his Friend for stealing his mistress.

A child was allegedly stillborn to Lady Penelope Rich at Leighs Priory in Essex in the early part of May 1594 (the month in which *Lucrece* was registered). In reality, did this infant survive, and if so was it brought to the Willoughby manor as the purported son of Henry Willoughby? Was it christened William Willoughby? Was it raised by Henry's elder brother William and his wife Eleanor, along with their own son Christopher? Was this infant the bastard son of the Dark Lady?

The scurrilous *Avisa* was republished in 1596 and 1599 and was quickly banned on both occasions. No copies of these editions survive. If we're to believe the 1596 date given in later editions, a poem appeared in the missing 1596 edition entitled: *The Victory of English Chastity under the Feigned Name of Avisa.* This poem which carries the vital clue to the identity of the real Avisa was ostensibly penned by Henry Willoughby's younger brother Thomas.

Further editions of the *Avisa* appeared in 1605, 1609 and 1635. Its success suggests contemporary readers 'in the know' would have been in little doubt which Elizabethan *glitterati* are intended by the innkeeper's wife and her would-be lovers, not to mention the innkeeper himself, the target of the cuckold's horns that decorate the title page.

The *Avisa*'s author must have considered Henry Willoughby minor enough to be mentionable by name, and Shakespeare could be hinted at with impunity as 'the old player' with the initials 'W.S.' Avisa's four remaining suitors and Avisa herself are identified less easily today, but I cannot believe readers in genteel Elizabethan and early Jacobean society would have had this problem. Their silence on the matter, at least in writing, only serves to underline how powerful the real-life Avisa must have been. While Robert Devereux was still the Queen's favorite his sister's influence must have been considerable.

When I discovered how famous the Dark Lady alias Avisa really was I understood why the cast of characters in the *Avisa* needed so much camouflage.

Let's take the dedication to Shakespeare's *Sonnets* and rearrange the words to see if they throw some light on the problem of who was the father of Penelope Rich's putative child, born in May 1594:

TO. MR. W.H.

THE. WELL-WISHING. ADVENTURER.

THE. ONLIE. BEGETTER.

OF. THESE. INSUING. SONNETS.

IN. SETTING. FORTH.

T.T.

347

WISHETH. ALL. HAPPINESSE.
AND. THAT. ETERNITIE.
PROMISED. BY.
OUR. EVER-LIVING. POET.

In this arrangement Mr W.H., whom we identify with Henry Willoughby, appears to be 'the only begetter'. If 'begetter' means father of a child, Thorpe makes Willoughby the father of a child who might be William Willoughby. Otherwise this arrangement suggests that 'begetter' means 'getter' and that Mr W.H. procured the *Sonnets* for Thorpe.

But look at this word order:

TO. MR. W.H.
THE. WELL-WISHING. ADVENTURER.
IN. SETTING. FORTH.
T.T. WISHETH. ALL. HAPPINESSE.
AND. THAT. ETERNITIE.
PROMISED. BY. OUR. EVER-LIVING. POET.
THE. ONLIE. BEGETTER.
OF. THESE. INSUING. SONNETS.

'Begetter' could mean creator of the *Sonnets*. It clearly refers to the poet in this version. But the poet was Shakespeare and he may have fathered Penelope Rich's bastard child whom we have called William Willoughby. Now we have another possible explanation for the fall from favor that Shakespeare alludes to in the *Sonnets*, an event that put an abrupt halt to his social ambitions.

There is no doubt that something happened to Shakespeare in 1594 which robbed him of the patronage of Henry Wriothesley, third Earl of Southampton. Wriothesley was a close friend of Penelope Rich and her brother the Earl of Essex. Southampton received the dedication of Shakespeare's *Venus and Adonis* in 1593 and his *Rape of Lucrece* in 1594. The latter dedication hinted at a third narrative poem which never appeared. In September 1594 the *Avisa* was published, a vague parody of *Lucrece*. Did Shakespeare's sudden climb up the social ladder end in scandal because his affair with Penelope Rich became known? Or because it was believed that he, or Willoughby, might be the father of Penelope's latest bastard child?

There is another explanation for the vulgar scandal. Perhaps the face behind Avisa's mask was also the face of the role model for Lucrece: Penelope Rich. In publishing *Lucrece* and daring to dedicate it to Southampton Shakespeare overstepped the mark. It may be possible to see Lucrece's rape by Tarquin as loosely based on Penelope's affair with Charles Blunt, who became eighth Lord Mountjoy in 1594. In which case Lucrece's husband Collatine becomes the cuckolded Lord Robert Rich. Shakespeare clearly sympathized with Tarquin, the not unlikeable seducer, as no doubt he did with Blunt, since they were both in the same position vis-à-vis Penelope, though Blunt had all the social advantages that Shakespeare lacked. A case of the lowborn Shakespeare pot calling the aristocratic Mountjoy kettle black . . . or simply gray.

On the other hand the *Avisa* may have wrecked Shakespeare's prospects simply by publicizing his affair, and Willoughby's, with Penelope. So long as such affairs were kept private no one worried too much, but the *Avisa* gave rise to scandal by holding Penelope Rich up to ridicule, making public her sexual peccadillos which would otherwise have gone unnoticed outside her circle, one to which Shakespeare had been briefly admitted.

The publisher Thomas Thorpe registered Shakespeare's *Sonnets* on 20 May 1609. At that date the seven ships and two pinnaces known as the Third Supply of the Virginia Company were already five days out of London, heading for Plymouth. The second charter of the Virginia Company was promulgated on 23 May 1609, three days later. On 2 June 1609 the nine vessels set forth from Plymouth, bound for Virginia.

Were Henry Willoughby and his hypothetical son William, fifteen years old by this time, on board one of the two pinnaces? On the death of Henry's father on 6 December 1608 the Willoughby estate had passed to the senior son, Henry's elder brother, as was customary. Without an inheritance Henry and his younger brother Thomas would have had to make their own way in the world. Had Henry Willoughby, the 'adventurer . . . setting forth' in the *Sonnets* dedication, decided to emigrate with the new fleet bound for Virginia and become an 'adventurer of person'? To become an 'adventurer of purse', an investor in the Company, would have cost a minimum of twelve pounds and ten shillings. Not that Henry would have been completely impecunious. For one thing he had probably just sold a complete set of Shakespeare's *Sonnets* to the publisher Thomas Thorpe.

The fleet destined to relaunch England's faltering New World colony ran into bad weather on 23 July 1609. Did Henry Willoughby transfer William, for his safety, from their small pinnace to the command vessel the *Seaventure*? Did Henry remain on board the pinnace? Sailing conditions deteriorated and the pinnace with its crew and passengers was lost from view by the *Seaventure*, never to be seen again. All on board were drowned. The *Seaventure* itself ran aground off Bermuda on the barrier reef. No one on board the *Seaventure* was lost at sea.

The remaining vessels of the Third Supply reached Virginia safely. This was the so-called 'Starving Time' when four out of five of those who made it to the new colony died of hunger or were killed by native Americans within the first twelve months.

Did young William Willoughby, fatherless now, reach Virginia on 23 May 1610 on board the *Patience*, captained by Sir George Somers, commander of the vessels of the Third Supply? The *Patience* was one of the two pinnaces built in Bermuda by the castaways. As all Shakespeare enthusiasts are aware that adventure was memorialized in the Bard's hermetic and final play: *The Tempest*.

Young William Willoughby would not have been alone for long. We can speculate that soon afterwards, Thomas Willoughby, possibly his uncle Thomas, arrived in Virginia on board the *Prosperous*. The facts are scant surrounding the Willoughbys who would now have found themselves in the New World. Thomas Willoughby may have died before 1625. A Thomas Willoughby who was possibly his son and appears to have had ties with the town of Barking in Essex went on to become the distinguished Virginia landowner Captain Thomas Willoughby, whose daughter Elizabeth eventually married into one of the *Mayflower* families, the Allertons.

I was more interested in what became of our putative William Willoughby, who would have been sixteen by the time he reached Kecoughtan in Virginia. Did he die in 1622 in his twenty-eighth year? There is no evidence that this William Willoughby had a wife. By the time he died did he have a son called Henry? If so, and if the child Henry did not die young, is there any theory which will explain why he should have disappeared from sight, except to

350

suggest that he was illegitimate and carried his mother's family name, whatever that was? The stigma of illegitimacy might have driven mother and child away from Virginia, perhaps to the new settlement in Massachusetts.

Perhaps Amelia Hungerford was right and the Willoughby – or Shakespeare – bloodline survives in New England today.

Can you, dear reader, help to throw some light on what remains of the mystery of the *Sonnets* and the Dark Lady?

Ian Wilson